WHEEL *on* *the* HAYLE

BASED ON
A TRUE STORY

A new novel by the author of *Village by the Ford* and *House by the Stream*, the real life story everyone dreams of – selling up and leaving to live in some remote and primitive place – struggling to survive and build a new, more risky, more exciting life.

Wheel on the Hayle finds the family living by candlelight in their beautiful but wild and lonely valley. Outside, only feet away, the crystal clear stream rushes swiftly by. There is power in that water – Can they harness it? This is a tale of ingenuity, humour and fun, not crime and violence, but there are problems, risks, danger! How did Sharon escape? Where is Margaret now? Will Billy survive? Life in the valley is unconventional but happy, lightened by children's laughter and perhaps a little mischief. Romance and a love of all things natural run through this true story as we recapture those marvellous times. A book every parent or grandparent will love!

To Ivy, Frank, Audrey and Jim,
and to parents and grandparents everywhere.

Printed and bound in UK

Cornish Books

First Published 1999

Reprinted 2001. Second impression 2003

IBSN 0 9537009 0 9

WHEEL *on* *the* HAYLE

by

GORDON CHANNER

Valley of Dreams series

CORNISH BOOKS
5 Tregembo Hill
Penzance, Cornwall, TR20 9EP

Press reviews
Wheel on the Hayle

...here is the book for you... transformed a deserted valley... heart warming tales of nature.
THE DAILY TELEGRAPH

...much charm and intrigue... inspirational development... waterwheel to harness energy... cannot help but delight... the children provide a source of entertainment...a deep appreciation of wildlife. THE CARAVAN CLUB MAGAZINE

Absolutely fascinating. RADIO CORNWALL

...weaves his magic... as near as Cornwall can get to Walton's Mountain. Wonderful. THE WEST BRITON

...another super read that should be enjoyed by caravanners and non-caravanners alike. CARAVAN LIFE

Recommended reading... why not treat yourself... I don't think you'll be disappointed. MMM

Live the Dream... adventure, humour and romance.
CARAVAN MAGAZINE

Pictured in CAMPING & CARAVANNING CLUB MAGAZINE

...his popular Valley of Dreams series... determine effort to make electricity from a waterwheel. BUCKS EXAMINER

...at the very top of my reading wants list... drama and some danger... and there is plenty of humour too.
THE CORNISHMAN

...we're sure this new book will keep you enthralled for hours. PRACTICAL CARAVAN

This series has now had 56 reviews, including the Daily Telegraph.

Contents

Chapter 1	Power	1
Chapter 2	Nessie	23
Chapter 3	Milk Tray	47
Chapter 4	The Billy	62
Chapter 5	The Dam	..81
Chapter 6	Old Relics	99
Chapter 7	Poor margaret	117
Chapter 8	S hark	137
Chapter 9	Spiderman	162
Chapter 10	Anne Arrives	181
Chapter 11	Bread on the Water	204
Chapter 12	Susan...	221
Chapter 13	Services	247
Chapter 14	Feathers	269
Chapter 15	Personal Magnatism	290
Chapter 16	The Pill	322
Chapter 17	The Dreaded Sewer	346

The Family at Relubbus

Gordon	Father
Jan	Mother
Chris	Age eleven (at start of book)
Sharon	Age ten
Stephen	Age seven
Jim	Grandfather (Jan's father)
Audrey	Grandmother (Jan's mother)
Max	The big yellow excavator.
Judy	The goat.
Olive and Ivy	Judy's kids

Period. October 1972 – April 1975.

Sketches and notes – see end of book.

Chapter 1

Power?

"Your father has decided to build a waterwheel."

Jan, her voice full of scepticism, addressed the three children eating breakfast. They paused, curiosity aroused, looking at each other in the soft flickering light. A candle stood at the table centre, attached by its own melted wax to a saucer mounted on an upturned blue and white striped mixing bowl, the flame throwing moving shadows behind. The hour was early and though still dark, Dad had already been out to tether the goat as dawn's first signs marked the eastern sky, these faint grey streaks not yet visible through the flimsy curtains. High on the far wall in the adjoining kitchen, a gas lamp hissed gently.

Letting her words hang in the air, Jan gazed back at the youngsters for some seconds, then spread her hands, palms upwards in a 'Who knows why?' gesture, before turning to stare accusingly at Gordon sitting across the table. The three children followed her gaze; she knew they would.

"Why?" Chris asked. "What can a waterwheel do?" The oldest at almost twelve, he had attended senior school in Penzance for little over a month. Sharon, two years his junior, had also opened her mouth to speak but hearing her brother's question, she waited.

Gordon looked at them and at Jan now sitting relaxed in her chair, a teasing smile on her lips, pleased to have put him on the defensive. She believed the venture futile, had told him so when he first broached the subject in bed the night before. Remembering well the nocturnal argument and all that had eventually followed, he glanced back at her, one hand stroking his chin. She had thrown down the gauntlet again, in front of the children this time, hoping to enlist them on her side. It promised to be interesting; he noticed the intonation when she had said 'Your father,' as if disclaiming any connection. Replying to Chris but speaking to all the children, he made a start.

"How long have we been here now? Over three years. When we first arrived in this wild valley there was nothing, not a clear space to put our tiny caravan, not a building as far as the eye could see; and no services, not even mains water. Remember your baths in the river?"

Sharon gave a shudder as Chris nodded solemnly. No sign had been expected from Stephen, the youngest at seven, a handful of trouble but quiet by nature. The room too lay silent, no sounds penetrating from outside, but that was normal in the solitary house beside the stream. Patiently the young family waited while Dad mentally organised his argument.

"Before a single tourist came, while still entirely alone, we solved those first problems; digging that half-mile trench for the water main and telephone cable, and finding a cheap caravan, one with a boiler to see us through the cold winter months. Since then we've shifted over thirty thousand tons of stony waste, laid out very nearly a mile of road, then levelled and grassed many acres of ground. During last winter we built this house together, just the five of us working alone, the blockwork, roof, plumbing, everything – didn't we?"

Heads nodded again. All had been fully involved in constructing the house, but none were yet strong enough to help much in moving those great heaps of waste; tailings left a century ago by Cornish miners digging for copper in the old Wheal Virgin mine. Watching the three children, Jan nodded too, but she stopped as if caught fraternising with the enemy when Gordon turned to her with a smile of success before resuming his case.

"Okay. If we can do all that, why not a waterwheel? Power is the only service that's missing; the thing other houses have and we don't. Waterwheels can produce electricity. The Hayle River may be shallow, but it's clear, fast flowing, and in the right place – a few paces from our own front door! So why not?"

Jan saw enthusiasm grow in their faces and knew he had won them over; but it would never work. As the children turned towards her expecting agreement, she leaned across, addressing them in a conspiratorial whisper.

"What do you know about waterwheels?"

"Nothing," Sharon admitted in a low voice as Chris shook his head. Young Stephen watched, eyes intent, but made no comment.

"Nor," Jan warned, "does your father!" Seeing doubts enter the children's faces, she swung defiantly towards Gordon.

He met the challenging stare; she looked fantastic with that broadening smile now spreading across her lips... the temptation to kiss her coming strongly – but he was not about to give up.

"I believe you were going to Penzance this morning, to the library, we agreed last night; you do remember last night?"

She looked back at him; that wasn't fair. How could she forget! "Yes, I seem to recall something." The reply was evasive, hoping the children would not understand; a quick glance flicked towards Chris, the oldest, then back as Gordon spoke again.

"A couple of books on waterwheels, you agreed to fetch them? I may not be an expert yet, but I *can* read."

"Really! I never realised. Two at once I suppose?" She stopped, suddenly remembering. Too late – he had broken into a huge grin and was replying already.

"'Corse I can, got two eyes haven't I?"

The very words little Stephen had used only weeks

before when he pinched Sharon's comic as well as his own, deliberately trying to annoy his older sister. The lad recognised the phrase immediately, a wicked grin spreading over impish features below curly, light brown hair that even now still showed almost blonde in places, bleached by the past summer's scorching sunshine.

The little conference broke up, disrupted by morning chores, weak dawn light now showing through the curtains. Gordon left to work farther down the valley, away from the few remaining caravans; they would all be gone soon, October was drawing on and the site must close in a couple of weeks. At least they would be free for a while from the mad things holidaymakers did. This would be the end of their third season, three years of gradually clearing more areas for caravans and tents; paying guests that had meant survival and a chance to eat! They had a house now, life was easier even without electric, but a greater problem lay ahead, something they were not yet fully aware of – and cash was still short.

While Sharon cleared and washed the plates, Stephen donned rubber gloves and headed off to check for rubbish. A fox still managed to overturn the dustbins from time to time; a squirrel or even a crow could also remove the light plastic lids, spreading visitors rubbish around. Chris hurried away to collect Judy, arriving back a few minutes later, guiding the goat through the house and descending the basement stairs. Jan led the way, walking ahead through dark underground corridors, a candle held out in front, the milking utensil in her other hand. This had started as an economy, a way to survive on less money, but with no electric and therefore no fridge, milk on the hoof, fresh twice daily, had proved preferable to a bottled supply. Judy, aided by a strategically placed carpenter's stool, jumped without help up onto the big bench, heading immediately for a nearby plastic bucket. The rolled oats it contained would keep her happily occupied. A special shelf recently bracketed to the wall, positioned the candle for a better angle of light. How much easier this task had become! Previously, the whole family had struggled to hold horns and legs, keeping the goat still and prevent it kicking over the pail as Jan milked. What a difference the bribe of those oats had made.

Later, the three children left for school, walking up the road together; Jan waved before leading Judy off to find a new strip of grass, following when the goat pulled towards a patch of bramble. Standing patiently while Judy ate, Jan absently cast an eye at the mountain of mine tailings still covering much the valley's western side and thought of their life by the river. It certainly seemed more secure now with the house, but last night had raised new doubts. Why did Gordon still work so hard, and why could they not have mains electric? She had asked that too, in bed when he first spoke of the waterwheel. The cost, he had said, it would take years and the road must come first. She disagreed, had argued strongly against; after all, trade had increased this year. They should have electric first! All right, so it would take another year or two, maybe more, but forget the road, bother about that later! Hearing no reply she thought he had dropped off, but after a while he had spoken again explaining.

Now, standing holding the tether rope, Jan turned back towards the bridge, remembering what had been said. Was he right? Those dust clouds that followed cars up and down the road, how long would people put up with them? Site standards everywhere were improving, that was true. Could they afford to be left behind? It was a long entrance road, a track really, road was too grand a title. Sites in Cornwall were in short supply at present but more were being created; lots more. Would their own numbers reduce? Could they still survive if that happened? Is that the reason he still worked so hard – more pitches could mean more money to surface the road sooner!

The rope pulled; Judy wanted to move on.

***

Saturday arrived and Chris was at a loose end; he had the day to himself. Work on the waterwheel had not yet started and his friend had left yesterday, a lad of 12 years, close to his own age; that was unusual in October but this boy's father also worked in the holiday trade and could hardly have taken time off earlier in the season. For the last week Chris had leapt from the school bus, raced off down the half-mile track leaving his sister far behind, and hurriedly eaten tea.

On the first such night, Sharon arrived at the house to find her brother missing, having already grabbed a sandwich and gone. She objected strongly.

"You shouldn't feed him first Mum, he should eat with the rest of us, not leave me to walk home alone! Dad's not back for tea yet."

"Do you really want me to make him wait? He has a friend staying at the moment and you know Dad will probably work until it's dark. You're not jealous because Chris has someone and you don't, are you?"

"No!" Sharon looked down at the floor.

"You are just a bit envious, aren't you? It isn't Chris's fault there are no girls staying."

"I know, but he shouldn't..." Sharon stopped abruptly.

"Ah! Thought of something have you?" Jan watched her daughter's eyes lower again, a small shake of the head telegraphing the coming denial.

"No."

"Don't fib to me. You've remembered that next time it may be your turn to have a friend and want early tea, haven't you?"

"Mum, I… How did you guess?"

"Thoughts show on your face just like headlines on a newspaper. There's an old saying, 'A great statesman thinks of the effect of his words before he speaks'. For a woman it's not just the words, your whole body speaks; how you stand, your face, everything. I've told you before, a girl should never be too transparent, a little mystery goes a long way!"

As the days passed, Chris had continued to eat early then disappear, seldom to arrive back until darkness fell and often not then. The young friends did many things together; they fished in the river, or ran the two miles downstream to St Erth to try their hand in the big pools, hurrying to reach them before the light faded, finding a way back in the twilight. They climbed various trees, tended Judy the goat and found ways into and through deep thickets to hidden places on both banks of the stream. Late one afternoon while his mother cut a sandwich, Chris walked into the office and from a drawer quietly pocketed the spare key to the service passage, a door normally kept locked as various tools were stored inside. Sneaking into the passage shortly after, he borrowed a Stanley knife kept there for trimming Judy's hooves, then selected two lengths of strong twine from an assorted swathe hanging on a hook. This string had accumulated over time from various parcels and packages for the family threw nothing away. Having obtained the necessary equipment, Chris and his friend hurried off, keeping to cover, running quickly across any open spaces, not wanting to be seen. Eventually they reached the downstream site boundary where a long row of nut trees formed a Hazel hedge. Choosing a spot that offered concealment from the riverbank footpath, they selected and cut suitable stems. Shortly each had a bow and several arrows. An hour later, approaching darkness interrupted practise, but their interest was already waning. The bows must be hidden, preferably under cover but not at the house where young Stephen would find them. Approaching the chestnut tree whose fruit was gathered each year for Christmas, Chris remembered seeing a large drainpipe, well concealed by a high bank behind yet more undergrowth. It was here that the boys chose to store their equipment, and promptly forgot it.

On Friday evening the visiting lad departed, his parents planning to drive home overnight, avoiding Saturday's traffic. It left Chris on his own. That was not unusual in October or indeed in any of the slacker months. The children had become used to losing friends, even Sharon who most liked company was well able to cope, to carry through a game or project on her own when necessary. That first year in the valley when their parents had been so busy had fostered a certain self-reliance which subsequent winters reinforced. The whole family would play cards and other games on a dark evening, but age and gender differences found them together less often outside the house. They had all grown accustomed to spending time alone. Even so, Chris felt the loss of this particular friend deeply. At tea, now eaten together again, Sharon and Stephen were little help.

"We weren't good enough when your friend was here, not that we cared, did we Stephen?" Sharon accused, preening herself. The younger boy nodded agreement. However, before the meal was finished all three were chatting together happily.

The following morning Chris was restless and eventually left the house. At first he had no particular objective in mind and walked beside the stream following a small branch bobbing along on the current, watching trout dart here and there from cover to cover. Coming level with the Chestnut tree he remembered the bows and picked his way across the intervening tangle of shrubs. Two large oaks grew nearby, one reputed to have the greatest girth in the parish; beyond this lay the hidden weapons. Crouching under a willow he trod carefully forward, sliding down into a dry gully. Some distance along to his right the tall sides came together and it was here, level with the gully floor that the pipe projected from under a steep bank. At some time it must have been a drainage course, possibly from the neighbouring slopes, but there had been no sign of water during the previous winter. Kneeling down Chris reached for the bows and was on the point of standing again when he bent lower. There was light at the other end, only a small irregular patch, but light none the less. Lying flat he peered into the darkness trying to see, arms stretched out in front. The pipe was bigger than his body! Easing forward, he felt farther inside, reaching ahead with both hands, fingers detecting what could not be seen. It was quite dry. The tiny patch of light still glowed somewhere ahead; was that tree branches crossing it and sky beyond? Would it be possible to get right through? The passage itself lay black and obscure. What about a fox, or even a badger asleep in the daytime? Should he shout and frighten it away? Hm, well... perhaps? Why not, probably nothing there! Something stopped him. That hole at the other end could be too small. Any trapped badger would certainly attack, even a fox might; and then there was… He snatched both hands back, easing carefully but quickly out, trying to make no rustle of sound; not admitting fear but not wanting to wake anything that might be lying just beyond where his fingers had probed. There were snakes in the valley when they first arrived! Vibrations from the big excavator had driven them away, but where were they hiding now? Continuing to tread quietly, he climbed the gully bank and hurried away; only when well clear did he slow to dawdle along indecisively, ducking under or around various vegetation until a fallen tree blocked his path. Sitting on the dead trunk kicking the ground, he pulled away a small branch, gazing out into space as the brittle twiglets snapped piece by piece between his fingers.

Looking down to find the branch gone, he stared at the ground then stood, fists clenched in resolution, head nodding to himself, and made purposefully for the house.

"Oh! So you're back?" Sharon's head came up as he entered. She and Stephen were using the three-quarter sized snooker table in the office, its mahogany covers taken off and leant against the far wall. "Do you want a game?"

"No, I've picked up a thorn." Chris threw a downward glance at his hand, holding it loosely against the chest as if injured.

"I'll do it for you." Thorns were frequent, Sharon reached for a needle kept nearby.

"You won't! You're not sticking anything in me!"

He made for the bathroom, closing the door and shooting the bolt, then eased back the sliding panel to the linen cupboard. Down one side was a rack of shelves; on one stood a small torch. Good. A little darkness in the pipe was fine, that was no worry but he must have a means of seeing inside, a reasonable chance of spotting anything venomous, coiled up and ready to strike! Slipping the torch in a pocket, he slid the panel closed and reached for the door bolt – but stopped. He had no thorn, it had been a ruse to deflect questions. Sharon would be suspicious! "Draw blood with a pin?" Discarding the passing thought, he pinched a finger trying to make it red. The effect was negligible. Reaching back into the cupboard he withdrew a bottle of Dettol. Unscrewing the top and holding it over the basin, a single drop splashed onto the finger – it should be enough.

"Show me!" Sharon challenged as her brother appeared again in the office, brushing by and making for the door. Chris thrust out the finger, deliberately near her face, blurring the focus. Threatened by the move and catching the smell, Sharon instinctively recoiled. In that moment her brother was through the door and gone.

Bolstered with success he raced along, slowing only at the big oak, slipping down the bank to kneel again in the gully. There was the pipe; not so close this time! It lay a full body length away, approached with more care, more suspicion. The dark circle stared back, a single unblinking baleful eye, somehow more threatening now his intention was clear. For a time Chris stayed silent, one knee on the ground, watching the opening, tense, listening, knowing what he had determined to do. A rustle behind and above whipped his head round sharply; a bird landing on the overhanging bush flew off again with a call of alarm, leaving the lad breathing faster.

Easing the torch from his jeans' pocket he bent lower, directing the light ahead. The weak beam showed little. Crawling closer, the inside became dimly visible. Nothing lay in the path, just a debris of dry leaf-litter in the bottom running forward evenly as far as the small torch penetrated. Beyond lay a shadowy area that might contain anything, and farther still, the irregular patch of light. Was it sky, or sun shining on the ground beyond? That small distant patch swung the balance. Lying there now flat on his stomach again he had begun to wonder, to hunt for an excuse, a reason to abandon the plan, pretending not yet to have decided, to be only considering it. This piece of light seen in the darkness bolstered his resolve. Pushing both arms ahead he entered the pipe, not exactly a tight fit, no danger of getting stuck but neither was it possible to rise onto the knees and certainly not to turn round. Whatever might be ahead it would be met face on. One hand gripped tighter on the arrow projecting in front, an arrow chosen for its stoutness and sharpened point. The torch showed stronger as pupils expanded with the loss of daylight. This pipe was smooth inside, smooth but not shiny for it carried the grime of ages, feeling uniformly soft to the touch like a fine moss, a surface without sharp edges.

After a while a darker ring indicated where two pipes joined, the second veering fractionally right, the deflection barely detectable. Chris tried to check behind but could see nothing, unable to raise and turn his head sufficiently, the pipe restricting all but the smallest movements. That patch of sky seemed unchanged... or was it bigger? He wanted to check without the torchlight but decided against switching it off. Something might yet slither from beyond the beam! Moving on again, the walls were changing, the smoothness ending abruptly. He heaved forwards, pushing with toes, knees, wrists – on into some kind of cavern, a rough irregular cavity with little extra headroom but wider; might even be space enough to turn! Across this cavern the aperture now showed clearly; not sky, but a patch of willow ahead, its leaves reflecting the light. Those were not branches that crossed the opening, but hanging roots. Above, torchlight revealed the whole cave supported by one immense root interlaced with a network of lesser ones. Crawling across he peered out; the opening was small, a rabbit perhaps? On a whim his arm reached through feeling the ground outside, testing – an urge to break free and stand again in the open air, but the bank was too thick! Beyond lay the chestnut tree and the wild undeveloped site; parts of the riverbank showed perhaps a hundred metres away.

"Hello!" He had needed to shout; proof that at least his voice could escape, but the sound inside that small underground chamber shook him. No one heard of course, no answering call came back. The valley lay deserted. It might be days before somebody passed. He lay for a time gazing out, ill at ease; then pushed the thoughts away and reached again through the small opening. Closer inspection suggested an exit might be possible – with sufficient tools! Dad would say "Take tools anyway, just in case. No he wouldn't," Chris corrected the thought. He'd say, "Don't go in at all!" But he had no intention of telling his father or any other member of the family. Tools would be good though, a small saw and a trowel? Should he dig a wider opening? Well... perhaps not! The concealment was good, difficult to detect from outside, there were possibilities here; something to show special friends next summer! Chris wiggled round, at one point becoming jammed, but managed in the end to force his body free. Good, much easier than going out backwards. Some tools certainly then, to work on the inside! And bring the bow in next time, held sideways it could be fired from here; he had the width – might even get a rabbit. Wriggling back along the pipe, a picture of Sharon's face as he walked into the house carrying tomorrow's lunch made him swell with pride, but memories of three baby rabbits fostered some years previously clouded the pleasure. Perhaps he would just watch? Emerging into daylight again and starting back towards the house, the sound of Max's engine approached from farther upstream. Not wanting to speak to anyone at that moment, he hid as another load of stone passed by.

Over the following days, Gordon continued loading stony material in the trailer, a long term task started soon after their first arrival and destined to continue for many more years. The aim was twofold; remove the unsightly heaps of mine waste, converting them eventually into grassy terraces up the valley side, and simultaneously use the surplus material to level uneven ground nearer the river. They had been short of flat camping pitches again in the busy school holiday period; more were needed.

As darkness fell, outside work was necessarily abandoned, thoughts returning to the waterwheel. Studying the books Jan had borrowed, there were undershot wheels, overshot wheels, breast wheels, Pelton wheels, backshot wheels, and even turbines and hydraulic rams – a bewildering array of choices! Unfortunately, despite copious photographs and flowery descriptions, there were few hard facts and figures. Turbines appeared specialised and expensive while hydraulic rams were suitable only for pumping water, or so the various writers seemed to imply.

"We must choose a wheel then, mustn't we?" Gordon asked a few evenings later, ostensibly to Jan and the children but really pulling the contents of some intensive reading together in his mind. "Well if a wheel, what type of wheel? First determine the maximum head available. That, at least, we know already!"

A natural fall of approximately eighteen inches occurred thirty paces downstream of the bridge. It marked the place where the dragline excavator that cleaned the riverbed every few years, always stopped work to avoid undermining the bridge's foundations. The river was wider at this point, nearly double its width elsewhere, with a natural weir, not laid squarely like a wall but jagged and irregular over which the stream, perhaps the cleanest in England, bubbled and swirled.

"If we put the waterwheel by the weir, it won't alter upstream or downstream levels and since the river there is so wide, it will never impede flow in times of heavy rainfall. You follow so far?"

The children nodded.

"Now, that eighteen inch fall is not much! An overshot wheel would be impractical, a breast wheel possible and an undershot simplest, that's the type where the water just passes under the paddles, pushing them round." Gordon's explanation finished, a gesture invited comment from the listening family.

Jan played with her wedding ring, looking directly back into his eyes, laughing. "Let's go for simplicity. I've always liked simple things!"

The children, missing her subtlety but delighted with the whole idea, fired off a barrage of questions. How big? At what speed might it spin? Would the water splash and spray around? When? When could work start?

"Never mind all that," Jan cut in. "Ask him who is going to make it and whether it will work?"

"I shall make it, and of course it will work."

"Hmm!"

"What if the river dries up?" Chris remembered the Misbourne, at the foot of the Chiltern Hills where they once lived. That river had disappeared, absorbed into hidden tunnels dissolved from chalky strata below.

"This stream never stops. If it ever does, the three of you can work it like a treadmill for an hour every day before tea."

"Great!" How easily children grasp for anything different, but as both parents well knew, five minutes of actual experience and the novelty would soon wear off! Fortunately, some older inhabitants of Relubbus advised that the river had never run dry. It was certainly a source of surprise that levels rose and fell so little in winter and summer; maybe those old mines farther upstream acted as a reservoir.

"Will it work the television?" Sharon asked anxiously. At school every one of her close friends had TV, the all-girl group frequently discussing programs and characters; talk from which Sharon found herself excluded.

An old set transported down by the removal firm with the rest of the furniture rested on a shelf in the basement. Gordon saw hope in his daughter's eyes and hesitated, reluctant to dampen her spirits, but felt compelled to be honest for the chances were poor. "Not the one downstairs, that's 240-volt. A small 12-volt set like those used in some caravans might work if the wheel makes enough, but it's doubtful! We can store current in batteries all day and night, that could provide limited viewing some evenings, but probably not. It's lights we're really after."

Stephen glanced up at the oil-lamp swinging from a hook in the ceiling as it did every evening after dark, and frowned, puzzled why another light should be needed. He knew other people had electric, had seen the lights at Jim's bungalow often enough, but was so used to the existing arrangement that it seemed to him perfectly satisfactory. Only one lamp was available, moved from room to room as required. Periodically, often when prompted by one of the children, Dad reached up, took it down and pumped in more pressure. It was difficult to start and when light would only be needed for a short while, like early in the mornings, a candle was easier and quicker. Candles were widely used, the boys always lit one at bedtime. Cooking was by gas and this had allowed a gas light over the stove and another in Sharon's bedroom, which backed onto the kitchen; but all the lights were dim. Jan often worried about its effect on the children's eyes.

"Will we ever have a television?" Sharon sighed, accepting there was no immediate prospect but still wondering about the future. Tea had been cleared away long since, and all homework completed; the family sat, piles of used matchsticks and hands of playing cards abandoned on the table, the game temporarily forgotten. The question was addressed to her father, to whom all heads now turned.

Leaning both elbows on the table, he looked back at the family, lips pursed. “Well... could do I suppose, sometime. If you mean a normal electricity supply, that’s a long way off. It’s money; costs a lot, we don’t have enough. One day perhaps, if the site wins a competition, becomes famous and lots of visitors come.”

Looks passed between the two older children, shrugs of disappointment, a clear belief that nothing would change. Seeing them, Jan spoke softly, in an easy gentle voice, explaining rather than lecturing.

“That’s why Dad works so hard moving the old mine waste and making new areas. It may not seem to change very much, but you don’t realise the... ” she stopped with a gesture of the hand, not sure how to make them understand. “It’s not so easy, laying out a site in such a special way, I doubt you’ll see another like it anywhere. If as much effort went into your schoolwork I’d have three very bright children. Did I ever tell you about *my* school days?”

Heads around the table shook, shoulders rising in expectation, gloomy thoughts pushed aside. The family talked a lot in the evenings, especially now as winter approached and none of the few remaining caravans had children to play with.

“You’d like to hear? Why not make coffee first?” She looked across at Sharon, who jumped quickly up, hurrying into the adjoining kitchen to light a gas ring under the kettle, blowing out the match and scraping off the burned end on the sink. Returning, she dropped the used stick onto her own small pile on the table, to cries of ‘Cheat’ from the boys.

“You can do it when you make the coffee!”

“We never...”

“Shall we sit here?” Jan interrupted, stifling the argument, “or in comfy armchairs in the lounge?”

Three small hands pointed to the doorway. As Dad rose to lift down the oil lamp, Mum laid a restraining hand on his arm. “Let’s take a candle?”

Sinking back into the big chairs a few minutes later, the flickering light was somehow appropriate for story-telling. It made the room much more cosy, removing the distraction of periodically reaching up to pump the lamp with more pressure. Hot coffee now close at hand, they waited for their mother to start.

“As you know, we lived in London when I was young, in Grove Park. Jim, my Dad, was a policeman. We had quite a big old house, three storeys high in a terrace. At about Sharon’s age I loved reading.” Jan turned to Stephen, “You’d be surprised what wonderful stories there are when you read really well. I read so many adventure books about girls at live-in schools, books like *Mallory Towers, Twins of St Clare’s,* that sort of thing, and I longed to go to boarding school myself. In the end my parents arranged it. Police pay at that time was not very good; to find enough money, Audrey, my Mum, took in medical students. Young men can be a problem sometimes, there were five of them but they always paid attention to me, made me feel special. I thought them wonderful.” Jan took sip of coffee – it was still too hot. Aware that Sharon’s eyes were shining, she smiled at her daughter and continued. “Once, these students hung a skeleton from the second floor window late at night, made the joints move with black string from the floor above, like a puppet; lit it suddenly with torches as people passed by. They did other things too, but Audrey liked them and Jim made sure nothing got out of hand.

“Anyway, off I went to Herne Bay in Kent, to a girl’s school run by nuns in an old convent. We slept in dormitories, long rooms with lots of beds. Each of us had our own little cell with a tall cupboard, some drawers and a bed. It had a wooden partition each side, not right to the ceiling; we used to jump up, hang over the top and talk to each other. The girl next to me had a sore foot from gymnastics. I was good at that; the only class where we didn't have a nun in charge. There were parallel bars fixed to the walls and ropes hanging down from the ceiling, strong thick ropes you could get a good grip on. I was one of the best climbers in our class. We climbed in bare feet; that was how my friend got hurt. She slid down fast and it took the skin off her big toe; they called it a rope burn. Anyway, with this bad foot she couldn't climb the partitions, so I and her other neighbour hung down from above, talking. We ribbed her a bit about being soft, she shouted back calling us names; the whole thing got so noisy they sent a nun with a chair to sit at the end of the dormitory and listen.

"They had given this girl a roll of cotton wool and strips of plaster because her injury kept weeping and the dressing needed changing regularly. She tore off pieces of the cotton wool, dipped them in the glass of water by her bed, then threw them over the partition trying to hit us. We threw them back of course, trying to be quiet, but when one piece stuck to the ceiling the outburst of giggling brought that nun out of her chair and marching down the corridor to investigate. Footsteps approached and my curtain was drawn back, I heard the rings slide on the bar at the top but I was in bed again, my eyes tightly closed pretending to be asleep. The main worry was that chunk of wet cotton wool stuck to the ceiling. Would it fall down, give the game away?" Jan stopped, not revealing the answer, watching the children's expressions as they sat in the candlelight, then sensing Sharon was about to ask, she spoke again.

"It didn't; not until ten minutes later and by then the nun had gone. That was the best thing about boarding school, fun with the other girls. I can't remember too much about the lessons, we did all the normal subjects; oh, and

Latin." Seeing the children's puzzled expressions, Jan attempted to explain. "Latin is what they call a dead language, that is, nobody speaks it any more. It's used by scientists for naming things; the nuns used it quite a lot, at prayers for instance. Everyone went to morning prayers."

"What was life like, living in dormitories away from home?" Chris asked.

"We rose early, had breakfast then off to the classroom when the bell rang for registry. After answering our names, we were marched in lines to the hall for prayers then back to the classroom to start the day's study. Most nuns were nice but one was very strict, made us work extra hard, wouldn't allow any talking, not a single word; none of the girls liked her. She stood on a raised platform behind this big table watching us, then prowled round the desks with a wooden ruler, tapping it against the palm of her other hand and hoping for an excuse to rap our knuckles. We had never found any way to rebel, to cause a bit of distraction, have a giggle; the punishment was too severe. I suppose it was good for us, but we hated it.

"Anyway, after the incident in the dormitory we decided to stick wet cotton wool to the ceiling over her head, exactly where she stood behind that table. Five of us rose early one morning, quickly had breakfast and sneaked into the classroom before registry. We had the stuff in a jam jar, large soggy chunks, damp but not saturated; didn't want any drips giving the game away. Doris was the biggest girl but the ceiling was far too high even for her. We stood on that table on the raised platform, all five of us; it creaked a bit, Doris was in the middle. With help from the others I climbed on her back; they steadied her while I reached up and stuck about a dozen pieces to the ceiling. There were several still in the jar but the girl we had left on guard outside banged on the door; the signal that someone was coming. I slid down as the other girls jumped! We rushed to crouch behind the door; it only had the one high window so anybody looking in should see an empty classroom. Crouching there, none of us could tell if anyone stood outside. We waited, whispering and giggling as young girls do when nervous and excited – afraid to move for fear of discovery. How long we crouched there I don't know, but suddenly the bell sounded. I rose carefully, checked through the window, then opened the door slightly and we walked to our seats as if arriving for class in the normal way." Jan raised her cup taking a long draught of coffee, signalling the children to drink.

When they were ready again, rather than speaking she peered suddenly upwards with concern at the ceiling above. It was a nice touch. Gordon, sitting on the opposite side saw the children's expressions change as Sharon looked up sharply, drawing in her breath, eyes searching. Chris, trying to hide any concern, glanced up more casually but leaned farther back as if to avoid some falling object. Stephen's face lit in a typically mischievous grin, remaining still with no apparent instinct to dodge, only the eyes swivelling first upward then towards his mother. Jan smiled at them as one by one they responded, then she continued.

"Those pieces were supposed to fall when the moisture dried out. You could hardly see them clinging high above, they were white like the ceiling paint. Our teacher knew immediately that something was afoot. We always paid attention in her class, frightened not to, but this was different. Everyone knew, all staring so intently to the front, waiting, aware they should fall – but they didn't! Our nun watched us; she was uneasy, trying to find the cause, sensing something irregular in the class but not knowing what. She glanced down at her habit once, that's the dress they wear, then round at the blackboard in case anyone had written something rude on it; but there was nothing. It disconcerted her, made her edgy. The register was called and we filed off to the hall for prayers. Far from asking the Lord's forgiveness for our sins, we just prayed the cotton wool pieces wouldn't all have fallen before we returned to the classroom. They hadn't, not one. That lesson went on and on. I'd stuck them too firmly! In the end one of the girls put her hand up. '*Yes*?' the teacher said, pointing with her ruler.

"'*It's hot miss, can we have a window open?'*

"They were big tall windows; the breeze soon dried our cotton wool and down they came, all of them, one at a time. Everyone giggled. She was so annoyed, livid, but didn't know who to punish, never connected it with that opening window." Jan lifted her cup, taking a final sip, and snuggled back into the armchair, twisting sideways, drawing up her bare feet, quietly observing the children in the candlelight. "Now what bad things have you been up to at school? I hope you spend most of your time paying close attention. You don't want to grow up like your father, unable to make a silly old waterwheel work!" She halted, folding her arms. Who would speak first? The evening was far from over.

Later, with the children gone to bed, the parents as so often in the evening, sat talking, books resting unread on the floor nearby.

"I never knew you were naughty at school, you've never mentioned it before," Gordon commented idly. They lay back in armchairs facing each other, bare feet stretched out and touching, playing with each other's toes, the candle now burning low on its saucer. "You usually encourage the children to behave in class, stress how important it is."

"Yes... true, I do." She stretched an arm lazily and wriggled to a new position. "Don't know why I told them really, but if you always say 'Be good', they stop listening anyway. Perhaps for a little while they'll take notice again now. That's my excuse anyway. And *you* can't talk – you were no angel at school! Your Mum told me about that girl's head."

"Girl's head?" Gordon asked defensively, feigning ignorance, surprised that Jan knew.

"Don't pretend. In your early teens when you were

interested in photography and developed your own films. You took a photo of a girl and fixed it onto the body from some naughty nudie magazine! I suppose that was A..."

"Never mind who it was," he cut in quickly. "Someone snitched on me for trying to sell copies at school. Enterprise see, but I kept one hidden in my bedroom, unwrapped it now and then, wondering. That was a big mistake. Ivy, my mum, threw a fit when she found it! She did look great though, the girl. Pity I never got to see the real thi... Hey! Stop changing the subject, we were talking about *your* school days. What else did you girls do to annoy those poor nuns?"

"Not much really or if we did I can't remember, or maybe I prefer not to. There was one thing; when the whole class read Latin aloud from our textbooks, we would shout *amo, amas, amat,* much more loudly than the other verbs; I love, you love, we love or whatever it was, trying to embarrass the teacher. Quite juvenile really."

"Young girls must think alike," he grinned at her. "My sister Jane once told me that at, er, Whitehill School in Chesham I think it was, one of the songs, a prayer that they sung at assembly had the words, *Mighty fences are down*. Of course all the girls sang very loudly, *My defences are down!"*

"It doesn't hurt." Jan raised her hand covering a yawn, not sure why she felt so relaxed and sleepy tonight. "Encourages team spirit when the whole class gets one over on the staff occasionally. I should think any good teacher could use it to advantage. Helps youngsters enjoy school; ours seem to, don't you think? They learn more easily if they're happy. I'll pop upstairs and check Chris put the candle out."

CHAPTER 2

Nessie

The season's end approached. Among the few remaining caravanners one couple had become like old friends, it was pleasant standing by the bridge or sitting on the low parapet chatting with them of an evening. On hearing of the need for an axle, the man remembered seeing many discarded shafts lying in a naval scrap yard near his home eighty miles away in Plymouth. He and his wife returned a few days later towing one on a trailer. It was sixteen feet long, two-inch diameter, with four large roller bearings.

The children arrived from school, saw the shaft lying near the door and enthusiastically helped carry it to the river's edge. Some large granite sections were already in position on the bank. These slabs would support three bearings to hold the shaft when it projected over the river with the wheel fixed to the end.

"Why three bearings?" Jan asked. "Four came with the shaft."

"Need to keep one as a spare."

Gordon collected his tools then spread a dozen stout bolts in a neat row along the ground. These would be cemented into holes in the granite; holes which must first be made! He started knocking straight away. It must all be done with a hand held chisel, there was no electric to work power tools. If drilling was complete by evening, then the children could help lift this axle into its final position. Jan, drawn by the sound of hammering, wandered over and watched for a few moments.

"Why use bolts so long and so thick? No, let me guess. They've got to be strong, right?"

He nodded. "Of course. There's not just the weight to carry, consider the vibration, and any impact forces if a floating branch gets suddenly stuck under the paddles."

"You sure twelve will be enough; they'll probably only take twenty tons each. What if a tidal wave brings an ocean liner up from the estuary? The Scilly Isles might go up like Krakatoa and create one, have you considered that? I suppose you intend finishing tonight?"

"Certainly. Why are you laughing?"

"All twelve. Really?" Knowing his eternal optimism, she turned and walked away.

By teatime, which coincided with darkness, he had to admit she was right, it would certainly not be done that evening even if he worked with the lamp. The granite resisted penetration, each hole took ages and there were many left to do!

In the morning he hammered on, continually rotating the chisel, periodically using the old bicycle pump trick to clear accumulated debris, boring slowly down to sufficient depth for each bolt. By lunch, all bearings were firmly held in place by cement grout poured and worked in around the bolts, the shaft left in position to protect the setting cement and ensure perfect alignment. He was pleased enough to sit on the excavator, loading the trailer and carting stone for the rest of the afternoon, and planned to continue with this work for several days while the grout hardened. The weekend, with the children home, would be time enough to make the wheel!

"Goodbye!" A hand waved from a window as the caravan rolled towards the bridge. Jan hurried to the door waving back, expecting the car to sweep on. When it stopped she ran lightly down the steps and across the yard, knowing they had something to say.

"Thanks for a great holiday." The woman stretched out

to clasp Jan's hand, the man beyond her smiling. "We've had a super time, you keep everything so clean! How is it that your sinks always have plugs in them? We've been to sites all over the country; half the sinks have no plugs but I've never seen one missing here."

"I don't really know. Gordon has a dozen spare ones, he buys spares for everything. You wouldn't believe the things he has in stock – just in case. You know that great thick deep sink just inside the door, a Belfast sink I think it's called, the one that's meant for washing dishes; he even has spares of those! But you're right about the sink plugs, none has ever disappeared; we've not replaced a single one yet. It's the nice people who come!" Jan said the last words as a joke, laughing.

"No, they are nice. It's because you don't have clubs. That's why we first came you know. You *are* lucky, living in this valley, the water's so clear, and the trees – hardly any have lost their leaves." A hand pointed through the open window.

"That's willow, those are always last to shed. I agree though, we are lucky – but it's lonely in winter."

After a few further pleasantries, the car started again and the outfit drew off. Something else was shouted back as it crossed the bridge, but carried away, lost in the engine noise; it might have been "See you next year!" Jan stood until it disappeared at the end of the track, a faint dust cloud rising even now with the ground no longer parched by the sun. It was the last; they were alone again in the Valley. How long before another vehicle would appear? She sighed. At least four months must pass before the next holiday visitors came. The site closed today, its licence expired until March.

At breakfast on Saturday both boys were eager to start the wheel; with the site now empty, no new young friends would arrive to divert their attention. Sharon was less keen, wanting it to work but showing little interest in the actual construction.

"I'll come if you boys get stuck," she offered, knowing they would never admit to any such thing, far less that they needed her help!

Jan nodded encouragingly, considering it a good sign. She had wondered when her daughter would start to make more use of that essential feminine quality – deviousness.

In the garage, from which the car had already been removed, Gordon explained as they worked. "The wheel will be six feet diameter and two feet wide. These..." he laid a hand on three marine plywood sheets leaning against the wall, "these are the biggest available locally, eight feet long, four feet wide. One is for paddles, the other two we must cut into big circles for the shrouds, that's what the outsides are called. Help me lift the first one."

With Stephen and Chris at one end, they lifted the large sheet, lowering it across two carpenter's stools like a tabletop.

"How can we find the exact centre?"

Stephen reached out, hesitated, checked from side to side, then poked a finger vertically downward, holding it firmly near the middle. His expression asked confirmation but he said nothing. Gordon reached forward, drew round the fingertip with a pencil, and turned to Chris.

"Can you be more accurate, more scientific?"

"At school, when making paper planes to throw..." he stopped momentarily, not prepared to say what they were thrown at, then continued. "What we do is fold the paper along the diagonals. The creases cross at the centre."

"Good. That way gives exact results." Dad held a hand towards Stephen. "Here, take one end each and stretch this string while I mark a line near the middle, then again from the other corners. As Chris says, where those lines cross will be the centre."

When this was done, Stephen's guess proved to be just over an inch out.

"Pretty fair. Now to draw the circle. You can do that with string too, but there's a more accurate way." As

Gordon spoke, he drilled a hole in a long thin strip of wood and loosely screwed it to the centre mark on the plywood. A pencil point held through a second hole three feet along the strip, scribed a six-foot circle in two arcs. Each arc reached the board edge in two places as the timber was only four feet wide, giving an incomplete disc with two flat sides.

"The missing edge pieces will be filled in with the ends we cut off." He indicated the area outside the circle in the eight-foot direction, then pointed to a stack of small wooden sections leaning against the wall. "We're using those one inch square teak timbers to fix paddles to shrouds. They'll fix the edge pieces too. Teak is good in water, it's used in boats. Lasts a long time, probably longer than the plywood."

Both children helped hold the timber while the circle was cut using a hand held keyhole-saw, the only flexible blade available. When work moved to the second sheet, Chris reached out to lift the saw, dropping it with a yell. The slender blade was burning hot. Axle holes were quickly cut and the third big sheet sawn into small paddle sections. Stephen had already ambled off to find other interests as the two shrouds and twelve paddles were assembled using brass screws to avoid rust.

At one point Jan shouted through the door, "Can I come in? Do you want coffee?"

"No!" They worked on, calling the family only when construction was complete. Seeing the finished work, even Sharon grew interested again. Though difficult to lift, the wheel rolled easily with many helping hands, down to the stream's edge. There on the bank, it stayed, right next to where an axle already projected out over the fast flowing water. But how could that wheel be placed on the axle without it being swept away down river?

The question was still being discussed when two electricity board men appeared from the north. They had been surveying for a pylon line much farther downstream and for convenience had parked their car in front of the house. Asked if they would like to help with a smaller scheme, both willingly obliged. One, a waterwheel enthusiast, exhibited great interest and considerable knowledge, telling of an existing wheel still in use at Charlestown, forty miles away.

"You don't mind a little competition then?" Jan asked.

"No. Not unless you want us to buy all your surplus current."

"Surplus?" she tossed her head. "Hm! I'll probably faint if it works at all!"

With the extra help, the whole assembly manhandled easily into position and was firmly fixed. The wheel turned handsomely! Water flowing swiftly beneath spun it rapidly, creating a flurry of flying spray; droplets of clinging liquid flung high in the air as each rotating paddle emerged on the downstream side. Long after the surveyors had left, the family stood together on the bank, silently watching this colourful display.

After a while, Jan, her arms round the children, leaned forward. "Might be quite decorative," she whispered, "so it may not after all be completely useless!"

On that dubious compliment, Gordon took his leave and hurried away to catch up on other work. Later Sharon raced across the field directly in front of the house, hurrying to open the office door and finding no one, shouted, "Mum, look!"

Jan appeared from the kitchen, summoned by the urgent call. Upstream, a young swan floated slowly towards them, not swimming but moving with the current. Stephen entered from another room as the bird disappeared, hidden by the bridge then sailed into view again directly in front of the window. Though full size, the mottled feathers of a not quite mature bird marked it as a juvenile. Gracefully it floated up to the new wheel, for all the world as if arriving deliberately at that moment to examine their handiwork.

"A River Board Inspector in disguise," Jan suggested

with a mock grimace. Both children stared again at the swan, swinging back at their mother's call of "Come on," as she made for the door, pausing once to warn, "Approach slowly, don't frighten it."

When the trio reached the bank, the swan drifted away, a few strokes taking it to the far side, dark webbed feet easily seen through the clear water.

"Fishing line!" Stephen lifted an arm, one finger extended to point. A slim strand hung from the beak.

"Do we need Dad?" Sharon asked.

"Probably, but not yet. He'll be in a hurry, find some excuse, say we can't catch it and go back to work. Where's Chris?"

Both children sped off at their mother's suggestion, racing against each other, giving no acknowledgement to the urgently shouted reminder to be careful. The swan eased towards midstream, coasted to the weir, the long neck curving over in examination as if wishing to float on down-river. Perhaps that was never its intention, or maybe the rough water over the drop formed a deterrent for it paddled slowly away, out of the mid-stream current to rest in slack water near the far edge. Sharon and Stephen reappeared at a run, dashing into view, Chris now with them. Having watched for a while, all moved back a goodly distance from the river. The swan was obviously unhappy but some deep instinct kept it on the water. What to do? A whispered conference discussed what action to take.

"Go in after it." Stephen offered.

He would certainly jump straight in, clothes and all, Jan was well aware of that; it was clear in his expression and the eager forward step. Quickly she moved to stop him.

"No! Even in that weak state, it's too fast for you in the water. On land we might stand a chance, but I doubt that's possible."

"Shout and splash the water from the other bank to

frighten it out," Chris pointed.

"Try if you like, I must check the lunch. Someone should hide on this side ready to jump out. Better be you Chris, can you handle it?"

He looked doubtfully at the big bird, obviously unsure. "I think so."

"Go for the neck," his mother advised. "That will stop any escape, but the wings are most dangerous – could break your arm! They're strong on the downbeat, but weaker at opening, that's what a bird needs for flying. Wrap an arm over them and hang on tightly until the rest of us arrive. Okay?" Jan made to leave and the younger two prepared to run round to the far bank, but Chris called them back.

"Wait!" He beckoned towards a thicket of willow bushes near the riverbank. "Come here first. We must all hide together."

"Why?" Sharon's single word had that quality of 'Why should I!', her natural tendency to refuse anything sounding like an order that came from her brother. But Chris had already gone, now kneeling hidden from the swan. If she wanted to know the reason, there was no option other than to join him. It was a tight fit, three children and Mum all huddled close together behind the foliage, for the bushes were not extensive. As they crouched there together, Chris attempted to explain.

"The father of one of my friends is a game warden. He says birds can't count, so..."

"What difference does that make?" Sharon tried to shove him into the bush but Jan reached out stopping her. "Let him finish."

"If I had hidden behind this bush on my own, the swan would know, but now, when you leave it won't realise someone is left because it can't count." Chris held out a hand indicating that it was obvious.

Sharon stiffened; her jaw clenched ready to argue... but as Stephen sped off she followed quickly, not wanting to be left behind, catching him as he ran over the bridge.

Entering the office door Mum saw them run down the far bank together, waving arms, shouting and jumping climbing the bank nearest the house. Stephen knelt at the edge, splashing water with his hands. The bird, distressed but not stupid, floated just beyond mid-stream and waited, moving with smooth grace in its favoured environment despite the dangling line. No one would catch or help it while on the water. In the end Jan re-emerged to throw bread on the grass and call them in to prepare for lunch.

Before washing they stood by the window. The swan glided easily towards the bank but had difficulty climbing out, all that graceful motion lost once the river no longer supported its weight. A dozen slow unsteady paces took it to the waiting bread; at one point a wing stretched sideways, touching the ground to maintain balance. Jim, Jan's father, could have walked faster with his bad leg. Forgetting the intention to wash, Chris crept through the office door, flattening himself against the wall, barely hidden by the house from the swan's field of vision. Working backward until well out of sight, he tore round the building to approach from the rear.

Peering from the opposite corner, only part of his face and one eye showing, he spied with satisfaction the bird's back, its head facing away. Tiptoeing stealthily forward with the intention of approaching undiscovered, proved futile. In that first step, even before fully breaking cover, the long neck straightened, swivelling to the rear and a warning hissed from the broad beak! Abandoning all caution, Chris dashed forward in a frantic effort to cut the Swan's retreat; in the heat of the moment he was prepared even for a flying tackle to prevent it regaining the river, giving little thought to how he would manage if contact was made.

The rush was wasted. Though his quarry tried to flee, it was not fast enough. As Chris stood blocking the path to the water, the swan faced him, standing tall and hissing with wings raised. It appeared bigger now! With the momentum of that first charge over, so too the determination to dive straight in deserted him. It was stalemate. The swan could not flee and Chris hung back, still preventing its escape but not yet finding the courage to step in and effect a capture. Flicking eyes to the windows beyond he saw the others inside. Even as he looked, Stephen turned away, hurrying towards the door and in a few moments came pelting round the corner straight at the swan. Chris had no time to think, he lunged for the neck, grabbing it as Stephen arrived at the other side. For all the swift approach, both lads handled the bird with some care, struggling to subdue it without damage. They had not long to hold on; Mum arrived, slipping an arm round the already trapped wings, taking the neck, then lifted and carefully walked to the office step.

"I'll hold it." She sat down, keeping one arm wrapped round the wings and retaining that firm hold on the neck. "Sharon, go and tend lunch, it's casserole – should be fine for a while but check on the liquid level and watch the vegetables. Dad will be back any moment. Chris, Stephen, you can stay here, try to calm our new friend down, talk to it, touch it gently but move slowly and speak softly, like we did with the Buzzard."

When Dad did appear from beyond the toilet building some minutes later, he missed a stride, hesitating in mid-step at the sight ahead.

"Problems? Who caught it?"

"Chris and Stephen. Look!" Jan pointed one finger without letting go as Stephen reached forward to hold up the loose fishing line. "See if you can locate the hook, it may be too far down."

The beak opened against weak resistance, a brassy glint reflecting sunlight from a point four inches below the opening.

"I'll need long pliers, can you hang on?" Unintentionally, he spoke as if she might not be capable.

"Of course we can – easily! Who do you think has been holding it for the last ten minutes? We're not helpless! Go find your tools." Jan admitted to herself the exaggeration, it had actually been less than five minutes but even in that time their captive seemed calmer. Gordon brushed past, moving carefully not to further fluster the bird, and headed off for the basement, grabbing a torch from a drawer behind the desk.

Descending the stairs he reached the workroom. "How is it tools are never where they should be? Where... Ah, there they are!"

Retrieving the pliers from an untidy pile on the bench, he hurried upstairs, dashing to the bathroom to dip them in a weak disinfectant solution before going outside. The swan tried feebly to escape again when its beak was cautiously but forcibly re-opened. The hook was simple enough to grip, but not so easy to remove without injury.

"Wish people would use barbless hooks."

He pressed gently downwards, twisting slightly to clear the flesh, then up and out. The merest touch of blood issued from a small puncture but close to the hook on the removed line rested several tiny clamped on weights. Seeing them Jan wondered if dissolving lead accounted for the bird's condition since the hook itself had inflicted only slight visible damage. She sat holding the swan while Stephen, having found some bread inside the house, tentatively held out a hand. Surprisingly, the large beak reached to take a piece from his fingers. Easing her hold on the neck, Jan stroked the feathers encouragingly. Sharon peered out from the office door, then quickly moved forward to take a piece. With eyes tightly shut, she offered the crusty morsel which was taken immediately from her open palm. Eating was a good sign, it usually indicated that a bird was not too disturbed.

"Treat Nessie with care," Jan warned as she passed the big bird over.

"Why Nessie?"

"Why not?" she shrugged. "Got to be called something, and it is big."

"We caught it." Stephen murmured as his father carried the now hook-free swan towards the river. The lad said no more. Detecting a touch of resentment, Jan glanced at Chris and seeing his expression, called "Wait!"

Gordon stopped as she signalled the boys to follow, indicating a spot on the bank not far from the river. "Sit there. Dad, bring Nessie over and put her down between them; don't let go until Chris has the wings and Stephen the neck."

With the swan in position the parents withdrew, going inside to watch through the window. Sharon, who had popped regularly to the door to check on progress as she tended the meal, joined them in the lounge. Nessie was now standing on Chris's outstretched leg and facing towards Stephen who had already released his grip on the neck, his fingers gently stroking the breast feathers. Gingerly Chris released the wings, talking quietly and rubbing a hand softly over the feathered back. For a time the boys and the big bird sat trustingly together as Jan appeared again to spread more bread liberally along the bank within easy reach from the river. After a while, Nessie stepped unhurriedly down, plodding ponderously towards the water's edge, entering the stream to drift on the current, the children slowly following. As they turned to go inside, Jan called over.

"Sharon, after lunch run up to the village before the shop closes. Ask Sampson if he still has a spare loaf. With what we've given the swan, there won't be enough for breakfast. Don't look so reluctant, you can tell Jim and Audrey about Nessie."

This inducement, the prospect of carrying the news, was more than sufficient for Sharon to happily nod in agreement. Their new friend stayed on for a few days, becoming obviously stronger and bolder. Now free, it never came quite near enough to feed directly from anyone's hand. Chris almost persuaded the bird, strangely enough because he took Judy with him, holding the goat on a rope to graze the bank while his other hand offered bread. The swan, sensing perhaps the goat's lack of concern at Chris's presence, almost took crumbs from his open palm, reaching out a long neck to within a hand's width but retracting at the last moment. It was already well fed, no longer needing to take risks.

The waterwheel looked great. As it spun, liquid droplets sprayed aloft sparkling with sunshine colours, wet shrouds glistened and constantly churning paddles smacked the stream with a pleasant rhythmic splash, releasing pulses of frothy water as each blade broke free at the downstream surface. Yet none but the family witnessed this spectacle, for the valley was deserted. Now, in November, no single person rambled by for days on end, nor could any caravan or tent be expected until the following spring. The whole wild valley rested, exclusively their own once more. Three children roamed unrestricted, calling, shouting across an empty landscape, making such noise as took their fancy; no one would hear, no visitor expecting quietness would be upset. Max, the big excavator, woke early; its engine starting with the dawn, no longer restrained by sleeping tourists.

Winters were different, a release from the pressure of keeping everything in order and sparklingly clean, of dealing with unexpected crises and of making people happy, or at least, trying to make them happy. Over the past season efforts had been intense; nothing had been out of order for more than twenty minutes, not a single tap, drain, door bolt, or hot shower had failed to function properly for longer than it took to grab tools and make the repair. Even the odd sink plug which came slightly loose had quickly been made secure again. Those busy days had been enjoyable, immensely so, but draining! Ten weeks ago more than three hundred guests lived in the valley, now there were none! Those little lights that had spread across the site as darkness fell, were gone.

For Jan there were all those jobs neglected during the summer; spring-cleaning that was never possible in spring, clothes to sort and mend, curtains to wash, rooms to repaint. Outside, the grass should have one more cut and the dustbin area needed attention; weeds had sneaked in over the busy period and trees must be trimmed. These tasks had already been started over the previous weeks, but she had not hurried, deliberately holding back for the lonely months ahead. Sometimes when needing the company, she would volunteer to drive Max, helping create new areas, wondering how Gordon could continue from dawn to dusk always working. He never let her load stone from the tall face of the old mine heaps; said it was too dangerous, but she would walk down the valley anyway, waiting for the return of another loaded trailer, or to find him digging out roots.

Feeling the solitude badly one morning even though it was only an hour since they had drunk coffee together, she set off to find him and on approaching, heard talking. The sound stopped her abruptly; that robin probably! Quietly stepping into deeper concealment and listening, a mixture of emotions tussled within. "He should be talking to me, not that bird – unfaithful brute! I've no one else now." The resentment was foolish, just loneliness, she knew that. "Rubbish, I can't be jealous of a robin!" But the thoughts persisted, tinged with anger as she made to move forward and confront him. His voice stopped her and she listened again, somehow sensing her own presence was not required. Creeping off and returning to the house feeling excluded, she stood for a long while gazing out along the river wondering, then hunted out an old light summer blouse and worked on the button holes.

At lunch they chatted happily enough; she made no mention of her earlier visit but as he rose to leave she brushed against him, apparently by accident. The blouse burst open to the waist – she had known it would, had practised the move a dozen times – there was no other garment beneath.

"Oh!" She drew in a sharp breath, grabbing his arm with a pretence of falling, stumbling against the table and leaning back to stretch the thin material tight against her figure.

Automatically his free hand moved to save her, his eyes drawn to the deep Vee of creamy flesh, one bosom almost exposed as she twisted sideways stretching an arm backwards apparently to save herself. For a moment he stood staring down, she could see the struggle in his face, the need for more progress, for another load of stone, or…

Letting the supporting hand slip backward, she twisted farther, feeling the blouse open wider, then catch and pull against a taut nipple. It could have been accidental, she covered the evocative movement well, a little roe deer, cornered and so vulnerable, looking up wide-eyed, the lips parting.

His arm had shot forward again, worried she would fall, supporting her between the shoulders but unable to tear his gaze away. She was breathing deeply, the smooth skin rising and falling, a small pink aureole peeping out where the material stretched tightly. Watching his eyes, she could sense the thoughts. For a moment he stood there... slowly a sun-tanned hand rose, the colour contrasting with her own skin as it reached for the blouse. No need to fake the tension, the excitement when he pulled the material free, exposing her. He would not escape now!

That afternoon she felt an inner happiness, a deeper contentment with the valley. Robin was not the only one who could get his attention! Try as he might to catch up, he would lose two trailer loads at least this day. She smiled to herself, folding the blouse and putting it in the bottom drawer; her secret. Perhaps one day she would tell – show him how loosely those buttons now fitted?

The swan's presence provided an excuse to postpone further development; the wheel temporarily forsaken in favour of landscape work, much to Sharon's annoyance. A rotating wheel was all very fine, it offered a start, but what about that promised electricity?

One morning Nessie was gone. A hurried search before school revealed no trace. Strong enough to swim off along the stream, no longer needing help? They all hoped so. Swans did prefer broader stretches of water, the departure was expected. That evening, the children's first question on arriving home confirmed the swan had not reappeared. The light was hardly beginning to fade when Max trundled into the yard for a top-up, having run low on fuel. Tea would be early.

The meal was all but finished when Sharon asked a question.

"Nessie won't ever come back, will she?"

"No, I wouldn't think so; not to a river this size."

Hearing her mother's confirmation of what had already been guessed, Sharon turned to her father. "You can finish the wheel now?"

"Probably. Do you know what we need next?"

"A generator," Chris prompted. "You mentioned it once before."

"Yes, but it's less straight forward than you might think." Dad looked around the three young faces. "I've decided what to do, but how would you tackle the problem; can you follow the reasoning? Most generators must rotate at constant speed, not easy on a river because of seasonal rises and falls. At one point I considered diverting water into a leat, that's a little channel, so flow to the wheel could be more easily controlled. These leats were once common in Cornwall. Did you know one served Carbis Mill, a mile downstream, in the eighteenth century?"

Chris nodded, "One of the boys at school says a millstone on St Michael's Mount came from there, I don't know if it's true."

"Really? Maybe it did; I think Carbis belongs to his Lordship. However, this leat idea; a Cornwall River

Authority Officer called last summer in response to my letter about building a wheel. I had to get permission you see. The chap was quite helpful. Apparently a leat would involve an extraction licence with an annual fee, so he advised putting the wheel directly in the river, like we've done. It avoids extracting water and we don't have to pay. He encouraged the project, wanted us to do it, said wheels are beneficial to freshwater creatures. They increase oxygen levels by aerating the water."

"You never told *me* of this man's visit!" Jan accused, pointing a finger as if it were loaded. "Not that I really want to know. Stupid idea anyway – but this site is not just yours! We do own it jointly, I am entitled to be consulted!"

Normally they discussed everything together, pleased with any topic to debate. Her annoyance at being excluded was showing as she stared at him, awaiting a reply.

"It was purely chance that he came while you were out. I do admit to keeping it secret and I did get the permission, but it was just a vague possibility then – didn't want to raise hopes without good reason. When the idea was abandoned, it seemed sensible to say nothing so not to disappoint you." He raised two hands in a tacit plea for understanding, or it might have been in self-defence in case something was thrown.

"Couldn't get yourself to admit giving up I expect. Anyway you were right, it won't work. No chance! But go ahead and try, give us all a laugh. More coffee?" Her good humour was restored.

"Yes please. It's getting dark, I'll top up the boiler." He lit a candle, there were several around, each stuck to its own saucer. Holding it out in front he disappeared, descending the basement stairs, round several corners and corridors and into a small room with the solid fuel boiler. The pile of coal usually stored on the floor was exhausted, a handful of dust remaining. He pushed the shovel into a nine-inch square opening above, a hole that communicated with a pit in the rear of the garage where the coal merchant tipped his sacks. The shovel came back loaded with black, somewhat dusty chunks.

Meanwhile, Jan poured the coffee as Sharon drew the curtains and Stephen lit another candle. Chris left the house, running round to check two large red gas bottles outside the kitchen window. He returned in time to hear his father mention the lack of coal in the basement.

Jan twisted from the stove towards the boys. "Whose turn is it? No good pointing at each other." She waited until Stephen raised his hand a few inches, accepting the task. "Okay. Tomorrow, after school and before it gets dark, shovel another hundredweight at least through the hole. Chris, hang that sheet on the nails over the boiler room doorway for him, to stop the dust spreading."

These small chores dealt with, the family settled again at the table.

"Good. Now where were we?" Dad scratched his chin, "Ah yes, this generator – how to make it run at a constant speed? In the old days, massive waterwheels used special devices to automatically lift or lower gates to control the water flow, but that's no good, it absorbs too much power. We could do like the Romans did on the Thames in London, float our wheel between two boats anchored in the river so it rises and falls with the water level. Good idea?"

"Hmm!" Viewing the entire project with scepticism and still miffed at being ignored in those original discussions with the River Board, Jan spoke with heavy sarcasm. "Did they need power for electric razors, or did Caesar want a washing machine for his toga?"

"Oh, clever! Know all about Romans do you, remember it well perhaps?" He ducked as she threw the newspaper. Much to the children's entertainment, it opened in the air and floated harmlessly to the ground but the little duel had put everyone in great good spirits.

"Romans had beards, they never needed razors," Chris claimed, only to be contradicted by his sister.

"That was Vikings, silly; beards and horns, we did them at school!"

The argument continued with some merriment but as usual when they disagreed, the exchanges threatened to become more acrimonious.

"Hold on!" Dad put down his empty cup, his timely interruption stopping them before the good humour was lost. "Mum was being facetious, er, sarcastic… She knows very well there was no electric in Roman times. They did use water power, but for other purposes, grinding corn to make flour for instance. Probably both Romans and Vikings had beards."

Stephen had watched the older two, at a loss. Romans? Vikings? Who were they? His vacant expression throughout the little war of words, caused Jan concern. Although never as talkative as Chris or Sharon, he usually joined in any argument. She disliked him being left out completely and attempting to bring her youngest back into the present conversation, asked what he had learned at school that the others might not know? The lad regarded her blankly, then a wicked little grin that he did so well spread slowly over his face. He spoke in almost a whisper.

"How tall is a dead fly?"

Silence enveloped the table as they looked at each other, then back at Stephen.

"Six feet in the air." His voice scarcely breathed the answer. From anyone else it would just have seemed clever, but from the little lad – amazing!

"Whoever told you that?" Jan gazed at the small face, the light unruly hair with no trace of a parting, blue eyes regarding her steadily, meeting her own, not turning away. Seeing the wilful expression, young lips compressed, she sensed he would say no more, and eased back with a sigh. Useless to ask again.

But she was wrong; he had not quite finished. The low voice came again, "Dead spiders are taller."

The interlude of light-hearted irrelevant chatter that

followed further delayed Dad's explanation, but eventually it died away allowing him to continue.

"Controlling the wheel's speed? Actually, the answer lies in a different direction; find a generator that doesn't need constant velocity but still gives a steady voltage. It's really quite simple – use the type that powers car headlights, they *have* to work at all speeds. Better still, we can get one from the scrap yard and it's bound to be cheap! Best get a couple, really – we'll need a spare."

Gordon had thought the design through to this point, but the gearing itself presented a real problem. He was about to speak again, but Sharon cut in first.

"If it's so simple, can we have electric tomorrow?"

"Hmm!" Jan's head shook. "Some chance!"

All eyes were on Dad, waiting.

"There's a problem..." his attention was diverted as Jan and the children looked at each other heads nodding, her hand held out, palm up, fingers extended in a 'What did you expect' gesture. The aura of disbelief was disconcerting. Drawing in a breath, he spoke defensively. "It's not insurmountable, just a gearing problem."

The family looked to Mum for their reaction, and when she nodded to them saying, "Yes, yes, of course it is," the words oozing with pretend sympathy, they nodded back, grinning, then turned as Dad spoke again.

"Car alternators need to rotate at more than a thousand revolutions every minute to produce any current. If you see a waterwheel turning at one tenth of that speed, run and don't stop. Centrifugal force will ensure its destruction, scattering debris like a grenade. Death from disintegrating flywheels occurred frequently during the Industrial Revolution. Now you've seen the speed that our wheel rotates at; it's approximately fifteen revolutions per minute, people usually say RPM. Check for yourself if you want. The river may rise several inches in mid-winter, spinning the wheel even faster; the water should fly off quite handsomely if it reaches twenty-RPM. Of course in midsummer it might slow slightly.

Our gearing must therefore increase rotations per minute by something like one hundred times!"

Chris frowned, "How can we make it turn so... Ouch."

"Don't ask!" Sharon urged, kicking him under the table. "We only want it working, not a six-week lecture on how it's done."

"Very well, I'll explain in the garage. Those who wish to remain ignorant, can stay behind." Dad picked up a candle, leaving the room. Only Chris followed.

The general principles involved were clear, but making it work would not be easy, neither would explaining the method but for that he had an idea. Entering the garage, he sought somewhere to perch the candle and having found a suitable place, crossed to a bicycle leaning against the wall in the far corner. It was one of the original Claude Butler racing cycles, still with the original Brooks leather saddle, bought many years ago while in the forces. He turned it upside down, and pointed.

"Look, this big cogwheel fixed to the pedals, the one the chain runs on. Count the number of cogs." They counted together, there were fifty, and on the smallest cogwheel at the other end of the chain there were fourteen.

"Right," Gordon continued, "if the pedal rotates once, the chain moves fifty cogs. Since there are only fourteen cogs on the rear wheel, each pedal turn makes the back wheel go round three and a half times. Try it?"

With a piece of string hastily tied to the back wheel as a marker, Chris rotated the pedal, counting. "Yes," he agreed slowly, "Three and a half. But a hundred times faster will take some gigantic cogwheel?"

"Not necessarily. A slightly bigger cog would give five times faster, then we can make the gearing like three bicycles coupled together, each one increasing the speed by five, giving 125 times faster."

Chris nodded dubiously, uncertain exactly how this could be done or if it would work at all, doubts that showed clearly. His father understood; he was himself unsure of success but if the family really wanted electricity then he *had* to make it work – could see no other way! Mains power lay far off, a penalty of living alone in the valley. The choice was simple; succeed or wait goodness knows how many years to accumulate money for the vast cost of a normal supply!

While Chris and often Stephen helped with the gearing, Sharon stayed well clear. Her interest, as always, lay not in construction but in results, in what it would produce. Here she had started to share Jan's doubts.

"Mum, if you don't think it will work, why do you let him do it?"

"Let him? Have you ever tried to stop your father when he has some mad idea?"

Never having given it a thought before, Sharon frowned, but she was beginning to notice boys and how they behaved. Helping prepare the midday meal, the growing girl for some reason felt a special closeness to her mother today, not like a parent exactly, more a friend, a confidante.

"Why should they have their own way always?" Sharon asked. It was hardly a question, more a thought spoken aloud.

"Do they?"

"The boys at school seem to expect it, particularly the bigger ones. Dad does too. He still hasn't put that curtain rail up in the hall but you never make him do it?"

"What do you suggest, I bash him over the head with a club, drag him into the hall by his hair and stand over him until it's done?"

They grinned at each other, Sharon signalling her enthusiasm, entirely approving of the idea.

"Some of my girl friends at school say their parents argue and fight a lot. You and Dad never shout at each other…" She stopped, remembering a couple of times over the past few years when voices had been raised. "Well, hardly ever. Is that why he always gets his own way?"

"Isn't it nicer not to be fighting all the time, worth

giving way for a smoother happier life?" Jan put the lid back on a saucepan and carrying a saucer with thin slices of raw carrot to nibble, she walked over to sit at table.

Sharon followed frowning, "They still shouldn't always get their own way."

Jan looked at her daughter, hesitating before offering a response, wondering how much to say, how much of her inner feelings to reveal – also sensing somehow the strange bond between them today. At ten years old perhaps it was time to be frank? She pulled absently at a sleeve, delayed a few more seconds, then spoke slowly.

"If you love someone, really love them, you want them to be happy too. And if they love you back, they feel the same. A man likes to know he's in charge, it's good for their ego, but that doesn't mean they get all their own way. You mentioned the hall. I don't really mind about that curtain, if it was something important, he would do it for me – but it's not, so I let it pass. It's hard for a man to like a woman who constantly nags. Anyway, we enjoy our small differences. While he hasn't done it, I can remind him of it if I'm loosing an argument."

The girls smiled at each other again, Sharon nodding her understanding before her mother continued.

"Disagreeing is not necessarily the best way to get what you want. Take those coat pegs on the hall wall. Your father wanted to put more the other side. That would have spoiled the entrance completely, but I never objected. I just said 'That's a good idea', then stood back, tilting my head one way then the other, and asked, 'You don't think that will make the hall look narrow do you?' He only shrugged, but no pegs were ever put on that side."

"Mum. That's..." Sharon searched for a suitable word.

"Deceitful?" Jan prompted. The two burst into laughter, Sharon reaching out to touch her mother's hand; an unintended, spontaneous response to the closeness that she suddenly felt.

Looking down at her daughter's dark hair, Jan spoke

again. "Actually, things like that are always happening. When we get better off and I want to change a carpet, I won't say 'let's buy a new rug'. I'll ask, do you think this room would be better with a different carpet?"

"He'll say no!" Sharon declared positively.

"Possibly, but he's not so insensitive as you think. Nor is what I do really deceitful. Mostly he knows. Those hooks for instance, he understood I disliked the idea, so he forgot it. It's how we make things run smoothly. Mind you, sometimes he doesn't know, then I feel deliciously wicked, but mostly he falls in line because he loves me. And I never press because I love him."

She stopped again, aware of the dreamy look in her daughter's eye, and felt a word of warning might not come amiss.

"Don't get too carried away. We used to argue a lot trying to score points off each other like you and Chris always do. Even now I could slosh him sometimes, especially when I'm angry and he just laughs. Do you remember that plate of egg and chips?"

CHAPTER 3

Milk Tray

All was ready! The moment of truth approached and the children expected success! Gordon hoped so too, well aware that Jan, sceptical as ever, just waited for the chance to say, 'I told you so!' She could do it without words, a glance and her expression would be enough. The waterwheel gearing had been arranged using V-belts rather than chains; they were cheaper. It had taken time to collect wheels, shafts, bearings, and fix them into a suitable pattern, but it should work – maybe?

For the first attempt, a car sidelight bulb was rigged to light up when the wheel started. At least it should – if the system produced any electricity! A meter in circuit would show the exact current. Dull weather might have been best to make any glimmer appear brighter, but listening to the small battery radio, clear skies were again forecast. Improvising, a cardboard box with one side cut away now covered the bulb, inverted over the circuit and weighted down with a chunk of wood, an attempt to create darker surroundings in which even a tiny glow would stand out. Tomorrow was test day, deliberately arranged for Saturday so the children could be present. Gordon told them at tea, attempting to defuse mushrooming expectations by explaining that alignment of the shafts was critical and large gear ratios inevitably led to loss of power.

"How big a loss? That, I can't tell you. Don't expect too much, but with luck you should see something."

They were jubilant, hungry for details. How bright?

How many bulbs would it run? Would there be one in *my* room? Would it give electric shocks?

"Hmm," Jan's head shook as she watched them.

The morning dawned true to forecast, with a clear cloudless sky. Sharon urged that the trial be made before breakfast, with the sun still hidden below the eastern horizon.

"Dad wanted a dull day so the bulb would show brighter, doing it early will be just as good."

Chris and Stephen held back, reluctant to agree with their sister, though they too, were much more interested in the test than in eating.

Jan smiled at her young brood as they gathered close, well aware of their desire. "You think this will work first time, with no trouble?" Seeing the eager nods, she shook her head. "You expect that bulb to light up..." she hunted for the words, at a loss how properly to express her doubts, then finding inspiration continued with a Tommy Cooper motion of the hands, "just like that." The children nodded again, oblivious of the inference that this too was something Cooperish that would fail to come off. Jan flicked a glance at Gordon, knowing immediately that he had understood, then turned back to her young brood. "Milking first, then breakfast. I want all chores out of the way, nothing to distract me when the fun starts – could be the best laugh in years!"

After milking, Judy was tied temporarily outside during breakfast. By the time Chris led the goat off to be tethered in a fresh place, somewhere away from young saplings but within reach of both grass and suitable roughage like gorse or brambles, the sun had risen over treetops on the gently sloping valley side. Though without strength now in winter, it reflected brightly from the unruffled surface of a still pool above the weir before the water cascaded over, foaming as it rushed off downstream. Temperature in the windless air remained high enough for shirtsleeves.

The little group approached the bank-top to look down on the rotating wheel, droplets of water flying out in its usual colourful display. To connect the gearing it must be stationary, unless someone wanted to risk a few fingers! This step had been discussed at length the previous evening. Dad's suggestion that the children might like to undertake the task had caused Sharon to shake her head in alarm, but both boys immediately volunteered.

"Oh no!" Jan had stepped in quickly. "You'll get filthy! That wheel will probably drag Stephen right over the top and pin him underwater on the upstream side! Dad started this; *he* can do it. I shall enjoy watching him get soaked; serves him right – stupid idea anyway!"

Now, bathed in morning sunshine, she stood with the children atop the bank as their father approached the river, hesitating just beyond the spray's reach. Bringing the speeding wooden structure to a standstill should indeed be an interesting venture in itself. It had never been done before but no other stopping mechanism yet existed. Lunging forward, Gordon grasped a paddle – only to have it torn from his grip, spray covering him liberally to above waist level. A cheer rose from above, drifting off across the empty valley. More shouted encouragement, happy eager young voices, rang in the air as he gripped the next, again snatched away with little change of speed. Doggedly he clung to each successive blade until it slipped under his fingertips, wrenched free by a combination of momentum and force from the river below. Gradually the speed reduced, until finally it stopped. He rested, leaning against the now stationary wheel, not daring let go long enough to connect that final belt.

Chris and Stephen, itching to join in, rushed forward. Sharon with a look of 'It's all wet and dirty,' written clear on her face, closed in more slowly. Jan moved to place her body in the remaining space next to Gordon. Straining back, attempting not to lean against his now saturated clothes, she spoke in a whisper.

"Well, they're enjoying it, but it won't work."

Releasing his grip he stepped away, swung quickly to

kneel over the shaft end and eased the final belt onto the temporarily motionless pulley. It was done! They could let go now but he delayed, putting off the moment, rechecking again the tangle of other belts and shafts with a swift glance, though they had all been examined beforehand – several times.

Rising, he turned towards the family still clinging to the wheel. "On the count of three, let go together. One, Two, Three!"

They jumped clear, Jan shaking her head, the children animated with hopeful anticipation. Expressions changed to disappointment as the wheel, contrary to expectations failed to resume its previous water spraying revolutions, but gathered speed more steadily, settling to a slower pace. They didn't realise it was to be expected, speed necessarily reducing now part of the stream's energy was directed to producing electricity, not just rotating a free running wheel.

"Look!" Stephen, again quickest, dragged his eyes from the paddles to notice the glowing bulb. Even so he uttered just the one exclamation and pointed. The meter showed less than two amps; it was a start. Two amps at twelve volts was only twenty-four watts, even stored it would be little enough. But it proved the system worked!

Gordon knelt near the bulb, the young family grouped closely around. With a smugly superior grin he looked up to Jan, the children following his gaze. Smiling back at the happy faces, she moved across, squatting daintily with one arm round Sharon, then to the youngster's increasing delight reached out to playfully shove Dad's shoulder.

"You're so clever – Bighead!"

And so the current flowed. A cable buried under the turf led this power to an old tractor battery beside the house. Another wire passing through a vent would operate the lights that were now rapidly introduced in various rooms. Jan had vetoed their installation before, refusing to have "bulbs that will never work cluttering up my ceilings!" as she put it. Well, that had been wrong – they did work, but all must be used sparingly. Modifications came thick and fast at the beginning. The alloy wheels were soft; they wore away to a black powder leaving the V belts touching the bottoms of the grooves then slipping to an uncontrollable degree. Cast iron wheels were the cure, some of a larger diameter and with multiple belts. These alterations proved moderately expensive, not only the cost of each new wheel, but machining of the shafts and hubs to fit. The effort was worthwhile; wattage increased to more than double the original output! However, Sharon was disappointed; this extra current was still insufficient for television.

Her father promised to attempt a further improvement in the power output, but for the moment could think of no way to achieve that ambition and excused himself, returning to the job of clearing those immense piles of mine waste that still covered the western valley side, the sunset side. How many hundreds of miners had spent their lives here in the quest for copper and tin? More to the point, how long would it take one family to remove the residue of their work? The site could never look its best while dominated by such barren spoil. Construction of the wheel, a few part-days snatched here and there over several weeks, had been a diversion, welcome enough but now work concentrated again wholly on the repetitive task of moving mine waste. Not that this stony deposit was a nuisance; undoubtedly it formed a valuable resource, making roads and levelling drastically uneven ground.

Occasionally young Stephen helped. The little lad, head hardly visible through the cab window, could now operate the big excavator, but only if the machine remained stationary. Like his older brother years before, he could reach the control levers to lift and lower the large front bucket, extracting roots while his father stood alongside, connecting up the chain before each pull. Chris was even more useful and could actually drive, helping at times to load and move the bigger stones, the pedals at last within his lengthening reach.

Sharon was different, she had never wanted to drive, showing no inclination to copy her mother in this one respect, for although Jan used Max less often now, she still did so from time to time. During the past holiday season, running the excavator was rare on account of noise but on one occasion Jan had driven it, the front bucket loaded with large stones to repair a spot where the riverbank had collapsed. The sight of her operating the lumbering machine had given rise to considerable amusement among the visitors. Fortunately, nobody fell over in surprise as one man had done during that first year in the valley, slipping down the riverbank to wet one foot in the water.

As work proceeded, the face of the waste heaps became progressively more steep; at such times Gordon forbade anyone to go near. At some unpredictable moment it would collapse, an avalanche of stone sweeping forward, sending the excavator charging back at maximum revs as he strove to avoid a stony grave. So far he had always succeeded, but now the bottom level had been worked until the gently rising soil of the original valley side had been reached. In one place this seemed like solid rock. Short of blasting, there was no way to continue. The loading position must move higher up the hill to what would be the first terrace; first of a series of broad flat shelves that would eventually cover the slope offering special pitches to visitors; River Valley's dress circle!

Naturally, this step upwards reduced the height of the working face. That was good, any slide must surely now be smaller and therefore safer. However, a counter-balancing danger arose. Previously, it was possible to reverse at speed for any distance when danger threatened, now that distance was limited; it terminated abruptly in a twelve-foot drop! A really major slide might carry the excavator, driver and all, over the edge.

An odd hour of most days was spent building a stone wall in front of the first terrace, partly as a break, partly to spread this particularly heavy work rather than leaving it to be done all at once later. Some of the stones were quite large. Lifting objects of that size over long continuous periods would be asking for pulled muscles. As luck would have it, the higher up the hill, the more reasonable became the size of the stones. It should have been expected. All those years ago when the waste was originally dumped, bigger stones were almost bound to have rolled farther down. For a while a pied wagtail began to frequent the stony area being worked. Alone again now for most of each day, naturally Gordon talked to the bird but never felt it understood like Robin and Blackbird, his regular companions over the years. They preferred work that disturbed the soil; only the wagtail liked hunting rocky areas, its longer thinner beak reaching easily into small crevices in the stone.

Despite the vast tonnage being moved, work proceeded in a sensitive way. Trees were preserved and saplings transplanted, banks retained for the badgers, rare flowers protected, changes of level and barriers of woody vegetation were frequent. On one of the areas being levelled, stone was tipped carefully to avoid crushing a tall plant, first noticed and marked for preservation the previous spring. In May it had been over two feet tall, with pale green leaves showing whitish or rather silvery from a distance. It bore no flowers at that time but had later developed little yellow blooms, a couple at a time, replaced by more as each faded. Research revealed the name Mullein. It still seemed rare, for no other had yet been located in the valley. Many wild places were deliberately preserved; rough grassy verges that were not cut until seeds had matured, small woods, clusters of bushes and whole areas of dense undergrowth. In these more secret places and on the spoil heaps, the children often played, returning dirty and scratched. It had happened again that very morning.

Stephen took the key and plastic bag from his mother's hand. Jan passed a tablet of soap and saw reluctance in his stance.

"Go on, you're filthy! I told you not to get dirty today. Been sliding down those heaps again, have you?"

The little face before her stiffened, lips firmly compressed, silent, but the eyes never wavered under her gaze. She wanted to stoop down, reach out and hug him to her, but he had grown to resist that now.

"Off you go then – your own fault, you knew the boiler was out. No good looking like that. It's full of clinker, it blocks sometimes, has to cool down so I can clear it."

Stephen marched off across the yard without a word. The toilet building was locked but inserting the key he entered, immediately reaching to press a basin tap, checking the temperature. At breakfast Mum had asked Chris to light both pilot jets in case she needed hot water. Shortly the basin ran hot. Good, probably the showers would too, but the air was cold. Stephen had intended using one of the footstools that resided under the basins for younger children to stand on. They were useful in the showers where both taps and hooks had been placed fairly high on the wall to avoid people hurting themselves if they slipped. However, the footstools were gone, stored safely away for winter. Inside the shower compartment he checked the contents of the plastic bag before reaching to hang it on the lowest hook. It was easy now; three years ago those footstools had been a necessity. Stripping, he threw the old clothes straight over the tall partitions to land where they would outside. One lodged, but he pulled it back by a sleeve, screwed it tighter and threw again.

At tea that evening Dad asked about the shower, concerned as always by anything affecting the facilities. How was the temperature, the water flow, had it run away properly, were the high windows open to stop steam condensing on the paintwork, did the door bolt slide easily and had the compartment been left clean?

The family smiled at each other during these exchanges,

which were answered in most cases with a single “Yus,” or an occasional, “’s alright.”

“Ah, but did you enjoy it?” Jan asked.

“No. Floor was cold.”

“Well what did you expect at this time of year? I did warn you not to get dirty today. Anyway, isn’t it normally cold?”

“No. Footstools are gone.” The family hardly expected more but shortly he spoke again with a certain pride. “I can reach now. Younger children should have a lower hook.”

Weeks passed and as Christmas approached, extra hooks had already been added low down in all the showers, tucked back in the corner where the door hinged so no one would catch themselves. This year should be something of a celebration, their fourth in the valley. Jan anticipated the event with considerable pleasure. She remembered their first in a 22-foot caravan and the following two in the bigger version taken over from Jim and Audrey. That one had been inherited when her father and mother moved to their new bungalow in the village of Relubbus, hidden from sight half a mile upstream. Now finally, she too, had a house. Last year the building stood gauntly empty, the structure complete but damp and unfinished inside. What a difference twelve months had made. She gazed round, comfortable in its present warm and cosy state, now boasting 12-volt waterwheel lights in every room, though they were not very bright and restricted to two small bulbs at any one time, or three if the period was short.

Shopping had, of necessity, been left until the morning of Christmas Eve – problems of keeping it fresh!

“Expense is no consideration. We shall splash out, show Dad and the boys what you can do!” Jan announced as they set off for Penzance. ‘Splash out’ was a relative term, she had no intention of being extravagant but was pleased with Sharon’s reaction, and seeing her daughter’s face light up, warned, “Don’t expect any praise from the males of this family, you know they'll find fault with anything you cook – but they like it really."

Sharon nodded. That was true, her cooking was enjoyed by everyone; annoying though, that the boys would never admit it. Unusually skilled for her age in the culinary arts, the ten-year-old girl used her knowledge and the bigger gas stove to good advantage later in the day, confidently baking cakes and pies, making jellies and trifles, boiling a ham and other pre-Christmas cooking; happy in the work. Jan, busy with more preparations, shared the oven but left her daughter largely to her own devices. The two chatted as they worked.

"Have you put enough water in that jelly?"

"I've reduced it slightly, makes them set better without a fridge, Mum. I'll do the same for the trifle jelly – use a fraction more powder in the custard too."

While Sharon enjoyed herself in the kitchen, Chris and Stephen with a few directions from their mother, hung decorations and cards. About mid-afternoon when Gordon arrived from his work down the valley, Jan called them to the dining room, an annexe of the kitchen, for coffee. Sharon walked over carrying a tray of mince pies not long taken from the oven. Had any alternative food been on offer the boys would probably have chosen that on principle. Jan seeing the hesitation winked at her daughter as Gordon reached to take a pie. Turning back to Chris, Sharon held out the tray, eyebrows raised.

"Well, do you want one or not? I'll put them away."

"Suppose I better try one, just in case they're any good." Chris's reluctant response was cut short as he lunged to grab one from the disappearing tray.

The action drew a quiet giggle from his sister and a knowing nod from Mum. Stephen, inspecting carefully, selected the biggest, put it on his plate without a word and probed suspiciously with a fork. Second helpings were accepted by everyone, to laughter from the female half of the family.

"We had a little wager," Jan explained, "after tasting one ourselves from an earlier batch."

It was proving an extremely congenial afternoon. At the boy's request Dad stayed in the house to fix the final decorations, then led them off to the underground work-room. The basement was also equipped with waterwheel lights, but again only two could be used at any one time without depleting the battery. Work on benches and shelves, sorting and sharpening tools, and secret Christmas cards made with the aid of pens, coloured pencils and scissors, saw the hours pass quickly.

Plans for the holiday had long since been made. Jim and Audrey, Jan's parents were to come down at eleven o'clock on Christmas day to exchange presents, followed later by the full family dinner. On Boxing Day they would in turn play host at their own bungalow beside the site entrance. Audrey had received extra help with her preparations, not that this help was needed, but Sharon enjoyed cooking and had asked if she could.

As expected, no one was allowed to oversleep on the great day. Stephen, waking first, pulled the switch to his light and leaving both doors wide open, crept into the adjoining bedroom. Soon all three children sat amid a pile of presents on their parent's bed, switching off all other lights to leave the rest of the house in darkness. Gordon, sitting up and leaning to the right against the wall, supported Jan's head on his shoulder, with Sharon near his left arm. Chris perched next to Jan, feet dangling, toes just making contact with the floor, while Stephen knelt back on his heels near the foot of the bed in a small space between his parent's legs. Presents were mostly clothes, with a few books, special running shoes for Chris, a dressing table set for Sharon, and several small toys for Stephen. All the items were cheap but no one noticed, expensive gifts never expected. Gordon unwrapped a large jigsaw.

"To keep me occupied, stop me thinking of work today?"

Jan nodded confirmation. She had a new dress, or

rather a skirt and matching top from all of them, but as an extra, Dad had smuggled in a box of Cadburys Chocolates. Who says advertising doesn't pay? Those scenes of the tall handsome fellow racing an avalanche down the mountain to bring his lady a box of Milk Tray had caught the imagination. He had seen it once, on the television at Jim's bungalow when he stopped to drop off some grass seed one evening. Problem was, how to give her the present in an equally impressive way. There were no such instructions on the label!

Jan was cooking lunch in the kitchen and would be there most of the morning. Gordon, down in the basement again with the boys, hunted out an old crash helmet, a relic of motor sport days, and passed it to Stephen. Picking up a length of strong rope, the chocolates in his other hand, he bade them follow, leading up the basement stairs to the ground floor.

"Chris, go to the kitchen and ask Sharon if she'll give a hand for a minute. Meet us upstairs in your bedroom." Gordon went ahead with Stephen and while waiting for the others, opened the high window really wide, leaning out to gaze north along the river then down at the kitchen window below and to the left. The ground looked surprisingly distant! Taking a deep breath he turned back into the room, donned the crash helmet, buckling it under the chin, and tied the rope round his waist in knots that hopefully would not slip. Chris and Sharon mounted the stairs swiftly and burst through the doorway, sensing something afoot but not knowing what. Ignoring eager questions, their father passed out the rope.

"Each of you take hold, Chris nearest, then Sharon. Stephen, you be at the back. The idea is this; I climb through the window, let myself fall outwards, walk down the wall like a two legged fly, swing completely upside down, then edge a bit sideways and end with my head hanging over the kitchen window. At least, that's the intention! If all goes well I'll surprise Mum with these chocolates. The only thing stopping me falling will be this rope – which is your job! Take my weight and lower me gradually so I don't hit those gas bottles."

Sharon showed alarm. "You're kidding Dad. You can't do that, it's dangerous. You'll fall!"

"Not unless you let go. Kick that rug away, can't have you slipping! Move it well clear. Yes, that's good. Now remember, I'll lay back horizontally, keeping my feet on the wall until I'm nearly there, that will take part of the weight. At the last moment I need to turn entirely upside down, legs straight up in the air; that's when you'll need to pull hardest. Are you ready?"

Dubious little nods from faces alive with doubt, anxiety, and an underlying eagerness, confirmed that they were. Climbing out on the sill, he cast a wary glance at the tall red cylinders directly below. The ground looked even more distant from here than it had leaning out a few minutes before; must be twenty feet at least. A pulse of misgiving tightened his skin, tensing the muscles beneath. Manoeuvring to face inward on the narrow sill, he leaned back over the void, body subsiding slowly towards the horizontal, taking two short steps down the wall to improve the rope's angle. Three little wide-eyed faces, clinging on, straining to retain a hold, disappeared as he dropped lower.

With the rope angle steeper, friction on the sill increased, enabling the children to hold more tightly. He was stuck, unable to descend, his body sticking rigidly out like some crazy inverted figurehead on a ship's prow, suspended just below the high bedroom window. Neither he nor the children could see each other, he must call up, take the risk of Jan hearing.

"Lower slowly." The kitchen window below was closed, with luck the call had passed unnoticed.

The rope moved again, descending – a climber on a rock face, feet somewhat sideways on the wall, body now sloping downwards, head nearest the ground. Approaching window level with hands cupped to direct the sound upward; he must judge the precise moment.

"Stop!"

The rope jerked slightly. Now for the final rotation! The bedroom no longer lay directly above; only sideways pressure on the feet maintained the off-centre position. Trying to move smoothly but hurrying in case little hands above should tire, he manoeuvred round and peered through the glass, head down, feet not quite vertically above, weight entirely taken by the rope. Tapping on the window he waited, aware of the hard stony surface twelve feet below; then tapped harder, uncertain how long the children could hold on.

Jan glanced up with a sharp intake of breath, startled, stopping in mid-stride to stare at a crash-helmet-clad head floating upside down in the top corner of her window. Rushing to open it, she looked up in alarm!

Just the right reaction! Bringing out the hidden box of Milk Tray, he held it towards her. Their eye's met. Fascinating; last time he had seen her from this upside down angle, she had been lying naked on the bed, her feet near the pillows, head draped over the lower end while he knelt alongside, massaging her shoulders and sliding his hands towards... Never mind about then, think of now! The message, remember the message! Hanging there he held the chocolates tightly, reaching forward expressively with the free hand, fingers outstretched, a yearning look of love on his face, love that he truly felt. Starting in a deliberately low and hopefully sensual tone, he spoke.

"Because the lady is…Oops…" He broke off suddenly. "...is so very beautiful!"

The final words lacked that certain panache hoped for – they came in a rush as the rope slipped. Jan reached despairingly towards him, and in that moment of lost balance he thrust the chocolates into her outstretched hand before loosing all contact with the wall, swinging away like a sack of potatoes, pendulum fashion and downwards, helpless, head still nearest the ground but spinning towards the horizontal as he went.

In warding off the big red gas cylinders, his foot took some of the weight, allowing the children above to get another grip. With the rope now firmly held from above, he hung stranded a mere five feet off the ground, one foot now sideways on the bottles.

"Lower slowly!" The shout came in a gasp as he struggled, trying to find purchase on the wall with his other foot, but the rope lowered sharply, slipping through the children's hands when they tried to ease it forward. Hitting the ground with a bump, he lay for a moment fighting for breath. Three little heads appeared at the window above, expressions a mixture of concern and excitement.

Perhaps not done with quite the aplomb of the chap in the advert, but when Gordon arrived indoors he could tell that Jan was pleased. With shining eyes she held the chocolates close to her chest.

The children were already there, having raced downstairs. Sharon thought Dad totally mad, but so romantic; she was definitely growing up. And the boys? They just wished they had been the one on the end of the rope!

Chapter 4

The Billy

"Eleven this morning? A new record?"

"Must be. It's Tuesday today, everyone's written off over the weekend," Jan looked up from the pile of letters scattering the desk, "I thought some might be birthday cards but they're all bookings, apart from three enquiries. You know what I think?" Getting no response, she tried again. "Did you notice the white tops on the grass yesterday morning?"

"Yesterday?" Gordon tried to recall. "Oh yes, the badgers were busy again, digging up turf. Why do they do that when there's frost? Divots all over the place, Area 15 mostly, near the setts. I trod them back in. No trouble this morning. How could that affect the post?"

"Frost on the line probably! There was only one letter yesterday; I expect the train was late and the postman couldn't wait. This may be two days mail in one."

"Um. Maybe. Even so, eleven is good!"

"Pity there are no cards though." Seeing him gaze at the pile of mail without comment, she spoke with resignation. "I suppose *you'll* forget again."

He made no reply but a small smile hovered on his lips, clearly visible before he swung away, crossing towards the window. She rose, following, standing close behind without touching, and saw his muscles stiffen waiting for her to strike. For a while they stood, both aware, a small battle of wills. On impulse she stepped to the side and forwards where they could see each other.

"You don't love me now I'm almost a year older," It was whispered with a small pout and a flutter of the eyelids, challenging him to deny it.

"How can you say that?" He reached a finger under her chin, lifting it slightly. "Wonderful! I always love you best at this time of year."

"Why?"

"Don't know really. As spring approaches you always do something for me."

"Oh yes. What?"

Hearing suspicion and a warning in her voice, he leaned forward kissing one cheek, then stepped towards the door.

"Well you paint the toilet buildings for a start!"

Something hit the frame with a thud as the door swung shut. He did not think it a good idea to stop and find out what.

As February came the waterwheel lights were still working well, if a little dim. Hours of daylight lengthened fractionally, so work on new camping pitches could start a few minutes earlier each day. Reading an article in *The Cornishman* as they drank mid-morning coffee, Jan put the paper aside with a frown.

"It says here, Hayle Parish Council have voted against the sewer. Will it affect our new planning permission?"

"Why should they vote against? Affect us? No, I shouldn't think so. I'll take an extra five minutes to browse through the relevant papers." Gordon drained his cup and reached for a box file.

"Switch the outside bell on when you go... no, switch it on now, you'll forget. I'm painting in the Gents, I'll hear if it rings." Jan picked up a paint-stained anorak and left. She reappeared an hour later to start preparing lunch, but stopped in the doorway, surprised to see Gordon still seated at the desk, papers strewn across the surface. This delay in returning to work was virtually unprecedented.

"Are you sitting here all morning?"

"I've a problem."

"Laziness?" Jan pulled up another chair and relaxed into it.

"Chance would be a fine thing. No, this is more serious. It's money, really."

"When isn't it? Last season was pretty good, what's wrong?"

"Yes, all right, we did well enough, but that may not last. I've found a flaw in the planning permission."

Jan had lain back in the chair as they spoke, showing no concern, well used to a shortage of cash and happy to wait for the following season. Now she sat abruptly forward, manner changing, tension in her face as Gordon continued.

"You remember they said we must join to the sewer when it comes through the valley, that we wouldn't be allowed to use the septic tanks any more?"

"Yes?" Jan watched as he leafed through some papers.

"Ah, here we are. Look, they gave us a new temporary permission until 1976 – three more years with a promise to extend if the sewer is late. It caused trouble because our original permission was permanent."

"Don't remind me! I thought we promised never to speak about that again. Anyway, the permanent permission is still good once we join to the sewer. That's what the Council said. We haven't upset them, they can't take it back can they?" Jan's anxiety was showing.

"I think they're quite happy with us actually, pleased with the way the site has developed. Even if the sewer is delayed we'll still be fine just so long as we don't refuse to join when it does become available, and we're not likely to do that. No, it's something else, something I've just discovered."

Jan felt a premonition rise that she tried to push away, a feeling that something bad was coming, something she did not want to know!

"It's to do with tents. See this!" He passed over a

document.

She scanned the print, 7th day of July, 1969. “Oh yes, the original permission, what about it?”

“Read what it says.”

“Land situate at Relubbus,” she read verbatim from the document, looking up anxiously then continuing, “namely the laying out of a caravan park, erection of...”

“Stop there. That’s it! Do you see?”

“No. See what?” Jan shook her head.

“Read condition two.”

“The chalets and caravans shall not be used for residential...”

“There! You follow now?” he interrupted again, and seeing her mystified expression, asked, “Where are the tents?”

Jan scanned the sheet, not understanding, “Can’t see anything about tents here, where is it? What about them?”

“You don’t see it because they’re not there, not even mentioned.” He waited but still she shook her head in bemusement. Slowly, he spelled it out for her. “We don’t have permission for tents in that original document!”

“But... How? The Council men have been round the site many times; they even bring people here now to show what a site should be like. They’ve seen the tents, lots of them, whole areas of them. You must be wrong – Please?” It was a plea for the news to be untrue.

“I’m not wrong. They just don’t realise. Funny thing is, this temporary permission we have, it allows tents. They can’t do anything until we connect to the sewer. The danger lies after we connect, when we revert to the original permission. If they find out, maybe they could stop us then.” Gordon shrugged, he’d hunted so carefully over the last hour hoping to find a mention of tents somewhere, but there was nothing.

“What can we do? How much would it affect us anyway?” She glanced again at the paper still in her hand.

“A solicitor once told me that if the Planning

department don't spot something for four years then it's okay! Let's hope that's true because we dare not ask. If they do try to stop us we can appeal of course but we could lose, and appeals take a lot of cash."

"Could we manage without tents? We've money in the bank; plenty surely to last until next season with reasonable care?"

"True, but what about the future?" He frowned. "We could probably survive on just caravans – provided they keep coming. But *will* they if we can't afford to surface that road in a few years? There are several things we'll need, the old mower won't last forever and visitors don't like walking far, we really should have another toilet building farther downstream. Other items may crop up, you know how standards and people's expectations rise every year. How could we pay for those things without the extra money from tents? Not only that, I'd hate to lose all our camping friends – some of our favourite people come in tents."

"Hm." Jan considered. "Tents are the future too, the young people very often, the ones who will have a caravan later on. When will we be safe?"

"I don't know if it's four years from when we first opened... maybe the time on this temporary permission wouldn't count? That would mean two more years after we connect to the sewer. Let's hope and save what we can, try to get the important things done first. However hard we try, even if we have good seasons, that tarmac will take several more years to save up for." He reached across for her hand and they sat together in silence for a while.

"What about the children?" Jan asked.

"Say nothing. Say nothing to anyone – it's too risky!"

"Well what then; be really, really, nice to all Council men?"

"Don't you dare!" Gordon warned. "Nothing more likely to make people suspicious! Mind you, we do get on well with most of them, several have been really helpful.

Just beware the awkward ones, don't seem to give way too easily. If they mention tents, talk about something else, change the subject, distract them!"

"Distract them? Wear a shorter skirt you mean, show my legs a bit whenever a Council man comes round? Some are quite good looking!" She smiled at him, knowing that his choice of words had been accidental and the situation was serious, but she could not resist this opportunity to tease, to break the tension.

It altered the mood. Smiling back and reaching out to touch the thigh where she had drawn up her dress to demonstrate a shorter skirt; he felt better. "Okay, what will you do if they send a woman? Tell me that."

"Depends." Jan considered, "If she's old and plain, you can distract her."

"And if she's young and beautiful?" Gordon asked.

"You're *not* distracting those. No way! I'd rather risk the tents!"

Two hands reached out across the desk to touch; the tension gone. And so it was left, a little tent time bomb hanging over them, thrust to one side but ticking quietly in the background, lurking, never to be entirely forgotten. They would push on, improve the site as quickly as money allowed and watch for anything that could make life more enjoyable for visitors. Press on with levelling more areas, not just for the extra pitches, but to reduce that unsightly mine waste – and always remember why people came to the valley – for peace and for the country. They might pray a little too, for the Council's continued amnesia; pray and try to forget – think of better things.

Late February did see a happier event looming, a family addition shortly expected, not from Jan, but Judy the goat. The previous autumn a four-mile journey by car had taken her to the billy. The same woman who sold Judy originally, led the male goat out, releasing the stout rope around its collar; a powerful beast with great sweeping horns. After the briefest 'getting to know you' motions, he went to work with an economy of effort befitting one who in his original wild environment might be responsible for mating a whole herd. In the fluttering of an eye he was through, and wandered off to browse again.

"Ungrateful cad!" Jan whispered. "Look at that, just like a man! Had what he wants, and that's it; off thinking of his stomach again. No foreplay, no affection afterwards, poor Judy."

But Judy pulled leaves from a nearby bramble with more contentment now than for several days. Glancing across to check they were out of earshot, Gordon leaned closer and spoke in a whisper.

"Judy's fine. Look at her. Wish all females were so easy to please!"

Restrained from taking action in the presence of the other woman, Jan crossed to the opposite side, ostensibly to be nearer the goats, treading heavily on his toe as she passed.

Mistaking this whispered conversation for a wish by her visitors to hurry away, the billy's owner cautioned patience. "That was only the first mating. Let Judy stay a while, just to be sure." With those parting words she left, promising to return shortly.

The waiting period on the common above Prussia Cove was pleasant, the lightest of breezes warmed by the sea wafted restfully soft on their faces. Lounging against an old stone wall, scanning breakers on the rocks below, they rested idly as the billy approached Judy again. Gordon, mind drifting as always when nothing important occupied his attention, wondered vaguely how patrons of River Valley would react to a sign fixed over the office door proclaiming, "Man at Stud." How should it look? A brass plate? No, something less formal, polished wood with nicely scrolled edges, knotty pine perhaps, the deeply carved letters tastefully picked out in red?

Another glance at the billy as it quickly performed and returned to grazing, banished the idea – he wasn't up to it.

The passing thought surprised him, how did such things spring unbidden into mind? A momentary mad association of ideas perhaps, it was apt to happen. Gazing vacantly at Judy as she resumed browsing, he recalled a couple of other strange notions that had suddenly surfaced at rare tranquil moments during the last tourist season, moments when most other people were asleep.

Disturbed by something in the small hours one morning, perhaps a demented fisherman off for a pre-sunrise catch, or maybe just indigestion, he had walked round the site, checking in the darkness. Not a soul moved anywhere, no light from a single window of all those many caravans or from the sprinkling of tents; no sound of man, not even a dog acknowledged his passing. Walking amid that sleeping world he had felt the need of a lantern, bell and three cornered hat, and an urge to stop at intervals, toll the bell and chant in a loud voice, "Past three o'clock and all's well!"

That should please the caravanners!

The other whim was an unaccountable desire to climb on the house roof at midnight in a loincloth, and from the very peak send Tarzan noises echoing across the valley. One day perhaps? He could picture those little lights springing up as folk struggled dozily to their gas lamps. A voice jolted him back to reality.

"What are you thinking?"

"Eh? Oh, nothing. You don't want to know."

"Yes I do." Jan insisted. The lady had failed to reappear, leaving them to keep an eye on the goats. They were content to wait, the congenial weather, scenery, each other's company, all conducive to laziness as they relaxed, continuing to lean against the wall.

"Go on. Tell me."

He avoided any mention of those thoughts about the billy; it left far too much scope for ridicule, and plumped instead for the roof at midnight.

"Tarzan?" she looked him up and down shaking her

head with incredulity that was only half make believe, "Don't you mean Cheeta?"

Ten minutes later the woman had returned. After a further quick, efficient mating, it seemed certain that Judy must be satisfied, if rather smelly having acquired a powerful, unpleasant odour – for the billy had sprayed his essence around with abandon.

Gordon sat in the back on the journey home, pulling Judy firmly against both knees in an attempt to prevent her soiling the upholstery, hoping rain would later make the goat less obnoxious. While grasping the coarse and sticky hair his hands picked the odour up strongly. At home, it refused to wash off though he tried several times. The children noticed at tea, asking Jan what it was.

"We took Judy to the billy so she can have baby goats next year. He made her smell. It got on Dad's hands getting her home."

"Why does a billy stink so bad?" Sharon asked, making a grimace and easing to the chair edge remote from her father.

Jan put down her knife, not quite sure how to reply. She had noted Chris's attempt to hide a grin, realising with surprise that he understood. Turning to Sharon she was preparing to attempt an explanation, but Gordon spoke first.

"The smell makes them attractive to female goats." He saw Sharon's nose wrinkle with distaste, and leaned towards her whispering loudly, "I'm hoping that tonight it will make me irresistible to Mum."

Sharon swung to her mother in surprise.

Jan, eyes wide and mouth half open searching for a response, was momentarily diverted by Chris's stifled laugh as he pretended to blow his nose in a handkerchief. Stephen, not understanding, looked from one to another, puzzled.

"Hm!" Mum turned from the children, drawing in cheeks to control her laughter. "Either get that smell off or you sleep on the floor! *Irresistible*? I'd prefer the billy!"

Since that long past autumn day, Judy's crushed oats had been increased and they stopped taking all her milk, discouraging its production until milking could stop altogether without causing discomfort. This had allowed the goat to put on condition as the months passed, ready for the coming birth. Aware of this pending event, the whole family, and particularly the children had been especially attentive, taking her for walks, offering handfuls of oats and rubbing those itchy places where she most enjoyed being touched. Even Dad showed extra concern, inspecting her feet more often, paring away any bad edges with a Stanley knife. Meal times usually included some talk of the goat's condition and the impending birth, together with news from school and odd snippets of local interest. Spreading an old copy of *The Cornishman* across the table ready for Stephen's homework, Jan read aloud an argument over the sewer outfall at Marazion; should it be increased by two pipe lengths, or extended to below high water? Gosh, such momentous decisions. Neither parent mentioned worries over their own sewer and how its eventual arrival might affect tents, but an anxious look did pass for a moment between them!

The kids were borne on 22 February, both female, immediately named Olive and Ivy after the grandparents, Olive being Jan's Mum's first name which she never used. Within minutes of birth they could walk round shakily and soon found the milk source. While young, they would be no problem, tether the mother and the kids could run free, but the time would come later in the year when they too, would start to chew bark off young trees; at that point all three goats must be tethered. Their arrival raised another problem. Previously Judy had slept in the lean-to shed attached to the ladies end of the second toilets, stretching half the width of that building, the floor specially adapted by laying down two inches of expanded polystyrene covered with a smooth cement finish for extra comfort. At the back of this shed were stored bottles of Calor gas for the caravanners. A two feet high sheet of plywood propped against the bottles had been enough to prevent Judy going near them, for older goats, particularly ones in kid, are not so inclined to climb on wobbly timber. This would certainly not be true of her offspring; young goats were known to jump on anything and might well hurt themselves. Besides, they needed more room. A new home must temporarily be found for the gas bottles.

"Store them in the service passage again, like the first season?" Jan suggested, addressing the idea across the lunch table.

"Go ahead, the children can help; no need for me to waste working time." Gordon continued to eat, not raising his head, doodling with a pencil sketching possible shapes of the next area to be levelled for grass.

Sensing he was only half listening, and not prepared to let go unchallenged the brusque passing of this chore without so much as a 'do you mind', Jan's responded with mild irony.

"You are switched on aren't you? Try to remember it's just for goats in future!" She turned to the children, "First time we need a gas bottle, you know what will happen. He'll go straight to the shed and come dashing back shouting 'Someone's stolen the Gas'."

Gordon looked up at the deep voiced imitation to find the family watching and Jan pleased with her success in having forced his attention.

"Mum's right, he *will* forget. Paint G.S. for Goat Shed, on the door," Sharon offered her support.

"Gas Store is G.S. too, stupid!" Chris paused, surprised to find himself arguing on his father's side.

Momentarily taken aback, Sharon quickly covered the mistake, responding with some dignity, "I know that! I only suggested it to save changing the sign when the goats grow up and the gas bottles go back."

Jan and Chris looked at each other, lips rounded in an "Ooh!" of disbelief; what a whopper! However, before either could respond, Sharon broke in again – no one could stop her, she bubbled with something that had to come out!

"Anyway, I shall spend lots of time with the little goats. It will be my special place – GS can stand for Gifted Sharon!"

Deep groans around the table did nothing to dent her jubilation. Young Stephen, who had struggled to follow the conversation, blew a raspberry on his wrist.

The incident however, retained its good humour as talk turned to old friends who might soon begin arriving. March and opening day approached, not that a rash of caravans was expected, far from it, but a few should appear. Jan had repainted the buildings, and the entrance road potholes were already being tackled. Finishing this particular job before visitors arrived reduced the danger that a car might suddenly appear round a bend and the risk of having to jump clear, possibly straight into gorse that lined the road in places. The repairs could not be started earlier since winter rain took its toll on the stony surface. Damage would happen in summer too, as fine material wafted away in dust clouds following vehicles along the track, but that was unavoidable. Filling had reached those final potholes near the entrance, where the track joined to the village's tarmac road right by Jan's parent's bungalow. Audrey leaned across her garden wall to call over.

"Gordon, I want a tree pulled out," she pointed to a decrepit specimen, affected no doubt either by lack of moisture during the previous hot summer or by the acid soil. "Can you manage it? There's coffee when you've finished."

It would have been the work of a few minutes with the big excavator's rear digging arm, but as usual this attachment had been removed to allow Max to tow the trailer. Twenty minutes with pick and shovel however, disposed of the offending tree together with most roots.

"Don't bother to fill in, I need to plant a new one," Audrey waved a cup through the open window. Jim joined them, sitting in that part of the bungalow with big windows that Audrey referred to as the sunroom. Having discussed the young goats' arrival, the children's progress, and work on the park in general, conversation turned to the village.

"Things move so slowly in Relubbus," Audrey shook her head, not in disappointment, but recognising the great contrast with the city they had left behind. "In two and a half years since we moved in, no more building work has touched the area; it's so different from London. Trudy and Charles," she pointed at her friend, Mrs Clouter's bungalow across the river, "say that theirs was completed about a year before ours. I don't think there's another new house anywhere in the village. Most are really old. How old *is* Relubbus?"

"I've seen a map somewhere," Gordon frowned, trying to remember. "St Michael's Mount I think, dated in the fifteen hundreds. The name was Reslehoubes then, or something like that. Res is the old word for a ford, we found that out before. It wasn't a ford at that time, there are records of a bridge back in the 1300's; the ford must have been before that. Back in the third century, there was a Roman outpost about a mile from here, up the hill at Bosence. There's something else from that age too, an inscribed stone inside the Church at St Hilary, carved to Caesar Constantine; It's thought to have been a Roman milestone from around 300AD. It was discovered when the church burned down in... er, the 1850's, can't remember the exact year – it was in the foundations of the earlier fourteenth century church. But this area must have been populated long before then; primitive peoples tended to live near streams for fresh water. Before many roads existed, rivers were used for transport too, for materials and people. Some of the Irish Saints are said to have landed down at Hayle estuary. They may have travelled up this river; St. Germoe for one is thought to have passed through the valley, let's see... that would be 1500 years ago."

"If this village was a settlement at that time, why did he go on to Germoe?" Audrey asked.

"Who knows?" Gordon shrugged, "probably people here were too civilised and educated, he thought a more wayward, more simple minded population needed his teaching – so Germoe would be an obvious choice – but maybe I'm biased! No, I've no idea really, why the great man went on, but there was probably a settlement here since very early times; Relubbus might be older than anyone will ever know. I'll see what else I can find out. Do you miss London much?"

"In a way." Audrey agreed, "More miss being young really, when you pass sixty, that's when the aches and pains start! This is nicer for us now; everyone waves, people walking to the shop, people sitting on the seat by the bridge, even people going to the chapel on Sunday. Hardly anyone waved in London."

"Probably get arrested if they did," Jim eased himself into a new position. "Better for my leg, here. We sit in the garden in summer, most of the caravanners know us, call in for a whisky some of them."

Draining his cup, Gordon trundled off downstream in Max, unaware he was seen from above. Sharon sat on a fallen log, high over the waste heaps in a flat grassy glade, sheltered on three sides by trees. Looking eastwards over the valley and the empty site below, she watched the yellow excavator and wondered if this weekend would bring any young girls down that stony track just visible alongside the stream. Thinking back to friends of last season, her hands continued to fondle the short coat of the little goat standing with two hooves on her knee. She loved the young kids, loved stroking the short lustrous coats and spent hours with them, laughing at the playful frolics. Although naturally gregarious, liking people to chatter with, Sharon sat often alone with the kids. The frisky young things were never content to remain still, to be mothered as the young rabbits had been some years earlier, but she liked their funny unpredictable antics. Whereas Judy was definitely Chris's goat, Olive and Ivy, being small and to a certain extent cuddly, were special to her. A head butted her left side, gently, not with force, as Olive sought a share of attention. Moving one hand from Ivy, she reached out, guiding the young goat nearer, rubbing its neck and shoulders. For a few minutes both stood, enjoying the probing fingers until without warning, Ivy raced off, bucking and leaping, stopping at the glade's far edge to browse an old bramble leaf, then reared round as Olive approached. Still sitting on the log, Sharon saw them face each other, rise onto hind legs like prancing horses, then drop simultaneously and crash sculls. Racing back, Olive jumped on the log to stand, both feet against the girl's shoulder, while Ivy pushed a way between her knees, rubbing a furry head against the faded jumper.

The young goats' birth coincided with other early signs of spring. All of a sudden, things were happening. River Valley was open again, the grass was growing, early leaves were unfurling, honeysuckle rambling along hedgerows, the bright spring green of hawthorn peeking through thorny branches, darker green elder leaves beginning to show, and everywhere the yellow blooms of gorse. Many taller trees remained bare, black ash buds not yet ready to burst, hazel with prominent catkins but no leaves, sycamore and oak needing time. However, all the buds were swelling; a promise of coming spring. Predominantly, the valley bottom nearer the stream was cloaked in willow, as yet with few leaves, the catkins in various stages of growth, many no more than little white blobs, others further advanced. These catkins fell into two distinct types, the females longer with a soft silvery green fur, the males more compact, some already showing a yellow coating of pollen. The whole valley was a hidden sheltered wonderland under blue skies dotted with broken white clouds. The river flowed sparklingly clear, birds were building, and rabbits nibbled with their young on grassy slopes, building up reserves no doubt for the next generation.

Suddenly, amid this array of promise, the electrical system began to fail! It would now support just one small bulb for a fairly short time. Not only that, but the long neglected oil lamp stored in the service passage since the wheel first ran, now refused to work. Rust or dirt no doubt had clogged the fine nozzle, but all attempts to clean it proved fruitless. There was no escaping the consequences – previously abandoned candles were hunted from draws and cupboards and stuck again to saucers!

Gordon was annoyed with himself! That three bearing arrangement on the waterwheel shaft was really most unsuitable since all the bearings needed to remain absolutely in line. Water always produced scour, and scour made things move! He should have known it would! The result – bearings no longer in a perfectly straight line so the shaft flexed slightly at each rotation. This absorbed a great deal of valuable energy, leaving hardly any for lights. But worse was to come!

On Friday morning about eleven, still pondering how to rectify the fault, he sat down ready for a coffee. Jan glanced out through the kitchen window while lifting the steaming cups. Turning away she took three steps towards the table before stopping abruptly, then swung back to look intently out again.

"Gordon! The waterwheel is sinking!"

How ridiculous! Better humour her. He rose, some soothing platitude on the tip of his tongue, ambling across to gaze at the river.

"Hell! It is sinking!"

Hard as it was to believe, there was no possible doubt! The granite block supporting the outermost bearing was giving way, no longer in line with slabs supporting the rest of the shaft. He dashed for the door, grabbing a pair of grips lying on the sideboard, shouting over one shoulder, "Find the adjustable spanner, it's quicker. Must release the weight before that shaft bends."

Frantic activity ensued. In perhaps thirty seconds they were both standing over the granite, Gordon loosening nuts, taking them off and passing them hurriedly to Jan. As he undid the last one the slab sunk at every turn of the spanner until water lapped over the top. Then it was free! But the shaft could yet be ruined! Still attached to the other bearings and gearing it could bend, forced aside in a downstream direction by the weight of water pressing hard against each paddle - this force continuing to spin the partially supported wheel.

He lunged for the wet rim. "Screwdriver!" the single shout, yelled as a drowning man might cry out, rose sharply above the sound of swirling water. Jan's drew an involuntary breath, muscles tightening, rooted momentarily to the spot – and then off! Galvanised into action by the urgency in that call, she departed at speed wearing old Wellies snatched in the initial rush, this clumsy, inelegant footwear contrasting with the vigour and energy above. Under normal conditions, the sight of her flying figure would have induced a different reaction, but there was no time! He caught a paddle, the wheel slowed marginally. Another slid free, and another – the fifth and he almost had it! The sixth held! He threw his chest against the downstream side, leaning at an angle, feet still on the bank, his weight helping to counteract the river's pressure.

Jan arrived back, thrusting the screwdriver forward, catching her breath, unable to speak. He seized it – screws that held the paddles were coming out fast. No chance of lifting the whole thing on their own, it had to be dismantled in position. Water from the wet timber soaked his shirt where his body pressed hard against paddles and the outer rim to keep the wheel stationary while leaving hands free. The first screws were passed carefully into Jan's hand, the rest disappeared in the grass, tossed on the bank to be found later – the waiting hand no longer available! It had become imperative for her hold the wheel, grasping the wet timber, one foot thrust on a lower paddle, striving to prevent it rotating as he slipped quickly into the foaming river, hurrying to reach screws on the far side. As a loosened paddle started to twist she reached with both hands to hold it steady while the final fixings were removed, then tossed it awkwardly onto the bank, still restraining the wheel's movement with that one foot and her chest. It gave new meaning to the word 'uplift!'

With three paddles cleared, that sector was turned to the bottom of the wheel. There was little now for the water to strike against and the pressure immediately reduced. Those remaining came free without any need to counteract the river's force, but still they worked urgently until the final paddle was removed, followed by sliding out and lifting off the two circular shrouds. Finally, releasing the other bearings allowed the shaft to be hauled clear.

Unable or unwilling to find the energy to go inside and clean themselves up, they sat back, wet and bedraggled, regarding the surrounding mess. Paddles, bearings, the big circular shrouds, the long shaft; debris lay everywhere, including those scattered screws still to be found. Holding hands seated on that grassy bank, they ignored the clinging dampness of their clothes, scanning the chaotic scene with mixed feelings. Dismantling the wheel without further damage gave a mere touch of success, a faint lift. However, as the blood still coursing through their bodies from those frenetic initial efforts subsided, any small feelings of triumph quickly gave way to depression – depression caused by the total loss of their electrical supply.

Panic over, what now? Pretty basic changes were obviously called for. Some system must be introduced which prevented the unstoppable scouring power of water from disturbing the set-up. The need to plan and construct a better, more durable arrangement unavoidably necessitated the loss of all power for a period. No point in hurriedly replacing this system with something equally short lived.

Later, when the children arrived home, they too were disappointed. Chris joined tentative discussions on a new design, understanding with difficulty but unable to suggest any solutions. Sharon's few comments were mostly sarcastic in content but with a touch of wistfulness that the already faint possibility of watching television had now receded out of sight.

"We should have proper 'lectric," Stephen advised; his only contribution.

Chapter 5

The Dam

Breakfast the following morning, a Saturday, lacked the cheerfulness generally present when all the family were gathered. Dad seemed detached, not responding, until Jan demanded, “Well, did you solve the problem last night?”

“Eh? Oh... No, I fell asleep playing with an idea. Still can’t quite get everything sorted.” His gaze shifted to the window, the fingers of one hand absently tapping a tattoo on the table.

“That’s pretty obvious. Couldn’t you leave…” She stopped, aware he was not hearing, his mind drifted off, eyes gazing sightlessly out. With a snort of anger, the butter in her hand thumped down hard enough to create tidal waves in the coffee cups. “I warned you it would go wrong. Forget that stupid wheel! And forget loading stone too, you’ve been at it all winter. Every single day – load the trailer, tow it away, tip it, then back for more – endlessly. Pay attention to your family for a change. Take us out for the day!”

Gordon looked up suddenly into her intense stare. His mouth opened to speak, gulped, searching for an answer, aware the children were watching. Perhaps he had worked on, ignoring the family, putting the site first.

“Lizard might be good?”

She blinked twice, taken aback at winning without the expected resistance. He had not even contradicted her claim to have foreseen the breakdown. What she actually forecast was, ‘It will never work,’ and in that had been mistaken. Never mind, if he missed the subtle difference, now was no time for confessions! Pleased with the turn of events, she went humming back into the kitchen, returning with more toast, chatting to the children about the trip and what to take.

"I think Dad only agreed because he's totally stumped on the new wheel design but doesn't want to admit it!"

"Hope it's better than last time!" Sharon turned to her father; "Will this one give enough power for television?"

The parents looked at each other, both noticing the implied criticism. What a curious effect the wild environment was having on the children's ideas. Sharon obviously thought instinctively that any Dad worth his salt should have no trouble making a waterwheel produce abundant electricity – and without breaking down! To her, that seemed a perfectly normal expectation.

A quick call confirmed that Jim would come down to watch the office and welcome early visitors in the unlikely event of any appearing. "Fifteen minutes," he said before putting down the receiver.

Judy had been tethered within sight of the office, her kids running free nearby. Sharon ran over to stroke and play with them, the young goats vying for her attention, butting gently as she knelt, rubbing and scratching their coats. One pushed a head under her arm, the other placed two small hoofs on her thigh reaching up to rub its face against her cheek. As always, neither were content to stay in one position for very long. With a last hug, pulling them both towards her, Sharon rose and hurried back to help prepare a hamper. The boys, keen to be off, waited with ill concealed impatience for their grandfather's arrival, hanging round, restless and interfering until led off to collect waterwheel paddles and other debris from the riverbank, a task which kept them busy until the car was loaded.

A little over forty minutes unhurried driving would have reached the destination, but they parked twice on the high plateau of the Lizard peninsula to ramble across this largely uncultivated landscape with its own special range of flora. Morning was well advanced when they reached Lizard, Britain's most southerly place, the spot from where the Armada had been sighted. Here, in 1588, burned the first beacon fire in a chain of such beacons that signalled from summit to summit across the country, news of the Spanish fleet's arrival. With the car parked, the family browsed among small shops; tourist mementoes, cards, shells, paintings, and everywhere carvings in Serpentine. This famous Lizard rock could be worked to a wonderful finish; various shapes, predominantly miniature lighthouses, shone with a greenish sheen or occasionally with bands of red. Attractive as they were however, this was not a buying trip! Plenty of chance for that after another season or so when some spare cash might have accumulated. Not that they were hard up like the first year, but the doubtful outlook for tents and that road surface held them back. It paid to be a little careful; or so Dad insisted! Chris was keen to walk to the lifeboat house not far away, and later they visited Church cove, following the coastal path to find a route down to a rocky beach. As lunchtime passed, hunger drew them back to the car. Jan suggested Kynance, another cove a little westward round the coast, might be a pleasant place to eat. Visitors had spoken highly of it during last summer.

The beach at Kynance proved strenuous to reach. Dad, well aware he would have to carry the hamper, offered token resistance before yielding, but insisted on leading the way down, restraining the youngsters' restive energy.

"When we know it's safe, then you can run to the top again and back – if you can!"

From the car park a steep path of steps stretched out, apparently unending, winding down to a tiny bay. The climb was well worthwhile. Sheltered by a big rock, weak winter sunshine radiated a pleasant warmth as Jan unpacked the food.

"Hang on to any paper, don't let it blow away. If a

place is special, why spoil it?"

The sea washed gently over the rocky shore, to roll part way up the small sandy patch of beach. Visitors' comments had been right, the little cove was exceptional, and how much more so it must have seemed to anyone arriving from a town. The children, discarding shoes, ran to play at the water's edge, dodging tiny wavelets, sometimes together, sometimes going their separate ways along the short beach, leaving parents to sit, waiting contentedly.

"I'm glad you decided to take us," Jan said quietly, "this is good for them. Our valley is great, but they need the excitement of new places."

"Was it up to me? Did I really have a choice?" he asked.

About to respond, she caught his concealed smile and relaxed expression. He was teasing. She smiled back.

"Okay. I prompt you sometimes, but I never insist. Anyway, don't pretend; you like to see them happy. I've been watching your eyes follow them. You don't have to look stern so often. They won't do anything dreadful if you're a bit lax." She reached for his hand.

"Didn't realise I was."

"You have been this week; gazing into space too. Stop worrying about that wheel, I always told you it would never work." She said the words affectionately, chiding gently, teasing as he had done, avoiding any ripple of discord on their tranquil mood.

They continued to relax as the afternoon wore on. Jan felt happier for the break, knew the children enjoyed it, but several times caught Gordon gazing sightlessly out over the waves. Even during the chatter, an occasional vacant look crossed his eyes, lost to all around, making her guess that either the wheel or some other task had returned to occupy his mind. She jabbed his ribs with a finger once, demanding to know his thoughts. The evasive reply and a certain guilty expression confirmed her suspicions but she let it pass, leaning over to kiss his stubbly cheek.

Starting for home, the children dashed off to lead up the steep stairway, only Chris reaching the top without being caught as first Stephen and then Sharon sat down on the steps to wait or perhaps to rest. Not another soul had been seen, not going down, not on the beach, nor climbing up again; hardly surprising so early in the year.

Arriving back in the valley, stopping momentarily on the bridge with its low uneven granite parapets, the view downstream missed something. Although the debris of paddles and miscellaneous pieces had been removed for temporary storage, the absence of the wheel which had for the past four months splashed happily away below, brought back the depressing problem of electricity. In any case, they could scarcely forget for long; tea was late and with approaching darkness, out came the candles. In the flickering light the family settled down to make decisions. Gordon set out the problem facing them, with his solution of how it must be tackled.

"Scour causes our trouble. As water washes through the paddles it also takes away little particles of soil from the bank. That's what caused it to collapse." Heads dipped in understanding, this part they had discussed before.

"The best way to prevent scour affecting the bearings, will be to mount the wheel in a concrete channel with one bearing on either side and the wheel between. Water pushing the paddles round then washes the inside of the channel instead of the bank. It can't hurt the concrete! Even if the channel moves slightly, the bearings will move together and not get out of in line." Dad looked to see if they still followed.

Stephen's frown and shrug of the shoulders were clear enough, he was lost. Sharon wore a neutral expression, not quite grasping the idea but not wishing to appear less intelligent than Chris.

Gordon walked to the bench, picking up a plastic sandwich box. Taking off and discarding the lid, he reached for a cotton reel, impaled it on a pencil and laid this across the sides of the box, giving the reel a spin with his finger. "You must think of this sandwich box with the ends cut out, so the water can flow through. We need a concrete channel like that. It will be heavy, too heavy to move after it's made. Somehow we must cast it above the river and lower it in!"

Intently watching faces and large round eyes indicated they were impressed, but after a series of questions the children drifted, one by one, back to their own pursuits. Jan reached for a book leaving Gordon to ponder the problem. That was the kernel of this issue, how to build the concrete channel? The rest should be relatively easy. Power would be taken off by leaving the shaft sticking out over the bank with a cogwheel on the end; a flexible chain would connect this cogwheel to the gearing. The only contact between the channel in the water, and the gearing on the bank, would be this chain. A little movement there would cause no trouble; the spacing could even be made adjustable.

Very well, so much for requirements, but how to begin? Working conditions were going to be difficult on the soft bottom. For a start, all those big granite slabs that had previously supported the shaft on the bank could now be sunk in the stream to form a solid foundation. Step one then; dig a large hole in the riverbed.

Sunday dawned with high cloud masking any sunshine and a chill northerly breeze sweeping briskly up the valley, not ideal conditions for prolonged immersion. A good fry-up should yield some fortification against the cold. Leaving Sharon to finish cooking, Jan lit a candle, descended the basement stairs, round one corner and on along a short passageway. Ignoring dark caverns ahead and to the right, she turned left into another corridor, striding along to take the first of four doorless openings at the far end. In the dim unsteady light, coal heaped in one corner was transferred to the boiler and the air intake control set higher. A warm house and plenty of hot water would undoubtedly be in demand this day! Hurrying upstairs she helped Sharon carry plates to the table and when they were eating, asked, "You realise what day it is?"

Heads shook and shoulders shrugged as they continued to eat.

"Fifth of March, St Piran's day. The patron Saint of Cornish Tinners. If he's watching over us," she cast her eyes upwards, "this should give him a good laugh!"

After breakfast, the entire crew assembled outside. Those granite slabs to be sunk in the bed were first moved along the bank and eased into the river a little downstream from where the hole must be dug. This done, Dad carrying a long Cornish shovel, stepped down lowering himself fully dressed into the water.

"How many people," he wondered, "have ever tried to dig a large hole underwater in a fast flowing stream where the bed is sand and gravel?"

Standing on the bank, Jan and Sharon were more interested in how wet he would get than in the actual task, though the boys were itching to help.

"Ooh!" Sharon winced, when water rose above his knees. "Is it cold?"

"No, hardly feel a thing! Do you want to come and help?" Addressing the invitation at all the children, he continued to wade cautiously forward, the level creeping gradually higher.

Stephen stepped to the edge and would have leaped straight in, but as his neck bent forward over the water to select a landing point, Jan's hand grasped his collar, yanking him back. "Not you. You're still too small. All *you* want is get thoroughly wet! Stay here, we'll watch."

Sharon dipped one hand in the water, withdrawing it quickly. "It's freezing! I'm not going in there!"

Chris slipped cautiously in, hesitating, numbly immobile for an instant when the cutting coldness struck, but stepped slowly forward again without a word. Pretending unconcern, he glanced covertly sideways at his sister on the bank, aware her eyes were following as his lower body disappeared. Taking the shovel and digging into the soft bed where his father indicated, the blade penetrated easily enough. Lowering one hand down the long shaft until his jumper submerged to the elbow, Chris heaved, attempting to pull the load clear. Failing, he reached lower for more leverage, one shoulder disappearing below the surface, but although growing stronger he was not yet big enough to apply the force needed to lift that fully loaded shovel.

"Good try." Gordon took the tool. The task was down to him; he always knew it would be. "You may be able to help again later."

Chris's expression showed no enthusiasm. Five minutes ago when expecting it to be forbidden, he had clamoured to enter the river. Now, with both opportunity and actual encouragement to stay, naturally he was no longer so keen. Rather than remaining in the water, he quickly made for the bank! Even Stephen, having witnessed Chris's efforts, was content now to observe from a safe distance. Gordon swung half a dozen big shovelfuls aside to be swept away in the flow, but to little avail. Progress was not so much slow as non-existent. Rather like trying to dig a hole where the tide had just reached, it kept filling itself up again. One might as well try making a dent in a bowl of water by taking a cupful from the middle. After a while he clambered out defeated. Down on the riverbed, all signs of the hole had already disappeared.

"A dam." He muttered to himself, gazing down and thinking half aloud.

"No good getting upset. Told you this would never work." Jan was laughing. "Don't give up yet though, have one more go, try to stoop lower like Chris did. Television we may never have but this is easily as good!"

"What you really want is to see me go right under, get totally soaked!" Nods of confirmation from three little heads and Jan's broadening smile made him glance at the wet sleeves and clinging trousers below. Perhaps the amusement was understandable, but they had misunderstood. "Sorry to disappoint you, I wasn't cursing. It's what we need – a dam." He went on to explain in detail, squatting on his heels with a squelch, bringing himself down to Stephen's level. "Not a dam to stop the river's flow and allow us to work in the dry, that's obviously impossible. We'll make a half dam designed to push the rushing water to one side." He pointed towards the far bank, sweeping an arm to follow the current. "That will create a pocket of still water here," he gestured again, indicating the general area they had already tried to excavate. "I should be able to dig then. I'm wet already and so is Chris, we might as well start now."

Chris looked up sharply to object, then caught Sharon watching him and stayed silent, masking his expression and following his father back into the water. They set to work borrowing stones from the weir to construct a quarter circular wall, just upstream of the wheel's intended position and about half the river's width.

"Curved walls are stronger," Dad explained.

It worked too! Even before the dam reached full height, the water's flow reduced substantially. Chris helped for perhaps fifteen minutes, then disappeared indoors. Due to the cold and without waders to keep dry, immersion time was best limited to less than an hour. Even fully clothed most feeling left the legs well before that time. Almost waist deep in places, Gordon whispered a concern about certain other parts of his anatomy!

"I shouldn't worry," Jan comforted, pausing before calling with some relish as he crossed again to the far side, "It's supposed to make you terribly virile."

"What does virile mean?" Sharon asked.

Gordon, lifting another large stone, glanced up with a grin. "Get out of that!"

Jan paused only briefly, "It means terribly energetic." Pleased at having found an acceptable answer with an approximately accurate meaning, she smiled at Sharon before wondering if the word would now appear in some school essay.

The dam was finished in a series of work sessions on that first morning, Chris twice returning for short periods. At one point Dad slipped, getting thoroughly wet, much to the family's amusement! Stephen helped by carrying old plastic bags, turf, and even armfuls of long grass to clog holes on the new dam's upstream face. Removing the weir on one side had the added advantage of lowering the river level; not much, but every little helped.

The afternoon weather showed no improvement, if anything the wind blew colder, or perhaps that was merely a depletion of bodily resources after the morning's chilling efforts. True to Dad's prediction, excavation below the surface became possible in the still water; not easy, but possible. The hole in the bed gradually expanded and deepened, though minor falls round the edge persisted. After the allotted time, he climbed from the water, made his way to the bathroom, stripped quickly and stepped into a tepid bath. Even moderate temperatures could make the legs tingle badly as circulation returned.

Forty minutes into the second session, the hole reached its full size and depth, but now, in spite of almost still water the edges tended to soften and flow back in. Postponing the planned warm-up break, he struggled to move the large granite slabs into position with a crow bar. The rest of the family was present, but standing on the bank offering only moral support. Jan said she wouldn't miss it for anything; the wetter he became the more loudly the children shouted encouragement. The extreme softness of that riverbed was unfortunate. Though it had aided excavation, obtaining leverage proved difficult. However, digging the bar in deeply, Gordon managed. The tendency of each stone to bulldoze a great pile of gravel in front as it moved, proved annoying but was overcome by shovelling these mounds away. A long handled garden hoe cleared gaps between slabs before each was given a final heave forcing it tight to the preceding one. Using the hoe, its handle shorter than the shovel, meant getting more of the body wet, bringing Ooh's from the children and a little shiver from Jan. Each time he straightened his back, water poured from the thick woollen sleeves. Although the rest of the jumper largely escaped submersion, the wet area gradually increased. Little splashes, contact with wet tools and capillary attraction all combined to spread liquid up the sides, then steadily to other parts. That March water, still cold from winter, felt freezing.

Stephen, lying on the ground, jumped up, ran along the bank and back again, then off over the granite bridge and down the small river's far side to watch the water beyond the dam rushing by. Totally unable to settle in his excitement, he raced back to the rest of the family and lay again on the ground, stretching out, far as he dare over the river, mere inches above its surface.

"Don't get wet!"

Ignoring his mother's urgent command the young lad deliberately lowered his face into the water, blinking eye's below. Unable to hold his breath longer, he rose again, flicking wet hair sharply right, intentionally showering cold droplets over Sharon who stood nearby.

Disregarding his daughter's scream of protest and Jan's scolding voice ordering Stephen inside to get dry, Dad worked on. His senses were in little shape to react; all feeling had left the lower body and above he shivered in the wind. Bent over, arm outstretched trying to co-ordinate the movement of that hoe blade was awkward, partly due to a cloudiness caused by the disturbed bed and partly because seen through water things appeared closer than they really were. Luckily, a gradual seepage still permeated the stone dam, drifting the cloudy water slowly downstream and preventing the river becoming too murky. The granite slabs were not of equal thickness, but shunting the wider ones backwards and forwards a mere inch or so with a crowbar, sent them down like a crab disappearing into the sand until they were all level. Having been in the water well over an hour, his legs were so rigidly unresponsive on climbing out that he entered the house and climbed stiffly into a bath of warm water, clothes and all. Gradually and painfully, the feeling crept back.

Foundation achieved, the group gathered for coffee in the kitchen. They stood together talking, glancing through the window at the river, lounging against the worktops, all waiting for the kettle to boil. Chris expressed surprise that his father had managed to move the great granite slabs on his own into their final position. It had taken all the family straining to the utmost with *two* crowbars to move those same slabs a short distance along the bank. Jan was laughing with Stephen and Sharon about the water that had oozed from Dad's clothes; they were half listening to Chris at the same time and stopped talking to hear the reply.

"Yes, how did you move them?" Sharon prompted when no answer seemed forthcoming.

Gordon, looking furtively over one shoulder then the other, beckoned them closer.

"Not many people know this," he whispered, "but I'm really superman."

Expressions in the ring of faces displayed instant and total disbelief, Stephen shaking his head, Jan saying "Rubbish!" with conviction, while Sharon reached out, triumphantly pointing a finger.

"Where's your costume then?"

"Never wear it! Modesty you know."

The entire family piled in! Short of hurting anyone he was unable to resist; going down under the weight of numbers, ending up with Sharon across his legs, one of the boys on each arm, and Jan sitting on his chest, her hair awry, skirt falling back to expose one shapely thigh.

"I know one thing he does better than anyone else," Mum offered. "Tells bigger lies! Now answer Chris's question!"

The evening was developing well. Being parents was a contact sport anyway, with everyone enjoying the turn of events hugely.

"You'll let me up if I tell the truth?" Gordon asked, making no attempt to escape.

"Only if we believe you?" Jan offered it as a question. The children nodded eagerly.

"Right. The secret is..." he let the expectations build, "Granite weighs less in water. Now let me up."

"Is it true?" Jan looked to the young faces. "Do we believe him?"

No one did, or if so, they concealed the fact. Everyone was smiling fit to burst, shaking heads wildly from side to side, encouraged by their mother.

"I can prove it!" Gordon protested grinning.

"Go on then."

"Can't show you lying here. I'll need something to illustrate the principle."

"He may sneak off and never come back," Sharon warned.

"Really? Quick! Let him go." Jan laughed as she jumped smartly to one side, followed by the children.

He did disappear, off into the basement, but returned shortly with a hunk of wood not quite the size of a small loaf of bread, one of the chunks saved for woodcarving.

"Catch!"

Sharon fumbled it, uttering a little cry and jumping her feet clear as it hit the floor with a thump, then bent to retrieve the fallen piece. At a signal, she passed it to Chris, who weighed the block in one hand before giving it to Stephen.

"Right, not very heavy, but weighs more than a big book would you say?" With varying degrees of reluctance they agreed, regarding it suspiciously, wondering what a piece of wood might prove.

"If it didn't weigh anything, it wouldn't have fallen when Sharon fumbled; instead it would have floated like a feather?" Again they agreed and Gordon continued. "What will happen if I put this in water? We can try it if you like."

"No need, it will float." Heads nodded agreement with Chris's positive assessment.

"Then a great tree trunk that ten men couldn't lift in the dry, will be easy to move on the river; even Stephen could give it a little shove?"

Again they nodded.

"So you agree; wood is lighter in water. Granite is too, not light enough to float but much lighter than it is on land. Early tomorrow, take a concrete building block down to the river's edge and try it for weight underwater. You'll find I'm right. Over sixty blocks will be needed; if we start early, you can all help before school – yes, you as well." He faced towards Sharon who had opened her mouth to object. "About time you helped, who's been most impatient for the new wheel?"

Morning saw the family awake early. Three lines of building blocks were needed, piled one above the other until the top ones showed in three little rows several inches above the water surface. Having checked that they actually were easier to lift underwater, the family had helped by passing each block into Gordon's waiting hands, but again only he worked in the water. The job was half finished when the children hurried inside to change for school, leaving their parents to continue alone. On top of these blocks, a platform was formed using nine-inch wide, three-inch thick timbers, 'borrowed' by dismantling the workbench. These and similar timbers upright at the edges, supported a layer of plastic film to stop cement grout running into the river. Strongly alkaline cement could kill the trout. Finally, reinforcing steel was tied into position, correctly spaced on little cement support pads.

"Why are these pads thicker than the ones we used for the floor of the house, Dad?" Chris asked that evening.

"One of the things concrete does is to stop the steel

reinforcement from rusting. In a dry situation like the house we need pads that give 1½-inches of concrete around the steel. This channel will be underwater, so it needs more protection. These pads are 3-inches deep."

Concreting the base had been delayed until after school to allow photos of the family standing on the platform. The half dam in the background would not be moved until the new channel had hardened and been lowered to the riverbed. Steel projected vertically near each edge ready for the channel sides. Due to a limited supply of timbers, these sides were cast in sections over the following few days. No section took long to complete and plenty of other tasks filled the intervening hours.

It was during one such period, with Gordon working on Max far down the site, that Jan, alone in the house, saw the season's first tourer appear along the track. It approached slowly, an incongruous outfit, the car with a recent K registration all polished and shiny towing something of great age. The old, decidedly tatty caravan hitched on behind, pitched and rolled a good deal more than was justified by the recently repaired track, one side listing heavily, its suspension partially collapsed. The paintwork, peeling in places, was stained and faded with age and a dark strip of some substance formed a thick diagonal line across the front window; adhesive tape covering a crack, perhaps?

"Wish Gordon could deal with this one," Jan sighed, moving towards the door. With one hand reaching for the knob she stopped abruptly, stepping back, restrained by an inner hope, "Wait! It may swing round and drive away."

Indeed this was not the type of unit that they ever accepted. Caravans were bound to arrive often enough covered in road dirt, and many were old, particularly those with young families just making their way in life. Retired people too, tended to hang on to their final caravan, either from shortage of cash or just sentimentality. However, age and superficial mud splashes were one thing, grime and dilapidation such as she now saw was something else. As it swung unsteadily across the bridge, the side came into full view. One panel had been repainted in a garish orange, not recently but at some long past time, a colour strong enough to burst in places through the green coating of algae and accumulated dirt. A tiny gutter strip along the roof edge flapped loose for perhaps one third of its length. She stood waiting, having quickly stepped back into shadow, into the hallway where the light was poor, willing it to drive round in a big circle and back up the track again.

Slowly the car drew to a halt. With a sigh she moved forward to meet the occupants, waiting for them on the top step, somehow feeling more secure with one hand clinging to her own doorway and standing with that extra height rather than being confronted on level ground.

"I'm sorry, we're not open yet. Try farther along the coast." Jan rehearsed the words silently as the driver's door swung open. An elderly gentleman stepped out, his head disappearing again as he leaned back inside obviously deep in discussion. Shortly a woman emerged from the far side and the couple, probably retired, crossed the stony yard.

"We're not really caravanners. Sorry about the state of it," the man waved a hand apologetically backwards. "This is just temporary. We bought it this morning, haven't had chance to wash it yet. Can you put us up for a while?"

"Well, I… We're not…" Jan hesitated.

"Perhaps I should explain." Taking advantage of the pause, the man spoke quickly. "We've been house hunting; didn't expect it to take so long, the cost of hotels… you know," he paused, his hands opening in an appeal for understanding. "Well, a caravan seemed better, cheaper; we can stay in one place, take our time to view an area, even lay-in some mornings. A garage we called at fitted the hitch so we could tow; they offered this old thing for almost nothing; wanted the space probably." He stopped, turning to his companion but she said nothing and he looked again towards the caravan. “It is awful, isn’t it? Did we make a mistake?” The pair stood waiting.

Jan moved uneasily, wanting to help, running her eyes again over the ruin. “I can’t!” the voice was in her head, nothing like this had been accepted on the site since that first season when tatty outfits had caused so much trouble. And this was worse than any of those had been; far worse – but the people were nice. “Ten?” The silent voice spoke again, half question, half suggestion.

Yes. Area 10, certainly; if anywhere. She gestured to the couple, descending the steps as she spoke. “Come. Let me show you a pitch, see if it’s suitable. This way.” The three strode off, round the second toilet building, bearing left through an opening onto a hardstanding area. “In here, this corner maybe? It’s very sheltered.” Trees surrounded the pitch on three sides, leaving it hardly visible except from the immediate area.

“Ideal,” the visiting woman was pleased. “The garage man suggested we choose a hard surface at this time of year, and it’s almost hidden. That’s good, I’m ashamed of its appearance!”

“Really?” Jan tried to hide her relief, but it was obvious from the woman’s expression that she knew. “All right, you’ve guessed. That *is* why I offered this pitch. I’m sorry but you’re right, it is pretty dreadful. We’ve found over the years that tatty ’vans make other visitors uncomfortable, nervous – makes them wonder what sort of site we run. Keeping a certain standard is important, people feel more contented, more relaxed, so we do try to hide any that are a bit...” Jan opened her hand apologetically, “Don’t worry, you’re the only ones here at the moment.” They walked back together to stand by the car, gazing again at the wreck behind. The silence lengthened. Jan could see they were uncomfortable, she had to say something.

“Ah well, it will never look great, may not even be very roadworthy but a good wash could do wonders for the appearance; give it a try! Must go now, I can see the children coming back from school." She pointed along the track, then made to enter the office but swung back to ask, "Have you used gas before? Do you know how it works?"

"No. All we've done is buy bedding. We'll eat out this evening." The man took a wallet from his inside pocket to offer money but Jan avoided it, pushing aside in her mind how long this caravan might stay – Gordon's problem!

"Pay my husband in the office tomorrow please. You may need your gas later. I'll send our son Chris to show you after we've eaten. Go ahead and tow it round. Get yourself pitched."

Chapter 6

Old Relics

"How long before it's working again," Jan asked softly, not pushing, just liking to chat as they so often did together after the children had gone to bed. A single candle flickered on the sideboard as she sat watching Gordon in the other armchair carving a chunk of teak, modelling another bird, a green woodpecker that had appeared on the riverbank the previous day. He lay the Stanley knife and wood on one side.

"Seven days at least. Last section tomorrow then the concrete needs to harden, should hate to crack it now. We need two new gear wheels anyway. Andrews in Redruth should have them."

"Sharon will be disappointed." Jan spoke softly, lazily, almost to herself.

"I can't see why? She's the only one with a gas light in her bedroom; better off than any of us. Probably still thinks it will run a television."

"Will it?"

"No... Well maybe, one day. Might find extra power, persuade it to produce enough. Anything's possible they say. In summer perhaps, with longer evenings and less lighting, provided river levels don't fall too much. No proper fridge either I'm afraid, they take a lot. We could buy a bottle-gas version, some caravans have them now."

"I'd like that," she smiled in the dim light. "A fridge would be great, especially in summer. Keeping food was such a problem last year. I never believed you could do it you know; the wheel. Been more difficult than even you thought, hasn't it?"

"I quite like difficult things." He smiled back, looking intently at her; she realised immediately he was not referring to the wheel, and reached out a slippered foot to kick him gently.

"It's strange," she stretched, arching her back then eased farther into the comfortable armchair. "Each time we manage something, like moving from the caravan into the house, I get that feeling, 'now we've got everything'; but in a few weeks, some new need, something else we must have, always comes along. When the wheel's working and if we do buy a fridge, what will be next?"

"Women are never satisfied," he shrugged as if everyone knew that. "Mind you, some things that seem utterly desirable at the time, prove afterwards to be a continual problem and expense. Take for instance the time I spent seven shillings and sixpence on..."

Jan's foot dug into his calf again, cutting him off, but he had never intended to finish. She kicked off the slipper and their feet rested against each other, neither moving from cosy relaxed positions. After a while she spoke quietly again, at peace, not aroused by his innuendo.

"I was worth every penny. How long do you think before we finish laying out the site. That first terrace is much better now the dry stone wall is finished, all those splashes of white quartz look good. Pity about the rest of the heap; it's still bleak, uninviting."

"I've set young trees above the wall, nothing special, just wild seedlings saved from other places, they may help. Another five years probably, before it's all moved. But this winter's work went well; more pitches, all the areas are better, more grass – need a bigger mower soon."

"We always knew this valley was special," Jan murmured, "Wouldn't it be great if we could win one of those awards for the most picturesque site. Pity that tent business is always hanging over us; will the Council stop us taking them?"

"I've been reading up. It *is* a four-year rule; that's part of the Planning law. After four years the Council can't object – I don't see why they should anyway. After all, what difference does it make if people holiday in a tent or a caravan? Doesn't affect anyone, only the visitors own preference or what they can afford. You'll like the next bit though." Gordon moved sideways in the chair, resting on one of the arms and leaning nearer to impart this important snippet of information. "Those four years don't make the use legal. It then becomes unlawful but immune!"

"What does that mean?"

"It's... uh... not legal but they can't touch you. So two years after the sewer comes and I think we're safe!"

"Unlawful but immune? Sounds like a house of ill repute run by politicians. I've never been illegal before. Hey! How do you fancy an unlawful woman?"

"Five more days?" echoed Sharon incredulously at lunch on Saturday. "I touched it this morning, the base feels really hard already!" A frown of annoyance displayed clearly her suspicions of deliberate delay.

Apart from the house-hunting couple, the site was empty; not unusual, March never a month with many tourists about. Moving stone would use up those seven days, but Max needed servicing. Stephen had begun showing an interest in things mechanical. Together they checked engine oil, transmission oil, and water. Stephen lubricated the lower ram bearings then passing the grease gun over, asked "Diesel?" His father nodded and the lad sped off. The 200-gallon fuel tank was too tall for him, but standing on a box he could reach the hand pump to fill the old, somewhat battered dairy churn used for carrying diesel to the tractor. His father would fetch it when he finished greasing.

Later, with fuelling complete and all nuts holding the shovel attachment properly checked, Stephen climbed on the bucket to be lifted high in the air. He hung on tightly while Max negotiated the stony surface to the spoil heap's working face. Now seven and a half, Stephen had operated the bucket levers occasionally for months, but though growing rapidly, was still too short to reach the foot pedals. He did drive sometimes, or rather steered, sitting on his father's knee, but usually preferred the bucket, liking best to be high in the air.

A minor landslip, a few hundred tons of old mine waste had fallen from the working face overnight. Projecting from this stone stuck a piece of wood. Discarded timbers cropped up occasionally in the waste, but casual examination showed this one had smoothly rounded edges, not just a broken plank. Working together, they moved the surrounding debris, pulling free a curiously shaped section, one end like a handle, the rest twelve inches wide at a guess. Delving carefully into the rocky pile from which this timber had been rescued, revealed three more pieces. When placed together, these parts re-constructed an old wooden wheelbarrow abandoned by miners probably a century before. The base was missing and the wheel, but all the sides were found, one carved with the initials WV in large capitals, obviously Wheal Virgin, the name of the old mine from which the waste originated. In spite of its age, the timber appeared sound, protected from rot by its burial deep in the waste heap where neither rain nor air penetrated. Though dry and solid, it was quickly photographed and carried back to be coated with preservative. Old wood was apt to disintegrate rapidly once exposed to air. When finished and fixed together again, they proudly took it to the office door.

Jan examined the carved initials with interest, then frowned. "More junk to store?"

"A genuine relic of Wheal Virgin Mine. Surprisingly good condition after all this time; we're lucky to have it!"

"Hm!" She rolled her eyes upward in an appeal to the heavens. "What use will it ever be?"

There must be some use for such a rare object. He hunted for a reason, looking towards Stephen for possible inspiration. The lad gave a shrug and turned away.

"You've no..." Gordon was about to say 'feelings' but remembered just how sensitive his wife could be under the right conditions and hurriedly tried another tack. "A hundred years ago, some Cornishman worked his hands raw wheeling this barrow along those narrow mine tunnels with his back hunched over – all to earn enough to buy mackerel and pasties for his family. No one even remembers his name now. The hand that held this lies buried, probably a thousand feet below!" Gordon pointed dramatically at the ground. "His bones may lay forever in darkness, never again to see the light of day. This is his legacy, all he left behind, his only memory."

"Oh, bring on the violins while I weep!" Jan gave a little snort, "Hm! A scoundrel who spent his money in one of the six Pubs Relubbus was supposed to have had in those days, what did they call them, um, kidleywinks wasn't it? Probably drunk himself silly while the family starved. It's rubbish! Anyway, what could you do with it? Mount the thing over our office door?"

Seeing him struggle for an answer, she laughed. "Can't resist, can you? Like a squirrel hoarding nuts, nothing must ever be thrown away. Genuine relic!" She stared at him for a moment, shaking her head, eyes flicking over his tattered working clothes. "Don't you think I've enough old relics already!"

A few extra caravans arrived as the days passed. Sharon had made friends with the daughter of a Jewish family, the Cowens. They were of similar age and being early season with no other girls staying on site, the two youngsters from greatly different backgrounds became almost inseparable. Jan stood by the window one morning, noticing the clothes. Sharon's were older, one elbow showing bare through a hole in the blue roll neck sweater worn under a grey pinafore dress, the red ribbon they had bought so long before still round her hair; her friend in pink over a green skirt. Each held a baby goat.

"There's very little more appealing in this world than a young kid," Jan sighed to herself as she watched.

Olive, her face brown, forehead marked with a white horseshoe-shaped crescent between two sideways jutting, alsatian-like ears, sat happily in Sharon's arms. Little ivory white hooves, almost hidden, peeped hobbit-fashion from white shaggy hair on each small leg. As the young girl leaned forward to rub her cheek against the soft mane behind the head, the little goat turned, lifting its nose upward to rub some itchy patch on the underside of its neck against her face. Jan stood, hidden inside the window, unable to move away, captivated by the closed eyes and expression of sublime happiness on her daughter's face as the little goat rubbed up and down.

Slowly the two girls moved off upstream and out of vision; the waterwheel channel in the river not far from where they had stood caught Jan's attention. It was ready. Actually, the hardening period had passed several days ago but Gordon insisted on finishing a small new camping area that had almost been completed. This was partly an excuse, postponing work in the river while a spell of cold northerly winds prevailed; winter having a last fling. Visitors from up-country seemed not to notice, even commenting on the milder weather; perhaps he was getting soft? Sharon in particular was critical at teatime on Saturday, seeing through his excuse and suggesting he was afraid to get wet unless the sun shone.

"You can start without me if you like," Dad offered.

"I would, but *ladies* just aren't strong enough." Sharon spoke in a delicate, upper crust way, chin held high; probably something picked up from her friends at school. A special emphasis placed on the word *ladies* had the boys choking on their food. Jan could only half conceal her delight at what she considered a very female accomplishment, both the quickness of response and the manner of its delivery; she raised her eyebrows questioningly in Gordon's direction, awaiting his reply.

"Hm. Since you put it so cleverly, I shall start in the morning!"

Absolutely swelling with pride, Sharon clasped both arms together with a little shiver, as if hugging herself. Stretching to sit erect, spine straight, shoulders back, she looked haughtily at the boys, wrinkling her nose slightly in their direction, an expression somehow embodying the essence of class and excellence. Recognising the implied inferiority both boys reacted with scorn. Chris, studiously ignored her, staring through the window in that 'Lord preserve us from girls' manner which he certainly no longer felt but reserved still for his sister on rare occasions. Stephen, more basic and with less finesse, drew a stern glance from Jan by blowing a raspberry on his wrist, something he had previously been told not to do.

Cleverly arranged by the delay, or more likely from sheer good luck, the sun shone brightly the following morning. In windless conditions, timbers under the now hardened concrete rested a mere three inches above the unruffled water surface. First task then, remove all these supports and lower the channel!

Substantial nibs had been cast on the concrete sides, short stubby projections sticking out fore and aft at the top of each wall, handles for some giant hand to lift. They were similar in idea, if not in shape or position, to the way poles projected from the sedan chairs of nobility in the seventeenth century. Without this feature, the old hydraulic jack would have been too tall to lower the structure all the way to the riverbed. As Gordon entered the stream yet again, three caravanners out for an early morning walk stopped to watch. Curious that anyone should wade in fully dressed they wandered over to join the family on the bank.

With the jack at one end, the channel was lifted and a packing piece inserted. A series of similar jacking and packing movements at both ends enabled the supporting timbers to be recovered one after another. Further jacking, extracting blocks then winding down, working backwards and forwards from alternate ends, gradually lowered the channel. Naturally, Dad alone received the soaking. With each layer removed, the next rested that bit deeper! The watermark crept gradually upwards, first his sleeves then the chest of his pullover as it became necessary to kneel in the water in order to reach underneath and grab blocks from the far side. Finally, he all but submerged, kneeling lower to probe under the narrow gap, grasping and dragging clear the last supports, hauling them to the surface and then to a pile on the bank. Lowering the jack one final time left the channel resting firmly on the riverbed, or rather on those large granite slabs already firmly implanted therein.

Indoors again, the family sat round the table, cups of steaming coffee near at hand. Dad had already dried out and changed to another set of working clothes.

"What made you think of those overhanging pieces for the jack to go under?" Jan asked. "I realise now that you couldn't have lowered it all the way without them; but how did you manage to think of it beforehand?"

The children had given this feature no consideration, but now the subject was raised they turned towards their father, not very concerned, but awaiting his reply.

"It's a long story; goes back to my school days. I'm not sure I should tell you."

The vague interest changed. Curiosity in the circle of faces intensified, particularly Sharon's at the hint that information might be withheld. Jan waited, a touch of suspicion in her glance, apprehensive least the children be led astray.

"You mustn't think I was bad at school," Gordon cautioned. "I paid close attention, was top in some classes, particularly in science. But there was one teacher that had no control, well usually he had no control, or perhaps we children just imagined it and took advantage. It was silly really, because what you learn at school often determines how well you do in life afterwards. Anyway, as I say, with this one teacher who taught geography, we were definitely naughty, and probably I was the worst of all." Dad sipped the coffee but in the silence of that room, no questions, no comments, interrupted the narrative.

"As a punishment, many teachers would give lines. You know; you have to write out one hundred times things like 'I must pay attention in the classroom'. They were all pretty standard, each teacher had a favourite; we knew what to expect – so much so that a group of us got together and wrote lines in advance. I used to keep the bank. Anyone given lines could come to me for the number they required and give them straight to the teacher. After a while, we had the whole class doing them. It wasn't a punishment any more, it was fun, but we took great care no one else should find out. Our class were probably the fastest writers in the whole school! We even experimented with a row of pens sellotaped to two school rulers so we could write six lines at once. It never really worked, they were cumbersome, awkward to handle and getting ink onto the nibs was difficult, you couldn't dip them in an inkwell. With most teachers we dare not play around, the cane was used liberally in those days, but in geography we were quite disappointed if some sort of trouble didn't arise." Dad stopped again, sipping more coffee. Jan took a drink, but the children remained still, glancing at each other and waiting expectantly.

"Late one afternoon, it was last period before the home-time bell, my class had a lesson with this particular teacher. Our desks were in rows down the room with clear aisles between each pair of desks so the teacher could walk by to examine anyone's work. My seat was near the back in this class, unlike most others where I preferred the front to be sure of missing nothing. It wasn't too long before there was trouble! 'Stand up that boy!' the teacher called pointing to me. I stepped into the aisle and stood by my desk. 'Take two hundred lines.' That was his normal standard, two hundred. The class knew which ones even before he spoke. 'Write, *I must behave properly during lessons*'.

"I had them written already. Using paper with widely spaced lines and writing on one side only there were fifteen pages; with the help of classmates we had glued them together, end to end. Coiled up like a toilet roll, they formed a little bulge in my inside blazer pocket. Before he could say more my hand had reached in and pulled out the roll! Raising it to head level, I let go but held tightly onto one end. We had weighted the bottom sheet and the paper unwound to the floor, momentum rolling it on up the aisle. He was walking towards me by that time and it stopped at his feet, that last sheet resting against one toecap before coiling itself back a few turns. It was marvellous! Only a few of the class were expecting it. The room was in uproar. My words 'There you are sir!' were lost in the chaos.

"Eventually he restored order, but the incident had been so unpredictably spectacular that I expected at least the cane. However, that teacher rose somewhat in the class's estimation, and especially in mine, when he smiled slightly and said 'All right my boy, do another five hundred and this time we'll have a new wording.' He walked back up the aisle and wrote on the blackboard *Systematic thinking must precede action!*"

Gordon paused for another sip of coffee. Jan tried to look stern, wanting to laugh as the rest of the family were doing, but unsure. School was too important. She was about to say something, but he continued again.

"Things improved in that class. The lessons somehow became more interesting. I took his warning to heart. Systematic thinking should precede action, after five hundred times it was burned in my mind. That's how, even before we started the job, I managed to think of those projections to fit the jack under."

***

"I could do with some help this morning," Gordon suggested when the children had left for the start of another school week. Jan followed him to the river. Before them lay a debris of timber strewn all round the gear housing; a mess of paddles and other parts carried from storage and deposited on the grassy bank late the previous afternoon in preparation. The two bearings were quickly placed over bolts projecting vertically from each wall of the concrete channel, and the nuts tightened. Recognising that lifting the complete wheel would be difficult, the new shorter axle was slid into position with only the circular shrouds adding to its weight. Paddles and various other parts were then rapidly assembled and immediately work commenced to remove the dam, placing the stones to re-form the weir. Smaller ones were thrown across to land with a splash, disappearing below the surface, but bigger lumps of granite were not so easy. In any case, the intention was to create a ragged natural cascade, not a precisely laid structure of artificial appearance. Restoring the former surface level was essential, so water rushing under the bridge would not undermine its foundations. Even in the few years the family had lived in the valley, river cleaning had lowered the bed level considerably.

Previously the wheel was powered merely by water flowing beneath, but the opportunity had been taken to convert from undershot to breast design. Little slots had been formed on the inside channel walls, which allowed pieces of boarding to be slid down into position an inch clear of the moving paddles. These boards stopped six inches below the surface, allowing water to flow over the top then rush downwards, taking advantage of the water's weight as well as its velocity.

The actual gearing could have remained substantially unchanged, but as shortening the shaft had necessitated rebuilding the gear house, it now also incorporated a more compact and improved layout. The first V-belt, the slowest moving, was changed to a chain because belts tend to slip substantially at slow speed. At the lowest point the chain dipped into a container partly filled with oil, keeping it constantly lubricated. Complicated calculations showed that by choosing one size bigger than necessary and taking advantage of several other favourable factors, this chain had an expected life of seventy years so long as the oil bath never ran dry.

"These chains are expensive, do you think I need keep a spare?" Gordon asked, torn between the twin passions of not wasting money but always being prepared. He was explaining the situation and asking Jan's opinion as they walked back for coffee having made the final connections.

She stopped, looked him up and down as if buying a horse, one hand stroking her chin, head shaking doubtfully, a ritual they inflicted on each other whenever an opportunity to be critical arose. "Seventy years? Wouldn't bother if I was you!"

Sitting over coffee shortly afterwards, conversation focused on the children.

"How did you dream up that story last night, what a load of old..." she hesitated, "...shoemakers! Couldn't you have admitted those nibs were luck?"

"Luck? Never! It was logic, genius... No; systematic thinking – that's what it was."

Seeing the word 'Rubbish' forming on her lips he reached a hand across the table. She met him halfway; they touched lovingly, grinning at each other as he spoke again.

"Can you think of a better way to make them listen so intently? Might even get *them* thinking ahead sometimes. Anyway it was true, every word. I did do that, everything exactly like I told it, and unfortunately many other things too."

"Well keep them to yourself." She smacked his hand softly, shaking her head, not entirely believing. "At least the wheel is finished, you can be top of the class for that – providing it doesn't break down again!"

Indeed, the new waterwheel arrangement was working well. The smooth channel walls, a reduction to two bearings and the timber breastwork, were a success. These features, together with horizontal screws to tension all the gearing belts, had increased output to almost 100 watts. Lighting quality improved dramatically, for the house continued to require less wattage than most homes on account of the totally white walls. Little light bulbs like those seen in buses in the old days, continued to be used. Three of these could now shine continuously without depleting the battery. However, the river was still high. As spring and summer progressed, the water level would fall a few inches and the power reduce. Never mind, darkness would come later each evening, shortening the requirement for lights. These small bulbs had now sprouted all over the house, individually or grouped in clusters to give the desired output. Low voltage meant a high amperage, so wires needed to be thicker, even to the extent of using cooker wire on some lighting circuits. Switches on certain makes of desk lamps tended to burn out, a problem overcome by switching on and off at the wall socket rather than using the lamp switch. Such technical considerations however were trivial compared to the satisfaction of wresting a power supply directly from nature. Over the winter, their own children may have viewed it as common place, but early visitors were definitely impressed when they discovered the wheel was more than ornamental. The reaction of the children's friends also began to change the outlook of both Chris and Sharon, who garnered a certain prestige by association, making them understand that producing power from the river was, after all, not such a mundane accomplishment.

"Can we have wallpaper now?" Jan asked.

"Sure, if you must. Paper every room if you like," he saw her face light up before adding, "So long as it's white!"

An arm flew out as she rounded on him. "I'm not

wallpapering if it looks no different!"

"Just kidding. It needn't be totally white, but remember the reply I got from ICI. Even the slightest of off-white shades reduces light by five percent. Find something with a white background and a sparse pattern; thin gold stripes or a trellis, or maybe the odd pink rose, again over white, something like that. White makes a room bigger too."

Everything in the house was far from being white the following day. Chris, interested for some time in cross-country running, had started to take the sport seriously during the previous autumn. The running season having recommenced with the coming of spring, he arrived home liberally coated in the mud. Seeing him cross the bridge, Jan hurried to the door. Lack of a washing machine, for no one made a 12-volt model, increased her concern.

"What an earth happened to you?"

"Cross-country. I came in the top ten out of nearly seventy – and that included a class of older boys!" Chris's clear pride in the achievement brought a dubious frown to his mother's face.

"Oh? Come inside, but don't touch anything! Surely they have showers at school when you do this sort of thing. Isn't it usual to wear sports gear?"

"Everyone else wore their normal clothes. Don't know about showers, the route's always been dry before. Had a new master leading; he got lost, took us through a stretch of marshy ground. Only just managed to catch the school bus."

"You're lucky they let you on!"

As spring blossomed Chris became increasingly enthusiastic and promising in his performance, inspired possibly by another local runner who competed nationally, representing the school at Plymouth and other places. Chris had ambitions of doing the same. He revealed one evening that his efforts to win had become so intense that he fainted after crossing the finishing line. On coming round the master had said, 'It's excess oxygen demand by the body not leaving enough for the brain. Nothing to bother about.' Jan, however, was far from convinced and expressed her worry strongly.

"Surprised it affected you at all!" Sharon muttered.

A man cursed as water swilled down the motor-caravan side. He was trying to replenish the internal freshwater tank using a large saucepan filled at the nearby standpipe, tipping it from some height and trying to direct the stream into the small inset filler cap. Most was washing down the paintwork to spill on the stony road surface below or splashing back onto his trousers. Chris, walking towards the vehicle gripped Judy's lead more firmly and called the young goats to him, moving out onto the grass to give it a wider berth as he passed. Olive however had other ideas and dashed forward, putting out her tongue to experimentally lick at droplets splashing below. The man tilted the pan upright to stop the flow and gazed down, his anger forgotten. Tentatively he tipped the saucepan again, watching the kid prance up, two hooves on the caravan side, trying to reach the main spout of water. As cold liquid covered the furry nose, it leapt backward turning 180 degrees in the air.

"Sorry," Chris apologised. "Come on Olive!"

"It's all right. Is she thirsty? Most of this is going to waste anyway. We forgot our hose – we normally push it on the tap and fill the tank directly. Good sites have one fixed up permanently."

Chris shook his head, about to explain it was curiosity not thirst that drew the little goat, but his attention was diverted as a woman descended from the passenger side, walking forward and bending to stroke the other kid.

"They're lovely. Good thing you came along; I go and sit in the cab when Bill gets annoyed. Sorry about the language. I'm the one who forgot the hose." Olive ran to the woman, seeking a share of attention, but she pushed it back, "Agh! Go away, you're all wet!"

Chris knelt quickly grabbing the kid, stopping it putting dirty feet to which road dust now adhered, onto the lady's dress. Seeing it restrained, she leant over to stroke the back of its head where the hair was still largely dry. Shortly after Chris left.

Ivy and Olive were taking almost everything mother goat could produce; little milk remained for use in the house. Never mind, bottles bought from the village shop now kept fresh in the new gas fridge. Judy was still led to the office door for milking each evening, where she ate with relish from the offered bucket of rolled oats. It had become a ritual, the kids came too, not following closely at their mother's heels but lagging behind, then on some impulse racing each other to catch up and galloping ahead until some bush to nibble or a patch of brambles caught their attention again. Usually Chris fetched the trio; Judy, by common consent, was his animal. She followed him with as much devotion as a goat's independent nature could ever give, running when he ran, slowing down if he chose not to hurry. Only occasionally did she dig in her heels, refusing to move forward until sure the youngsters were given time to catch up. The kids were much less controllable, being free and naturally curious. That motor-caravan visit just now was typical, anything could divert them. Whenever they did lag behind, more interested in something else, it seldom proved possible to attract them with food, since they had taken their fill from Judy throughout the day, nibbling tentatively at any piece of greenery that took their fancy. Nor did calling them prove very effective; sometimes on a whim they would come but just as often they would not. Chris, however, had found something much more irresistible. Kneeling on all fours he faced towards them, head down in a challenging position. From right across a grassy area they would race each other to reach him. The first time, the impact had knocked him clean over, leaving him dizzy and unable to remember which kid had made contact. After that, he stood up at the last moment holding both hands down, palms forward to act as buffers, held sideways to avoid impact with his shins. Small they might be but their heads were hard; bullfighting in miniature. Sometimes the ploy failed when for some unknown reason they were just not interested, but it only needed one to start, the other would always follow, neither prepared to be left alone. When they both caught up, Chris usually spent a few moments scratching itchy places to encourage them to come next time.

With the arrival of Easter and a small influx of tourists, Judy's visit to the office at a regular hour became a magnet for children and adults alike. The kids loved the attention they were given, and liked human company. One man, persuaded along by his wife and children went up enormously in their estimation when, not really paying attention, he bent to tie a shoelace. Quick as a flash Olive was on his back, balancing easily as he wobbled to cheers from his family and a round of applause from all those present. Just as quickly Olive jumped down, bounced with straight legs in that way young goats have, as if on springs, and dashed off to someone else. The man rose, gave a little bow to the audience and basked in admiring glances from his children.

Both kids blissfully submitted to being handled and cosseted. One young mother with two toddlers approached Chris, who everyone considered in charge of the goats.

"Can we touch the little black and white one?" she asked.

"Yes, that's Ivy. She's anyone's for a rub behind the ears." Chris responded casually.

The woman stiffened, taken aback.

Chris, old enough to realise how it had sounded, blushed brightly, glancing up quickly at his mother standing nearby, hoping she had not noticed. Jan moved her head, looking sideways at him in surprise and then towards Gordon; had he overheard? She watched him gaze casually round as if nothing had happened but detected a silly grin on his face and knew that he had.

Later that evening with the children asleep, or perhaps reading in their bedrooms, Jan sat down and reached for her book. Gordon came into the room from the kitchen and stood behind her chair. She sat, eyes on the page but not reading, refusing to look up. Would it be one of those battles of will? A hand reached out and rubbed her gently behind the ear. She didn't understand at first, but when he changed to the other ear, a memory of Chris's words returned. She could scarcely contain the smile. Rising slowly, she swung gracefully from the chair with a dreamy look in her eye and moved towards him sending little kiss signals with her lips. Eyes shining in anticipation, he opened his arms to her.

At that precise moment, she lowered her head, and driving off the back foot, butted him hard in the chest. "Baaa!" The bleating cry of triumph might have been more sheep that goat, but Jan was higher than a kite all evening on her success.

Chapter 7

Poor Margaret

The initial appearance was important. It affected trade. Moving into the house and selling the old caravan early in the previous year had done much for the site entrance. While still far from perfect, the improvement and its effect on arriving visitors was marked. That move had other advantages, benefits not seen by guests but for the family alone. Copious kitchen space and the new full sized stove had gradually made Jan's cooking more adventurous. Of course, it would revert to snacks later when peak season arrived, but the better quality could still be enjoyed now in April with customers relatively sparse. After an especially appetising meal with empty plates littering the table, she was pleased to observe contentment and a reluctance to move by those seated round the dining annex. A feeling of well-being pervaded the room.

"Far better than school dinners." Chris paid the doubtful compliment without thought, not intending to understate the quality.

"It's not bad," Gordon agreed, "but I expect no less, having invested seven shillings and sixpence on a..."

He got no further. Jan hit him with a cushion, but it was thrown only in fun.

Sharon's praise flowed with more enthusiasm; genuine certainly, but perhaps also expecting to garner a certain prestige herself for she finished by mentioning casually, "I often cook when Mum's busy." The boys looked at each other, Chris putting one hand to his mouth in a pretended yawn. Sharon glared at him fiercely and turned on Stephen to demand, "Meals *are* much tastier since we left the caravan, aren't they?"

"Yus." A single nod of conviction accompanied the word.

Jan smiled, content with his natural reticence, but Sharon, still angling for an acknowledgement of her part in the food preparation, wanted more.

"What do you like most about our new cooking?"

"Proper chips."

No one could argue with that. It had perhaps been the thing most missed in the caravan where the gas flame had never been hot enough to make them brown, apart from one occasion where Dad had managed with some dangerous assistance from an ancient paraffin blowlamp. Jan was pleased. She had put extra effort into this meal and would have been disappointed if nobody commented. Nevertheless, it had not been possible to do all of the things she had wanted.

"Glad you enjoyed it. If my food processor would work, I'd do milk shakes too, and meringues... occasionally even puddings with whipped cream high on top; that sort of thing would be easy then." She spoke, moving her hands to the various shapes then spreading them sideways, palms up, sighing with a certain sadness.

The children nodded vigorously. Puddings, anything sweet and gooey, was definitely favourite. Sharon turned to her father, "Why can't you fix it, Dad?"

There was a way. He knew that, but had tried to avoid spending the money. It needed a Transverter, an expensive gadget that converted 12-volt DC to 240-volt AC. (from car type electric to house type electric, you might say). There was cash available in the bank but it would already take several years to save enough for a proper road surface and this would set it back further. If River Valley was going to be the best site in the southwest, those dust clouds on the road would have to go, and that meant tarmac! However, in the end Gordon gave way to the family's wishes and sent off a cheque. The equipment arrived a week later and by using it, about half a kilowatt of normal current could be obtained. Fixing it in the basement and running the necessary wires to the kitchen above, he issued a warning.

"This uses current extremely fast; you can't run it for long at any one time. Try not to use it when darkness approaches or the lights will be affected. Our battery is not so good as it used to be!"

"Buy a new one?" Jan suggested.

"No point. It would soon deteriorate. Lead-acid batteries don't like the way we use them, running them flat then charging up again – it affects the plates. We'll make do with this one for a while, it's okay if you manage it right."

"Hm. If it affected the site, you'd have a spare!"

Jan's food mixer, the vacuum cleaner, the electric drill, all of which they already had, would now work but only for short periods, ten minutes at most for the vacuum. Providing these implements were only used in the morning, the battery would still be topped up again before darkness descended. Television however, was not practical; it required more than the wheel could produce and would very rapidly have drained the old battery. It was hardly worthwhile to buy a 12-volt TV set that could only be used for such a limited time – and it would dim all the lights too.

The move to a house had caused other changes. For one, the reception area was much better. Although this room remained part of the normal living accommodation, there was more space, a chair for arriving visitors to sit in, and a desk to transact the business more easily. On this desk sat the telephone, a facility that had received priority treatment during the move. It had been re-connected less than an hour after disconnection from the old caravan, in order not to miss those precious incoming booking calls. During the previous season many visitors had asked to use the phone and at first this was readily agreed to by whoever sat in the office. Overhearing such one-sided conversations while sitting working at the desk often made concentration difficult. Try as one might to shut it out, the mind unconsciously furnished those missing answers. Hearing a distraught young lady having an apparently torrid conversation with someone had spawned the natural assumption that the person at the other end of the line must be a young man. "Lecherous beast!" Jan had thought as a tear crept down the woman's cheek. Only later, while unavoidably eaves-dropping on yet another call, did she discover that the tear had been for a cat, which on being let out at night had lost itself for a few days.

These calls were not only distracting, but requests for them had regularly interrupted meals and worse, blocked incoming telephone enquiries and bookings. This year they had resolved to send visitors to a public phone in the village. The change aroused some resentment and had already caused complaints from villagers regarding numerous cars parked outside the local telephone box at six o'clock each evening when cheap rate calls started. Relubbus was such a small village. The road, not particularly wide anywhere, was extra narrow by the kiosk and the old granite bridge. Even three or four cars parked there created a potential hazard. Obviously matters would become worse later in the season. Something must be done! There was still time. With Easter over, caravan numbers had dropped considerably. The site telephone cable had fourteen lines, and only one in use. Left over from other buildings were sand, gravel, concrete blocks, roof tiles and several short timbers; everything needed for a kiosk except a few bags of cement and the door arrangement. Cement had risen to the ridiculous price of over fifty pence for a one hundredweight bag but in spite of this the total cost would be less than £40.

Even with waiting a couple of days for foundations to harden and a further two days until the blockwork set, Gordon had it finished, complete with door, roof and cement rendering inside and out, in little over a week; moreover the work had been done with special attention to quietness. Excavation to extend the cable had been the only noisy operation. That short trench he dug, then laid the cable inside a plastic duct and refilled again one early afternoon while all the customers were out. An arrangement with the Water Authority allowed the water main to be extended at the same time. There remained just the door to be hung and a coat of paint.

"Looks like a sentry box," Chris observed, standing back to stare critically at the structure.

True, it did. One could see what he meant, but with the kiosk complete, what could be done? Very little!

"We could use invisible paint!" Gordon suggested.

"There's no such thing – is there?" Chris looked doubtful.

"Not really, but old painters used to pretend there was. Inside a building for instance, any pipework fixed to the wall was usually done with invisible paint. I've even seen that written in specifications. What it really means is paint the pipe exactly the same colour as the wall behind. Makes it hard to see; it's still there but no one notices, or at least, not so much."

"Yes, but..." Chris stopped indicating the kiosk and the trees behind with a sweep of the hand and a shrug that said, "How?"

"I know, the background is all different colours so we can't do that exactly, but let's change our mind and use dark Cuprinol to stain the door and the other bare wood surfaces, it will preserve them and blend in better than white paint."

As a final touch, cutting the outline of a telephone from sheet aluminium and fixing it above the newly stained door revealed the kiosk's purpose but did little to soften the shape. With the work complete the family stood back studying the effect. The addition made little difference, the sentry box impression persisted, reminiscent of those in children's toy soldier sets! Deep discussions on the appearance yielded nothing beyond the conclusion that a single person kiosk must necessarily appear this way unless made mainly of glass and painted red in imitation of the real thing. Not the great improvement sought for, but a solution to the practical problem of visitors phone calls; the facility would no doubt find great favour in the season ahead. When those trees behind grew a bit and branches hung over the roof, perhaps it would look better. Jan planted ivy along one side.

"Camouflage!" she said, confirming her dislike of the present appearance.

Stephen first made use of the kiosk, though not for its intended purpose. An American family had arrived on site, a rare event. As usual with people from the States, they drove a hired motorcaravan or as they called it, an RV, a Recreational Vehicle, and were staying only one night. In the afternoon they would visit St Michael's Mount and Land's End. Tomorrow they must see Plymouth, home of the Pilgrim Fathers, then on to Dover and the ferry for France. No doubt they would return home professing to "know Cornwall – stayed there in '73." This family of four was pleasant and easy to chat with, another American trait, and even before choosing a pitch the camera was out for photos beside the waterwheel. Since they too lived near a river, an account of its construction interested them greatly. The son, a boy of about 12-years called John, was particularly taken with Chris's part in building the temporary dam. However, because of school the two boys were never to meet. Chris had already left for his bus the following morning when the motorcaravan stopped to say goodbye, but John passed three American comics through the window, one for each of the children.

Waving as the vehicle crossed the bridge, Jan carried the glossy-covered booklets inside, glancing at the lurid pictures of a powerful masked figure before dropping them on the desktop and picking up a pen. As she wrote in the ledger, a woman entered to book an extra night. While taking the money Jan noticed her eyes rest several times on the magazines. Not wanting other customers to think this was her normal taste in reading, she moved them to the dining room sideboard after the woman had left.

That evening Sharon stayed at Jim's bungalow to walk home with Chris as she had often done recently. She would be attending senior school herself before long and was anxious about the change. When they were alone with no appearances to maintain, her older brother was usually more talkative, more prepared to reveal what went on and to treat her better. Stephen, therefore, reached the house first and alone. He was talking with his mother in the office, answering her questions about his day at school with mostly one-word replies, when another customer appeared. Sauntering off to the dining room while the visitor was dealt with, Stephen found the comics and picked them up. Guessing the older two would each forcibly take one away when they arrived home, he slipped out unseen while Jan was fetching a gas bottle. A large rock behind the house provided a place to sit as he scanned the pictures at leisure, reading only enough of the short captions to understand the gist of the story. Little time had passed before he heard his name shouted angrily inside the house. He was sitting near a vent that led to the basement as Chris's voice floated up, "He's not here!"

Mum must have told them about the comics. He was being hunted! They would soon exhaust the house and start searching outside. Dashing off to seek a more remote hiding place, he was racing across the yard as the office door opened.

"There he goes!" Sharon yelled.

They were after him! Stephen sprinted round the toilet building but instead of running on, he swung open the telephone box door, entering and closing it barely in time. Crouched low behind the wooden panel the sound of running feet passed close by, Chris and Sharon calling to each other as the steps faded. Obviously seeing nothing through the clear glass panel above they had assumed the box empty. Stephen delayed another minute before rising to look through the glass, then opened the door a fraction and listened. They were gone. Hearing a shout from farther down the valley, he slipped out and raced for the office, knowing they had already searched the house. No one was inside as he entered, shutting the door behind him – the first time he had closed it quietly in weeks. Dad would be out working of course and he had banked on his mother being in the kitchen. Creeping stealthily across the room his eye caught the phone – he almost stopped. "Don't ring," the thought came suddenly, aware it would bring Jan running. Still moving with caution he entered the hall as the bell rang out! Three steps and he leapt for the staircase, knowing the concrete treads would not creak. One more step up and he froze, flattened against the wall. Below, soft shoes sounded, walking on the carpet and the bell stopped as someone picked up the receiver. Taking advantage of the diversion, he tiptoed lightly up the stairs, stepped over the last two treads which were timber, entered the room that he shared with Chris and crept across to lay on the floor on the far side of his own bed. This room would be the first place they had checked, they were unlikely to try again; even if they did he would only be seen if they came right to the window end. Carefully he rested all three comics on the mat. The sound of the phone put back in its cradle was faint, but he heard it. Soft steps approached the bottom of the staircase.

"Chris?" His mother's voice floated up. The call had a tentative quality, as if not expecting a reply; he kept silent. Below Jan walked away, back to the kitchen. She had no idea what made her call, nothing had been heard, it had just been a feeling, but never in her wildest dreams would she have considered Stephen capable of entering and closing a door silently.

Above, the young lad flipped a page to scan more

pictures, reading snippets of text, pleased with himself, pleased to come out on top against his older brother and sister; that seldom happened! They were still searching, that would annoy them; he smiled realising how angry they would be if they knew, if they could see him lying there. He tossed one comic aside and opened another, flicking through, not reading any more.

The office door opened and closed again.

"Has he come back?" Sharon's called.

"No. Tea's ready, come and sit down."

Stephen lay listening to the voices below, then quick footsteps mounted the stairs. He kept very still, not seeing but aware that someone now stood in the doorway. The footsteps departed again. Scraping chairs told they were sitting down to the meal. What if he went down now? What would they do? What would happen if he walked into the room holding the comics? That would make them really mad!

A little elfin grin crossed the young face. Silently he rose and headed for the door.

***

Not working in the rain was one of the few special favours Gordon now permitted himself, a favour not often possible in previous years. Invariably there were enough inside jobs, for rainfall in the valley was infrequent. Should tasks in the dry ever run out, Jan would undoubtedly find more; only that morning she had issued another reminder.

"You still haven't fixed a curtain rail over the front door in the hall."

Several wettings did however have to be endured in a rush to level some late deliveries of topsoil. The seed needed setting while April showers lasted, before May with its hot, dry days terminated the grass-growing season. One Saturday in particular he arrived back at the house soaked to the skin, expecting a certain amount of sympathy from the family who had themselves stayed inside, comfortably warm and dry.

“Ugh. Don’t come near me, you’re all soggy.” Sharon shrieked, backing away.

“Skin is supposed to be waterproof,” commented Chris, though whether to Dad or Sharon was unclear.

“Save having a bath,” Stephen muttered into his chest.

Jan said nothing but her expression, as usual, encouraged the children, nodding with agreement and approval.

“What does a chap have to do to get a little consideration and a coffee around here?” Gordon asked, “Come back carrying my head under one arm, I suppose.”

“If you do, try not to drip blood on the carpet,” Jan suggested, winking at the children, “and you wouldn’t be wanting coffee then, would you?”

Shutting himself in the bathroom to dry off and change, he remembered a similar incident where she had shown an equal lack of any proper feeling, egging the children on at his expense. It was earlier in the year, when building the half dam of stones for the waterwheel. This construction had made the stream rush through one half of the river, leaving relatively motionless water on the near side. He had been working in the placid section, placing the final stones in position, water level part way up his thighs. Since the dam was right in front of the house, Jan had brought hot coffee in a cup rather than using a flask, and walking carefully to avoid spilling any, had approached the bank accompanied by the children. She called loudly, shouting to be heard above the noisy water rushing by on the far side of the stream.

He had looked up, pleased to see them, pushing both arms outward in a long stretch and arching over to relieve aching shoulders. Whether stepping back to admire his own handiwork, or arching too far and taking a rearward pace to avoid overbalancing, he could not afterwards remember. Whatever the cause, this sudden careless movement took him out of the still water, directly into the full force of concentrated flow outside the dam! He was unprepared; not braced against the pressure as he had always taken care to be when lifting stones from the old weir. The soft bed had crumbled under one foot, further unbalancing him; he staggered, trying to stabilise, but had been long past the point of no return! Hands windmilling in the air, trying desperately to recover, his body had fallen headlong with a great splash, rushing water closing over him where it ran deepest. Heaving off the bottom to surface again with a struggle, he had stood fighting the current, spluttering, totally saturated, and clawed a way back into the sheltered pool behind the dam.

Did the family dash down the bank to help their poor old drowning Dad? No, not a bit of it! They had stood helpless with laughter, doubled up, tears running down Jan's cheeks, young Stephen jumping up and down as he did when over-excited. The coffee might have been anywhere, certainly none remained in the cup! The ingratitude of it all.

"Would you like me to do it again?" he had asked indignantly.

"Oh yes please!"

Jan's reply held such honest desire, such conviction, such emphasis, and three little heads nodded agreement! He had clambered up the bank, stuck his nose in the air, sniffed loudly, ignoring them all and walked dripping through the house.

Gordon smiled at the memory. Drawing on a dry shirt called to mind the response on that previous occasion when he had donned dry clothes and returned to the kitchen. Just the sight of him re-entering the room had generated further irrepressible chuckles, and his enquiry "Where's the coffee?" had received a facetious response.

"It spilt." Jan, standing by the sink, had said simply. "A glass of water instead, perhaps? You seem to like that!"

Giggles and smirks all round from the children at the table.

"Perhaps we could all do with a swim?" he had suggested mildly, eyebrows raised.

"Couldn't possibly. I've just put the kettle on." Jan had responded as she hurriedly lit the gas.

He remembered the angelic expressions on those three young faces, now apparently engrossed in books. Chris's was upside down. Moving over to the edge of the table he had gazed down at them, just stood there saying nothing as the children strained to keep back bursts of laughter that everyone knew were totally uncontainable. All it had needed was patience. Sharon peeped from the corner of one eye; a small sound escaped, somewhere between a hiccup and a broody hen. That did it! Everyone was off again curled up and helpless. He had struggled to maintain a severe expression but couldn't make it, ending up somehow with both arms round Jan, children on all sides.

His thoughts returned to the present, to the family sitting warm and dry inside the house. Outside against the windows, the rain continued. That was where he must go again shortly. Oh well, as Jan would say, 'What else are Dads for?'

Days passed and another area was levelled and planted. Those April showers might be ideal for newly set seed, but how they made the established grass grow! Mowing had become a problem. The old Haytor mower, its blades powered by the petrol engine but muscle power alone providing forward motion, had been fine when the site first opened for there had been little grass to cut. Now that the number of prepared areas had much expanded and still grew, it was definitely not so good! Hours of effort were required pushing the machine; time and energy better spent on other things. Nor was the lengthening period during which the noisy engine must run any help to the site's reputation.

The old horse drawn mower, the one collected with such difficulty in the first year then dragged around by the excavator, had long since been discarded. It had been useful only for cutting long vegetation on level ground, and none of the remaining uncleared areas was remotely level. After the first season and the difficulties experienced in preventing visitors' children playing on this rather dangerous toy, they had dug a large hole to bury it. What else could be done? Whoever would want a horse drawn mower?

With money coming in again and the season ahead, Jan pushed for the purchase of a better machine. This new cost would be yet another setback to future road surfacing, and there was still the old worry that the Council might discover their planning discrepancy. However, any tarmac was still years away and there seemed no possibility of the old mower lasting that long. Better perhaps to buy one now before prices increased again? In spite of a reluctance to spend, he agreed in this instance, showing only token resistance. Jan was surprised, but pleased nevertheless to have achieved her purpose so simply. The new mower looked more like a Dodgem from a fairground than a grass cutter; a little petrol engined ride-on machine called a Gilson. It could also pull a small trailer. Storage would be in the garage in front of the car, there was plenty of room. The old Haytor could also rest there Gordon insisted; it would be a spare, a standby in case of breakdown. The new machine cut superbly, far more quickly and quietly; so easy to use that Jan and Chris between them took over much of the grass trimming.

Gordon entered to the office one afternoon, having found a pitch for two caravans travelling together. He walked with Jan to the bridge, watching her toss a handful of bread to the trout. Stephen's deep annoyance at not being allowed to drive the new mower fell under discussion, as did the speed with which it had been purchased.

"You did virtually all the mowing with the old machine, and now we do most of it; that wouldn't explain how you came to part with the money so easily would it?" Jan demanded. Seeing him look away and detecting a slight grin, she sighed. "I might have guessed. Wish you were as easy to persuade when *I* want something new!"

"Yes, but you're only a wife, why should I want to spend money on you?"

"That will cost you next time I go shopping," she vowed quietly but audibly, trying not to smile, allowing herself to be pulled gently towards him and returning his kiss. Resting comfortably close, cheek to cheek, she slid a hand upwards, fingers finding the short hairs on the nape of his neck and brushing them softly against the grain. Feeling a warm response against her body, she stretched up on tiptoe, leaning forward to bite the lobe of his ear softly against her lower lip, and whispered, "Just let me catch you spending money on anyone else! One day I'll ask for something really expensive, like a new car."

***

"Everybody likes wasps!"

"Well I don't!" Jan replied firmly. "Must you bring it in here?"

It was early May. Gordon entered the door, carefully carrying a small object on the palm of his hand. The nest had been discovered while spreading the last remains of a dozen loads of topsoil tipped by a friendly lorry driver in April, the same soil that had caused him to get so wet two weeks before. The job was almost finished, most of the newly spread area already seeded, though with dry May weather likely to persist, germination was now somewhat doubtful.

Jim was not really helping, he seldom ventured this far but had come to inspect progress and picked up the spare shovel largely to lean on. Suddenly, a queen wasp zoomed from the ground to fly tight, and one could easily think somewhat menacing circles around their heads. Jim hated wasps; long ago he had been stung on the back of the tongue after eating one on a slice of bread and jam, and had almost choked when the flesh swelled. In an uncharacteristically adroit but most regrettable parry with his spade, Jim killed the assailant when only a temporary strategic withdrawal was needed. However, the damage was done and they bent down to investigate the soil from where the unfortunate insect had appeared. In a hollow under a partly rotted turf, the nest, smaller than a tennis ball, hung with its entrance at the bottom. Without the queen, the sole egg laying machine, this nest was no longer viable. Prising off the attachment to the turf and handling the delicate sides with great care Gordon had carried it back to show Jan. As he quickly became aware, she was less than thrilled!

The nest had reached a stage where the first grubs had pupated but none hatched. Jan, inspecting it guardedly and with positive disapproval, was nevertheless intrigued by the little paper ball. Assured of the absence of any live wasps, her concern relaxed and it remained on the desktop for others to see. The children, curiosity aroused, peered into the small opening. They had never seen such a nest before. It was surprising that grubs inside the tiny cells continued to move. To help compensate for loss of the queen's body heat and the insulation that surrounding soil had once provided, the desk light was shone on them. No one knew if wasps needed extra heat but this nest was exceptionally early; most wasps appeared in the warmth of summer so they must like a higher temperature. The small 12-volt bulb emitted considerable heat as well as light but its use, while easily met by the waterwheel during daytime, did unfortunately reduced the lighting available for evenings.

A day later the first wasp emerged and was immediately given the name Anne; they often called their pets after Royalty. Usually Jan approved but in this case she was, to say the least, uncertain.

"Had I known one would hatch out, I would never have agreed to the nest coming indoors. She will probably sting you, serves you right! She had better not come near me!" Jan's lips compressed in the tight thin line as she issued the warning, waving a rolled up newspaper threateningly, but there was a hint of humour in her flashing eyes.

They knew the wasp was female; the males, drones for mating, were only bred later in the season. Gordon put his hand protectively over Anne until Jan left the room, still making swishing sounds with swipes through the air at an imaginary foe. After she had departed, he cleared a space on the desk for a small wooden drawing board, and on this arranged the nest with Anne inside, and some flat plastic lids containing water, jam, and meat. Several small pieces of old dry wood were added for nest building. Wasps' nests are entirely made from wood, pulped up in those strong jaws then moulded to form horizontal layers of downward facing cells inside a spherical paper envelope. Each cell layer hangs from the one above by little ropes of paper. The nest is usually made underground, often under a tree among the roots.

Anne became more active, but rather erratic! She spent much time with her head in one of the apparently empty cells and in spite of plenty of wood around, made no attempt to repair the slightly damaged nest. Probably she could detect the absence of the queen, around whom every wasp's life was normally organised. Gordon felt sorry for her and except when Jan was around, seldom bothered to keep the clear plastic dome in position. (It was one of those propagation domes with vents at the top. Matchsticks provided an improvised air gap underneath). Later in the day Anne tried her first flight, only to fall on to the floor, her wings not quite perfect. He carried her back to the nest clinging to a pencil-sized paintbrush.

Jan, seeing the incident, put on her 'We are not amused' expression and wagged a finger in air. Opening her mouth to say something, she hesitated as if lost for words, pursed her lips in determination, then repeated the warning.

"Just let her fly into *my* kitchen!"

A further day passed and Margaret emerged, closely followed by Elizabeth; all very similar in appearance. To ensure he did not offend by getting the names mixed up, a tiny dab of quick drying enamel paint in different colours was placed on the thorax of each. Names are so important! Watching the wasps, Gordon's mind drifted again, as it so often tended to do. He recalled an incident that occurred several years previously when they were still leading a normal life. He had taken Jan to the firm's Christmas dinner party. For the first time they were on the top table with the directors and senior designers. Jan was sparkling in an evening dress, her hair perfect, lots of shoulder showing above the plunging neckline, lips very red and slightly moist he noticed. Following tradition, everyone presented their partners, the rest feigning polite interest during each introduction. Being most junior, Gordon's turn was last, and awaited with a certain nervousness, though he felt proud to present the best looking girl in the room.

"May I introduce..."

He froze, hunting frantically for the name. No good! It was gone! They had been married five years and he couldn't remember her name! The polite interest changed. Tension hung palpably round the table. Now there was real attention, real curiosity, even envy. Jan had suddenly been promoted to the rank of Mistress; beautiful, naughty, and therefore utterly desirable. That, without doubt, was definitely the men's reaction. The ladies lifted their noses a little higher, as if something malodorous had appeared suddenly in their midst. Jan grew even prettier in the red that slowly spread across her cheeks. Probably his own colour was no better. Suddenly he had it!

"This is my wife Janifer."

It came out in a rush. No one was convinced, but politeness and convention saved the day, Jan becoming the recipient of much male attention throughout the meal and afterwards in the guise of kindness and concern, and he never realised that his own standing among the chaps was quite so high. Apparently being able to 'pull' a 'belle fantastique' as the French might say, carried merit far above merely marrying one!

His thoughts returned to the wasps. They too, might well be offended if he got their names muddled, they were after all female, and females can give you hell later if you get their name wrong!

Paint dots should prevent this. Using the stronger colours first, Anne was yellow, Margaret crimson, and Elizabeth white.

"Yellow," Jan insisted, "is totally inappropriate for Anne."

"No, no! The colours have absolutely no significance. I chose them solely for their brightness," he insisted.

The latest arrivals also spent much time with heads in apparently empty cells, listless and with no apparent desire to undertake the normal, well-organised, industrious work of a wasp's nest. Gordon had persuaded all three, with a little encouragement, to eat syrup off his finger. Margaret, the only one so far who could fly really well, became so fixed on hands that it was necessary to replace the plastic sandwich cover to protect the occasional nervous visitor, and especially when Jan was around.

Two of the girls were being fed when Margaret took her first long flight finding her way to the kitchen.

"You want to be careful," Gordon whispered as he carried her, clinging to his finger, quickly back towards the nest. Lifting her near to his lips so that they would not be overheard, he warned, "That Jan will swat you with a newspaper if she catches you in her kitchen."

Ivy hatched and was given a dab of blue, followed by Olive, metallic blue; these were the names of mother and mother-in-law, names used also for the young goats.

"It's an insult," Jan said, only partly in jest. "I insist you change them!"

"No, no! It's a sign of affection. You might even get to like one if she's named after your mother; besides, don't you see the resemblance?" He ducked low as a dishcloth whistled past his ear to squelch wetly on the wall beyond, but it was thrown in fun, not anger.

Later there was Audrey and Sophie in orange and green. All fed happily from his finger, liking particularly the syrup left at the bottom of glacé cherry tubs. He always fed them on his left hand because after eating they were often quite lazy. If the hand was turned over, the little creatures happily slept hanging upside down under the palm, no doubt feeling warm and secure while he carried on writing with the other hand. At first he let them stay, hidden and asleep while talking to visitors, not even mentioning their presence, but this did not always work. After a while it became necessary to put the wasps back under their dome if anyone entered the office, for they were apt to wake up and were equally friendly towards strangers. One lady got quite upset when a wasp settled on her finger, and didn't seem to wish to listen to the explanation that Elizabeth only wanted feeding!

Gordon started to take the better flyers outside for short trips. One day Margaret never returned. He was miserable and suggested that they wear black armbands and put an obituary in The Times. Jan, with creditable logic, pointed out that there was no corpse, therefore death could not be certified!

"Margaret might have gone off with a Henry or George or Charles," she suggested, and added with a touch of malice, "Although it's far more likely that one of the visitors has swatted it." A short swinging action of her right hand thumped the table top with a book, demonstrating Margaret's probable fate.

"No! We have a nice, friendly class of visitor. How, could anyone possibly pulverise poor Margaret, who only wanted a little warmth and affection, just to curl up in the palm of a hand and go to sleep?" He also pointed out that wasps, other than Queens, do not chase after males because although female, they are sexually inactive and only attend to collecting food, feeding the young and keeping the nest tidy.

"Some women," he suggested, "could learn a lot from my little pets."

Jan stood looking down at him, flicking a glance across at the wasps, now all safely under the dome. "Ah! But they're ordinary females. In this household, I'm the Queen! And don't you forget it!"

Struck by a further idea, she stepped closer, lifting her left foot onto the edge of his chair and allowing the skirt to fall back exposing a shapely leg.

"Hope I won't have to wait until autumn arrives for *my* drone."

When the last grub hatched, the nest and occupants were carried outside and placed deep in an ivy covered tree to lead the best lives they could manage without a queen.

Chapter 8

The Shark

Taking another cup from the draining board and wiping it with a teacloth, Sharon flicked a glance towards the boys. She had watched for some minutes, wanting them to move but saying nothing, knowing they would stay if they guessed. As Chris made to leave and Stephen followed, she waited a few seconds then stepped to the doorway, peeping out along the corridor, checking. The office door banged shut; Stephen obviously. They had gone outside.

"What's the matter with Dad?" Sharon asked as Jan lowered a pile of big plates stained with the residue of baked beans into the bowl of soapy water.

"You noticed? I'm surprised, I don't believe the boys did. What made you think something was wrong?"

"He was kind of quiet, Mum."

"Isn't he usually? Sometimes he doesn't even hear when we speak to him – when he's thinking about that wheel or some other thing." Jan shrugged.

"Yes," Sharon searched for the right words. "I know he never shouts, well not often, but usually... I'm not sure how to explain. When the boys started flicking beans at each other at tea, you stopped it. Normally Dad would have just looked at them, it would have been enough."

"Is your father such an ogre?"

"No, not exactly, but he does give extra jobs sometimes if we misbehave."

"Like moving all those building blocks for the house?"

"Yes Mum! Like that. We hardly had to do a thing to

get another fifty to shift!"

"That was special, he needed the help, was very tired; people do get intolerant when they're tired. But that's not what you noticed today, is it?"

"I... no. He saw them do it, but seemed not to mind; had that look like when the goat kids do something naughty, sort of almost a smile, as if they don't know any better."

Jan studied at her daughter for a while, wondering how a girl not quite eleven could be so discerning. "He looks at you children like that when you're playing together on the floor or at the beach, when we went to Lizard for instance, places you can't see his expression. But this evening is different. Something went wrong on site; that teenager who all the complaints were about, the one who dashed round on his bike all over the grass areas and near the younger children. It's too dangerous."

"I know!" Sharon's hand rose fractionally as she spoke, an unconscious movement, one finger pointed towards the front field. "My friend's young sister was knocked over late yesterday evening; just frightened not injured, but she could have been. Her Mum was angry; went to the boy's parents but they used swear words and let him carry on doing it. I told Dad. I thought he'd go and see them, but he didn't."

"Dad had already spoken to them, to the boy and to his parents. This morning he turned them off, made them leave. You could see from here; the man was waving his arms about, walked right up close and shook his fist but your father just stood there. He gave them the balance of their money back and waited until they pulled out."

"Is that why he was quiet at tea; he was afraid?"

"I asked him that." Jan paused, remembering. "He just said, *Probably. I'm bound to get clobbered one day*. But it wasn't that; I know him better. This was the first caravan we have ever actually evicted. A few, three I think, were not allowed to extended their booking last year, but no one has been asked to leave before – not that I'm aware of anyway. That's what affected Dad. He blames himself for not handling it better, for not persuading the boy or his parents to co-operate."

"Where is he now?" Sharon asked. "Should I say something?"

"By the second toilet building fixing a tap and hose for motorcaravans to top up their fresh water tanks. Someone spoke to Chris about it, a man had forgotten his hose and said good sites had hoses already fixed. Dad altered the pipework midday while most people were out – had to shut the water to the men's basins off for a while. There are only the brackets and the hose left to do. Finishing it will make him feel better, a penance for not managing the other matter – but I think no one could have done anything with that family. Say nothing, don't mention it, you're not supposed to know."

Numbers declined a little as people left at the weekend. Only ten caravans and three tents now graced the site, the expected influx for spring bank holiday still several weeks away. These visitors were mostly retired couples, as was usual in spring, but they included three older children and there were half a dozen of junior school age who played together frequently. Jan and Gordon, standing on the bridge feeding the trout with bread, saw them coming from a distance, dashing along the riverbank in a group, the three youngest struggling to keep up.

"There's a shark in the river!" The children shouted breathlessly as they approached. "A big one!" At least that was the gist of it, heard with difficulty as they all spoke at once between gasps, full of excitement, expecting everyone else to be excited too.

"Oh yes, well never mind." Jan's tone, while not actually saying 'Rubbish', clearly indicated disbelief; a polite version of 'Pull the other one, it's got bells on'.

Not satisfied with this placid reaction, expecting their news to be greeted with concern if not amazement, the band rushed off to tell their parents.

Following along slowly in the youngster's wake, an elderly couple wandered up the path and onto the bridge.

"Did the children tell you about the shark? It's in the river a hundred yards downstream," the woman raised an eyebrow in a manner that asked, 'Is that normal?'

Obviously, however impossible, there must really be a shark! Stopping only long enough to exchange a few pleasantries and speculate as to the fish's origin, Jan threw a last handful of crumbs on the water, caught Gordon's arm and started downstream. Shortly, the same group of children came charging by, running at full speed, racing on ahead after persuading parents of the shark's existence.

Reaching the spot where the youngsters now stood pointing, a single glance down into the clear water was sufficient. Sure enough, there it was! The big fish swam, nose facing upstream, tail swinging lazily from side to side; definitely a shark, and a good deal bigger than any of the children. As other parents arrived, a small conference developed. What does one do with a big shark in a small river? A few pea-sized pebbles failed to frighten it, in fact were treated with complete disdain, either that or it was really on its last legs. Can a shark survive in a river ten feet wide and less than eighteen inches deep? How did it get past the tide flaps down at Hayle estuary? They tried prodding with a flexible willow twig ripped from a nearby bush. Still no reaction. Perhaps it was dead?

"But why does that tail keep wagging? Maybe it's gone to the happy hunting grounds; the wagging tail indicates how happy it is?" Gordon was not happy! Someone had to remove it, decomposing in the river would be bad, but then it just might be alive. Another thought occurred. "This big shark in a little river, what does it eat? The fool who tries to pull it out perhaps?"

Gingerly he placed one foot in the water behind the moving tail fin, watching it carefully and waiting. A hush descended over the parents and children above. The tail continued to flap but otherwise no reaction. Just lulling its prey into a false sense of security? Taking a deep breath, three more quick steps and his hands reach for the narrow waist from which the big tail fin sprouted. Grasping firmly he lunged for the bank, heart rate rising, a little prayer on his lips.

"Keep going feet!"

Considering its weight, that fish left the water in a truly athletic movement, energy fed to muscle fibres by apprehension, or more honestly by a mixture of fear and panic. The achievement drew a ripple of applause. That was before the odour hit! Dead? Very definitely! And really high. The shark, strong when alive, was even stronger dead! Some fisherman had probably caught it on a long range trip some twelve miles or more out to sea, for who hears of sharks inshore around Cornwall? Seals are quite common, and dolphins, yes, every few years one plays with bathers somewhere round the coast, but never sharks. The intrepid fisherman probably took it home to show his family, found it becoming a bit obnoxious and slipped it over Relubbus bridge in the dead of night. The current had done the rest, and must have been responsible for wagging the tail. Why do dead sharks not float belly up on the surface like other fish? Perhaps a lower fin had hooked into weed on the riverbed. Be that as it may, they now had one very dead shark! What should be done with the carcass?

"There is one thing," a father with his hands resting on the shoulders of two children, suggested. "You *can* claim to have taken the biggest fish ever from the River Hayle. How about some photos?"

Naturally everyone wanted a picture - conclusive proof that they were the ones who had made this monster catch! A hurriedly fetched wheelbarrow solved the transport problem, pushed towards the office by various people sharing the task as others nipped ahead for cameras. With the photo session in full swing, Stephen appeared, running down the road to see what everyone was doing. After the guests had finished, the shark was lowered temporarily back into the river by the bridge, allowing the lad to be snapped catching it with a small child's rod and four-pound line! His strength would nowhere near extend to holding it up by the tail like the adults had for their family photos. At five feet the shark well exceeded Stephen's height. Sharon and Chris were out with friends and missed the opportunity.

Photos over, the pressing need for disposal remained. Remembering the difficulties involved with their sewage system, Gordon explained briefly to the assembled visitors.

"Our waste water goes into a big tank where bacteria decompose all the solids. With only ourselves here in winter, most of those bacteria die. When we start getting busy in spring, there aren't enough bugs left to eat all the debris, so we get smells. Well, it's coming up to that time of year. This could help!"

Surrounded by guests, he lifted the septic tank lid and slid the odorous shark into the thick, foul smelling, crusty scum below. That should do a super job of increasing the bacterial count! They hoped that as the weeks passed and trade increased, the system would now work superbly; without the faintest niff of a smell. However, that might be wishful thinking, and other things needed attention!

Standing on the bridge, gazing over the site as any arriving caravanner would see it, Jan pointed at the house, sweeping one arm in an arc towards the nearest toilet building. "If we're ever going to win a top site award, we need *something*! Something to take away the bareness, to soften the appearance. Maybe flowers, or shrubs; perhaps both?" She turned questioningly to Gordon at her side.

"Um. All road and buildings you mean. Yes. The house front is… it's very square." His head tilted, surveying the scene – at a loss, searching for some way. "Can't see how we could change that. A Cornish wall round the toilet building maybe?"

Cornish garden walls were two lines of stone with varying amounts of soil between. Stones were no problem, the stockpile remained substantial and grew regularly as more were collected, picked out while moving the large waste heaps from Wheal Virgin, the old copper mine. This waste was diminishing, but slowly! A mass of stony material still partly covered the valley's western side. Further discussion and the experimental placing of four long wooden battens determined the position. The new wall would be four feet wide, allowing room for an ample width of soil between the two stone facings. In this soil would be planted a colourful array of flowers and shrubs.

So much for the intention. With few people on site and the weather sunny, it was easy to find times when everyone was out and to use these opportunities for the noisy task of transporting stones and soil in Max's bucket. With these dumped nearby, work could then proceed quietly as the afternoon wore on. By evening, the shape was emerging and people returning from the beach were stopping to comment and chat. Construction resumed next morning; lifting the irregular shaped rocks and fitting them carefully into position caused no noise and continued for a further day. The project made a change; it was good to work with the soil together – if the telephone should ring with a booking, it lay within easy reach. When the last stones had been placed, the finished effect even in its bare state, did soften the lines of the building.

Several types of conifer were chosen, carefully selected for contrasting sizes, colours and textures. Modestly sized erect forms like Chamaecyparis Lawsonia Elwoodi Gold with gold edged green leaves, contrasted with the lower growing blue-green Juniperus Squamata Blue Star and the taller Cupressus Macrocarpa Golden Pillar. This last was not really golden at all, but much more a bright spring green. To create balance with contrast, a dozen different conifers were used. Jan suggested the wall be extended later to include more. Prostrate prickly Junipers were particularly attractive, and she liked the evenly rounded shape of the golden Thuja Aurea Nana. Between these conifers a mixture of other shrubs were set, together with an array of more colourful annuals. The final effect looked great, but more than that, it should improve year by year as the trees grew nearer to their mature size. The front of the house had retained its squareness, but neither parent nor any of the children who were also consulted could quite fathom how to improve it. Perhaps extra walls? Maybe wider steps? The ideas were discussed but it needed more thought. Never mind, the purpose had been achieved, the entrance already looked much better for the coming spring bank holiday.

More visitors were starting to arrive, and with these greater numbers came a problem. Nothing ever stands still; standards were forever changing. Many new caravans now used electric pumps for water and even low voltage tubes for lighting to supplement their gas mantles. Most were operated direct from the car via those multi-pin plugs that also fed the caravan's rear lights, stoplights and indicators; a few even carried separate batteries. Whatever you have is never enough, and so it was with electric. The hundred watts that had seemed so marvellous at first, dwindled to a mere eighty watts as dry weather shrunk the river's size. Simultaneously caravanners' batteries were carried to the office for charging in increasing numbers; those who had run them flat overnight could not start their cars until at least a token charge was restored.

Attempting to unearth the relevant information, an amazing numbers of books on waterwheels were discovered. These publications told how pretty they were, where to find them, the original uses, diameter, width, materials, but absolutely nothing of a basic theoretical nature to assist in improving performance. Edinburgh University Library eventual yielded a book "*Mills & Millwork* by Fairbain 3rd Edition 1871." How Penzance Library had located this publication the family had no idea, but gave the librarian top marks for efficiency! A little worn with the odd loose page, it was nevertheless a truly knowledgeable volume, laying out optimum paddle spacing, the best shape and the most favourable angle for striking the water. All examples referred to giant machinery of the last century, typically fifty feet diameter, twenty feet wide, a far cry from River Valley's six feet diameter, two feet wide wheel. Interpolation downward to this extent could never yield accurate results but did give a starting point for experimentation. Angles, lengths and spacing of the blades were all altered, resulting finally in double the number of paddles, each with a slight tilt, lifting the wattage from 80 to over 100 in the low river. With luck it would be 25-watts higher in winter when water levels normally increased.

The uninitiated might think no considerations arose except making the wheel go faster, and having done so, that was that. Other concerns did exist however, like being able to stop it! At first this had been achieved by grasping the flying paddles, gradually slowing the wheel as each successive blade slipped away. Next came a brake made from two stout balks of timber clamped loosely around the steel shaft. These timbers were hinged together at one end where they rested on the ground, and joined by a long bolt at the other. Tightening this bolt squeezed the shaft like giant wooden pliers. The timber heated quickly, on one occasion starting to smoulder, and hardly managing to hold the original low powered wheel. Such a system offered no chance of stopping the present more powerful version and had now been discarded, but the parts were still stored – an alternative way to kindle a fire Gordon insisted, if the world ran out of matches!

The new concrete supporting channel made provision for pieces of wood to be slotted in near the upstream edge, blocking the water flow; effective but time consuming. Something better was required. Another visit to Eslea Lashbrook, the St. Erth blacksmith, provided an answer. He fabricated an ornamental steel guard to surround the wheel and prevent injury. Fixed to this metalwork hung a sluice gate that could be lowered from above by a handle and screw thread, thus enabling the wheel to be stopped in seconds! It also allowed greater control when needed, by checking the water flow and hence reducing the wheel speed. Chris found it strange that anything other than maximum flow should ever be required, but the wheel now produced more than could be stored overnight, and reducing its speed each evening avoided overcharging the battery. The new channel arrangement also supported a grid to prevent damage by debris and floating logs.

When Gordon collected the metal guard from St Erth, the blacksmith warned: "Be sure you keep that screw thread greased or it will rust," then spoke of the mystery it caused for his customers. The assembly consisted of four parts, made separately for ease of transportation but intended to bolt together around the wheel. Being fabricated from steel, with all the curly swirls that wrought iron work traditionally has, the two side pieces looked much like a matching pair of gates, but with a difference. Instead of being square, one side of each was slanting to roughly follow the wheel's shape. They had been standing in the smithy leant against the wall, the two slanting sides together, touching only at the top. Instead of appearing to close as gates should, they left a tall triangular hole between.

"One of my customers asked what idiot wanted gates made like that. *'Don't 'e know they stupid things won't keep nothin' out'*, was what he said," the blacksmith repeated with relish.

"I suppose you told him it was that mad couple living down Relubbus caravan park?" Gordon asked.

"How d'you guess? I was tempted, but no. I told him they were for a chap who kept pigs that used to grub about in the orchard next door. If any come home after he locked up for the night, well then, they pigs could still get in. An' he believed me!"

The sections were, of course, sent off to be galvanised

like all other metalwork on the site – it would stop them rusting and keep them strong! Soon after completion of the guard, a new timber breastwork was installed in place of the rough wood strips previously slipped into the slots in the channel. It was much smoother and a closer fit, directing more of the water's force onto the paddles. These and other small improvements increased the power to as much as 120-watts in the low river, opening up new prospects. Gordon admitted some power increase to the children. He would have preferred to say nothing, but they were too knowledgeable about waterwheels to keep these improvements completely secret. The full extent of the gain however, he revealed only to Jan.

"If we charge caravanner's batteries only until teatime, then our own battery can charge up a little and we'll have the wheel's full output just for ourselves in the evenings. Before we go to bed, I can go outside and reconnect any batteries that are still waiting; they'll charge overnight. If there are several to charge, then I won't slow the wheel down, I'll leave it running at full speed."

In a coffee break sitting in the lounge overlooking the river, they discussed the possibilities, plotting the clandestine purchase of the cheapest 12-volt black and white television that could be found. The following day Jan returned from Penzance, waving through the car window.

"I've got one! A twelve inch screen," she called out, drawing the vehicle to a halt.

Gordon hurried to meet her, leaning in to retrieve the set from a back seat and carrying it inside. Having fixed an aerial in the roof space, invisible from outside, he ran white co-axial cable down the corner of the white wall; it was almost invisible at a quick glance. Together they tried the set, checking reception was tolerable before disconnecting and hiding it in one of the darker recesses of the basement.

Tea went ahead normally when the children arrived home from school, but later while they tackled homework at the kitchen table, Gordon slipped down to the basement and smuggled the new television unseen up the stairs across the hallway and into the lounge. He tuned in to Blue Peter which Jan had previously decided on, and leaving the sound inaudibly low, crept towards the kitchen. Inching forward to peer carefully round the doorpost, he caught Jan's eye and quickly disappeared back into the lounge to stand in front of the small set, one hand behind him on the volume control, the other arm straight down, increasing the width of his body to help hide the screen.

Seeing the prearranged signal, Jan counted a ten second delay then rose, carefully controlling her impulse to laugh with delight. "Stop homework!"

Three faces shot up in surprise. This was new! Never before had she said stop; often start, often get on with it, or concentrate, or stop talking, or other more dire threats, but never stop. Something must be wrong, but what? They could detect no signs of worry or anger in her face, the opposite in fact; was that a hidden smile? What could it mean? Intrigue was written clearly in their expressions.

"Follow me." She turned to the door. They scrambled from the table, scraping chairs on the floor in a rush to be first, no enticement so strong as a secret one! Entering the lounge Jan stepped aside to watch their faces, and saw puzzlement. Nothing appeared new, just Dad standing, one hand behind his back. The children knew something had caused the sudden interruption and Mum's strange behaviour; they could feel the air of expectancy, stood uncertain, looking again round the room and questioningly back to their parents. Jan delayed a few seconds longer, heightening the tension before giving a small nod. At the signal Gordon adjusted the volume and stepped away in one movement.

The children gasped. Sharon's eyes opened wide enough to fall out, Stephen punched one fist into his other palm, and Chris, while managing to maintain some reserve, could not prevent a broad smile of pleasure crossing his face. Evenings were normally happy but this one excelled.

The children watched delighted, unable at first to stop asking questions, especially Sharon. Even warnings of viewing limited to one hour each night did little to dent their mood. After the programme Jan produced coffee, Cornish heavy cake, and a paper showing forthcoming programmes.

"There, decide between yourselves on tomorrow's viewing. That's reading practice for all of you. If you can't agree, I'll decide!"

Over the following days, Jan would not allow viewing until after six thirty so homework would not be rushed, but nevertheless there ensued a noticeable change from entertaining themselves to being entertained. The best of both worlds perhaps, television available, but a natural limitation on excessive viewing. In spite of Jan's warning, the children did of course argue about what programme to view, so the choice was shared. This overcame disputes over programmes, substituting instead disagreements on whose turn to choose. The parents smiled at each other in a guarded fashion when the boys were unusually nice to Sharon on her first night in control. She played them along, developing further what Dad called, 'The natural deviousness of the female.'

As time passed, having mostly a pleasant nature Sharon usually accommodated her brother's wishes, especially when, as often occurred, they coincided with her own – but not always! On occasion she enjoyed her mastery fully, almost giving way to the boys' choice, then, having drained the last ounce of submission, suddenly changed her mind to another programme, not necessarily one she wanted, but something she knew they would hate. Revenge was sweet, revenge for the ribbing and insults they usually heaped on her cooking, although now, neither brother made such derogatory statements on her choice nights unless they had forgotten the day. Chris was even heard to refer to some mince pies as 'Quite good' on one such evening.

Funnily enough, it was the battery more than the river

that limited electrical power; the wheel could now produce more than it was possible to store. On those days when no caravanner brought in a battery for charging, the TV could be watched in the morning, again at lunch and still be ready for the evening – if anyone had ever found that much spare time! Viewing however, could not be continuous. The TV took more current than the wheel produced and relied on the battery to make up the difference. Whatever time of day it was used, little more than one hour's viewing was available before the battery lost its charge. Films posed a problem, for most were longer than an hour and therefore were generally avoided. If one seemed particularly desirable, then the last hour was chosen, not the first. Even so, sometimes the end was missed.

A new battery would extend viewing considerably but would soon deteriorate – no lead-acid battery will stay in good condition if continually charged and discharged! A nickel-alkaline set would solve the problem, but they were too expensive at the moment. Winter should help; the wheel would produce more then, provided the extra was not all used for lights.

"This milk tastes terrible!" Dad complained, pushing the cornflakes away. The children, sitting down for breakfast, showed no sympathy. Jan had been milking Judy properly again for the past month, but she was not yet back to full production; the kids, though mainly eating grass and bramble, still took a share.

"You're too fussy." Sharon pulled up her chair.

"Rubbish, I'm probably the least fussy person in all the world."

A storm of protest and ridicule greeted Dad's statement, with a long list of past instances reeled off for proof as they nodded backwards and forwards to each other agreeing and confirming every example.

"Don't give him anything else Mum." Sharon urged.

Jan frowned dubiously, knowing he would need the

energy, and asked, "Okay. What do you want? Eggs?"

"No, I'll wait until you and the children have finished, you'll find it will save work."

Jan shrugged, about to sit down when her attention was again diverted.

"Ugh!" The sound could hardly be called a word, more a nasal intimation of disgust. Unable to speak clearly with her mouth full and not knowing whether to swallow or spit it out, Sharon dashed suddenly to the toilet. The chain pulled and she re-emerged.

"That's horrible!"

Chris, being more cautious, had probably held back deliberately, letting Sharon try first after Dad's earlier warning. Now he lifted a tiny portion on a spoon, sampled carefully, pulled a face and lay the spoon down. Stephen bent over to sniff the bowl, then copying his older brother, took the smallest possible taste. The little head shook and he pushed the bowl away.

"Come now, eat up. There's nothing wrong with it, you're all too fussy!" Attention swung to Dad as he spoke with that '*I told you so*' tone in his voice.

"Clever Clogs," Sharon muttered under her breath, the expression, set of her shoulders and voice such a copy of her mother that Jan had to laugh. In seconds everyone including Sharon herself, joined in.

Smugly, Gordon spoke again as the laughter stopped. "Eggs all round. Told you it would save work if I waited."

Jan smiled from the adjoining kitchen. "So you did. And Sharon was right!" Another round of laughter engulfed the table as she re-lit the gas and bent down for the frying pan. "What's wrong with the milk anyway, is it off?"

"I don't think so, it's not that taste, more... I don't know, sort of goaty?" He shrugged, inviting the children's suggestions. Blank looks and shaken heads indicated no ideas were on offer.

"Perhaps..." Chris paused, "Perhaps it's ivy. The past two days I've tethered Judy within reach of some. She seems to like it, maybe because apart from grass there were no other big green leaves within reach. Do you think it could affect the milk?"

"We can find out," Jan broke another egg into the pan. "Make sure she can't reach any more ivy for a few days and let's see what happens. I'll take an extra pint from Sampson tomorrow." Sampson Polglase from the shop in Relubbus, delivered bread, milk and newspapers to the caravanners every morning throughout the season, except very early and late in the year when numbers made it not worthwhile.

Chris nodded. Though Stephen helped and Sharon often spent time with the kids, he was still the one who did most goat tending. He cared for Judy, settling her with Olive and Ivy comfortably at night in the lean-to shed and taking them out again most mornings. Since the gas bottles had been removed to the service passage, Judy liked the shed more, leading her kids in each evening with seldom any trouble. Jan usually did the milking, Sharon having largely given up, and the boys conveniently 'forgetting' a job that they had never liked or been proficient at. While family life was generally harmonious, with considerable laughter and fun, disagreements and friction did occur. It was not only milking that the boys had dodged; other jobs too, they tried to avoid. Ash and clinkers were deposited in a metal bucket near the boiler in the basement, a bucket that regularly required emptying. It was the boys' task on alternate mornings; to carry these ashes up the stairs and out through the office door, adding to a great pile steadily accumulating behind the house. At the same time they were supposed to check the coal and if necessary push more through the hole which had been cut in the basement wall to connect with a pit in the garage where the fuel merchant emptied his sacks. Mostly it worked well, but there was a tendency on the part of Stephen to pretend it was not his turn.

This was not the only source of trouble. The basement

ceiling was reinforced concrete, it needed to be, it formed the ground floor of the house above. An opening, two feet square, had been cast in this concrete ceiling when they built the house. It formed an 'alternative means of escape' from all those underground rooms as required by the fire regulations and had therefore been placed as far from the basement staircase as it was possible to get. This was a considerable distance for the cellar was large, extending under the whole house, every room above having another identically sized room below. The escape hatch emerged in Sharon's bedroom, lying in one corner of her floor near the bed, and was covered by a timber lid. Naturally none of these underground rooms had a window, but each one now sported a single small waterwheel light making them more useful for storage.

The boys in particular spent time at the workbench down below, being allowed to use the various tools that were now kept in boxes and drawers or hanging on the wall. Both learned after a time that it paid to put these tools back in the correct storage places, for Dad, particularly when he was tired, could become quite annoyed if he needed a tool in a hurry and it was missing. One evening a tap had been wrenched from an external wall, bending the pipework. It emerged later that some idiot had hung a three-gallon bucket over the tap head while it filled! Dad had been levelling topsoil all day. This was unusual once the season had started, but a driver they knew had drawn his huge lorry up at the office and had offered it free. They could hardly refuse; the soil was badly needed, but due to the vehicle's size it had to be tipped in an unsightly heap well short of its intended destination. Not wishing to use the noisy excavator, Gordon had spent the entire day trying to spread and level this soil with spade and wheelbarrow. The distance it needed to be wheeled and many interruptions to pitch caravans had lengthened the task. Plodding back to the house after a long day, the sight of water gushing from a broken tap, drew a silent curse! There was no alternative but to fix it immediately. Most of the tools came quickly to hand but the hacksaw needed to cut a new length of copper pipe was not in its correct place! Eventually the implement was found in the boys' bedroom and Dad had been severe on the lads, cancelling part of the coming weekend's freedom and giving them work to do instead. When he trudged off leaving the rest of the family comfortably sitting in the house, Chris spoke to his mother with some bitterness.

"Dad leaves tools around all the while. There are piles on the bench, in the service passage, everywhere. We get in trouble if we forget just once!"

Jan looked at her son, wondering; she had felt the same resentment but deliberately said nothing. Now she must explain. "You're right in a way. We all know he leaves his own tools around sometimes, when he's rushed, meaning to put them away later. When that happens and he can't find something, I think he's angry with himself too, but at least there is a chance of remembering where they are, where he used them last. That's not possible if you've taken them. Often enough I collect up odd tools that he's used and slip them back in the proper places without saying anything. I do that for you sometimes. You must be more careful, either don't use the tools, or put them back. It's not fair I know, but did you see how tired he is tonight, and the job still has to be done, there's no putting it off. That water can't be allowed to spew out all night – think what it's doing to the meter. There's another reason; the tap must be available for anyone who wants it. I know there are others but they're farther away and we never let things stay out of order here – you know that!"

Something else that caused friction was the leaving on of lights, especially basement lights since these could go unnoticed for long periods, and it was Sharon who proved most lax in this respect. One evening, the family sat down for the television hour, parents having overruled the children's choice in favour of a wildlife programme they particularly wanted to see. It was later than the usual viewing time and although the light had only just begun to fade, Jan drew the curtains in the hope of avoiding any interruptions. After a short while the picture deteriorated, dark borders appearing around the screen, a sure sign of low power. Shortly the programme was lost. Investigation revealed three lights in the basement had been left on! These had been sufficient to prevent the battery recharging after Jan used the vacuum earlier.

"It couldn't have been me," Sharon protested as the boys pointed accusingly. Jan knew her daughter had shown a friend around earlier, she had seen the two young girls descend the basement stairs and noticed Sharon return without her cardigan. After some discussion it was clear beyond doubt that nobody else had been below since breakfast time, when the boiler was last topped up and the ashes emptied. It had to be Sharon.

"Well all of you forget sometimes," she protested, "You're horrible to me. I'm going out to play with my friend!"

"*You,*" Dad ordered sternly, "are going to bed my girl, to remind you not to leave lights on next time!"

"You left your cardigan down in the basement," Jan prompted. "Go and find it first, you'll need it in the morning."

Colour deepening in anger at the boys' jubilant faces, Sharon rose from her chair, stamped from the room and off downstairs to collect the garment. While there, she quickly but without making any noise, moved the stepladder from its normal storage position. Returning up the concrete stair and regaining the hall, she marched off to her bedroom, glancing into the dining room in passing. The rest of the family were settling at the table with a pack of cards. A single 24-watt bulb glowed more dimly than usual near the ceiling. That was another feature of waterwheel lights; when the battery condition was low the voltage dropped and everything shone less brightly.

"Use your gas lamp, don't switch on another light," her mother called as the door closed.

"They're using one, but I'm forbidden!" The resentful thought caused a sulky frown. Night had not yet fallen; it was gloomy outside, the light fading but still easy enough to see. Sharon lit the gas and drew the fawn curtains, a spare pair from Audrey that had been altered to fit the window. She wanted a darker colour but had been refused; at least now these drapes were different. Every other curtain in the house was a lemony orange mixture, a sunshine colour, bright and attractive certainly, but all identical.

"A girl should be able to choose her own colours, not have the same as everyone else! Dad would have all the curtains white like the walls if Mum hadn't stopped him," she thought sullenly. "He should have made a bigger wheel, then we could have whatever we wanted and I wouldn't keep getting in trouble! My friends at school can leave lights on whenever they like, several even have a television in their rooms! Well I not staying in *here* all evening!"

There was no way out through the door; her bedroom lay at the end of a narrow corridor, to escape that way she must pass the open dining room doorway where the family would, no doubt, continue playing cards for some time.

"Well, at least I anticipated that!" she told herself with a determined nod, putting one ear against the door and listening, clenching her fists as a muffled burst of laughter sounded. After a while, she judged it safe; nobody would come to speak, she was in disgrace. "Good!" Kneeling at the foot of the bed, she prized up the basement emergency hatch, silently leaning it against the wall, and looked down. *Yes!* The stepladder stood directly beneath. But it was dark down there; only light from the gas lamp on her wall spreading a faint glow below. Sitting on the floor, legs dangling into the basement room, she tried to reach, but failed. Although tallish for a ten-year-old, the gap was too great. Taking the precaution of bringing the lid closer so it could be reached from below, she turned over, kneeling on the edge, lowering one leg at a time until resting on her tummy, hips hanging down through the opening. Easing backward, one hand still stretched out gripping the bed, her feet swung, frantically searching for contact but found only air. She tried to go up again, but couldn't. Stuck and with arms tiring, there was no alternative but to slip downward. The tip of one toe, pointed like a ballet dancer, brushed something! With a huge sigh of relief the young girl let herself slide until the top step gave solid support. Reaching back up to grasp the lid, she lowered carefully, descending the steps until it dropped tightly into place, shutting off all light.

Moving down another step, Sharon clutched the ladder, now in total blackness; not just the darkness of a cloudy night – in that basement no light whatever penetrated; even an owl could have seen nothing. Small fingers gripped the wooden sides harder. The light switch lay on the far side of the room but she must avoid at all costs knocking anything over; that would mean immediate discovery. Careful steps descended until the floor was firmly underfoot. A tentative pace and she felt backwards, reaching for the stepladder again, disorientated, trying to work out in which direction lay the door. The cellar, although it was virtually identical in layout to the house above, had never seemed like this when the lights were on. The need to make no noise didn't help, she found herself listening, imagining...

Holding arms out ahead in what might be the right direction, a few careful paces and one finger bumped a solid surface. Moving closer and probing to left then right, the wall seemed continuous. Where was the opening? Why was she trying to breathe so quietly? No one would hear through the concrete floor, unless something was dropped… or unless she screamed!

"Don't be silly. Why should I scream? Whatever made me think of that?" But the thought would not entirely go away. Stretching to the right, her hand encountered an opening. "Ah!" Feeling for the other side, she reached upwards, searching, and with relief found the bottom of the switch. Suddenly the hand recoiled as if burnt; her heart skipping a beat!

They would know! Of course they would know! How could she nearly have made such an error? If a light was switched on anywhere in the house, all other lights dimmed. They would investigate, would go to her room! She stood there, pulse throbbing, trapped in the darkness! To go back, or forward. It had to be forward, she could never hoist her body up through the trap door again. Forward, or shout for help and take the consequences! The way ahead must be found entirely by feel. Follow the walls! Yes, that's it… but what else might she touch? An involuntary shiver raked her body, one hand stretching again tentatively towards the switch. How long she stood unmoving in indecision she could not tell, as seconds ticked silently away. Nervously, with an unconscious motion, one hand brushed goose pimples on a bare forearm. Something was out there, something sinister, drawing near in the curtain of blackness, she knew… could sense it… knees beginning to shake, gasping a deep breath, the scream rose in her throat…

Little fists clenched as she fought for control, forcing such thoughts away, then reaching out experimentally into the void, careful fingers brushing something... the hand snatched away! Reaching again, touching nervously the surface felt hard and kind of rough? Cement! She knew that texture and stepped forward, determined now to go on. Three slow, careful steps and the narrow corridor walls were on both sides. That was better! More quickly each leg slid forward, stretching to probe ahead before transferring the weight... and then the left-hand wall disappeared. Ah! Those rooms opening off the corridor! She had reached them - dark caverns even if one had a candle, but now with no light at all, just a sense, a change in quality of the air, of the sound as her foot slid out again. A ripple of tension tightened the skin; slowly she eased forward, on round a corner into the second corridor. Still the blackness around was complete. She must be near, but couldn't quite shake the sense that something was following… would reach out and touch her back. She arched slightly at the thought, nerves taut. One toe stubbed against the bottom step abruptly blocking her forward advance. Momentarily she felt something else had stopped her – sheer panic strangled her breath as she stood frozen, petrified, strength draining away in the blackness! Gradually she got a grip, feeling gingerly for the step with one foot, then onward, winding round and up the concrete staircase. Here she could move more freely. A faint light showed through a crack under the door, hardly a glimmer but bright enough to inspire confidence after the darkness below.

This stairway opened into the same corridor as her bedroom, but farther along, not visible from the dining room in which the remaining family were busily playing cards. However, the doors were barely seven feet apart; any small sound would be discovery. Slowly she eased down the handle, opening the door a crack, listening. At a burst of laughter she slipped quickly out, closing it softly and in a few dainty steps was beside the office door. Would the breeze when it opened alert them? She waited. It could be fatal to hurry! For a while no sounds came from the other room; she was tempted to chance it, but waited on. Without warning a gale of renewed laughter rang round the house. Sharon was out through the door, closing it with a slight click, racing across the yard and round the toilet building, hurrying from sight, hidden now from anyone who might have sensed a draught and come to check through the office window. Slowing to collect herself and allow her pulse to steady before reaching the friend's caravan, she sauntered along with a certain glow of achievement, pleased with herself.

In the house, the games were a great success; after an

hour Jan rose to make coffee. Catching Gordon's eye when the boy's attention was elsewhere, she lifted a cup, pointed to the adjoining room and signalled her intention to call Sharon in for the drink; seeking his approval. They tried to act together in matters affecting the family, avoiding open disagreement, even supporting each other when one had doubts; less confusing to the children than having parents who constantly disagreed.

Seeing a nod, Jan walked into the corridor and called through the door.

"You can come and drink your coffee with us, Sharon," Not waiting for a reply, but returning to carry the five cups to the table, she signalled to Chris, who grabbed a stack of coasters from the sideboard and spread them around. When Sharon still didn't reply or appear, Jan looked at Gordon with raised eyebrows.

"Sulking?" he asked.

"I'll check. If she's asleep I'll turn her gaslight off." Jan moved across, opened the door softly, paused, then called out in surprise, "She's gone!"

Everyone rose, making for the doorway to peer in at the empty room. "That's impossible!"

Chris moved to check the window. Finding the latch shut, a thing not achievable from outside, he turned, "She must have sneaked by while we were playing." Voice and manner indicated Sharon had risen in his estimation.

"Must have," Jan agreed, shaking her head, "but I don't know how she managed it."

Ten minutes later, Sharon squinted round the toilet building. The house front appeared empty and unlit. Having given little thought to getting back, she approached the office uneasily, crouching below the window and waiting before rising to peer tentatively through the glass, then using her key, opened the door and entered, closing it silently behind.

Unbeknown to the young girl, her advance had not been managed in secret. Two eyes watching anxiously from the dark hallway had seen her approach in the glow of the toilet building lights, her silhouette outlined for an instant against the Gent's window. Feeling relief at the safe return, Jan called quickly to the rest of the family, who now stood together in the recess by the front door. They remained alert and motionless as Sharon entered, but when she tiptoed into the hall, preparing to creep along the corridor to her bedroom, Mum pulled the light cord and a chorus of questions hit.

Sharon gave a great jump then stood rooted to the spot like a cornered rabbit. When the hubbub died down, Jan spoke clearly and alone.

"Just where have *you* been? And how did you leave without being seen?"

Sharon swallowed, glancing furtively to one side, then brushing hands nervously down her dress, shrugged. "I kind of slipped out, across to use the toilet."

"What's wrong with our own?" Jan demanded, as Dad and the boys looked on accusingly.

Realising they had not yet found her escape route, and thinking the stepladder must be moved first thing the following morning, Sharon drew herself up to respond.

"There's no light in our toilet, at least not one *I'm* allowed to use!"

CHAPTER 9

Spiderman

A shout rose from the riverbank. Gordon, sitting at the desk opening the morning post, glanced up. The late spring sky was clear and bright, grass not yet showing brown, the trees still retaining a hint of new season freshness. "Good day for site photos?" The thought came unconsciously, triggered by favourable weather, but were those conditions really right? "No, I want fluffy white clouds in that blue sky. There's a distant haze too, the best photos are after a shower when the air is crisply clear; and we need more visitors for a really good shot." Not many caravans yet stood on the grassy field near the office; an area used by families with children. Most visitors were still retired couples who chose the 'oldies' section, downstream of the house; the geriatric section some regulars called it and nothing would persuade them to go elsewhere. During the earlier months of the year, the difference was not usually explained to people arriving for the first time and they were actively encouraged to choose this front field, since a few caravans near the entrance made the site look more inviting. It was strange that although most caravanners hated crowded sites, they shied away from being completely alone. If the valley appeared empty when they arrived, some swung round and drove away again; whether due to a fear of isolation, or a suspicion that no people indicated bad toilets, was never clear. It would have been useless to ask, for who would admit to being afraid?

More cries from the river drew his attention back to

the present. Several children were running along the bank pointing. What had they seen? A floating log perhaps, it sometimes happened. Opening another letter the noise increased and youngsters were racing now towards the office. Several ran to the door, not entering, but standing in a small group on the step, shouting urgently. Piecing together the clamour of words it appeared that some small bird was struggling in the river, drifting downstream on the current. Gordon rose immediately, running to follow as this excited band led towards the bridge. Looking upstream, a bundle of black fluff floated clearly visible, struggling weakly against the flow. Rushing back to the workroom, he grabbed a big net and raced to the riverbank, gaining the weir below the bridge barely soon enough! The small black bundle approached the brink and must surely be washed over.

No time to climb out on the waterwheel channel! Still on the move, a headlong dive along the grass took him horizontal, overhanging the river's edge, lunging one handed at full stretch – but the net was just too short! Calls to hurry, to be quick, rang with urgency from many young voices, but he had already acted! Instinctively digging the fingers of his free hand into the turf and leaning a few extra inches, the tiny bird was scooped from the weir's crest, snatched in that instant of plummeting down the cascade.

Swinging the net to one side he wriggled backwards then stood, reaching in and gently retrieving the chick. Holding the little creature in one cupped hand against his chest for warmth, Gordon climbed to the bank top and sat down. It showed no inclination to escape. The children, jostling for position, seated themselves on the dry ground in a half-circle before him; none had any idea what had been saved.

"Look at the size of those feet," he pointed, "almost bigger than the bird's body. Feet that size have to be for treading on reeds in the water or on marshy ground. It's a baby Moorhen." The tiny fledgling was passed from hand to hand, the little group having first been shown how to support the bird. Not one child treated it with anything other than the greatest care but again the young girls were most open with their affection. Extracting a promise that they could come to visit each day, the youngsters dispersed as the tiny black bundle was carried into the house.

"Where is it going to live?" Jan asked, in the office, and hearing his intention to keep it on the desk, warned, "You can clear up the mess. I suppose this is another bird you'll be talking to, won't your robin be jealous?"

He looked up, about to protest, but thought better of it; this was a no win situation. Normally they discussed everything, but he had tried to prevent her finding out about Robin. He had started talking to the bird during long hours of lonely work in their first year by the river when hardly another soul entered the valley, and had continued ever since, even imagining at times that the bird replied. Jan had found out of course, caught him on several occasions when bringing coffee. However, she still knew nothing about Blackbird, he took some satisfaction from that.

Covering the bottom of an old shoebox with newspaper topped by a tea towel for softness, the chick was placed inside and the desk lamp adjusted to shine down for warmth. The waterwheel could feed a single 24-watt light and still have some 80-watts (it varied a bit with the river level) left for the house and to charge any batteries carried in by caravanners. Special food for young chicks from a pet shop in Penzance or Helston was needed as a regular diet, but some temporary substitute nourishment would see it through until Jan went to town the following day.

"What does it normally eat?" Jan asked, "What can we use?"

"It's a seed eater, or at least partially a seed eater. A few soft bread crumbs should fill the bill."

She made to move off in search of a loaf, then grasping the double meaning swung back lifting an arm in make-believe wrath. A tray at one end of the box provided water; after forcibly dipping its beak once or twice with gentle pressure from one finger, no further encouragement was needed. The black furry ball soon drank and pecked crumbs quite happily, the bulb's warmth aiding recovery. After tea, before homework started, the children gathered round making a fuss of their new lodger. Jan, who had slipped outside, returned with an assortment of small leafy twigs and added these to the box.

"Will it eat them?" Chris asked.

"Possibly. It's omnivorous!" Jan smiled at the children and at Gordon's surprise. "That means they eat any type of food – plants or insects. They probably like marsh plants best so I picked a selection. Did you know they often have a second brood? That may be why this chick's rather late."

"Clever!" Sharon sounded impressed.

"Not really, I've been reading up!"

That evening the lamp was switched off, Stephen holding the fledgling in his hands to keep it warm and save current during the TV hour. The moorhen quickly became accustomed to voices and to hands as the family cradled it in turn. This bird would not be shy of people! Would it also be a tele-addict?

Over the next days, it roamed the desk, placing those incredible feet a little unsteadily at first. Perhaps such large feet absorbed warmth or it may have been a mother fixation, whatever the cause, the young moorhen liked best to stand on an upturned hand. Its plumage sprung out long and black, an insulating layer of fluff; the feathers would come later. This hairy appearance led to the universal nickname Spiderman, an appropriate title for the long toes sticking out from under its spherical body gave exactly that impression at a quick glance. The similarity on closer inspection proved less than perfect for only three toes on each foot projected, the rear spurs being shorter, and spiders, as Stephen pointed out, have eight legs.

Spiderman lived on the desk for a week, but like all

birds, its digestion was rapid and uncontrollable, in need of constant wiping up. With the tissue supply very nearly exhausted, Jan in a flash of inspiration, produced a toilet roll. These they had in abundance, purchased wholesale by the thousand for use in the toilet buildings. Gordon took it with raised eyebrows.

"It is what they're made for." Jan shrugged.

"Funny thing to have on a desk though, when customers come in." He frowned.

"Pretend it's a sample from some sales rep. Anyway, I wouldn't worry about it being unusual. You can't say a moorhen chick that tries to stand on customer's hands as they sign the visitors book is absolutely normal!"

Closely followed for droppings, Spiderman walked on the carpet in the evenings, which he liked, and even at such a young age exhibited the typical jerky Moorhen movements. No fear of man existed, he had become completely fixed on humans and in particular human hands. Stephen lay on the floor, holding out an arm. Spiderman ran out from under the low sideboard to the extended hand, then along the inside of the arm up to the armpit where it formed a sharp angle with the body, a cosy nook in which to snuggle.

"Poor thing has no sense of smell," Sharon commented, rising from the chair to sit back on her heels on the carpet. After a short time the restless black bundle came to investigate her bare knees, taking a few slow steps, followed by a quick run, then more slow steps on final approach. The family watched; it was uncanny how this little bird had found its way so deeply into everyone's affection. All the children, particularly Stephen, treated their house guest with great tenderness and care.

An introduction to a wider world came one weekend shortly after midday with no visitors around. The young bird quickly took to running on grass, and though now able to move quite fast, it made no attempt to leave. Stephen, who Spiderman particularly liked to follow, led it in and out of the office door four or five times on Dad's suggestion, feeding a small morsel each time they entered to ensure familiarity with the way home. It now seemed safe and more convenient to let the fledgling enter and leave at will so the office door could remain open, propped back to avoid it blowing closed and injuring the chick. Towards evening, people returning from the beach walked to the bridge, drawn by those waiting trout. Spiderman chased after them and finding someone with sandals, the young moorhen climbed on an exposed foot and sat there. It caused quite a commotion. Jan was called from the office by the man's wife, and walked over to the group on the bridge.

"Why does it do that?" the woman asked in fascination. Several people had gathered in a small circle round the occupied foot, awaiting an explanation.

"No one really knows. Perhaps the warmth, or maybe it feels safer with people?" Jan, at a loss what more to say, bent down and reached out. Seeing the extended hand, Spiderman left the foot, pausing first to leave a little gift on the instep. Ignoring bellows of laughter from happy spectators, the bird ran quickly across to climb aboard. Feet apparently formed a good substitute only when no hands were available.

News travelled through the park; gossip in the toilets, neighbours talking, strangers meeting at Sampson's van when buying milk each morning – in a dozen different ways. One woman even stopped a car that was going rather fast and told the driver off severely, warning that he might hurt the little chick. As everyone quickly grew familiar with the bird's idiosyncrasy, more people visited the bridge and it soon became standard practice for many to wear scandals. Word had got round that any little present it might leave was lucky.

"Why should it be lucky?" a woman asked, pointing to a deposit on her instep as Stephen walked by with Judy, the two kids following behind.

The little lad stopped to look down, regarding the blob, wondering why the lady had not removed it. He shrugged, “Lucky it wasn’t a turkey?”

Spiderman, having selected his host, would cross from one foot to the other, or to some other person close by, but only if they were wearing scandals. Most people became convinced it liked the warmth. During the following weeks he became a great favourite, feathering up as he rapidly grew in size, ranging steadily farther from the office and staying away for longer periods. Then suddenly, it was gone. Where, no one ever knew, but as Chris said to a group of young visitors, “If a Moorhen ever stands on your foot, see if it answers to the name of Spiderman.”

All the family missed the little bird but had expected it to leave eventually - only natural; in any case there was little time for sorrow with the site becoming steadily busier. At the start, when they had first moved into the valley and lived in the tiny caravan, all work had been well within shouting distance, for tall vegetation stretched right to the single door. Jan had found the adjustment difficult then.

“One of the hardest things to get used to is having you working nearby all day,” she had said. “After years of seeing you leave around seven each morning and not return for nearly twelve hours, I find it hard to adapt,”

Now the change was even more pronounced. With caravans arriving at unpredictable intervals, Gordon tended to work either within the house or at least within call. During the coming peak season, she knew they would be almost constantly in each other’s company. Jan had warned in that first year, that sudden total intermingling of lives had been responsible for many a marriage break-up and they should be on guard, resisting the antagonism such changes could cause.

In the event, far from causing discord, the increased contact brought better understanding, greater contentment with life, and deeper love. Almost every stage of the site’s development was talked over, discussed and probed until their ideas met. Not only did this produce a better site, it resulted in a blending of minds and purpose. Gordon listened to Jan because she offered a different point of view, a new perspective, particularly on topics related to the likes and dislikes of lady visitors. She picked up points he might miss, points that could cause extra work later – but most of all he listened because he loved her and liked to hear her talk.

Sometimes in the kitchen while she cooked and he studied a plan or drawing, waiting for a not quite ready meal, she would chat, and on getting no response would suddenly round on him.

"You're not listening to a word I say!"

He would look up startled, think a moment, and then repeat her last sentences word-perfect. She was right, he hadn't been listening, hadn't taken in a single word. They both knew it, but part of him always listened to what she said. Often he could replay her words from memory like rewinding a tape. On these occasions she never knew whether to be angry or pleased.

"You devil!" she came at him with arms outstretched, hands held as if to go for the throat but only in fun, and invariably her soft warm lips made the contact. Probably neither fully realised how important this fondness had been in combating both the winter loneliness and the pressures that came with each peak season – the next one just over a month away!

Towards evening, new motorcaravans arriving for the night and people returning after a day out, created a late afternoon flush of activity. Gradually this died away and the two parents could walk again along the riverbank, one of the children staying in the office until they returned. Recently, work had started on a line of pylons that would march across the valley some distance downstream. The nearest one, tower nineteen the surveyor called it, was now under construction just beyond the site boundary on the stream's opposite bank. Fortunately no noise had reached the site from this activity.

"Why have you changed into old trousers?" Jan asked as they set off.

"Thought I might wade across the river to inspect more closely."

"Why? Don't think it's strong enough I suppose? Want an extra thousand tons of concrete round those steel legs, perhaps?"

"No. They promised to plant trees to screen it from the site. I wonder if they've put marker pegs down? I'd like to see where each will be."

"I may walk back on my own if we meet anyone," Jan threatened, "You look bad enough now. Wet, trousers will be even worse; I'll pretend you're nothing to do with me, that I don't even know you."

However, when they arrived at the embryo pylon with only its first lengths sticking in the air, a surprise awaited. Among the piles of material laid on the ground was the curled up shape of an Alsatian dog, apparently fast asleep. It was wrapped round so that the head was hidden, tucked somehow under the body. Shouting in the hope of rousing the animal to reveal its disposition, friendly or otherwise, failed to have any effect. They stood for a while, watching, but never so much as a twitch moved the sleeping form. Could it be stuffed, not a real dog but left by the men as a deterrent to anyone pinching materials? There was only one way to find out – wade across the river!

"Are you going?" Jan asked.

"Ah well, I..." Gordon looked at the dog again then turned away. "Never mind. It's not important, we shall see soon enough."

Jan chuckled as they headed back upstream.

Frequently when an evening remained busy, the walk was missed or on occasion just postponed until dusk sent visitors safely back inside their caravans. Darkness was no problem; by the stream, no matter what time of night, even with no moon and heavy cloud cover it was always light enough to see without a torch. Only deep in the woods did it ever become really dark. Nevertheless they liked moonlight best, particularly on a still night, hearing the whisper of water as here and there it babbled over hidden stones. At certain points the moon's reflection from the surface revealed movement, in places turbulent, in others a smooth fluid flow where the bed dipped deeper. Arm in arm, or arms around each other's waist, they strolled slowly back towards the house, stopping occasionally to stand motionless, listening.

Night noises were few, the occasional cricket but no bird song except the solitary hoot of a tawny owl with sometimes an answering call. On rare occasions the bird itself crossed the river; a silent darker shape outlined against the already darkened sky. Once they thought a Nightjar called, but were never sure. The romantic setting wasn't needed, but it helped. Darkness was friendly, a torch beam would have shattered the illusion, the sense of being two people alone on earth, the feeling that trees and the countryside were their habitat, not houses, cities or people. Even when the peak of the school holidays arrived next month, this solitude would still be available a little farther downstream. Why do so few people like to walk in the dark?

Approaching the bridge, they noticed the waterwheel had slowed. Slipping inside for a lamp while Jan leaned on the guard rail watching the water, Gordon quickly returned, passing over the torch. In the circle of light now pointed at the grid, the accumulated reed stems were removed using a hooked length of steel rather like a shepherd's crook. It took a few seconds only before the wheel resumed its normal speed. He would have moved off then, but Jan held him, just laying her hand on his arm.

"Look, near the bank and three yards in front of the grid," she whispered. "A small circular ripple spread from there in the moonlight while you were fetching the torch. Must be a trout lying below."

They stood for a time in silence, partly for the trout, partly for the closeness of each other's company. No more ripples appeared. Moving forward carefully, Jan pointed the torch downward and switched on; it cut through the crystal clearness, highlighting a gravely bottom. After a short search, there it lay, a small brown trout perhaps seven to nine inches long at a guess. More surprising, it showed no reaction to the light. They had expected the fish to dart away but it ignored the beam completely, even when they knelt for a closer look. Does a torch seem like the moon to a fish? Gordon rolled up a shirtsleeve tightly to the shoulder and lowered his hand carefully into the water a few feet downstream from the slowly moving tail. Cautiously he inched forward, until with great patience his fingers lay under its belly. Tilting the hand fractionally he stroked the trout's underside. A quick grasp of the gills and it would be on the bank, but that was not their mood. No word was spoken, but he knew Jan wanted it left in peace. Lowering the wrist, he slowly withdrew the hand, bringing it sideways over the bank edge so no drip should disturb the surface. They rose in a single movement, the torch extinguished, together stepping away from the river. Jan's eyes shining softly moist in the moonlight as they stood, speech unnecessary. Leaving the trout to its watery bed, they crept away, quietly but with a certain eagerness, to find their own.

All last winter, Max, the big excavator had continued moving those waste heaps on the valley's western side, using the spoil to level drastically uneven ground elsewhere. That work had stopped early in the season after a sizeable landslip left the heaps in a safe condition. Good earth to cover these new areas however had been hard to obtain. Despite a policy of avoiding such work in summer, topsoil was too valuable to refuse. One large load had already been received and when a smaller lorry arrived with two further loads, that soil too was gratefully accepted.

Three days later no signs of the recent tippings remained, all moved quietly by hand, the finishing touches now complete on another section. Seed had been scattered but it was late, the ground dry – more would probably be needed in September. Never mind, grassed or not it looked much better. Some visitors found the numbering system puzzling. Area 15, the one just finished, was next to Area 14 naturally, but next to 14 was 6, and 6 had 3 on one side and 16 on the other; all very systematic. The reason for this seemingly illogical sequence lay simply in each section being numbered only when work on it actually commenced. It had to be done this way, for areas were not laid out on a drawing in advance but were formed as the work proceeded, the various shapes resulting from luck, inspiration, whim, call it what you will – helped perhaps by a few thumbnail sketches drawn over coffee. The layout was intuitive rather than designed!

With working round trees and at different levels, sometimes filling with stone, sometimes finishing with topsoil, the areas were not tackled in geographical order starting with the nearest, finishing at the farthest. Rather, those needing least work were prepared first, allowing space to come into use more quickly. Starting an area and giving it a number did not guarantee that it would be finished in the same order. Area 16 for instance had only been started that winter, but being a riverbank pitch it had received priority when topsoil became available and was actually ready for use before some earlier numbers. Renumbering would be possible when all the areas were levelled, but since many of the visitors knew and asked for favourite pitches by these existing numbers, they would likely remain unchanged. A certain satisfaction could be drawn from this chaotic layout. Nothing in nature was well ordered. The more diverse and unregimented the development, the better would be the final effect. Uniformity and order were in this context, the enemy.

In addition to these numbers, some parts of the site

acquired names as well. Primrose Corner for instance, where primroses surrounded the foot of a big sycamore in a pale yellow spring profusion, and Bluebell Wood, its complete carpet of vividly blue bells too early for most visitors. Yet others were named, not from any natural feature, but after folk who had stayed there, like Mad Hatters corner, a name bestowed on it by a group from three caravans who regularly took tea together in the sunshine. It should be said that Fairy Dell did not fall into this category and did not obtain its title from people who had stayed there! Sharon had named the small glade soon after their arrival, a hidden, almost circular clearing amid a tangled mass of bramble, bracken and young saplings.

Some parts of the site had special features. Areas 8 and 15 were adjoining but separated by several large trees. Area 8 had been started the year before, hence the low number, but the suspicion that water might percolate down the valley slope from higher ground caused a trench to be dug on one side to divert any such seepage. This trench would be filled with medium sized stones as they became available, those too small for building walls. This had delayed further work on the area, but now it was nearly finished. Lying immediately in front of Bluebell Wood with the waste heaps to the West, these pitches caught some shade as the sun sank each evening. Not a place for sun worshippers, but sheltered, and being raised above other site levels by a small stone wall perhaps four feet high, gave fine views of the sunrise across farmland to the east. Another stone wall rose on a bank behind, at the edge of Bluebell Wood; a wall of great age and unknown origin.

The adjoining Area 15 was carved from a mound of fine sand. These washings from ancient mining operations had a special attribute discovered several years earlier. Much of the big sandy bank on the northwestern perimeter of this area remained untouched and provided a home for several families of Badgers, their setts opening close by at two separate points. That facet alone would make these pitches irresistible to many visitors. Wild creatures and an abundance of wild flowers were part of the valley's attraction; both were nurtured and protected. Here again, too much order and neatness were destructive. It was not the closely trimmed, spick-and-span appearance of a city square that visitors wanted, but the chance to appreciate nature's diversity. One couple, regular visitors and friends, John and Anita, had been working for over a week to tame a young jay, feeding it regularly, throwing small titbits, gradually enticing it nearer. They were pitched on a large oval of grass fringed by bushy trees downstream of the house. A couple of other caravans dotted the area, their owners watching with interest as days passed and the young bird came gradually closer. It was intriguing, for jays are normally cautious and shy. Towards the end of the holiday, John actually succeeded in enticing the young bird onto his hand and picking it up! It had taken hours of patience to be sure, but where else could you find the conditions, the peaceful tranquillity that such an achievement needed.

One feature not attractive to guests, particularly those with children, was the existing bonfire patch where hedge trimmings, fallen trees and cleared vegetation had been burnt over the past years. Though hardly visible from any of the pitches, the extending site had crept steadily nearer and plans had been made to relocate it after the season. However, two women suddenly complained; the only two on site with young families. No one had foreseen that children would find their way to this black ugly mess, far less that they would play in the accumulated ash that swelled to a muddy porridge after rain, clinging to little feet and walking in when they returned to their caravans. If these youngsters could do it, what trouble lay in store when the school holidays arrived? It had become an embarrassment that must be removed and a new burning place found downstream – and the farther downstream the better! Moreover, this job needed doing now, for they would soon be too busy. Life was still relatively easy in these early weeks of June; they had twenty-four caravans and seven tents on site at the moment. Jan could probably manage the office alone after lunch, at least until the children came home from school; mid-afternoon was normally a slack period with many visitors still at the beach. Today should not see many arrivals, Tuesday was normally slow.

When Gordon walked down the site dressed in old clothes and carrying various hand tools, one or two guests raised a friendly hand. Days of hot weather had caused some visitors to remain on site; they sat shaded beneath awnings, or under large colourful umbrellas set between reclining chairs, idly observing the birds or reading. This handful of people remaining in the valley showed little inclination to climb in their cars and go out. Part of the site's beauty comprised the temptation to do nothing, to sit and unwind for the day, enjoying the peacefulness. Never mind, working with only hand tools, clearing a path through the undergrowth to a lower region could be done without disturbing these visitors. Later, when the route had been cleared, a few quick trips with Max on some less sunny day when everyone was out, should safely dispose of the ash.

As the afternoon progressed, he worked on, cutting brambles and digging out gorse, stripped to the waist in search of coolness and perhaps a deeper suntan. Slowly he forged onwards, out of sight and beyond earshot, forgotten no doubt by guests on their sun loungers. Robin arrived quickly, as was normal early in the season before handouts from caravanners had completely diverted his loyalty, but an hour passed before Blackbird showed up. Farther back a fern had been discovered, a type not seen on site before. Deflecting the cleared path to one side and by-passing the clump, preserved it for identification later. Since then more hours had rolled by with nothing else unusual being found. Jan had not appeared either, they had agreed there would be no coffee this afternoon. Normally she avoided pitching caravans since people were sometimes difficult, but she had promised to handle any new arrivals today. That was good. At this time of year opportunities to be alone were rare – usually a welcome change but for some strange reason a feeling of depression slowly grew as he worked. There had never been reason before to cut so narrow a path, barely tractor width, not straight but winding to avoid that newly discovered fern and around the bigger trees. It was different from clearing whole areas. This narrow track forging into largely untrodden ground felt... He wasn't sure what created the unease; was it the boxed-in feeling, the claustrophobic effect of thick surrounding foliage, or perhaps a sense of work unending, that the site would never be finished? Progress along the slender pathway only emphasised the areas still to be cleared on either side and in all those acres ahead.

He forced away the morbid thoughts and tried to push on, but after four hours of continuous physical effort, the warmth and declining energy induced a certain lethargy. Must be that missing coffee! Easing down to sit on a south-facing bank forming one side of the cleared track, he relaxed for a brief breather, watching the Blackbird feed not far from his feet. Robin too, ventured closer, totally unworried by his presence. How tame they had become; did they enjoy his company as much as he liked theirs? Would they always return, or perish in the winter as so many did? Come to that, he would go himself one day; what would happen to the valley and its creatures then? He gazed sadly at the bird on the ground, almost at his feet, the background blurring out of focus as his mind wandered.

"*Sombre today?*" The Blackbird looked up seeming to speak… or was it just the stance?

"No... " Gordon shrugged, "Well yes, I suppose. Wondering what will happen to this valley when we leave?"

"*Urge to migrate?*" The bird's head cocked on one

side questioningly.

"Not really," he eased a hand on the ground, glancing at the enclosing vegetation. "This clearing does seem endless. I enjoy it, but will I ever finish, or die of old age first?" The facetious thought had just a touch of truth.

"*Ah.*" The bird's head moved, almost a nod of understanding. "*Little worries on immortality? Let me tell you about that. Some creatures have few thoughts, you might call them semi-intelligent if you were charitable. Take long tailed tits, following one another in groups, hardly an original thought among them. One moves to a new bush, the others trail on behind, unable to make their own way, only one mind between the lot, brains largely vacant, always happy, never brooding, not bright enough to realise there is danger all around. Perhaps from them you get the expression 'bird brain', which by the way is highly offensive to Blackbirds. You could never fall into that category of happy non-thinkers.*"

"Thanks. I'm glad to hear it, but do go on!" As Gordon spoke aloud, the bird moved slightly at the sound, bright eyes regarding him closely.

"*Let's try. Chemically, nothing in this world can be destroyed, apart that is from a tiny loss on conversion of matter to energy that one of your kind named Einstein has at last realised, but you had better not try to think about that. Just take it that nothing can be destroyed. When a favourite drinking puddle dries up in the sun, the water has not gone, but changed to water vapour in the air. If a forest fire burns a tree that you plan to build your home in next spring, the substance of the tree is still on this earth, as ash, smoke and more water vapour, and the total weight is identical to the tree's weight before the fire.*

"*Now consider something else. Suppose you were granted a wish to live a million years. After the first few hundred you would have done everything, experienced everything, and your best moments would be thinking back to younger days. After 500 years the boredom would be hardly bearable. One of your scientists might find a way of wiping your mind clear so that you could have all those experiences afresh. What a great achievement!*

"*But that is what the Good Lord has arranged when you die. Your body will not be destroyed, just dispersed. The chemicals from your tissues will become many things; maybe part will grow a new tree to give my descendants pleasure. If you are very lucky you could even become part Blackbird.*"

The bird gave a sudden start, stepping back a pace, beak open. Gordon turned his head carefully wondering as to the cause and seeing nothing, whispered, "What's the matter? You look as if you've lost a pound and found sixpence."

"*The expression is 'Lost a worm and found a flea', but you are right. A desperately degrading possibility has occurred to me. In the course of time I may come back as partly human!*" With a chattering scream of alarm, Blackbird was off, a low twisting flight through the bushes.

Gordon roused himself, stretched and rose from the bank, still not seeing what had startled his friend. Some distance away, the face of a fox backed softly into the undergrowth to make off in pursuit of easier prey.

Determined to clear another six feet before tea he worked on with a will, trying to forget, but the morbid thoughts persisted. Being buried would not be good. Every scrap of his body would lie dormant for centuries under six feet of earth. Cremation then, ashes scattered around rose trees? Better, but only a route back into the plant kingdom, and nothing other than aphids eat rose bushes. How would it go; leaf, aphid, ladybird, mantis, crow – where then? What eats crows? Ah! Four and twenty blackbirds baked in a pie… I doubt it, that was only for kings. Anyway, they must have been rooks, crows go in pairs, not two dozen at a time.

What else? Sprinkle the ashes in a field of spuds perhaps? Now we're back in a more direct route to the animal kingdom. But surely there must be a quicker way? Hector would have done better if Achilles, after dragging the carcass three times round those walls, actually *had* thrown his body to the dogs at the gates of Troy rather than just thinking about it. Sweeney Todd got it right, but that too was not fact, only some fourteenth century French legend.

Later at coffee with Jan, he appeared brooding and unresponsive to her questions.

"What's the matter? What are you thinking about?"

"Hm, nothing you want to know," he turned to stare evasively through the window.

"Yes I do, we never keep secrets from each other."

"Okay." Spreading fingers on the table his shoulders shrugged with an expression of resignation. "When I die, instead of being cremated what are the chances of getting my body secretly used in a meat pie factory?"

Jan's face hovered between humour and distaste, "Why not a pâté factory, be eaten by a better class of people. What gives you these mad ideas?"

"I told you, you didn't want to know!"

"So you did," she sighed, shaking her head in disbelief. "I'm sure it's stupid to ask this, but just for curiosity tell me anyway. Why would you want to be eaten?"

"To get back in the human food chain – be part of life again!"

"Couldn't you just be an organ donor?"

Chapter 10

Anne Arrives

Almost imperceptibly, life in the valley was changing. Fortunately, the ashes of those old bonfires had already been removed. Each day now a few more caravans dotted the site and foreign tents had started to arrive, young couples mostly, each staying only a few days, anxious to see more of the country. Motorcaravans, having booked one night, were staying longer. Other changes had crept in, hardly noticed as the weeks slid by. Evenings were even lighter and courtesy of some splendid weather, the grass lay limply brown while the river ran more shallow. People were happy; faces smiling with approval visited the office to book extra days or ask advice, and compliments flowed, particularly about the showers. Approving remarks covered a hundred different things, the layout, the new telephone box, the quietness at night, the cleanness of the toilet buildings.

"They don't smell like toilets, how do you do that?" one visitor had asked. How indeed? It would have been a long answer. Jan showed her pleasure at the compliment, and replied to the effect that visitors themselves were largely responsible, all the nice people staying in the valley who helped keep everything special. And that was true, or at least half the truth. This year too, there had been no smell from the septic tanks, not even early in the season, thanks probably to the shark. But there was more to it than that. Few of the caravanners realised that both toilet buildings were cleaned at six o'clock each morning, before the site owners ate breakfast; even before they had a coffee. It was out of bed with the alarm and five minutes later both were at work cleaning loos, basins, and showers. Nothing was allowed to be in less than top condition; a blocked drain, dripping tap, a loose plug, anything out of place was fixed immediately. During this season so far, no item once it was found faulty, had ever remained out of order for more than fifteen minutes and most were fixed in five! This was only possible because of the spares; spares for everything. Few people can claim three toilets in their basement, but River Valley could – not fixed up of course, but standing incongruously against one wall together with hand basins, sinks, four spare doors, pipes, taps, manhole covers and a dozen other items all waiting patiently to be used.

As each day became more busy, the pace of life increased in one respect and diminished in another. In the slacker periods like early afternoon, an odd hour of work preparing new areas might still have been possible but it was never worthwhile. Not that a little silent cutting of undergrowth far down the site would cause customers any annoyance; that was not the reason. It just took too long to return, clean up and change clothes now the tempo of life had picked up. Even though there would be unpredictable idle periods, reception could no longer be run single handed with any efficiency. Greeting new visitors and showing them to a pitch with the office left unattended, risked an unanswered telephone and guests waiting at the door – not good! Having two people on call removed this problem. Besides, if there was the odd slack period with nothing to do, what did it matter? Even busier times lay only a month ahead; reserves of stamina would be tested then! Better now to relax in any odd free moments, to take advantage while that possibility still existed.

Of necessity, Jan rushed out occasionally in the car to collect food, bleach, toilet rolls, or any of the many things an active site requires. Early afternoon was the usual time for these quick sorties, and on such days Jim came from his bungalow to sit in the office taking phone calls. It saved any lost bookings while each toilet building was give the midday clean and Gordon was still within call if a caravan came. Sometimes arriving visitors prevented the work, keeping him busy pitching. On such occasions, Jan would go cleaning after unloading the shopping, but this was later in the afternoon. As teatime approached, working in the toilets became more difficult with people returning from the beach so the Gent's door was always opened carefully. One day, hurrying because it was late, her mind was elsewhere worrying about the evening meal. A bucket of cleaning materials and brush in one hand, she entered sideways, pushing the door wide with a shoulder and stepped right in. A man was drying himself outside the shower! He stood bent over with legs apart, completely naked, head fortunately facing away but his pink bottom pointed straight at her, other little attributes dimly visible below.

Groping for the handle, catching hold as the door began automatically to close behind her, she pulled it open again, backing quickly out before he became aware of her presence! Running to the house, abandoning the bucket on the step, she arrived in a state of collapse and sank into a chair.

"What is it?" Something had obviously happened, but Gordon could extract no intelligible explanation. It began to emerge eventually, between quiet chuckles and bouts of helpless laughter, how she had approached the door without the ususal caution. Breaking off in another spasm, Jan wondered what it was that had caused her to lose control. The shock possibly, in that first moment of realisation? Certainly she had drawn a sudden breath and for a second been at a loss. Embarrassment perhaps? Involuntarily a hand moved to her cheek as if fingers could detect colour; but no, it couldn't be that. The escape then, the success of leaving undetected? Or was it fear of the man swinging round in surprise as he could well have done, exposing himself fully – then perhaps leaping sideways into the nearest cubicle. She didn't know, and Gordon was eyeing her suspiciously, waiting… Clenching fists for control and attempting to continue, she dissolved again into laughter.

Irrepressible little giggles bubbled forth at intervals, even after the children arrived home. While preparing an evening meal, with Dad and the boys already sitting at the table, Jan again burst into laughter. Sharon, who was helping and already annoyed at not receiving an explanation, put her hands on her hips, regarding her mother in exasperation.

"Mum! Tell me!" A little foot stamped the floor.

"It's nothing." Jan insisted, then catching Dad's eye, dissolved again into tears of laughter. Sharon practically burst with anger, but efforts at inducing her mother to talk failed totally. During the following days she several times asked again, but two of her young friends arrived on site and what with more sunshine and long light evenings, the matter was gradually forgotten.

June was a splendid month. People attending the Royal Cornwall Show the previous week had reported a great success, so much so that rumours suggested a three-day event next year. Anything attracting extra visitors must be good! Caravans were still increasing, yet more tents, and long hours of sunshine; people were so easy to please. Of course, a week of rain would soon change that! At the moment however, the site owners could do almost nothing wrong! Visitors were happy with their neighbours and generally obliging in every way; even when approached about a dog running loose, reactions were apologetic, rather than surly and resentful.

However, always there is danger. The risks of two people running a big park without help were driven home by a more serious incident which in a circuitous but unpleasant fashion, also highlighted a danger to all Cornish visitors. In an act of gross stupidity, Gordon stood up under the digger. He had been servicing the big excavator, something needed occasionally even in summer when it was idle. Lying on the ground to inspect the lower bolts of the rear digging arm, he was caught on rising. A peculiarly sharp piece of metal projected under the high seat at a level seemingly designed to allow his head to reach maximum velocity. Crunch!

Blood welled up from the wound and presented the possibility at least, of splintered bone and internal bleeding. The injury could not be ignored; Truro hospital was the nearest accident unit, an immediate visit unavoidable. Had he the good sense to wait a few months, then Penzance casualty would have opened. Jan refused to let him drive, and the children were at school. Leaving the site unattended in summer was ridiculous and had never been done before, but Jim would have to cope somehow! Stopping at the bungalow only long enough to shout 'Help' to Jan's Mum and Dad, they set off. Forty minutes later Jan drove into the hospital at Truro. The wait for treatment was to some extent confidence building.

"I only need to worry if they rush me to the head of the queue," Gordon thought. In this case he was right, it wasn't critical. When eventually cleaned up and treated, no severe bone damage had been sustained.

"So. There really are advantages to being thick!" Jan muttered, covering her relief with the flippant remark.

Apart from the doctor's warning of uncomfortable nights to come, which might involve difficulty lying on the pillow, all should be well. As they left the hospital an ambulance arrived and from it were stretchered three of the worst sunburn cases ever seen. One was overheard telling a nurse they had fallen asleep on the beach, but had only been there for three hours. Three hours! On a sunny day in Cornwall! Without a suntan for protection, you can get overdone in a fraction of that time; the air is so clear and free from industrial pollution. If a light breeze is blowing off the sea, you don't even notice. "Beware! Human Lobsters!" as Chris had once said.

Back at the site, the heat was having other effects.

"Over there!" Jan pointed. "Another one-o-four to change, on the second building. Where's it all going? While you're fixing it, check in the Gent's, the first shower head seems twisted."

Gordon rose, reached into a desk draw for an adjustable spanner and hurried outside. Removing one of the big red gas bottles, another was rolled into its place, connected up and the valve opened. The bottle empty indicator changed from red to black again. That was the third in as many days. He headed for the Gent's, and shortly returned to the office

"How can they use them so fast?" Jan asked "It *was* empty I suppose, not a fault with the indicator tag?"

"Yes, quite empty. Must be this hot weather, visitors feel sweaty – sticky is a better word for the ladies I suppose; makes them take more showers. Nothing we can do about it."

"Some places have slot meters?"

"Hm." He shook his head. "Sites right on the beach can get away with anything. Move a couple of miles inland and it's different. We fight for our trade. The most important thing in *our* lives is keeping the customer happy, not taking extra pennies. Where's the coffee?"

"Have you earned one? Did you fix that shower head?" Not waiting for a reply, Jan walked through to the kitchen. Gordon followed, moving in close as she bent to light the gas under the kettle. Feeling a comfortable contact from behind, she raised the burning match for him to blow out, holding it forward so his face rested against her cheek as he blew.

"Well? Did you fix it?"

"Yes. Wrenched to one side as if someone couldn't be bothered to step clear while they lathered their hair. I got it back, but looser now, not good for the joints."

"Don't tell me it's not strong? Thought you said they were bomb proof! You must be..."

A voice calling from the office broke the conversation and the contact. A woman, finding the door open, had stepped inside with two ice packs. She held them out but Jan, entering from the hallway, shook her head.

"No, not here. Take them up to Audrey, my mother; the bungalow at the entrance with the black Delabole slate front. Riverside it's called."

"Couldn't you do just these two? My husband forgot them, he's gone by car to the beach. I'm on my own for a restful afternoon; no transport."

Jan explained the electrical system to the woman's evident surprise, pulling a cord to light one of the little twelve-volt bulbs above. They conversed for a while and the woman went away happy enough, asking if she could bring the family back and show them that evening, or perhaps the following day if they returned late.

Not knowing what time that might be, Jan called to the children when a lull in activities gave a brief respite.

"Chris! Dad and I are off for a walk. If that family comes who want to see the wheel, will you show them. Sharon, can you stay for half an hour?"

"Yes Mum. If my friends arrive, can they play snooker with me in the office?"

"They can, provided you all look respectable."

An evening walk was still a feature of the day, even as business became more hectic. Walking off downstream away from the caravans formed the only chance to escape; a brief respite from the continuous demands of customers and that unrelenting phone bell! Not that they really wanted a quieter existence; both enjoyed the constant activity. It was their life, making people happy, keeping order, satisfying conflicting demands. They did it well – most of the time! However, Jan in particular reached a point on some evenings where she wanted to throw something! Fortunately, Chris and Sharon certainly, and to a lesser extent young Stephen, were all capable of minding the office and the phone for a while. Leaving the youngsters in charge, the parents slipped out.

Over the years of living in the valley, their knowledge of natural history had increased, partly gleaned from the expertise of customers. What they saw depended to some extent on how early they managed to get away. On those rare occasions when a late afternoon lull allowed an earlier break, they could watch the last butterflies, those, which had not yet retired to a safe nook for the night. They found other things too, a patch of nettles covered with spiky black caterpillars.

"Peacocks I think. Bit late aren't they?" Jan asked. "How do those beautiful wings originate from such ugly creatures?"

Red Admirals were still rare and particularly liked the flowers of hemp agrimony just beginning to bloom in bunches on the sloping bank sides. Later they would be more common and would target buddleia bushes that sprouted at various points, growing from roots hidden in imported topsoil. Less glamorous types such as Gatekeepers and Speckled Woods fluttered among tangles of bramble in shady patches, while small blues and coppers favoured the shorter growing sparse grasses found in places where strongly acid conditions stunted taller growth. A great many species, some resident, others just passing through, flitted happily in a natural environment for no spraying occurred along the valley bottom. These colourful insects, together with many different birds and various flowers coming successively into bloom, combined with the clear water flowing alongside to make this the most pleasant of footpaths. They walked far enough to see the strange brick path that crossed the riverbed underwater, and found it half-hidden by shingle washed down on the current. This oddity led from nowhere, to nowhere; its origin and purpose still a mystery, lost in time and passing generations. Farther on, the pylon now stood complete but as yet without wires above and naturally with no trace of that mystery alsatian! Stopping at this point, they strolled slowly homeward.

To discourage interruptions while eating, the office door usually remained closed during meals, this ploy only moderately successful. At other times normal practice left the door open. As a consequence, those butterflies found along the riverbank would now and then enter the house and flutter against the glass trying to escape. All the children knew how to catch them, carefully carrying the delicate creatures between cupped hands to be released outside.

The following day, Saturday, shortly after lunch with the children not yet departed to play, a Small Tortoiseshell, brightly colourful with fancy blue wing boarders, floated through the open door. It sailed easily around the office and into the lounge, to flutter against the window facing the river. Sharon made to catch it.

"No!" Stephen pushed his sister aside, thrusting against her shoulder then stood before the window, little fists clenched and ready for action.

Caught by surprise, Sharon staggered back. Recovering balance she turned angrily, reaching out with the obvious intention of forcibly removing her younger brother – but stopped at a signal from Jan.

Stephen looked from one to another then ran to the door, disappearing down the corridor. Sharon and her mother followed, reaching the kitchen to see an eggcup snatched from a cupboard. Catching a dribble of water from the tap, the young lad added a teaspoon of sugar, stirred vigorously then shot past them to the bathroom. Returning with a small tuft of cotton wool, he dipped it in the eggcup and was off again, still without a word, hurrying back to the lounge. Here, moving forwards cautiously, he stood close to the window holding out an arm; the cotton wool on one extended finger pressed against the glass close to the butterfly. As they waited, Jan asked softly, "Who showed you that?"

"Dad did." The words were whispered without the slightest nod or movement.

Eyes swung to Gordon.

"Yes. I did; one day when you were out. Somehow butterflies must survive the winter, otherwise they would become extinct. Some lay eggs that hatch in spring but others hibernate. The sleeping ones may wake on a warm winter day to feed. People who breed butterflies sometimes deliberately waken certain types, and use sugar water to feed them. It's supposed to be possible to train some species to come to hand and…"

He stopped as Chris and Sharon's attention swung back to the window.

Stephen, who had not moved a muscle since returning to the room, watched his finger intently. The Tortoiseshell touched the cotton wool. For a moment it did nothing, then a long delicate proboscis uncurled, slender, like a wisp of hair, to probe and suck up the liquid. No one stirred. After a while the tongue withdrew, coiling up and retracting, but reappeared shortly as the insect moved, its feet stepping gingerly onto the wet wool. Very carefully Stephen turned, bringing his hand away from the window with the butterfly still feeding. Moving slowly, his young face a mask of concentration and pride, he crossed the room, heading towards the office door. Halfway… three quarters… nearing the opening where lounge and office met… the family held their breath. Passing between the two rooms a sudden movement of wings carried their new friend back to the window. Jan reached to open a side panel, swinging it wide then stepping back, inviting Stephen to manage the final escape. As the lad moved forward cupping one hand to guide it out, she stood waiting, the scene triggering a memory.

"I read in a magazine that Churchill had hundreds of newly hatched butterflies released at Chartwell for a garden party once; must have been an impressive sight don't you think?"

She waited for Stephen's comment but he gave no indication at all of having heard his mother's words and stood gazing out, watching as tiny wings fluttered off into the distance.

Dad, sitting watching, made no comment either but later that afternoon, thinking to imitate Churchill's display on a smaller scale, he dug a root of tall nettles, replanting them in a large flowerpot then hurried along the river bank to locate the black peacock caterpillars seen the previous day. There were masses to choose from, a dozen of the fattest were selected, those that seemed almost ready to pupate. They were introduced to the pot of nettles and carried back to the office desk.

Jan, approaching from the kitchen, talking as she came, stopped suddenly in the doorway. "Oh yes. What is it this time? Silk worms?"

"Now that's a good idea."

At the evasive reply she moved towards him, a smile on her lips but trying to look fierce and threatening, a game they often played together.

Lifting a hand in pretended defence he hastily explained. "Okay. They're peacock caterpillars. *You* remember; we saw them near the riverbank. I had to do it now, they'll all be gone shortly. Anyway, we'll be too busy when the school holidays start. We're going to breed some."

"Are we really? How nice! Caravanners may all leave in case madness is catching." She waltzed out towards the kitchen speaking in a deep voice as she went, "Mad? 'Corse I'm not mad. Everyone else is though!" A peal of demonic laughter followed.

"Stop taking the Micky." Gordon called after her, "You'll like them when they hatch."

She was right in one respect, the caravanners did exchange glances. Though a few became interested, most were too polite to ask and left the office quickly. Caterpillar droppings seemed to accumulate on the desktop like hail-stones in an Arctic monsoon, only smaller and blackish. The poor nettles disappeared with great rapidity, which didn't much matter, but when they woke one morning, so had all the caterpillars. Jan noticed first.

"Where are they?" she waved a finger. "You find every last one, or cook your own meals!"

What a threat. Fried egg sandwiches and tinned rice for life! Gordon stepped quickly into the office to check. She was right. Bare nettles, most stripped to the leaf ribs, stood forlorn and empty. He was in trouble! Try to humour her.

"Don't worry. They won't be crawling about, they'll just form chrysalises in some dark corner. In a couple of weeks you'll have dozens of beautiful butterflies flitting about the house. A girl like you should have beautiful things around her." That should do it, flattery usually worked!

"I don't care if they shine like gold and glitter like diamonds, get them out of my house… Now! And get rid of those bedraggled nettles before any more visitors see them!"

She might be laughing, but that outstretched arm with pointed finger and the other hand clenched into a small fist held ready at waist level as she approached to stand close, left no room for debate! However, try as they might, only five were found.

"I've heard certain types can be cannibalistic," Gordon suggested, inventing the story in self-defence. "Probably when the nettles were all gone they ate each other. No good hunting anymore, these five are the only ones left."

Unsure whether to believe it or not, Jan regarded him suspiciously – but where else could they have gone, all in twenty-four hours as if leaving together on a signal? Sharon, on learning of the disappearance, searched long and thoroughly but without success and was still concerned the following morning. However, Chris had more important news.

"More trout have disappeared from under the bridge."

The family were seated round the breakfast table. At least this meal usually went without interruptions for it still wanted a few minutes to 7am. The loss was not unexpected, it had happened last season too, and no one believed the heron was to blame.

"Shame." Jan frowned. "Children love feeding them. From our bridge and with the water so clear, it's one of the few places a young child can actually see the fish – first time for some of them the mothers have told me. Can we do anything?" She looked towards Gordon.

"Don't ask me, I'm not the fisherman of this family."

Eyes automatically turned to Chris, who shrugged his shoulders. "We could have ducks, won't stop anyone but does make it harder to fish. What else is there – unless you want to stop people fishing that stretch?" He looked back to his father.

"Not really. It might become necessary one day to keep a section unfished if more children come. At some point there won't be any trout left otherwise I suppose, but I'd rather not have more rules. It's difficult enough persuading visitors to keep dogs on a lead and lift ground sheets. If there *is* another way, let's try it first."

Jan nodded agreement. "I've always wanted ducks on the river. Wonder why there aren't any? People like ducks; even if they didn't succeed in protecting the fish, visiting children would love them – adults too, everyone would."

A copy of *The Western Morning News* provided the answer, a tiny advert for ducks near St Just. Jan had really expected to find them in one of the weekly local papers, but that meant waiting two days and she was impatient, knowing the school holidays were imminent. With the children off to catch the school bus, Gordon prepared to leave, but Jan held his arm. "I want to come."

"Jim can't manage alone. Don't you trust me?" He grinned down at her.

"Yes he can, for a little while."

"That's stupid! We've never left together at this time of year, except when I hit my head. There's too much for one person. Jim will never cope – not with his bad leg."

"He'll have to. He can ring Audrey if we get a rush but it's Tuesday, the slackest day and it won't take long – or you can stay, because I'm definitely going. And no, I don't trust you. I want nice ducks and several of them, not one mangy specimen because it's cheap!"

At Gordon's insistence the trip was postponed until early afternoon, usually the least busy time. Leaving Jim temporarily in charge they drove away.

"Slow down!" Jan shouted, as rounding a corner at speed, a tractor towing some wide agricultural implement appeared before them, scarcely leaving room to squeeze by. "I told you, Jim can manage! Stop driving like a madman. The site won't blow up because you take an hour off!"

The St Ives to Lands End road, narrow and winding but picturesque, soon disappeared behind with little chance to admire the sweeping sea views as they rapidly located the farm in the advert. Five Muscovy ducks and one drake were purchased at a cost of 75p each. Jan approved each one, running a hand over the feathers and examining the birds carefully as the farmer slipped them into ventilated cardboard boxes in the car boot. It had always seemed strange that no ducks lived naturally on the river, and although Muscovys were a farmyard rather than a wild duck, closer to a small goose really, it made a step in the right direction. There would be ducks on the Hayle again. These new companions rode home more sedately, the urge to get back being modified by a need not to shake them about, the slower pace raising comments that ducks must be more important than wives! That was true; at 75p new money they were twice as valuable as a wife bought for seven shillings and six pence old money. Pointing this out in the close confines of the car may not have been too bright! On arrival home, three caravans were waiting in the yard and people stood talking outside the office. Jim had obviously pointed to the arriving car, for the group descended almost before the doors opened.

“Hold on. Give us a moment please, to get these ducks comfortable. Anyone want to carry the other boxes?”

Two men volunteered and the ducks took residence in the goat’s quarters, the lean-to shed which stretched half the width of the second toilet building. Leaving them to settle, Gordon hurried off leading the first caravan, stopping part way along Area 3.

“Come and book in when you get settled. Sorry you had to wait but Jim has a bad leg, he doesn’t get around enough to know which pitches are best. How would that one over there suit you? Can you reverse or shall I?”

Shortly all three were sited. Jan had served two other customers with gas bottles and worked through the list of phone calls, checking with her father before he left. A full twenty minutes passed before they were free and returned to the shed. The floor ran with water from a low trough filled only that morning; the ducks were enjoying themselves. “Keep them in for a day or two and feed them inside so they know where home is,” the farmer had advised. This was the only suitable place; the goats must stay in the garage, they would make less mess than six Muscovys; goat droppings were less adhesive, easier to sweep up cleanly. The car could stand outside and the mower too, covered with an old dustsheet.

Stephen, as usual, arrived home first. Jan showed him the ducks, taking along a bowl of poultry corn from a bag she had purchased earlier in the day at Cornwall Farmers, the local farm wholesalers in Penzance. Only one duck would take food from the hand, a mainly black female with a deep green metallic sheen on her wings.

“Anne. We’ll call her Anne.” Jan said, and went away to prepare tea leaving Stephen with the remains of the corn. When returning ten minutes later, she approached slowly, stopping some distance away and standing still. The lad sat astride the doorway, a chunk of wood providing a seat above the wet floor. Several ducks were eating from his hand. Anne was standing on his leg, his other hand stroking her back feathers ever so gently. His eyes glanced briefly at Mum and the hand stopped. Anne ceased eating, her beak rising towards him, then resumed feeding as the fingers moved again on her back. Stephen looked up with a shy smile, but said nothing.

When Chris and Sharon arrived home together, Jan let Stephen show the ducks; she liked to see him assume the senior roll occasionally even if only for a brief period. On returning to the house for tea, Chris voiced his concern for the goat's welfare.

"What about Judy and the kids, can they live in with the ducks?"

"No." Gordon shook his head. "Might not get on. The goats can have the garage for a time. Mum's left the car outside. I'd planned to extend the lean-to shed the full width of the toilet building anyway – that will more than double its size. The new part was for mower storage but the goats can have it instead. We've enough concrete blocks and roof tiles, only a few timbers need be bought."

The ducks were a lucky choice, for by ignorant good fortune Muscovys were a silent breed, virtually never quacking and very idle, both praiseworthy features for free ranging ornamental fowl.

"Is that why they took to Stephen so quickly? Did they sense a kindred spirit?" Jan asked.

"Hm. You mean the quietness or because he's idle sometimes? Probably my fault, I tend to give the heavier jobs to Chris because he's stronger. Stephen may do less than the rest of the family, but he probably manages more than most boys his age. Still, I agree, he does wriggle out of jobs."

The Muscovys, when they were released from the shed, tended to stay near the house, too lazy to wander far. Occasionally they swam in the river but mostly slept on the grass, which provided much of their food intake for they grazed a great deal, unlike most ducks. This stay at home tendency could be helpful later in keeping other species, ones more inclined to wander. Ducks like to be with other ducks, at least, most breeds do; a flocking instinct designed by nature to reduce the chances of a predator catching any one particular duck, many pairs of eyes giving earlier warning of approaching danger. The family derived great pleasure from feeding them. Soon, not just Anne but the other ducks and Francis the drake ate from anyone's hand, big cold beaks nuzzling around the palm to pick up the last grain of corn. They were still shut in at night in case one of the resident foxes developed a taste for duck. It became apparent later that most preferred to sleep floating on the river but they would need the shed for nesting anyway, so it did no harm to get them thoroughly used to going in.

In less than a week, a couple of hours work in the middle of each day had extended the shed as promised. Working neatly avoided any mess that might inconvenience visitors, and being near the office, Gordon remained quickly available to pitch arriving caravans. Instead of bedding the blocks down with the end of a trowel, he tapped them silently with a rubber hammer, and any block that needed cutting to size was carried to the basement where the sound would not he heard. Only right at the end, driving a handful of nails to fix the roof, did he make any noise, but it was quickly done when most people were out. With this separate compartment, Judy and her kids no longer slept in the garage. After some vigorous floor cleaning, both car and mower regained their proper home.

Arriving visitors increased, the families now containing a higher proportion of older children. Many were scarcely children any more but in their late teens, probably finished A-level exams and left before the official term end. All were with parents, most having paid only the children's rate for site fees.

"Why do we charge less?" Jan protested. "These young girls stay in the shower longer than any three adults. They keep asking for hair dryers too."

Jan wanted one for the home as well, and had raised the matter several times with increasing force but received only evasive responses. She had experimented before, washing Sharon's hair then sitting her close to the boiler in the basement, flapping a large towel to simulate a current of hot air. It failed to work. This time, she decided Gordon must make a serious attempt to rectify this deficiency. By the weekend it would be too late; the hordes would be upon them! But how to persuade him? At coffee she mentioned again the various teenage girls' requests for a hairdryer, and described her own attempt with the towel, and its failure.

"Yes, I ought to think about that sometime," he replied, obviously without the slightest intention of doing so.

Continuing to walk about tidying the kitchen, she shook her head, "No, no. Hair drying is a female thing. Men don't understand it. You wouldn't have a clue."

A direct challenge to masculine brain power. Right! He knew her well enough to realise this was not the casual offhand remark it appeared. "This attempt to goad me into action... it must be important to her ." The thoughts came silently. "She'll guess I'll see through it, but she won't be sure. A little deception is fun anyway between consenting adults."

Hair dryers were a real problem, they needed power as anything with a heating element did. Current in that quantity the water-wheel could not produce. There must be other ways of drying hair. All it needed surely was a little thought, some exercise for the little grey cells. A good flow of warm air would do it! Gas could provide heat, but how to blow it at someone's head? He sat, not speaking but continuing to think, sipping the hot liquid.

"What do I know about heat? Hot air rises. Stick a blowlamp in the end of a long vertical pipe and it should shoot out the top quite fast. But then the person with wet hair will need to be high up. Sit them on the house roof? Rubbish. Think again."

Sipping more coffee, he developed another line of thought. Still use gas for the heat, there seemed no other option, but how about a big hand operated fan for the air current. A bicycle wheel perhaps, with aluminium fan blades fixed to the spokes, and rotating inside a casing, sucking up hot air from the gas flame and blowing it out inside some sort of cubicle. A handle outside would turn the bicycle wheel. Problem – who would do the winding? Well, ladies were usually the ones who wanted hair dryers; so each lady must bring along her own man to crank the handle. Novel? Oh sure! And bound to be popular with the chaps! Guess who would wind that handle when Jan wanted her hair dried, and probably Sharon too! "Think I better think it out again, as Fagin would say." Gordon muttered to himself, looking up to catch Jan watching him.

She turned away, unable to conceal the slight smile on her lips, aware that he had seen and understood it, aware that he knew that she knew – the wager had been taken up. At stake, pride!

He sat, a hand rubbing absently over stubble on his chin. She would not let him forget easily if he failed! That much was clear. There would be no criticism, no constant complaints; that was not her style. Rather she would be sympathetic, consoling; but whenever the question of mental capacity arose, he sensed what would happen. She would smile and stroke her hair, pulling forward a strand to rub it softly between finger and thumb with a questioning look on her face. No words would be necessary; they understood each other far too well.

He needed a current of air! Heat was no problem, only how to transport it. What then, a blower, a fan? A low powered fan. A car! Yes! Vehicle heaters used 12-volt fans!

A quick visit to the local breaker's yard about twelve miles away, yielded a considerable choice. He chose one from an old Rover, a powerful unit costing £1 and taking 60 watts, the equivalent of nearly three small light bulbs.

Even with the river now lower, the wheel could handle that without help from the battery. If it worked he would get another later as a spare. Smuggling this fan down into the basement workroom, he screwed it to a frame over the bench then connected up their 12-volt supply simply by plugging into a light socket. It worked fine, a solid blast of air much greater than any normal hairdryer. Good! Now to get it hot. With the biggest nozzle attached and the recently purchased gas blowtorch set to its fiercest heat, he pointed the flame at the fan inlet from a good distance away. Tepid air blasted forth. Moving the blowtorch nearer, the temperature grew increasingly pleasant. Who said men didn't understand hair drying. Masculine brain power had solved it – naturally! Calling up through the concrete floor above bought no response, Jan couldn't hear. Turning the gas off, hurried paces headed along dark corridors and up the concrete staircase.

Leading the way back down, he pointed, "Stand there," and waited while she moved to the spot. Pushing a plug into the light socket started the fan. Cold air whistled out strongly at a height somewhere above waist level – her hands rose defensively.

"Oh! But it's cold!" She moved sideways out of the blast, leaving only her fingers to test the breeze.

"Wait for it! I haven't finished yet." He lit the blowlamp, pointing it at the fan.

"That's better! Can you fix it higher up?" She sounded pleased, shouting above the lamp's roar.

"No. Not at the moment. It's Stephen's height, fixed to the wall. Squat down."

She did, letting her hair stream out in the wind; he moved the hissing lamp nearer to the fan inlet.

"Hey, it's getting hot!"

His free hand reached out to check the airstream and at that moment Jan cried out! Trying to move back from the heat, she overbalanced, falling awkwardly to sprawl on the workroom floor. Gordon swung round in concern, the blowlamp moving in his hand.

Somehow the fan caught the flame, boosted it, and threw it forwards like a dragon's breath. Whether the blaze went through the actual fan, or the nozzle got in front of the outlet, was never clear. It singed the hair off his right hand that was still held in the air stream checking the temperature. Reflex action snatched the burnt limb away very quickly indeed! The motion was unconscious and he stood momentarily transfixed, an acrid smell hanging on the air.

Jan, still struggling to rise, nearly stood in the burning path. She let out a shriek. He snatched the lamp away and the fan's flame died.

For a moment neither spoke. They were breathing heavily. Extinguishing the blowlamp and laying it down, he rubbed the knuckles. It felt peculiar, the hairs burned to a strange texture, but the skin appeared unaffected.

Jan steadied herself, rose and stepped towards him.

"Did you hurt your hand?" she enquired softly.

He opened his mouth to reply, but she cut him short with a glare.

"Good! Serves you right! I told you men were useless at hair drying!"

With those biting words she drew herself up, left the underground room and strode off towards the stairway, magnificent in her scorn.

Later at tea, Mum commanded, "Look at Dad's hand." Three heads swung towards him.

"Nothing wrong with my hand," he said holding it out.

"Show the right one!" she insisted.

"No."

Nothing was more calculated to gain the children's full attention. Sharon rose and leaned over trying to see.

"Don't worry, he'll show you in a minute." Jan lifted plates of beans on toast, putting one in front of Chris and another before Dad. "See if you can eat *that* one handed."

He reached forward with both hands, picking up the

knife and fork to an "Ooh!" from Sharon and curiosity from the boys. Jan, bringing over the other three plates, embarked between mouthfuls on an embroidered version of events in the basement, pausing before the end.

"Whoosh! This enormous flame shot out as I was about to get up. Only a second later you'd have come home to a bald Mum. Instead it scorched Dad's hand; serves him right!" She pointed an accusing finger.

"Chris couldn't have told it better," he replied, nodding.

The children seemed puzzled but Jan understood, knowing there had been a little exaggeration. "Well perhaps quite a lot," she admitted, concealing the thought and turning to Sharon. "We'll wash your hair tonight and try the thing out. Dad worked on the details again after the accident; it may even be safe now."

"I've had mine washed this week already, it's not good to wash hair too often, Mum. Must be someone else's turn." Sharon, alarm in her voice, looked hopefully round the table.

Stephen nodded, silently putting himself forward as a volunteer. It was true as Jan said, the arrangement had been worked on – in odd moments snatched here and there, for the site was becoming busy with the school holidays only days away. A fixed grid now prevented the flame reaching the fan and a few experiments seemed to indicate the system was now safe at least for the family, but such an arrangement could never be offered for use by caravanners. Even with the blowlamp firmly clamped in an immovable position, people might leave it burning after use and melt the fan, or someone would turn it on letting the gas accumulate while they hunted for a match and eventually having found one, would strike it and barbecue themselves. Apart from the safety aspect, if rigged in the toilet buildings it would run almost continuously; people would not only use it for drying hair, but for their washing, for bathing costumes, towels – it had even been known for people to dry dogs with site hairdryers! Even a single dryer in the Ladies would absorb much of the wheel's output, leaving little to charge caravanner's batteries, and the young lads were bound to want one too. No, this new device must be for the family alone. When Stephen tried it later the system worked to perfection; fast, efficient, a nice feel of warm wind in the hair. Everyone watched as he stood, exactly the right height, an expression of pride on his face, just like when he alone had ridden in the digger bucket nearly four years before – half a lifetime ago for him.

CHAPTER 11

Bread on the Water

Only a handful of trout remained below the bridge, the numbers continuing to diminish though more slowly now, depleted no doubt by keen young fishermen in spite of the ducks. Standing at mid-span tossing bread to the water below, Jan saw a woman cycle round the toilet building, pedal slowly across the yard and stop close by. Still astride the saddle, steadying one foot on the low bridge parapet, the lady checked over one shoulder obviously expecting company, and finding no one, turned to speak.

"Relubbus is a quaint little village, pity about the steep hill."

"Which way are you going?"

"We went to Marazion yesterday, it was fine after the first half-mile. The children insist on avoiding that hill, so this morning it's St Ives." The woman straightened. "Have I said something funny?"

"Sorry, didn't mean to laugh, but the hill – there's a bigger one the way you're going today." Seeing the visitor's rueful shrug and a small sigh of disappointment, Jan asked, "When you booked a holiday with us, didn't you guess there would be hills each side."

"No. We chose you for the river mostly, River Valley sounded nice; and because you have no clubs and things. My family wanted somewhere peaceful. It's certainly that, ideal in every way, except for those hills! What makes you think we should have guessed?"

"It's what rivers do, water runs to the lowest possible

level it can find. Whenever you camp by a river you have to be at the lowest point and that means rising ground when you leave – hills." Jan stopped, wondering whether to say more, and seeing the woman nod a little shame-facedly, decided she would. "Don't blame yourself, I thought the same thing when we first arrived. What I just said, that was exactly how my husband explained it; told me as if talking to a child, smirking all over his face. I could have sloshed him!" The women were laughing together when a man and two children appeared round the toilet building with bicycles.

There were actually three hills leading from Relubbus. Turning left from the site entrance, the road forked after a short distance. Tregembo hill led on to Townsend while Gurlyn hill provided a shorter route to the Atlantic coast but narrow and winding, definitely not for caravans or anyone wanting to hurry on corners.

In the opposite direction, across the Hayle River and heading towards Marazion and St Michael's Mount, the route led past the old Post Office and the ancient village pump. At this southwesterly end of the village, two houses, one on each side, jutted almost to the road edge; a dangerously blind corner but serving to slow any traffic. The route continued up Relubbus Hill, at the top of which lay St Hilary from where the parish took its name, or more correctly both parish and village were named after a French scholar, Bishop of Poitiers in the fourth century.

The St Hilary Institute was young by comparison, a mere century or so old, a derelict oblong of stone, its corrugated iron roof liberally perforated allowing rain to trickle down inside. This building had received much attention back in the winter; most of the visitors staying at River Valley passed it daily en-route to the coast but none were aware of the strange way these renovations had assisted in milking Judy the goat.

The institute stood at the road edge. Stepping from its single door left a person standing on the carriageway, for no footpath intervened. That carriageway was called New Road, it must have been new once of course, but no one could remember when. The building, deserted many years since, had in its heyday been the working man's club, a totally male domain, a meeting place where billiards and the company of other men provided relaxation after the day's work. Of course, there were alternative places to spend an evening, like the six pubs Relubbus was rumoured to have in mining times, though none remained open today and most of those buildings were gone. The village was bigger then, many small dwellings having since disappeared; the plot on which Jim's bungalow now stood for instance, once contained no less than five small cottages. Life in those days was hard; the miners had no need to wonder if drink would damage their health, so many died young from other causes.

Stanley Thomas had a great interest in The Institute and hoped to bring it back into use. Stanley ran an agricultural repair workshop farther up the valley and had often welded cracks in Max, the excavator when the family first arrived in Relubbus. He asked a handful of people, including Gordon, Jim, Mr Curzon and several others to help. They had met in the Institute on winter evenings after dark, using an oil lamp for lighting. With the roof temporarily patched pending re-roofing later, some form of heating became essential to disperse the accumulated dampness. The existing solid fuel stove should suffice if someone provided fuel. Other problems included disposal of the battered remains of what had once been a full sized billiard table. The slate bed was missing, removed at some past time for who knows what; the baize and pockets gone, the joints loose and the woodwork bruised and damaged.

"Next farmer that comes for a tractor repair, can cart it away to burn." Stanley promised confidently.

Jim, always good with a saw, offered to cut the frame to firewood for the stove, solving both problems at once, but it seemed unlikely to last more than one evening.

“We’ve a mountain of logs already sawn, seasoned wood from fallen trees mostly, Gordon offered. I could use this wreckage, swap it for logs instead. Pity to burn something so historic, how old is it anyway?”

“Dammed if I know, saw it here as a child.” Stanley gazed at the wreck in the corner, long memories obviously stirred.

“Must be 200 years then, at least.”

Stanley came out of his reminiscence fast. “You cheeky young bu…” He went on for some time.

“Sorry Stanley, I don’t understand all those long foreign words!” Gordon tried to keep a straight face.

Stanley let rip another crisp string of uncomplimentary expressions, leaning back and grinning as he become more serious. “I’ll tell you about those days. We children weren’t normally allowed in, only the men. When I first went, must have been in the 1920’s, I saw them, all dressed in Sunday best. Younger chaps kept their place, gave way to seniors and quick about it. Didn’t need no police to keep order then. One word from an older man was enough! I seen a young chap, sixteen or seventeen maybe, knocked senseless by a man once, just for moving while he was cueing on a ball. The lad pitched up in that corner there,” Stanley pointed, “Out to the world. Nobody cared. Carried right on with the game, left the body lie, ignored it completely. Could have been dead. None of us younger ones moved a damned inch in the next half-hour!”

Over a period the building had dried out, been cleaned up and the lighting switched back on. Stanley did get it completed and organised a series of events to be run there; Whist Drives and the like. That had been back in the winter. Once the lighter evenings started Gordon was no longer able to help, but that old billiard table probably in use at the turn of the century had lived on. It now formed a sturdy bench in the basement at River Valley, a bench on which Judy the goat was often milked. What stories could that table tell of those days shortly after the fall from grace of copper and tin in Cornwall, when miners and their sons left to find work in far flung corners of the world?

Judy was not always milked indoors. On most evenings during the tourist season this task was performed outside for the benefit of visitors. The ducks too were great favourites; they had become quite at home by the river. While free to leave, they showed no inclination to do so – certainly not while an increasing number of visiting children fed them regularly. When most tourists were out, the ducks sat for long periods sunning themselves on the bank, close to the water's edge. Choosing to cluster in a little group, some would sleep with head under wing while others nuzzled a beak lazily through a neighbour's feathers. Should anyone approach, each duck's reaction depended solely on its need for food.

A young girl walked towards the bridge early one morning, several slices of bread in her hand. Jan, glancing from time to time through the window as she worked, noticed six heads shoot suddenly upright, beaks all facing in the same direction. Was it a fox? As the girl came into view, the ducks rose, dashing forwards in a mad scramble, surrounding her with upturned beaks. One snatched a whole slice, making off with it, two others in pursuit. The remaining three took smaller pieces from the girl's hand, pulling her little skirt with impatient beaks if she kept them waiting. All were totally forbearing when their feathers were stroked – so long as the food kept coming.

Later in the morning, much more bread would arrive, distributed by little hands until every duck's appetite was well and truly sated. Then they would gather in a group on the grassy bank and sleep again. Children arriving after that time might warrant the opening of a single eye, or a curious glance with raised beak, but no more. Even this meagre movement would be abandoned and the beak promptly buried again in feathers once the duck decided no danger threatened. Jan had watched children, particularly young girls, approach the over-fed birds, kneel down beside them and stroke the feathers. If the hands were gentle, the attention was often tolerated, almost ignored.

As midday passed, with most visitors off to the beach and no more food forthcoming, appetites progressively recovered and the Muscovys would graze on grass or dabble underwater, feeding around the roots of rush and sedge. At this time of day, Sharon, if she was home, often sat on the riverbank with bread in her hand. Anne, the almost black duck, would stand on her lap picking the soft centre from a slice while the crusty edges were fed to other ducks and to Francis the drake. Some people were not so keen to be near those hard beaks; often bread was cast on the water instead. Ducks have a natural preference for wet food. When anyone sat on the bridge parapet they would anticipate being fed, and wait paddling gently, keeping station in a line just downstream. This was particularly good for small children or anyone nervous of feeding them directly. As a bonus, trout lurking in the current below would dart to snatch morsels from under a slower beak, each fish disappearing quickly with its prize. As the season continued, the number of trout seen rising for bread had gradually decreased. The shoal that should have been waiting in an arc had reduced to a handful, but nevertheless a few fish could still clearly be seen by anyone looking down from the bridge; one was almost a foot long, good for so small a river.

Knowing how much the younger children enjoyed these trout, something most of them had never been able to see before, a no-fishing area had reluctantly been introduced for an equal distance upstream and downstream from the bridge; a belated attempt to stop the rest disappearing. It had not proved easy in those first few weeks, for the trout were so tempting to boys, and in this single respect it was always boys, never girls, who were difficult. Those that were knowledgeable about angling, generally understood conservation; a few even gave support, commenting that unless part of the river remained unfished there would be none left to breed in the autumn and they wanted to come back next year. For the most part however, boys of all ages live for the moment and are very competitive; consideration for other children or the future seldom a high priority. A plea that younger children would be unable to see the trout from any other place, cut little ice. However, the suggestion that it took more skill to make a catch downstream and that no decent fisherman would stoop to taking tame fish, was much more successful!

Those without that skill, who failed to catch anything in other parts of the river, could be very sneaky! Several had sauntered up to the bridge, slid down behind the parapet, and quietly taking a hand line from their pockets, commenced to fish in secret. As the number of children began rapidly to increase, keeping an eye on the river became less easy. One little girl dashed towards the office, reaching out to ring the doorbell urgently, not pausing between rings but pressing continuously, both thumbs hard on the button.

"He's trying to catch my fish!" she gasped, breathlessly indignant, pointing to the far side of the bridge.

Gordon, having sat down for the evening but not expecting to escape without interruptions, said "Thank you," smiled at her, and ran quickly to the bridge in his slippers.

"Not here. Beyond the waterwheel!"

The lad fishing below shot upright, almost falling in the water, taken by surprise as the voice called down from above. Recovering to climb up the bank with a guilty expression, he rolled up the line, sliding it back in his pocket.

"Down there," Gordon pointed. "Look for a place where the water is smooth on top; that will indicate it's deeper, trout like those places. Don't make any noise or you'll frighten them away. Big hooks are not much help either, a size ten or smaller would be better for this river."

Opening his box and asking which was size ten, the

lad picked out the indicated hook and ran off happily enough. Pity they were not all like that. Recently one persistent teenager had been a nuisance, catching two of the bigger trout in spite of having been warned off several times before; totally inconsiderate of the younger children, the type on who reason and kind words were entirely wasted! Ah well, nothing ever works perfectly; into every paradise, sadly, a little evil must fall – not really evil, just selfishness. It was only to be expected; much as Adam may have suggested it was all Eve's fault, boys are not angels!

Certainly there would be proof of that over the next few weeks. As teatime approached Jan pointed up the road. "Here they come, look at them run! All three together, they must have waited at Jim's bungalow for Chris to arrive. It's about to start!"

They both knew that only too well. Friday evening; schools everywhere were closing for the summer recess. Tomorrow should be great, and tough! From 7.30 am or shortly after, both parents would be caught up in a ceaseless struggle to pitch new arrivals and satisfy the demands of those already present. Before that they must clean the toilets, prepare for the day and eat.

The children of course were delighted, knowing their help would be needed at times but excited all the same at the prospect of meeting old friends, wondering which ones would arrive and what new faces would appear. They must fend for themselves too, be left very much to their own devices including cooking breakfast unless they rose early.

***

Jan woke at 5.45am, peeping down from the bedroom window to see a yard full of caravans, the owners mostly asleep in their cars. Another pulled in five minutes later as Gordon opened the office door. He walked over, speaking in a low voice to the occupants, a couple with two children curled up on the back seat.

"We'll be a while yet. Need to clean the facilities then

have a quick breakfast. Probably won't get a chance later," a sweep of the hand indicated the other waiting caravans. "I try to avoid pitching this early, it wakes people up. Everyone here gets a good night's sleep!" The couple nodded appreciatively. Asking them to pass the information to anyone else who woke, he left.

The busy period had begun! Brief and unpredictable breaks would occur now and then, sufficient with luck to swallow a quickly drunk coffee and at sometime a snatched meal, but neither would have missed these weeks for the world! Jan opened the duck shed door, the three regular occupants made for the water, joining those that habitually slept on the river. Judy would be milked after breakfast, but the three goats required more attention; one of the children would tend them.

Stephen appeared in the kitchen having risen early, aware some friends might arrive that day. He looked at the stove, but left without eating. Sharon would be preparing something later; she would cook for him too, though he would wait for her offer, only asking if he had to. Seeing the yard full of caravans and his father moving dustbins, he took the padlock key, remembered for once to close the office door without slamming it too loudly, and headed for the shed. The goats were pleased to see him, Ivy butting a leg gently as he reached over, picking up three loose ropes for tethering then threw the door wide leaving them to run free. In spite of hay in the shed, they were hungry for greenery and ran after him, stripping mouthfuls of bramble from hedges as they passed. Goats did not bark trees when they were hungry, he knew that. Later, having satisfied their immediate appetite, they would gnaw at such delicacies if allowed to run free, but for the moment they were safe. Leading them round to the west side, walking away from the morning sun and into bluebell wood provided brambles in abundance; the bluebells were long over but their leaves still carpeted the floor. He pushed some vegetation aside to penetrate deeper, calling softly to Olive who had stopped to munch near a fallen trunk. As the ground began to rise, he reached a particular tree, clambering and swinging his body upward onto a rough wooden platform well above the ground; the tree house, a place built by Chris and Sharon several years before when he was still only four, unable to climb without help. Chris never came here now, not since he started at senior school, nor Sharon either, concerned about her dress probably, though she could still climb as quickly when she wished. He had somehow inherited ownership; it was his place now, somewhere to be alone, at least early in the morning. Some of his friends knew of it if they came back this year, but few would wake at this time. Climbing down again, Stephen led the goats back, making for the riverbank across a flat area of sparse grass, then ran upstream towards the house. Judy must be milked after breakfast; finding somewhere conveniently near, he tethered all three within sight of each other but not close enough to become tangled. Chris would find them a better place later.

Sharon was alone in the kitchen when he arrived back. "Where have you been?" Stephen didn't reply; she had guessed anyway. "Do you want an egg?"

He shrugged. "All right."

She reached in the cupboard for another, expecting no show of gratitude, and crossed to the stove breaking it into the pan. Stephen took a slice of bread and disappeared through the doorway.

"Don't be long!"

The lad must have heard but there was no response. One was not expected. The ducks were in a huddle farther along the bank. Seeing him and guessing his intention they tumbled into the water some distance down-river as he hurried to the bridge, casting a handful of small pieces quickly on the stream. These were not intended for the muscovys; they would never be fast enough, the scraps would disappear far too soon. He saw with surprise the bread drifting on untouched until reached by the oncoming ducks. Taking aim, he cast a single piece, then another on the surface below, targeting open spaces away from the ducks, fooling them by switching suddenly from one side of the river to the other, all the while staring intently into the clear water. Returning to the house he entered the kitchen to find the family all there, most now seated round the table, eating.

"About time!" Sharon stood by the stove, one hand on her hip. "I gave yours to Chris but these are ready." She took the pan to the table and flipped an egg onto his plate. "You want beans with it?"

At a small nod, she fetched another saucepan and ladled some with a wooden spoon, emptying the rest on her own plate with the other egg. Jan's warning finger elicited from Stephen a mumbled, "Thanks."

For an interval they ate quickly, without words, a habit borne of constant interruptions at mealtimes. With the food rapidly diminishing, odd questions were asked and answered, mainly concerning the coming day, the conversation intermittent but necessary; there would be little time for chat later.

"The fish are gone." Stephen spoke without emphasis, continuing to eat, scraping up a final forkful of beans.

"What do you mean the fish are gone?" Sharon demanded.

He ignored her question, finishing the beans before flicking a glance under his eyebrows at the surrounding faces, deliberately pursing lips tightly closed and looking down again at the plate. Sharon swung to her mother, aglow with indignation. She wanted to know!

Jan watched Stephen. Was that a grin on his face? How different her children were. Sharon could never have contained herself until the meal was almost finished before imparting such news; she would have come in shouting it to everyone. Stephen caught his mother's eye, the stern expression made it clear he must tell.

"No fish this morning. Not one. All gone."

Swallowing a last mouthful, Chris put his hands on the table to rise, looked across at Jan and seeing her nod, scrambled from his chair and dashed for the door. The rest followed, Gordon grabbing a slice of bread as they left. Two minutes on the bridge confirmed Stephen's discovery was true. So far as could be seen, not a single fish remained. Pity, but there was no time to worry, the caravans were waiting. Only at mid-morning when a break in arrivals allowed the Suggestion Box in the telephone kiosk to be opened, was the mystery solved. The top message, a small dog-eared slip of paper, written untidily in childish print revealed the fish's fate.

"*You was a meen old burger so I took them fish what were under that brige. I aint comin back.*"

A name was scribbled at the bottom. Jan hastily examined the daybook; the boy, almost a young man, caught several times fishing in that section. He should leave that morning the book said; probably already gone. Good!

"One of my failures," Gordon waved a hand in disappointment. "They were so tame, anyone could catch them. Wonder when he did it? The trout were there yesterday, must have been late evening, or very early today, it's light about five. Damn shame for the younger children. More should come back eventually, but not very quickly."

There was little time to brood, a truly enormous motor-caravan, longer than some coaches, appeared along the track. As it approached the bridge another caravan came into sight some distance behind. This could be trouble! The bridge had plenty of width but the track ran beside the stream then turned on an arc to cross it.

"Don't let it stick," Jan thought as the vehicle slowed. If the crossing proved too tight and it had to go back, there was nowhere to turn for half a mile. Could the driver reverse that far? What about the caravan behind, and how many more would be coming down the track by then? But the driver was competent, it should have been expected, he would hardly have chosen such a monster otherwise. It crossed with inches to spare and drew up in the yard.

"Jan, book in the other caravan," Gordon called across. "Don't think we can take this one. I'll talk to the driver."

He strode across to the big machine, trying to think of a suitable place. It would have to be hardstanding, for although the weather was dry, the thin soil layers were compacted enough by car tyres without adding this sort of weight to the problem. Really, there was no suitable place. A man came round the corner carrying a gas bottle and stopped close by, regarding the vehicle.

"Phew. Make a great removal van." He shouted up to the face at the high window, "How many gallons does it take to the mile?"

The man above shook his head, "Miles to the gallon you mean. It's not bad, nearly twenty." He turned, asking, "You've a pitch for us?"

"Sorry, hang on a minute." Gordon called across the yard, "Chris! Change a gas bottle please," and seeing a hand lifted in acknowledgement, signalled the man to follow. Swinging back he addressed the driver again. "You're too big. I'd only put something that size on hardstanding but it wouldn't be fair to the next pitch. Out of season maybe, but not now."

"We just need one night, could I pay for two pitches?"

Another caravan was already drawing across the bridge; it would not be easy to turn this big one round now.

Gordon shrugged, "Okay, Leave it there, come and have a look first, see what you think. If it's suitable, book in at the office while I pitch the other caravans, you're never going to manoeuvre unless the yard is clear."

Fifteen minutes later the monster was in position, diagonally across the pitches, not exactly filling them for they were large, but both had been paid for anyway. It didn't matter, the man was pleased with the hard surface and extra space, and in any case others were waiting! More caravans had arrived, someone's car would not start, another lady had found a leak in her water carrier and was there a way of mending it? Someone else wanted to change pitches because a big tree they chose to be next to was now throwing a shadow in the wrong place – and as if that was not enough, the telephone started ringing again.

Late that same evening, lying in bed tired, exhausted and happy, sleep would not come. The body needed rest, wanted the release of complete oblivion, but for some contrary reason the head would not let go. Calculations trundled around inside, of caravans arriving, gas bottles, people asking help, and all the while these figures churned. How many feet of tarmac would the money buy? That man in a dark suit walking among the tents earlier; who was he? A Council Inspector checking into their planning permissions perhaps? Would he spot the deficiency? The questions kept coming. He had walked over twenty miles, been on call for more than sixteen hours, stood up for at least fourteen – "Oh, shut up brain! I need rest!"

Of course, eventually sleep came. Lying awake was exceptional, rarely a problem. Once head touched pillow at this time of year, both parents usually went out like switching off a light.

Earlier in the season, when extra caravans had suddenly begun to appear, Gordon recommenced his evening walk, covering the entire site as the light faded. These patrols had been intermittent, a few times each week, seldom more unless some complaint from a visitor indicated that all might not be well. Now, with caravans and children rapidly increasing, the late inspection was regular, every night, and it took longer. Jan waited in the office peering at intervals through the curtains, never quite sure when he would appear or what might happen in the darkness. That darkness, fortunately, was beginning to fall a touch earlier, but they seldom retired before eleven; less than seven hours before rising again, for at six next morning the toilets must be cleaned! The days were long, not strenuous like digging trenches, but always on the move, seldom a moment to truly relax, to be free of demands. Meals were eaten even more quickly. By the time darkness fell, there was a constant inclination to forget, to leave events to themselves, to lock the door and retire. After all, for the most part nothing dramatic happened on the evening rounds, any problems that did arise were mainly small. However, this temptation to let things slide was always resisted.

On most nights, pairs of visitors walking together in the twilight would offer a friendly greeting, or some group sitting beside a caravan would wave a salutation, signalling him across for a chat and the occasional glass of sherry. A few, knowing he rose early, expressed surprised to see him still about. This part was enjoyable and in a way, important. Tourists chat together and often become quite friendly, sometimes with immediate neighbours, at other times with someone met completely by chance. Discussion of the site was a typical introductory gambit used to strike up conversation when such strangers met. In this way, knowledge that the park was patrolled at night passed between visitors. From odd snatches of conversation, off the cuff remarks, notes in the suggestion box, it was clear that most visitors approved, were pleased and reassured; it may even have prompted a few to avoid such late night anti-social actions as over-loud wirelesses, shouted family arguments and the like.

Helpful though this was in maintaining the proper atmosphere of safety and order that most people expected to enjoy, such problems were only reduced not eliminated entirely. Three things in particular, required attention from time to time, and demanded a certain amount of tact. For all the apparently casual way he handled these events, Gordon found this part far from easy. The first was noise from children playing games in the dark, taking advantage of the valley's relative safety to run slightly wild, shouting loudly to each other from considerable distances. In general, this was the easiest to deal with for children are innately reasonable, not having yet developed the resentment adults sometimes feel when anything adverse is drawn to their attention. Such an incident had occurred on the previous night. Hearing shouting and finding one of those concerned, a boy, probably about twelve or in his early teens, Gordon had approached him.

"Try to find your friends please, I'd like a word with them."

After a short while a small circle of seven children, three of them girls, gathered near the second toilet building. Feeble gas light from a window partially illuminated the faces.

"Sorry to spoil the fun, but I need your help. There are quite a few babies on site, and younger children who go to bed early. Their Mum's want them to sleep so they won't be miserable in the morning. Would you mind breaking up the game now; you don't have to go in, just be real quiet. Sit on the riverbank and chat or something if you want."

The group looked at each other, one of the older girls nodded. "Sure."

"Thanks. You may notice ducks still in the river," he spoke in hushed tones. "Did you know they sleep floating in mid-stream in case of foxes? Several prefer it to being locked in the shed. Goodnight."

A chorus of quiet 'Goodnights' replied as he walked away, raising a hand in acknowledgement. That was the nicer part, when all went well and everyone was happy. Children are just younger adults and should be treated in an adult way. Good and bad in degrees like everywhere, they mostly reacted favourably to a well-reasoned request.

Other things were not always so easy, those loud radios for instance, and dogs. Even people who were good with their dogs in the daytime, occasionally pushed them out through an open door at night, not expecting anyone to notice and forgetting the mess they might leave by another doorstep. A thin leather lead carried in the pocket helped to deal with such pets. Having called the animal softly and clipped the lead to its collar, the dog would act as a guide back to its owner. Reactions were mixed, from profuse apology to deep annoyance. It was particularly difficult when the person responsible was an old customer, someone who had become a friend, and even nastier when it happened more than once. An apology could be accepted gracefully and made light of, but backing down to a belligerent response just asked for more trouble! Burying ones head in the sand, pretending not to see the dog wandering, was worse still. He had tried for a while the previous year. Amazingly quickly, dogs started to run loose everywhere, even in daytime. An avalanche of complaints from concerned mothers had resulted.

Returning one evening from a longer than usual walk round, he discussed the problem with Jan over late coffee.

"Keeping some sort of decent behaviour is so difficult. I have to force myself to speak to people; but is there any alternative? I had one tonight where the radio could be heard ten caravans away. I deliberately walked in both directions and listened. Turned out the chap is slightly deaf. I felt bad, but what do you do? Let everyone else suffer?"

"I knew there was something," she reached for his hand. "You were tense. Was he difficult, did he tone it down?"

"He was fine. But did I do right? It was nearly eleven, and there were toddlers in caravans nearby. If we stay for twenty years I shall never do this really well."

Chapter 12

Susan

The first Saturday in August saw a second wave arrive. Many from the previous weekend had already booked a fortnight and some three weeks, so those few pitches previously remaining empty were now mostly full. Foreign tents were constantly coming and going, several of the happiest accepted isolated spots beyond the developed site, places not yet prepared as proper pitches where the ground purely by chance had some semblance of flatness. Most were quite difficult to reach and suitable for only one tent, offering the compensation of being alone; real camping in the wild. These visitors were delighted, a few even rescheduled their tour to stay extra days, finding the site and the southwestern tip of Cornwall so very much to their liking. The extra pitches created over last winter were not so adequate after all; something to rectify later in the year.

A woman walked across the stony yard in bare feet, bright red nail varnish contrasting with the light tan. The Gaz bottle in one hand gave a fair indication she was staying in a tent. Several people were already in the office. Jan seeing her arrive, offered a greeting, "Be with you shortly," and continued talking to a family standing round the desk. Stephen stood to one side; he was on duty, Chris out with friends and Sharon in the kitchen. It was his job to run errands or to guard the office and help any customers if his mother had to leave temporarily. He cast an eye at the woman's feet and seeing her turn in his direction, looked away. Jan too, had noticed the feet, but had been more discreet, not making it obvious, continuing to write in the ledger, recording those extra days just paid for and giving the family their change, raising a hand to wave as they left.

"Have you one of these?" Mrs barefeet stepped forward and held up the blue cylinder.

"Certainly. Stephen, fetch a full one please; take the empty with you."

The lad moved forward to take the bottle, hesitating momentarily as he stared again at the bright red toenails, then took a firm hold and carried it to the door, glancing back as he went out.

"Your son?" the woman asked, and receiving confirmation , moved her hands, not knowing quite what to do with them. Starting to make a gesture, she reached instead into a purse for some coins. "He seems to find me er... unusual?"

Jan took the money then looked directly at the feet, "I wonder why?"

"Ah. Yes... Well we have a small problem inside our tent."

"Don't worry, when we first lived in the valley we went barefoot often, he was only three then, too young to remember. Not many people come to the office like that now, the stony surface puts them off – expect you've found that out. What went wrong with your tent? Anything we can help with?"

"It isn't wrong really. When I said a small problem, I meant small, very small, a mouse! We have one in the tent. I keep all my shoes in a box in one corner. Mostly I wear sandals, hence the varnish – new colour, bit brighter than I thought it would be – not too strong is it?" The woman glanced down, shrugged, and continued. "We went out last night, left our sons in the tent. I wore something a bit less casual, court shoes; got back late, tired, dropped them straight in the box on top of the others. This morning when we woke, one of the boys saw a little mousy head poke out.

We all went over to look thinking it would run away but it curled back up in the toe of my shoe, wrapped its body in a circle, tail round the outside, head tucked in, and just went to sleep. I've not seen one that close before. They wouldn't let me put it out, want to see if it will make a nest they say, so I can't get at any of my shoes."

"My older son Chris will move it if you like?"

"No, we're keeping it, I'm interested, never mind the shoes. Actually I do have another pair hidden away, but that's where they're staying – hidden. Jack, that's my husband, has promised new ones, we're off to the shops this morning. Whatever happens I don't want that mouse moved until then! That's why I'm barefoot, let him find out for himself what good shoes cost! Don't tell your son, he may talk to my boys."

The door opened and Stephen carried a new cylinder in, passing it to the woman who thanked him, turned to wink at Jan, and left.

"She's no shoes on?" the lad looked questioningly at his mother.

"No, she hadn't had she." Jan studied a paper on the desk.

"Why?"

"Wants a deeper tan to match that bright nail varnish."

Stephen looked at his mother for a moment, then without comment drifted through to the kitchen. Sharon was preparing lunch, a salad with eggs – it would be eaten individually, not as a family meal, each person grabbing the opportunity in any lull, the occurrence of which was totally unpredictable. Smacking her brother's hand as he reached to take a piece of chicken, she continued filling the plates, covering each with a cloth and wishing the little gas fridge was bigger, working quickly – many children had arrived, friends were waiting! Finishing and glancing round the kitchen to check everything was tidy, she made ready to leave. In the office a group of people were talking at the desk; hesitating, Sharon sought to catch her mother's eye.

“Is it ready?” Jan asked.

“Yes. I’ll be back in an hour. Okay?” Receiving a nod, Sharon opened the door, calling to two waiting friends, girls of about 11 years, her own age, who were kneeling on the riverbank surrounded by ducks. As they called back, a caravan swept round the corner from the toilet building heading out towards the bridge, its holiday over. Sharon flicked a glance in that direction, ready to wave; everyday friends were arriving, others leaving. Seeing only an elderly couple in the car, she was about to turn away when something caught her attention. Dashing forward and waving, she ran at an angle to reach the bridge first, trying to flag the vehicle down. At first it appeared that the car would drive on, but the woman inside leaned towards the driver and he drew to a halt, the car’s radiator just on the bridge, blocking the road.

A window opened. “Did you want something?”

“Your front caravan leg is still down, it’s almost touching.” Sharon pointed. Another car had already drawn up behind.

Unlocking the caravan, finding the winder and raising the leg took a few minutes, it must have hit a bump for the threads were twisted, stopping it from fully retracting but the man forced it far enough to be safe. Several cars were now waiting. He put the tool away, locking the door, stopped to say “Thank you young lady,” and hurriedly drove off allowing the traffic to clear.

Sharon returned to her friends who had stood on the bank, surprised by her instant action. Around their feet slept the ducks. None had bothered to stir when the girls rose, nor did they move as the three bent again to stroke them before moving off to sit talking on the bank nearby until it was time for the meal.

The following day lunch was hot, not anything special but maybe the only proper lunch of the week; a joint effort, Sharon and her mother working together, though

Jan was constantly popping away as the office doorbell called. However, at 12.30, Gordon hung a roughly scrawled sign by the bellpush, "*Having Sunday Lunch. Open again at 1.00pm. Do ring if you are dying!!!*"

For five minutes they ate in silence but conversation soon sprang up, nobody waiting to empty their mouth before speaking; such refinements were for those with time on their hands.

"What will you do if someone does ring the bell?" Chris asked.

"Send you out to tell them we're full?" Jan phrased the reply as a question.

"Um?" Gordon considered the suggestion. "Perhaps I should have fixed a plastic bucket full of water hanging outside the bedroom window above the office door, with a rope over a series of pulleys, the end hanging down here." He reached out and pulled the imaginary cord, eyes swinging to the ceiling, startled, throwing hands above his head in imitation of a customer drowned by the water.

Little heads nodded, smiling together. Sharon, catching Chris's eye, looked quickly away throwing her head in the air and sniffing loudly.

"Trouble?" Jan asked.

"I'm not talking to my brother," Sharon had adopted a haughty tone she used sometimes, but was fighting to keep a straight face.

"Why?" Jan turned to Chris, surprised to find him embarrassed, cheeks reddening as he looked down, concentrating on the meal. Sharon's smile was open now, delighted with her success and with the attention it brought.

"Well, he shouldn't steal things!"

"Steal things?" Jan was mystified, for both her older children were grinning, though Chris's colour still showed. Stephen continued to eat and listen.

"Yes. Steal things. I had something very special, and he took it away!"

"Took what away?"

"Susan, that's what he took away. I shan't introduce him in future. My friends wanted to meet the boys, so I took them across to Chris and his pals. My special friend Susan, she's a bit older than me and kind of… well… grown up; her hair is sort of special. We were all talking together and suddenly *my brother* is walking off with my best friend!" Sharon stopped, looking at Chris, putting him on the spot, raising a hand to her mouth to smother a giggle.

Chris, finding himself the centre of attention, turned away, moving an arm in a half gesture of protest, "Well… I… She wanted to learn to fish!"

"Is that why you wandered off talking together along the riverbank? Why couldn't you have shown her by the bridge?"

"Er… You know the trout don't bite when there's noise and people." All the family, including Chris himself chuckled at this neatly reasoned answer, but Sharon had not finished. She pointed a finger, speaking with triumph, certain of winning the point.

"How come you didn't stop to fetch fishing gear! And don't say it was in your pocket, I know you never carry line and hooks normally!"

"Ah… Well, Susan didn't actually want to catch any, she's sensitive, thinks it's cruel. She just wanted me to tell her how it's done, show her the sort of places where trout might hide. So of course, naturally we had to walk farther down."

"Oh naturally. Susan's *so* sensitive! Oh dear!" The tone was exaggerated, mocking. Seeing Chris's colour rise Sharon paused glowing. "Thinks it too, too cruel, does she?" Again the derisive tone, before a jubilant final demand, thumping one small hand on the table. "Then why does she want to know how? Tell me that!"

For a moment Chris sat, stumped, aware that his parents were watching though neither had spoken. Vainly he searched for a plausible explanation.

"She wants to borrow my line, tie bread to the end without a hook, and see how tame they will get."

"Brilliant!" Sharon leaned forward forgetting herself, putting one elbow on the table, chin cupped in her palm. "Just as you went out of sight, didn't I see you holding her hand?"

"No! How could you see if we were out of sight? It's possible I was showing her how to grip the rod. Probably go down this evening to try, trout feed best at dawn and dusk as you know. I wanted to fish with the boys, but I'd better go and help Susan, see that she gets the hang of it; after all, she is my sister's best friend."

"Dad found something today," Jan interrupted, feeling the matter had reached an evenly balanced climax and what had been fun might well go sour if continued. "Look at this, a foreign coin. Someone used it in the telephone. Although we empty the box, the money goes to the phone company; we shall be paying for this! Anyone know what it is?" She rolled it to the table centre.

Sharon grabbed at the coin, inspected it shaking her head, then passed it to Chris.

"Dutch?" Chris offered it to his mother

"Looks more French. What makes you think it's Dutch?"

"We get millions of Dutch visitors."

"Millions?" Sharon jumped in quickly

"Well… Thousands anyway, hundreds at least. You wouldn't know, probably think Holland is in Yorkshire."

"*I know* where Holland is, it's where the tulips grow…"

"Hold on you two!" Jan stepped in. "A clever thought, we do get more Dutch people than any other nationality."

"Oh, he's always clever – bet Susan thinks so." Sharon muttered half under her breath.

"She probably does but let's drop it Sharon." Jan flipped the coin over. "Whatever this is, the value must be low, nobody would use it in the phone otherwise."

"Can I have it then?" Stephen had taken no part in the

conversation up to this point, and even now spoke in a low voice.

His mother tossed it over, seeing him catch and slide it into a pocket. "What do you want it for?"

Stephen made no reply, glancing up once under his eyebrows, then looked deliberately away.

Jan sighed. No chance now that he would tell. He seldom asked for anything; what could he want with a useless coin? Something different to show his friends probably.

The bell rang. Fifteen minutes had passed since they sat down but it spite of the chatter, the food was gone! Gordon hurried to the office, Jan rising to follow. A woman at the door wanted matches, she had arrived an hour earlier in a hired motorcaravan and had expected the gas to light automatically like her stove at home. While she explained at length the hired vehicle's differences and shortcomings, another caravan drew into the yard, three more approaching the bridge. The matches were quickly found, a new box, and passed to the lady.

"How much?"

"Nothing. If you happen to be in town shopping, buy me another for the next caravanner in need, but it really doesn't matter."

"Oh, thank you." The lady left, walking away.

Jan followed to the door, removing the sign, waving it at Gordon. "Didn't work very well, I don't think she even saw it. Hardly an emergency – matches. What's this about giving them away free?" She spoke with a touch of criticism, looking out as the other three caravans parked in the yard. "Thought we were all supposed to be stingy until we've saved up to tarmac that road!"

"I've got a generous nature."

"You...!" Jan stopped, lost for words. Outside, people were climbing from cars to huddle in a group, deep in conversation. A dog stuck its head from one window. This could be difficult. "They're together, you'll have to book them all in first then take the lot at once. I'll be in the kitchen." She left.

Eight people walked towards the office, three children and the dog remaining in the cars. Gordon opened the door, waiting for them.

"Can you fix us up?" a man asked. "Four caravans, three with awnings."

"Not together, you'll be lucky to find four together anywhere in August without booking. How long did you want."

"Just tonight to start with, until we get our bearings. If we stay longer could we move together then?"

"Not the red car, we have a separate area for dogs; it's near the river walk. The other three, possibly, I'd have to check who's leaving. Come and see before you decide." Receiving a nod, Gordon led the group away. This preview was not normally offered but with four caravans it seemed advisable. Besides there were other points he needed to discuss that would come better while they viewed the pitches.

Two places, side by side near bluebell wood were quickly accepted, a warning given that these pitches lost the sun in late evening raised no difficulties. The next was not so near as they would have liked, for all the closer pitches were full; in fact, few on the whole site were empty. When they gathered in front of the final pitch on the area reserved for canine visitors, Gordon put his other conditions, speaking to the dog owners first.

"You can't take the dog when visiting your friends, that's the first thing. I've promised mothers that those areas are dog free." He waited, seeing the man frown then a nod of agreement. "Another thing; obviously you'll want to get together in the evenings. Could you leave your cars on your own pitches please. A big party like yours can make life difficult for neighbours; do what you can to help. That's all. Come back to the office; I'll book you in, then give a hand with the pitching."

"We can pitch ourselves. We will be able to stay longer if we want to?"

"You can stay to October provided no one books the space before you do. Look around, there are hardly any left. About the pitching; I'm sure you *could* handle it alone, but humour me, I need to check the spacing for fire regulations. Put your questions while we manoeuvre the caravans: which way is sunrise, where do the TV signals come from, are all the taps drinking water, which are the best beaches? – all the things people usually ask."

Seeing the shortage of spaces on the way back to the office, they decided to pay for a week immediately. Naturally, when it came to pitching, the two who were sited together wanted their awnings facing each other. Fine, the first caravan quickly parked where indicated but when Gordon paced out eleven steps they protested. "We wanted to be close together!"

"Park it where I say, then when your awnings go up, there will be the correct six-metre space." Seeing the frowns, Gordon tried again. "Look, give me three markers and I'll show you."

The lady from the first caravan leaned inside and produced three plastic mugs. One was placed where the second caravan's jockey wheel must be, and the other two where the awnings would come. "Okay, that should give a gap of seven paces. Watch!" Gordon stepped out the distance and found half a pace short. "Six-and-a-half, near enough. Now, you two are together, so very likely the others will visit you in the evenings. Right? Well then, you're going to need at least this space to sit in. Agreed?"

They were happy now. He went away to pitch the others. It was soon done, for both were good at reversing. When Gordon returned to join the family seated again at the table, Jan addressed the children.

"Your father just gave a box of matches free to a woman from a motorcaravan."

"Cheek! I can't have a new dress!" Sharon glared at

Dad, awaiting his reply.

"I told her that if she's in town, she can buy me another box for the next caravanner who needs help." He waved a hand as if that made it okay.

"And if she doesn't go to town, or if she forgets?" Jan asked.

"Matches are cheap, only a few pence. I said not to worry."

Jan leaned towards the children, mischief in her face. "You know what Dad said to me in the office? He said *'I've got a generous nature*!' Can you believe that?"

"Mum!" Sharon stared with incredulity.

"We should have a vote," Jan suggested, confident of getting full support, lifting her own hand as she spoke. "Who says Dad should not be more generous to other people than he is to us?"

Two other hands immediately rose in support but Chris sat still, looking from one parent to the other, obviously uneasy but not raising his arm.

"Chris!" Sharon prodded him, but he shook his head.

"Why?" Jan was surprised; usually all the children supported her against Gordon, it was almost a tradition. She had hoped to create some family fun.

Chris drew in a breath, aware that everyone round that table was waiting. "You said it was a motorcaravan..."

"What difference does that make?" Sharon demanded, banging a small fist unconsciously on the table, not heavily but with righteous indignation, angry with her brother for breaking the normal custom. Jan glanced at her daughter, the expression warning not to interrupt again as all eyes turned back to Chris.

"Motorcaravans are different because most book one night at a time. They don't know themselves where they may end up next day or whether they'll come back. This woman will be pleased that we gave her the matches, it will make her feel better about the site..." Chris paused, working out how best to express his thoughts. "More than that, Dad said to replace it if she could for the next visitor who might need help. Even though she doesn't have to do it, she'll feel obliged. She's grateful we helped her and wouldn't want the next person not to be helped because she didn't return the matches. That's more important than you think!"

Dad was smiling, nodding, but he said nothing. Chris waited for someone to ask why. He really hoped it would be his sister but he must not let her see what he wanted. The pause lengthened and in the end Sharon could not resist, she charged in challenging him, still annoyed and with every sign of disbelief.

"Why? If she doesn't bring them we lose, if she does, we gain nothing. What's so important about that?!"

"Where would she get them?" Chris asked.

"In town probably."

"That would have to be tomorrow, most shops are closed now. In that case she will have to come here again tomorrow to give them back. That will mean another night's fee worth a thousand matches!" Chris punched a fist in the air in triumph, gloating over his sister's defeat.

"Hm!" Sharon's face coloured as grins passed round the table, eyes swinging in her direction. "Well... he's exaggerating again. Worth a thousand... Hm!"

"I'm not so sure. Toss me those matches Stephen." Jan pointed to a box on the sideboard, caught them and read the packet. "Average content thirty five. Now site fees average just under a pound, and a box of matches... two pence I paid for the last one. How many is that?" She held out a hand, passing the calculation over to Gordon.

"Er... say forty boxes with thirty-five matches in each. Now, half the forty and double the thirty-five, do it again; that's ten by one hundred and forty. Easy. One thousand four hundred matches for one night's stay. So he wasn't exaggerating."

A good deal of merriment followed at Sharon's expense, Chris being particularly jubilant, having won in every direction. Seeking to protect her daughter and divert the attention back to Dad, Jan leaned forward, whispering a question.

"You know what I think?" she paused, "I believe your father realised about that extra night right from the start!"

The family turned to find Gordon smiling quietly.

"Like I use flies to catch trout?" Chris asked, but his father gazed casually through the window, not replying, the smile still on his face. A ring at the office door saved him from further interrogation.

"He did know, Mum." Sharon insisted when Dad left. "I hope it doesn't come back now!"

"Do you really? Every extra visitor puts a bit more towards surfacing that road, and once that's done, guess what?" Jan held out a hand inviting an answer, continuing when Sharon shook her head. "You get a complete new outfit then. I shall insist!"

"Can I choose it?" Receiving a nod of confirmation from her mother, the young girl beamed with happiness. "Well, I hope it comes back, but if it does and Dad's out, hide it so he doesn't know!"

The following day it did return. Jan, following Sharon's suggestion, sited it quickly in an almost hidden corner, but the ruse failed.

"I see that motorcaravan came back again," Gordon commented as the family sat down at tea later. "Why has it changed position?"

"They asked for somewhere more private." Jan fibbed while the children looked down, hiding their faces. Dad nodded, lifting his cup to drink as she spoke again. "The woman brought your matches back. I thanked her and said you'd left instructions that she was to have the night free for being so honest!"

"Whssss!" Gordon twisted choking into the corner; the coffee already in his mouth going down the wrong way. It was some time before he recovered, time in which the children turned to Mum in delight and amazement. They had all been in the lounge and seen her take the woman's money.

"You let her in free?" Dad gasped, still trying to clear his throat.

"She was ever so grateful," Jan smiled. "I told her you were like that – had a generous nature!"

Audrey, Jan's Mum up at the bungalow in Relubbus where the track to the site left the tarmac road, also felt the effect of greater numbers. Visitors bringing in ice packs for the chest freezer in her garage had reached almost unmanageable proportions; some brought several, expecting three or even four to be frozen each day. Finding any particular pack among so many was no easy task. She had started to refuse those that were not clearly labelled, offering a marker pen and making visitors write their name clearly on every item. Even so, the lid was now opened too frequently and stayed open so long each time while searching for the correct name, that packs were no longer freezing in one day.

"Jim, we need another chest freezer, one is not enough, some blocks are still soft when people collect them the day after. One man was quite rude me this morning."

"Who? Let me at him tomorrow!" Jim struggled to his feet.

"Don't worry, I put him in his place. Went away with his tail down, probably send his wife tomorrow. Anyway, he was in his thirties, what would you do against a younger man?"

"Kick him straight in the goo… where it hurts most!" Jim grinned, reaching for his walking stick.

"You're not boxing for the army now, those years have long gone. We're supposed to please the customers, not cripple them. Anyway, most are nice, we never had so many visitors for coffee back in London. Half of them drink whisky with you; don't be so touchy. I can handle any grumpy ones. What shall we do about ice packs? It's having the lid open so much that causes half the trouble."

"Charge ten pence a go, put it in a tin towards a new freezer. Any that stay soft can be free. Stick a few in our fridge, we don't use the ice cube compartment."

"Ten pence will probably stop some bringing so many too," Audrey nodded agreement, "Perhaps if we ask people to mark the packs more clearly with bigger letters, I'll find them quicker, but young Stephen has run off with my marker pen. I told him to bring it straight back. If he knew what I'm thinking his ears would burn!"

But Stephen was blissfully unaware, half a mile away downstream, the borrowed marker long forgotten. He stood waiting in the hall as a group of people were talking to his mother on the doorstep. They came from two caravans that had drawn up near the office. Carefully the young lad opened the basement door, slid through and closed it behind himself. There was a light switch on the wall, but he descended the stairs in darkness, using his hands to follow the walls round and along two corridors before switching on a light in the workroom.

Extracting the foreign coin from one pocket, he moved to the bench, clamping it in the big vice. Reaching for a hand-drill hanging from the wall, he pulled it free and hunted for a suitably sized steel bit. A hole quickly drilled near the coin's outer edge was small, barely sufficient for a needle to pass, but adequate for the intended purpose. He had wanted to make such a hole in a penny the week before, but Chris said it was wrong to damage coins of the realm, treason to deform the Queen's head. That had sounded bad but this coin had no Queen, that was why he asked for it; not to use now, but later when the evenings were not so light.

Darkness was already falling earlier, only a little each night, but noticeable. Numbers held steady during the first weeks in August, they could scarcely go higher for there were no more pitches, but no one was actually refused; no one, that is, other than a party of young lads 'looking for action' as they put it. In spite of difficulties with ice packs, it was a contented site. Although nothing special was done to attract children, all those that did come seemed happy enough, forming small groups, finding sufficient in the valley without the need for more artificial amusements. Chris had been very quiet one morning, staying in the house, rather listlessly.

"Susan left last night," Sharon whispered to her mother, "My friends say he's lovesick. Do you think he is?"

"No." Jan spoke automatically, thinking him much too young at not quite thirteen, then paused wondering, trying to remember herself at that age. "Just a normal close friendship; don't you miss friends when they leave?"

"I suppose; but some of my friends are Chris's age, they say things sometimes."

"What sort of things?"

"Nothing, just things." Sharon turned away, obviously uncomfortable.

The office doorbell rang; it always did at the wrong moments. Jan strode quickly along the corridor to find Chris entering the office and a lady in jeans with a towel over her arm standing by the doorway.

"One of your showers is blocked, there's water two inches deep on the floor. It was dry when I started, but just built up. I did nothing different?"

It sounded like an apology, but was not necessarily her fault. Jan was on the point of saying "Thank you for letting us know," when Chris spoke.

"I can fix it Mum."

"You can?"

"Yes, Dad showed me. That plastic waste pipe which takes the shower water away; there's a trap in it, a section that bends down then up again to stop smells getting back. Things lodge there. I know how to dismantle and clean it."

"You're being brave, working in the Ladies?"

"No, it's inside the service passage where it doesn't show. The toilets can still be used and the Gents side isn't affected, but you'll have to stop people using the ladies basins and showers while I clear it."

Jan checked through the window, counting three caravans in the yard. Gordon was off showing a tent round and would be back soon to guide them to other pitches, but that meant he would be tied up for a while. She glanced across the field, wondering if Sharon was around before asking, "Will it take long?"

"Dad cleared the last one in under four minutes, we timed it. A lady's hair grip had jammed in the bend, a wad of hair collected around it; but I need the tools first." Chris hurried off towards the basement.

"Could I help?" The lady asked. "I can stand outside and tell people to use the other building."

"Do you mind, that really would be a help. It's difficult for me to leave the office..." The phone started ringing. "See what I mean?" Jan shrugged, "Thanks." She reached over and lifted the receiver.

Life was hectic; constant changeovers, visitors arriving and leaving, others asking for help, wanting advice or gas bottles or mantles for their lights, a whirl of activity; but considering all this the site ran smoothly enough. Little hiccups like the blocked shower pipe were bound to occur, some people even used wads of toilet paper to plug the outlet, deliberately creating a pool to soak their feet while showering. When the paper softened and pressure built up, that temporary plug washed down the pipe. No great problem, the facilities had been designed to make every pipe accessible, every drain easy to rod and unblock. The slightly sloping floor took away any water that did spill to another drain point, dripping taps could be replaced in minutes with spare ones and the washers replaced later at leisure. Even in this busy period and with no outside help whatsoever, nothing was allowed to remain in less than top condition for more than a few minutes once it was discovered or brought to the family's attention. And yet, few of the visitors ever gave this matter a thought. It was no less than they expected. None remarked on the closers that automatically shut the doors silently, without a bang to wake them in the night; none noticed the nylon hinges on every cubicle door that would not squeak or rust. Even the extra toilet rolls handily stored behind the downpipe in case the one on the holder ran out raised no remark. People were happy, one could say delighted without exaggerating – with the facilities, the site, and the pitches – but few ever wondered why. The only things that did raise regular comment were the dog hitches low on the toilet building walls that Stephen had suggested years before. They were actually drawer handles, an old cast iron type, and gave the impression of being there to lift the building.

However, nothing is perfect, some new problem would always appear! Jan returned from topping up toilet rolls shortly after lunch one afternoon.

"How do they use so many? That's fifteen more since this morning!"

"Which side takes the most, Ladies or Gents?" Gordon asked.

"The Ladies, always."

"Thought so. Pinching them for their make up. Still, you females need it far more than we do! Chaps are so thoroughly reliable. Why can't a woman be more like a man?" He jumped back quickly out of range as an arm shot out.

"I'll 'ave you 'enry 'iggins!" She faced him, one small bunched fist held out in front. "It may have escaped your notice but ladies naturally use more; they're built differently."

"Tell me about it."

"You've forgotten? So that's why you fall asleep directly your head touches the pillow this week!" Jan thumped the table, beaming with success. She had won; there was no answer to that! They stood looking at each other; pleased as always with the little duel. Gordon offered a bow of defeat and pulled her to him, kissing with a great show of passion. “I’ll try harder!”

“Save your energy, someone’s bent the shower head in the Gents first cubicle again. Saw it while topping up the toilet rolls. Why don’t you write it in the daybook, like a diary of faults? We might work out who’s doing it if they’re staying a long time.”

“And if we find out, what then? Another job for me I suppose?” He drew himself up, pointing at an imaginary visitor, “‘You, Sir, are a vandal; kindly don’t do it again.’ Then what do I do? Strike him with a glove and say ‘Pistols at dawn!’ No, I don’t think so! But after the season I do intend to fix those heads so they can’t be moved. Then I won’t need to speak to anyone.”

“Oh yes? What will you use this time?”

“Something appropriate, it’s got to blend in – but strong of course.”

“Of course. Ten tons of concrete and half a mile of armoured steel be enough?”

August was passing, ten days to go, but the site still hummed with activity. The evenings were darker now. A group of small children, most around seven years old and mainly boys, stood quiet but excited, hidden by bushes behind the second toilet building. In their midst crouched Stephen, one hand on the stepladder which earlier in the day he had surreptitiously removed from the service passage while his mother was busy with the midday cleaning. She had taken a brush and bucket of materials, leaving the door unlocked and hurried off to start work. Stephen, hidden and waiting for the opportunity, had run forward, pushed open the door again and struggled out with the ladder, dragging it to the concealment of wild vegetation behind the house. He had returned quickly, taking the spare broom, hoping neither object would be missed.

Now, as darkness fell, the small band stood in the shadows, whispering, checking the coast was clear. Stephen no longer carried the load; that job had been delegated to two other lads. At a signal, they ran awkwardly forward, erecting the steps in front of the duck shed door then raced back to join their comrades. More whispered plans were interrupted by an adult walking towards the bridge, causing them to crouch lower in silence, small eyes following, watching intently. The man veered left, strolling off downstream along the river path. As he passed from sight, two of the children, one carrying the spare broom, sped off to the far side of the building, the side where visitors entered and left the toilets.

For a moment there was silence again; then three boys ran forward. Two grabbed the ladder, steadying it, while Stephen quickly mounted to stand on the top step. Too short! Placing one foot on the apex of the triangle formed by the sides, he pushed upwards, grasping the low roof edge, the pair below struggling to hold the legs steady. Heaving upward again, his small figure stood on the duck shed roof, momentarily outlined against the faint gaslight glow from a high Ladies window. Then the silhouette was gone, clambering onto the main roof low down near the eaves and running up the slope, dark clothing hidden against the tiles. A small head poked carefully over the ridge line, turning right and left, cautiously checking. Below lay the road, and beyond that a group of trees. One boy dispatched earlier, clung almost invisible in the branches. A movement below caught Stephen's attention. His head ducked, shoes slipping on the sloping surface; one hand grasped desperately for the ridge tile, the arm extending to full stretch as feet scrabbled for grip.

For a moment he hung, body flat on the tiles, then rose slowly, eyes again coming level with the ridge to peer cautiously over. What had moved? Only the boy with the broom stirred in the shadow, otherwise the stony track lay deserted. Heaving up to sit astride the ridge, Stephen slid one hand into a pocket, producing a reel of fishing line, 'borrowed' from Chris's tackle box – only he had forgotten to mention it to his brother.

“Catch!” He threw the end, weighted with a lead sinker; it flew through the air. The reel, held on a pencil, whizzed round paying out line. Below, the waiting lad made a grab, draped it over the broom and hoisted up to his friend in the tree. A small hand reached out from the branches, seized the fine nylon thread, climbed as high as he dare and secured it. “Right!”

On the call Stephen took up the slack and eased down the roof, careful not to lose his footing again, following the same route back to the ladder and down, unwinding extra line until he stood once more, firmly on the ground. Quickly, those holding the stepladder moved it part way along the same roof edge. Stephen followed, ascending the steps to eaves level, measured roughly and used his teeth to bite through the plastic line. Threading it round a gutter bracket, pulling taut and tying it tightly, he glanced down at Chris’s almost empty fishing reel still in his hand, then turned at a soft warning call from below. Someone approached up the riverbank! The reel slid into a pocket as three small figures dropped to lay low behind the Cornish hedge. Operation stage one was complete!

A woman passed by, walking away towards the tents on the rear field. All clear! Stage two was underway. A low whistle brought a flood of small children from the waiting bush, one running on ahead to scout the corner. This group quickly joined the pair waiting on the access side of the toilet building, all grouping round as Stephen produced a reel of black cotton and the foreign coin which earlier in the month had been drilled with a tiny hole near one edge. Threading cotton through the hole and tying several knots, he laid out ample slack and threw it upward towards the fishing line now suspended high above. It failed to reach.

“More slack.” The boy who had climbed the tree, bigger and more muscular, picked it up and threw again, feet leaving the ground with a mighty heave. The coin flew over, falling to dangle above their heads. Reaching up, it was grabbed and pulled down to lay just clear of the Ladies door, the group retiring into the bushes, unwinding more cotton on the way. They reached their hiding place none too soon.

A woman walked up, pushed the door and entered. They crouched patiently, whispering. In a few minutes the door opened and the woman stepped out; Stephen gave a sharp pull, immediately letting the cotton go slack. Lighting was dim at ground level but the dropping coin clinked unmistakably. The woman stopped. What had she lost? The small silver disk was barely visible but she peered more closely then bent reaching out. At that moment the cotton moved again, the coin jerking four feet out into the roadway. Foiled in the act of picking it up, she leaned forward fingers outstretched, but the coin spun away. This time it lay more visible where light shone directly through the glass. She lunged, determined, but the coin hopped from under her grasp – rising clear as her hand slapped down on the dusty road, seen in a brief glint of reflected light as it flew off to be lost in the dark foliage beyond. Mystified, she stood up, looking this way and that. A faint snigger caught her attention, then a childish whisper. Crossing the road she pushed the bushes aside, stepping back quickly as a storm of laughing children dashed by in every direction.

It took time to locate the coin again when the woman had gone, but they persevered, then settled down to wait, setting their trap for another victim.

People came to the office next morning with strange tales. News of the incident spread across the site, but the steps had been used again to remove the fishing line and no evidence could be found. No one thought to check the stepladder and if they had it would have been too late, for Stephen had risen early, slipping it back soon after 6am while his parents were busy with the morning cleaning.

Another day passed before Jan learned the full details. One young boy had let something slip, and under questioning by his family the whole story came out. Jan, having listened in fascination to a second-hand account by the lad's mother, challenged Stephen at tea. He said nothing, just sat, a little satanic grin on his face beneath a mop of curly tousled hair, but no words forthcoming.

"It's no good you clamming up, I know all the details. One of the other mothers told me; said you climbed up the roof. Did you?" Jan watched her son's lips purse together, that wicked grin breaking through again as he looked back at her saying nothing. A good spanking was really needed but she felt an unaccountable urge to cuddle him. "Now I know why you wanted that silver coin, you planned this weeks ago! Whoever gave you the idea?"

"Dad did." Sharon accused. "He told us once of something that happened years ago when he worked in London, about a Polish friend of his who did it as a child, in Warsaw I think it was. Threw black string over telegraph lines and stood on the other side of the street."

"I might have known Dad was behind it." Jan turned accusingly as the family laughed together, but a ring on the doorbell cut the merriment short.

Although site numbers were reducing, the welcome but tiring stream of arriving visitors continued, sending the family or rather the parents, to bed that night, as every night, near the end of their reserves.

"We are doing well," Jan commented, snuggling nearer, contentedly happy at the upturn in fortunes. Feeling pressure from his hand on her shoulder, she twisted onto her side. They were both lying naked, the rooms in the roof hot in the summer night. The hand slid down her back pulling forwards until she lay against and slightly over him, one leg resting between his, and he reached to kiss her. After a while their lips parted.

"Don't tell me you've still got the energy?"

"Not really," he lay back with a sigh, his hand on her back relaxing. "Just like you near me."

"I can feel that!"

"Take no notice. Bits of me get over optimistic sometimes," he dragged his mind back to the subject she had raised. "Like you say, we are doing well, but certain things still need improvement. The dust-clouds that follow cars; even with the better season, no way can we afford tarmac yet. We need more water points too, and more pitches for campers. Did you notice how much the proportion of tents has increased in mid-season? Losing them would really hurt if the Council should find out. People do seem happy though; gives you a good feeling when their faces, what they say, how they behave, tells you they're really pleased."

"They ought to be happy, the way we work to give them a good holiday. But you get very depressed if things go wrong. I don't mean plumbing or anything like that, but when you have to choose between two people; who is right and who wrong. You take too much on yourself, trying to make everything perfect."

"Didn't realise it showed so much."

"It doesn't to other people. Some of them think you don't care, but I know you better." She leaned forward to kiss him again. "No good blaming yourself if other people make a noise and keep neighbours awake at night. You do what you can. I'll bet not many site owners walk round every night to check on things."

No one spoke for a while. They lay together, he gently rubbing a hand over her back again, up and down between her shoulder blades as she lay pliant and relaxed, enjoying the pleasurable sensation.

"The children are mixing better this year," Jan spoke softly, as if the boys in the room across the stairway might hear. "Chris and Sharon particularly. I think they deliberately bring their groups together now. Chris undeniably likes meeting the lasses, and Sharon knows he does; he's very polite to them. I think she gets a certain standing with the other girls, particularly the ones who are a little older, by introducing them to Chris and his friends. Stephen moves with the younger children, he never seems to be in charge like Chris but I think he's the one who leads them astray. Little devil, up on that roof, making women chase coins. Your fault!"

"Not my fault. Anyway, shows enterprise. You liked it too, I was watching your face, a proud Mum pretending disapproval to her naughty son."

"Perhaps?" Jan smiled. "What would you have me do, let him see I'm pleased? It was just a prank, not destructive, not something to hurt anyone; quite well organised really. I didn't think to check the stepladder when the woman first told me but I slipped out later to see; it was there, exactly where it should be. Young boys do that sort of thing, his friends are mostly boys now, only one or two bring sisters. A few years ago he didn't care, but this year girls are out unless they're very tomboyish. That's one of the few things he doesn't envy in Chris, his tolerance of girls. I don't suppose you even noticed."

"No, can't say I have – but I expect you are right."

"Off course I'm right, aren't I always?"

"Neve…" He drew in a gasp, a small warm hand had suddenly reached out and… What a hell of a way to win an argument! Suddenly he had forgotten exactly what it was they were discussing. Leaning back in the darkness, he knew for absolute certain the laugh that would be on her face at the effectiveness of the action.

In the morning both were late rising; six-fifteen already! They threw on clothes and dashed out to clean before most people were about.

Late August saw numbers decrease further, caravans and tents more spread out but still using a good percentage of the grassy areas. The fine weather continued, such rain as did fall was mostly during the night; night rain was best, it evaporated more slowly helping to green up the sun-browned grass, earlier evenings already improving its colour. Some guests who had visited other sites took the trouble to call at the office and congratulate them. Such praise did more than any pep pill to compensate for long hours that were only now beginning to diminish. Four people, two couples travelling together, were particularly effusive, not only about the site, but the surrounding area. They had been to Godophin House, to a pageant using local actors and actresses to recreate a type of garden party as it might have been four hundred years ago in the reign of Elizabeth I.

Complaints were few. One family leaving for home suggested a car wash; seeing their vehicle it wasn't hard to understand why, but they promised to be back next year. A new arrival enquired tongue in cheek, where to buy aqua-roll water carriers as they were pitched three hundred miles from a tap! These broad hints were all in good-natured banter. They continued to live on quickly taken meals, combined with a large measure of natural adrenaline, a rarefied existence impossible to sustain in the long term – but there would be no long term. The end was in sight; each day would see a reduction now. In another fortnight it would all be over bar a trickle of caravans with couples; September was never busy, a nice relaxing month to wind down, with more time to talk to old friends among the visitors.

Chapter 13

Services

A car drew up in the yard.

"It's a rep," Jan offered, gazing through the window from the shadow of the hallway. "Man on his own in a suit, new car with no towing hitch. Must be a rep. Yes, he's getting out; here comes the briefcase. What's he selling?"

"Cigarettes probably, that will be the third this season; they expect us to have a site shop. I'll send him to Sampson in the village." Gordon stayed in his chair scanning a sewer pipe catalogue, but rose when the bell rang.

"Good morning. Janitorial supplies?"

"Pardon?"

"Toilet rolls, and cleaning fluids," the rep explained, stepping onto the mat inside the office door without being invited. "Can I show you samples, quote you prices? You do buy toilet rolls?"

"Thousands. Don't know what they do with them."

"Tried flat packs, have you? We supply the containers free provided you order a certain number of cases with each. Just a minute, I'll get one."

The traveller put down his case, strode smartly across the yard, collected something from his car and returned carrying a white-enamelled, metal container.

"They can't steal a whole roll with these, the sheets come out individually." He made a motion, pulling free an imaginary tissue from the bottom with one hand.

"Um," Gordon took the container, examining it. "Can you leave this with me?"

"Sorry, only one I have." The rep shook his head. "They come with the paper, one for every five cases. You can buy extras."

"No. I need to try them first. Never mind, I'll make one, leave me your pricelist and details." Gordon laid the container on a clean sheet of paper and drew the outline, tipping it over onto another sheet to draw the other sides.

"We do regular rolls too, it's all in here. Ten percent discount on these prices if you order now, delivery whenever you want, next Easter I expect?" The rep passed over a small glossy leaflet. He failed to make a sale, but wrote his name on the pricelist before leaving.

In a quiet spell one morning a few days later, Jan entered the office to find some sort of box under construction.

"What are you making? A nest for that robin?"

"Remember the rep who wanted to sell us flat toilet paper? I'm making the container he showed us; it's finished now." Gordon held up the white cardboard box, then delved in the drawer for a screwdriver. "Come on, we'll try it. Bring the selotape and scissors."

They gathered the tools, called Sharon to watch the office, and left.

"Why not the Ladies?" Jan asked as he pushed open the Gents door.

"A chap like me has to be careful. I could..."

"Don't tell me, I remember. You might get attacked by a screaming hoard of young girls all after your body? You wish!"

When screws fixing the existing holder to the wall in one loo compartment were removed and the new box sellotaped temporarily in its place, Jan entered closing the door, sitting down, rising again and leaving. The box was dislodged and needed replacing with more selotape.

"Makes the cubicle smaller I think; difficult to get past without brushing against it. You try."

Gordon entered and at the same time the outer door

opened. A man stepped in, stopped, muttered "I'm sorry," and hurriedly withdrew. Slowly the outer door opened again, the man's head peering round.

"Come in," Jan called to him, "You're in the right side. Don't mind me, I'm only waiting for my husband."

Gingerly he stepped in, stopping as Gordon reappeared from the cubicle. Still surprised at finding a woman in the Gents toilets, the man expressed curiosity and was asked his opinion. These three were standing near the cardboard mock-up, discussing its effect when another man joined them. It was a happy foursome that experimented for several minutes, entering and leaving the compartment, Jan's presence adding that touch of novelty. A consensus was reached; it did make the cubicle smaller. One of the men made to leave, but stopped with his hand resting on the outside door handle, and turned back to Jan.

"Can I ask you something cheeky?"

"That depends!" She looked at him suspiciously, but feeling somehow supercharged, well aware she was the centre of attention. The unusual, slightly naughty circumstances enhanced her attraction; the men had all asked for her opinion, wanting to listen and talk to her. Somehow the presence of a pretty woman in that forbidden place had lifted the chance meeting into almost a party spirit. "Go ahead. Ask."

"My wife is outside, waiting to be taken to the beach. We had an argument this morning and she's not speaking to me. Would you mind walking out on my arm? Don't explain, just wave to her and walk away. Muriel will have to speak then, she'll never be able to resist."

Jan hesitated, head on one side with an amused smile, wanting to agree but unsure, turning to Gordon with eyebrows questioningly raised, asking silently if she should.

"Go on, keep the campers happy, you could have quite a reputation by evening!" Gordon turned, "Good luck, er...?"

"Derek." The man answered the unspoken question.

"Good luck, Derek, this will either cure the quarrel or

we'll fish your body from the river tomorrow. By the way, when you came in here, didn't you have something in mind?"

"Oh! I..." Derek glanced at the urinal, then slid self-consciously into the farthest cubicle. He emerged quite quickly to wash at the basin, glancing up with perhaps a touch of nervousness.

"Let's go in style then," Jan held out a hand.

"I'm still wet..." he flicked his hands at the floor.

"That's all right, I'll hold your arm." Jan reached out and they made for the door. Gordon and the other visitor grinned, watching them go.

Derek stepped out. Jan, one hand still round his arm, saw a woman standing across the road by the trees. Her expression was electric!

Separating, Jan took half a dozen steps then paused, turning to call sweetly, "Goodbye Derek!"

Derek, already walking towards his wife, stopped with jerk, as if hit with a cattle prod. Swallowing, he raised a hand half-heartedly, unsure, stopping at waist height as if to conceal the movement, the fingers giving a little flutter, an intimate motion which pleaded "Go away!" He had started this little charade, but hardly expected such co-operation. Guilt oozed from him. No actor could have done it better but this was no acting! Struggling to keep a straight face, Jan walked off towards the house, heart racing, something within bursting with excitement, with the achievement of being considered *the other woman*, mincing her step to appear more feminine.

The long summer holidays were over. Visitor numbers had diminished drastically during the past weeks and currently stood at twenty-three units, only six of which were tents. Sharon had learned that '*The Importance of being Earnest'* was now showing at Minack, and tried to persuade her mother that they should attend the open air theatre.

“You said we should see places our visitors ask about, I’ve never even been there. We don’t have many people staying, couldn’t we go?”

The attempt had been unsuccessful, securing only a promise to visit sometime. Sharon made a show of being disappointed but she was restless, not really sure what she wanted to do; tomorrow would see her starting senior school! At mid-morning with her mother not yet ready to commence the midday meal, she set about preparing for that important first day. Inspecting the bottom of the ancient iron, she placed it on the stove and lit the gas, then draped a doubled over blanket to protect the kitchen worktop, the one by the window overlooking the river. A glance downstream to where the boys had gone fishing, confirmed they were not in sight. For some reason she hoped they would not return, did not want them seeing these careful preparations; would like to pretend the occasion meant nothing, certainly not the turmoil she felt within.

After a time, a few spots of water flicked at the old implement sizzled satisfactorily – hot enough. Donning the specially padded oven glove that her mother always used, she lifted the iron but left the gas burning. A white blouse already lay, precisely arranged under a dampened cloth; the new school uniform, skirt, blazer and special tie in a neat pile nearby. At intervals the iron required re-heating, sooty deposits carefully rubbed off after each session on the gas. Every inch of each garment was painstakingly covered even though they had never been worn; never that is, if one discounted those many times she had slipped them on in secret to inspect herself in the mirror.

The following morning, hearing her parents leave the house, Sharon slid from her bed. Thoroughly washing in the bathroom then slipping back into the bedroom, she closed the door tightly before dropping the blue dressing gown and donning her panties and vest. Reaching into the wardrobe the young girl carefully removed a hanger containing a blue cardigan, white blouse and school tie, lifting each one off separately and laying them carefully on the bed. The cardigan she appraised critically, the only garment not ironed because of its woollen texture. Was it good enough?

Donning blouse, then the skirt from a separate hanger, she held up the tie, glancing in the mirror. Dad had shown her how to tie it; Chris could have but she wouldn't ask him.

"Now how does it go?" she lifted the collar and draped the tie round, making sure the wide end hung lower. "Over, round and under, right round again, up, down through the loop, tighten up and turn down the collar." The reflection in the mirror was fine. "Good!"

Jan entered the house to prepare breakfast, leaving Gordon to organise the dustbins, part of the regular routine releasing the children from these tasks now the site was less busy. Chris had finished tending the goats, having led them off, selected a location that had everything they would need and tethered all three securely on long ropes. Stephen struggled up from the basement carrying a bucket loaded with ash; no one offered to help. The boys swapped jobs sometimes, agreeing between themselves who should do what. Sharon was still in her room, combing again the long dark hair that hung down below shoulder level. She tried it in front, hanging equally each side, showing almost black against the white blouse. A flick of the head sent one side flying to the rear. The lopsided style was rather good, film star like; would Mum approve? Maybe, but the boys would scoff and pass derogatory comments. Hearing her mother call breakfast, she pushed the rest behind with a deft sweep of the fingers and opened the door.

An hour later, Sharon, now eleven and smartly dressed in the school colours, left the house with Chris for her first day at senior school. Chris would be thirteen in December, almost a man. Setting off towards the village, Sharon was nervously proud, chin up, very conscious of her new clothes.

They strode away talking, keen for the first day of the new term, not even trying to score points off each other as they often had in the past. Mum, Dad and Stephen watched them go.

Stephen followed shortly after, on his own for the first time. He passed no comment, if anything was quieter than normal striding off across the bridge. At the far side he turned once; his parents, still standing in the doorway, raised their hands and waved. Stephen made no direct acknowledgement, perhaps his head tilted slightly but it could have been just part of the natural movement as he continued to walk along the stony surface. The young lad, eight in a few days, did not look back again though they stood until he disappeared three hundred yards away.

"What are you doing today?" Jan asked as she lit the gas under the kettle.

"Some clearing I think, the weather's good. If the remaining visitors all go to the beach or sightseeing later, I might start the digger. I feel... I don't know; sort of deflated, left behind by events. How did they grow up so fast?"

Jan answered with a soft smile, and slight surprise.

"Getting sensitive aren't you? About time you noticed." She sat at the table next to him. "Did you see the way Chris and Sharon got on this morning, not a single word of derision or argument. I think she's glad to have an older brother at her new school; reassuring perhaps. But why was he so amenable? Sharon looked very smart, was that the reason? Is he thinking ahead, thinking it could be an advantage to have a well-dressed sister; more introductions maybe? Chris is sensible, he'd consider things like that; he already knows the facts of life!"

"Did he say so?" It was Gordon's turn to look surprised.

"Of course not. But he does try to conceal a laugh occasionally, when anyone says something with a double meaning. A woman can tell, take my word for it!"

The end of the school holidays coincided with another,

more ominous, event. Confirmation that the main sewer would definitely be laid had come in the spring, with surveyors checking terrain and gradients. It would follow the river, traversing the entire length of the site. Now the first signs of disturbance began. Fortunately, major works were not scheduled to start until the following autumn but one preliminary sortie occurred; a digger prematurely ripping turf from the path. The big bosses came down and it was sent away, but the stay of execution would be temporary at most! Was it really accidental, or specially arranged to soften the family up for a main assault later.

"How much mess will they really make?" Jan asked.

"Can't tell. Depends on so many things; how good the workmen are, the weather, the trench depth, will the pipes be laid above or below the natural water table. Who knows? A well organised firm shouldn't do too much damage, but there's bound to be quite a bit."

"I suppose the trees and all those heathers along the riverbank will be affected," Jan murmured, sighing. "It won't affect the trout, will it?"

"Only if they drop cement in the water. That will kill fish. They shouldn't, but it has been known for workers to dump material that's not been used when it's time to go home. Just hope we get a good gang. We need to lay some more service pipes ourselves too."

Although the new telephone box had only come into operation part way through the season, it had been well used and greatly appreciated. The selected position opposite the centre toilet building, or rather what would be the centre one when the third was eventually erected, had proved a good choice, conveniently near to the entrance yard with plenty of parking space. Helpful as this addition might be however, it was obvious that with the site expanding, more services would be required, particularly water points to serve the farther pitches.

Jan and Gordon talked a lot together, discussing the site constantly. With the few remaining customers mostly out and the children at school, who else could they talk to? Jan knew he spoke to the robin when believing himself alone. Sometimes, particularly in good weather, she still took a flask to where he was working, choosing to have coffee on a sunny bank rather than inside the house. On these occasions she made a point of approaching silently, hoping to catch him chatting to the bird. Once, while feeding the ducks she caught herself telling them of Prince Charles recent visit to the Scilly Isles, and stopped in mid flow, wondering, "Is it catching? Winters do tend to be long and lonely since Stephen went to school; is it beginning to affect me too? When all the work is done, will I still like this wonderful wild valley, without a soul to talk to?"

Something nudged her knee. Anne raised a hungry beak expectantly, the other ducks close by, every one now prepared to eat from the hand. Jan sighed. Isolation was fine really, even pleasant after the busy summer. The ducks were like friends; she loved the feel as they let her stroke their feathers. Why shouldn't she talk to them? People talked to their dogs.

As the visitors diminished further, husband and wife chatted together more and more, at meals and over coffee; that recent first landing of a helicopter on top of the Wolf Rock lighthouse, the builder of the new Scillonian ship for the Scilly Isles going bust; anything and everything was discussed. Often they walked round, admiring the site, talking about progress and what remained to be done, basking in their own achievement without really realising it. Work was not over, not by any means; nor ever likely to be it seemed. Both were fiercely determined River Valley would be the best site in the Southwest, but in a peaceful country way, avoiding anything that might detract from the natural surroundings. Side by side with the continuing clearing of yet unlevelled areas went a constant quest to improve convenience and pleasure for customers.

"Did you notice Derek's wet hands?" Jan asked.

"Derek who?"

"I forget his other name. The man who asked me to walk out of the Gents toilets with him to upset his wife?"

"Oh... Yes, I remember." Gordon grinned, "Wonder what she did to him?"

"Very little. We met the following evening on the bridge, he introduced her as Muriel; we spent some time together. Apparently they drove right to Marazion without speaking, but on the beach she couldn't keep silent any longer – had to ask him, had to find out what he was doing in the Gents with another woman; she hadn't recognised me." Jan paused, smiling. "Derek strung her along for a bit at first, asking 'What woman?' pretending not to remember, being evasive as if having some guilty secret. In the end he told her the whole story. It had to be true, Muriel said, because no one could invent so improbable an excuse! Anyway, it worked, did bring them together again, made their holiday. They hardly argued all day – evidently that was unusual. If one became moody about something, the other whispered 'Loo paper', and it worked like magic. Two other caravanners joined us on the bridge towards the end, so they went all through the explanation again in more detail. We all had a good laugh together."

"Funny way to make people happy but who cares how we do it!" Gordon shrugged.

"By the way, Muriel wants to know when she can meet you in the Ladies?"

"Never! No, wait a minute. Tell her next year, that should make them come back."

"Trust you to think of money." Jan took a pace backwards, pretending to inspect him critically. "Frighten them off more likely!"

"I suppose it might. What were you saying about Derek's hands?"

"After he washed, did you notice him flick them at the floor. When we used the basins before the house was built we always carried a towel, most people do; but if they just nip in for... well, a quick one – there's nowhere to dry your hands. Perhaps that's where some of the toilet rolls go. Could you rig something up? We ladies probably need it more than the Gents do."

"Roller towels, you mean? I could enquire. Not very hygienic. Hand dryers would be better. Same problem as hairdryers though; the waterwheel could never handle it. Anyway, there are more important improvements to make during this coming winter."

"Such as?"

"Services!" Gordon cast a glance towards the areas farther from the toilet building. "You notice how many retired people come here – for the quiet I suppose? Some are quite old. I help when they arrive by reversing or even pushing the caravan into their chosen position, but they carry their own water. No visitor should go too far for a tap or to empty waste. We need to take drinking water and an emptying point within easy reach of every area."

At tea that evening, they told the children of the planned expansion of services. Gordon explained briefly, expecting to elicit a certain amount of sympathy.

"It will be hard work but more water points are really needed. More than that, the Council has insisted our site be connected up immediately the main sewer is completed. That's supposed to be next autumn; we won't be allowed to use the septic tank after that. If we're late, they might be really mean and try to close us down. So we're taking no risks; we'll do it this year. Our pipework will be ready a year in advance!"

The three children watched, a certain apprehension in their expressions. This was not something that affected them personally as the earlier work had done. While living in the caravan, they had been anxious to help construct the original toilet building with its promise of hot showers and flush loos, a facility they had all longed for. With the house too, they had all helped, keen for rooms of their own. This latest project however, promised more hard work but no equivalent benefit to themselves.

"Will we have to help?" Chris asked, putting all their thoughts into words.

"Not really." Gordon saw relief on the children's faces. "There's not a lot you could do. Much of the work will be through areas that are already grassed. All those I shall dig with a pick and shovel to avoid making a mess. Too hard for any of you, even for Chris I suspect. I'll take the turf off carefully first then put it back afterwards so no marks will show. The pipes will be covered with sand, to protect them; you could fill the digger bucket with sand and drive it round to me at weekends if you like. You could learn to use the levelling instrument, but Mum will be doing both those things most of the winter, and..."

"Most of the winter? The water pipe from the village only took a couple of weeks!" Sharon looked suspiciously at her father, not believing it could take so long.

"This is more difficult, several different pipes, lots of junctions, inspection chambers, and it's deeper. Besides, I can't work at it all the time. At least half of each day must be spent preparing new areas, we were short of space again with all the extra caravans this year. Hand digging takes longer too. From the telephone box, trenches will carry pipes to many places; a six-inch sewer pipe, the three-inch water main, and a spare two-inch duct for any future services, just in case."

Seeing a query concerning the spare duct in Chris's expression, Dad paused. "You think that's extravagant? I know the extra duct might never be needed, but plastic pipe is cheap... Well, not the bigger sizes, they're quite expensive but at least the small two-inch size is cheap – and digging trenches is strenuous! All the water pipes will be laid inside ducts, inside bigger pipes that is, for better protection and easy renewal. Let's do it well, and do it only once!"

Heads nodded freely in agreement. Having understood that little of the work would fall on them, the children were happy, quite prepared now to approve.

"Right," Dad continued. "How will we lay it out? I'll tell you. The main pipework will head straight down the valley. Lateral trenches..." he stopped again, seeing more puzzled expressions. "Lateral means sideways, they'll spread out to all the other areas to provide services everywhere. I plan to put standpipes for fresh water within easy reach of all pitches, near road edges but close to trees and bushes; accessible but unobtrusive. I can't complete the emptying points because our sewer pipe will lead nowhere; the end covered in soil to await the main sewer's arrival. Now tell me, when I bury that end, what is it I mustn't forget?"

Heads were shaken; young Stephen opened his mouth to speak, thought better of it and stayed silent.

"I must measure carefully from two well separated trees. Can you imagine Mum's sarcasm if when the time comes to join up, I can't find the pipe end?" It was clear from their expressions that they dearly hoped he would not be able to. Typical! No respect for a father's efforts.

"This means a lot of extra work for me, digging and filling the trenches."

No one made any comment. He could not see Jan behind him, finger to her lips warning the children to stay silent. Apparently Dad's were made for work! Just a normal state of affairs, not worth remarking on. He tried again.

"I'll have to work long hours, won't have much time to sit indoors and talk to you."

He heard Jan say "Good! Peace at last!" and out of the corner of one eye, caught her signalling to the children.

They nodded back, agreeing strongly, grinning from ear to ear.

Depth, or course, was the critical factor; dictated by the level of the main sewer. Since that would not be laid at least until the following year, this depth must rely on calculation and a willingness by the Local Authority to divulge the figures! Would they be co-operative? A visit confirmed that they would! More than just being willing, they were encouraging and helpful, quickly approving a drawing of the planned pipework, pleased and surprised that it would be ready early. Gordon told the family as they ate that evening.

"Right. They want us to do it! Apparently it's important that a good volume of liquid should flow down the pipes as soon as possible once the sewage works opens. The more volume the quicker the flow. You know what the Council Officer said to me? He said, *Fresh sewage is so much nicer than stale sewage*!"

"Ugh! How can any sewage be nice; filthy water with lumps of..." Sharon, dunking a biscuit as she spoke, waved her free hand to indicate that they must all know what floated on sewage. Her repugnance was such that she forgot the biscuit held in her other hand; part of it broke off to float in the coffee. Grabbing a teaspoon she fished it out; the piece was too big and hung dripping over the edge at both sides, threatening to stain the tablecloth. Leaning quickly forward she drew it into her mouth with an unintended slurp.

A titter of laughter round the table and her mother's comment, 'So elegant', put her on the defensive, but before she could say anything her father spoke again.

"Only comparatively nice. The Council man meant it gets even more smelly and obnoxious if it takes longer to reach the treatment works, and sticky sediments can build up in the pipes if the flow is slow." Dad broke off as Chris asked "Why?" then launched into an explanation of sewage deposits and blockages, rounding off with a brief reference to Barnes Formula for Slimy Sewers and how to calculate flow velocity. The family munched happily away as he came to the main point. "Now then, the big question is, can we trust the figures, will they be correct or will some official alter them before the sewer reaches us? Even if they remain unaltered, will the workmen get them right?"

Over the following days, the deepest drain run was started, the one farthest down the site. This section, not yet seeded with grass and lying farthest from the remaining caravans, could be dug by Max, the excavator, without risk of disturbing either turf or visitors. That should make it easier. It did, but the trench was deep and the top material loose! Many men have died in trench collapses. This one really needed timbering; that is, upright planks with cross-timbers to prevent the sides falling in if the ground should slip. Gordon inspected the excavation, knew it was unsafe, thought of the cost of timber – and eased himself gingerly down to stand on the uneven bottom. The unsupported ground stood sheer and close on both sides, so close he stood partly sideways to stop his shoulders brushing the soil. He could see over the top, but only just! A vertical coffin? Should those sides collapse he would be helpless.

First task, level the bottom; he reached for a shovel. It should have taken an hour but was finished in half that time, a healthy apprehension having driven his muscles on, anxious to complete the job and get clear! As he climbed out, Jan drove up in Max. Lowering the front bucket, which was full of sand, she switched off and swung herself down from the machine, landing lightly on the ground, her skirt swaying.

"I still think it's too deep. Are you sure it's safe."

"Quite safe," he lied.

"Why are you sweating then. Fear is it?"

"Shovelling is hot work, you don't get much breeze in a trench."

They worked on, Jan passing down pipes then helping with the levels, reading the instrument and calling out the figures as he crouched down making joints and adjusting the depth. These were the worst moments, his head many feet below ground. It went without mishap, this first length completed by evening. When the children arrived from school, they ran through the site together, aware the pipework had started that morning and wanting to inspect progress. By this time Jan had already returned to the house. Later, seated round the table eating beans on toast, she asked,

"Well, what did you think?"

"Hasn't done much today," Sharon frowned.

"Did miles more when he laid the water main from the village." Chris concurred.

"Slowing down in his old age?" Jan suggested. Grinning faces agreed, Stephen wrinkling his nose.

"Naturally it takes me longer. There's much more to do in this trench. Did you notice the first inspection chamber base is concreted?"

"Yes," Jan interrupted, "And who mixed that concrete? I did!"

"Mum!" Sharon stared for a moment, then swung round accusingly to her father.

"Well, why not? Marriage is supposed to be a partnership. I didn't sit in the armchair with my feet up while she mixed it; I was working too! Anyway, your mother offered. What did you think; that I stood over her with a whip?"

"Mum?" Sharon asked again, looking to her mother doubtfully for confirmation, not really believing.

"Yes, I offered. Sympathy really, poor old chap!"

Young smiles erupted, awaiting Dad's defence. He studied the ring of faces, realising nothing in the children's eyes would justify these drains moving more slowly than the water pipes had, and decided to change the subject.

"Poor old chap, eh? Well so I am when my daughter wouldn't even walk back to the house with me, not even a hug of greeting."

"I should say not! Have you seen the mud on his working clothes Mum? They're horrible. Why can't we pay someone else to work in the trench, then you needn't mix concrete either?"

Jan faked alarm, "Pay someone else? Be careful, you'll give Dad a heart attack!" She turned to Gordon. "Well, why not? The season was really good, don't deny it. Come on, let's have the figures!"

"Okay." He left the room, returning shortly with a roll of paper, spreading it on the table to reveal a graph with rows of numbers across the page.

"Now let me see," a finger slid along the data for 1972. "Last year we had 5048 caravan days in total, that includes tents you understand. Now this year... where are we? Ah yes, the green line, 6278 already – and still three weeks to go before closing. A 25% increase! Beware though, much of that increase is in tents." He glanced significantly at Jan, not attempting to explain why that should be so important.

Jan nodded thinking about the planning flaw and the possibility that still existed of the Council refusing to let them take tents once the sewer was completed; it was something that seldom left their thoughts completely. But the figures were good, she was still pleased, "The extra advertising is paying off."

"It's certainly bringing new people," Gordon agreed, "especially the club magazines and the monthly titles, we should try to spend more with them each season; but the big difference is all those coming back from previous years! No good just getting new faces, take good care of the old ones too."

"I had more foreign friends this year, from Holland and Germany. 'Tot ziens' is Goodbye in Dutch." Waving a hand in farewell motion, Sharon addressed her father. "They say it's cheaper in England now?"

"That will be the exchange rate. The pound is down, its value has fallen. A low pound helps us in two ways; makes it cheaper for foreign visitors, and it's dearer for our people to go abroad, so more may stay in Britain."

"I didn't see any young French girls on site this year," Sharon frowned. "Well, there was one, but she didn't speak English!"

"You think she should?" Jan asked. "You say that as if it made her an imbecile. What about your Dutch and German friends, did they think you stupid because you can't speak their language?"

"No, suppose not. I hadn't thought of that. We've

started French at school."

"Vous parlez bien?"

Sharon looked blankly at Dad before appealing to her mother for help.

"It's French, Sharon. Tell him to stop showing off, he only has a few words himself, enough to show someone to a pitch. Visitors from France are rare; nice people but not great travellers. Can't you see what he's doing? Putting one over on you by changing the subject. Well *I* still remember what we were talking about!"

Chris was laughing quietly at Sharon. She glared back at him, then turned indignantly.

"Dad, that wasn't fair. Our class has only had one lesson. Anyway, I *hadn't* forgotten. If we've done so well this year, why can't we pay someone to work in the trench?"

It was no surprise that all the children supported Mum. To an extent they were right, extra help could probably be afforded now, but only if one turned a blind eye to the future. Other expenses were coming, essential things that must be saved up for. Gordon wondered how best to reply.

"Well, we could pay someone else, I grant you that, but I'd prefer not to. There are several reasons. First I have to admit a reluctance to letting some stranger have a hand in developing the park; this is our creation. Would they make the joints properly, put enough sand round and over the pipe, get the levels right…"

"Make it strong enough?" Jan interrupted.

"Well yes, if you like. I think that even though they will never be seen, a line of pipes is something to be proud of; it should stretch along the trench in a perfect line and should last without any attention at least for the rest of our lifetime. But that's not the main reason. We've done really well, yes, but expenses have risen and there are many months to go with no money coming in. The pipes have already cost quite a lot and more are needed. We don't know how much damage the sewer will do, and there's still the cost of tarmacing the road to find sometime. We can't expect visitors to put up with the dust clouds forever. We started saving for it last year but the new drains and water points have had to take preference."

The ring of young faces showed no sign of agreement. Ah well, he had tried to explain but knew there was little chance the children would be convinced.

The year wore on; darker evenings were in one way a relief. Even dividing the day in two and spending half sitting on Max loading stone, those other hours digging trenches by hand, much of it through hard stony ground, certainly sapped the energy. The children were progressing at School, Sharon flourished a few new French words now and again but Chris seldom responded, finding greater interest in practical things. Following the autumn river cleaning, television viewing had increased by fifteen minutes, and he wanted to know why.

"Dad, when the River Board clean the river with their dragline, the bed sinks down a bit each time, but only downstream of the wheel. They can't use the dragline on the upstream side because of the bridge foundations, so our water level there is unchanged – right? Well then, I understand it makes a bigger drop over the weir, but surely it's the upstream level that affects the power. Why have we suddenly got more?"

"That's not quite true. Remember that the downstream water level covers the paddles by six inches or more. That creates some resistance to rotation, not much but a little. Since the last cleaning, the downstream level has fallen as you say, so there's not so much resistance, the paddles come out of the water more easily, giving the wheel extra power. Mind you, once that lower water level drops to the bottom of the paddles, no more benefit will come no matter how much the bed goes down."

"We could lower the whole wheel then?" Chris asked.

"No we can't!" Jan who had been half listening raised her head in alarm.

"Let him Mum, it was fun to watch."

"If it ever gets that low Sharon, you'll be old enough to help, not watch," Dad warned. "But it may never be needed. Remember how I persuaded the last of those granite slabs underneath the channel to go down until it was level? I moved it fractionally backwards and forwards with the crow bar and down it went. Well I wonder if, over many years, vibration from the moving wheel might do the same and the whole thing settle gently. Now wouldn't that be a perfect design if settlement of the wheel kept exact pace with lowering of the bed by the River Board? What do you think Chris?"

"Don't know. How much does it go down each year? Can you tell?"

"I've taken levels on the riverbed." Gordon picked up a folder and flicked through the pages. "At 200 yards downstream the bed is eight feet below the bank top; at 500 yards it's only six feet below. That's approximate, but we've got the actual levels written down, we can check again at any time in the future."

Chris pulled at his earlobe thoughtfully then remembered something. "The river cleaning did some good, it frightened a few trout back to the bridge. There were half a dozen when I fed the ducks this morning."

Into the long pause that followed another voice spoke.

"How d'you make a fish go mad?"

Young Stephen had until that moment remained silent during the conversation, eating, listening, turning to follow each speaker. Now he sat, cheek propped on a hand, only his eyes moving from one person to another.

"Well? How do you?" Sharon demanded.

"Send it to Paris."

The family shrugged at each other, but Stephen would say no more, not then or over the following days.

As work proceeded towards the site entrance, trenches became shallower and almost totally through grass covered areas. These were worked by hand. After every dozen turfs were re-laid, traces of soil on the grass were swept with a stiff broom into the open trench ahead making the finished work almost invisible. Perhaps the regular visitors would think the family went on winter holidays, so little evidence would show of this work. Of course, farther down the site they would see a change; several new areas had already been levelled and this work was continuing.

Building manholes at each change of direction and junction of the sewer pipes had taken time, and there was still a coat of cement to apply inside. Achieving a smooth finish often meant lying on the ground working at arm's length, head down inside the small chambers. Gordon struggled at the full extent of his reach on a particularly difficult manhole, not only his head but chest too, hanging down inside, only his legs and backside visible from above. It lay next to some hazel bushes, the deepest one on site. A good smooth finish proved elusive, the cement's texture a little wet and his arm muscles were starting to tie up in knots.

He heaved upwards, extracting shoulders from the chamber, rolling over to lay back and let both arms flop to the ground. Strong sunlight caused him to swivel round so a bush shielded his eyes. After a while the muscle pain began subsiding but five more minutes wouldn't hurt! "Laziness!" his conscience accused, "No, cement needs time to stiffen," the body countered. Giving way and relaxing completely he let his thoughts wander as Robin appeared on a branch above.

What was that ornithological saying? 'One does not observe our feathered friends when directly overhead'. Would his frequent companion sitting vertically above, involuntarily target him?

"*You won't find worms down at that depth.*" He had known the bird, as always, would be preoccupied with food.

"It's not for worms, it's drains for human wastes," Gordon responded aloud, then wondered if Robin would understand what human wastes were. Should he have put it in blunter terms? The reply came to him quickly.

"*If your customers had digestion as quick as birds, you wouldn't need drains and you'd have wonderful grass.*"

Seeing no prospect of food, the bird flew off. Was it right, was all this underground pipework strictly necessary? Perhaps they had made difficulties for themselves by putting the small water pipes inside ducting; such pipe was normally laid directly in the soil. Ducts however, as well as protection, offered other advantages. To repair a leak usually entailed digging up the ground; not at River Valley. Just undo the leaking pipe, pull out that length and slip in a new one. No mess, no inconvenience to the customer, and very quick. As a bonus, increasing the pipe sizes would be easy if ever needed, and there was room in the duct for other services too.

Chapter 14

Feathers

"Did you know the spire on St Hilary church was a day mark for ships sailing along the Cornish coast?" Chris asked as they ate. The light had faded outside but this early darkness as Christmas approached troubled no one, certainly not Dad after another day swinging the pick, digging yet more service trenches.

"What *is* a day mark?" Sharon asked.

"Something ships can see to know where they are, like a lighthouse marks a place at night. That's why the spire was painted white. We were doing discoveries by sea; guess who found America?"

Sharon shrugged, looked to Stephen, then at Mum.

"Columbus?" Jan offered.

"Yes, 482 years ago in..."

"Wait a minute! How did it go?" Jan tapped a knuckle against one cheek, trying to remember. "Ah! In fourteen hundred and ninety two, Columbus sailed the ocean blue! That's it, 1492."

Chris, happy to have the display of his new knowledge so well received, sat back, chest expanding, smiling in anticipation. "But what was his Christian name?"

"Sebastian?" Jan winked at Gordon and leaned over to whisper in Stephen's ear. Teatime was often a source of fun, everyone joined in offering a barrage of names but carefully omitting the right one. Chris, soon understanding that they knew the correct answer, sniffed loudly, sensibly refrained from quoting it himself and continued his history.

"Columbus was Italian but worked for the Spanish. Another Spaniard, Cortez, conquered the natives in South America, then plundered the native gold. British ships took it sometimes from the Spanish galleons. There were many rich wrecks off the Cornish coast over the following centuries. That was the time of Francis Drake!" He half glanced to the window, thinking of their own Francis drake and the rest of the ducks but the curtains were drawn. Most likely they would all be asleep floating on the river.

"What use is history, they're all dead." It was hardly a question, Sharon needed only the small hesitation on Chris's part to force a way in, not liking her brother to monopolise the conversation. Having stopped his flow she hurried on. "We did science, the effects of heat. Mum, you remember that explosion in our first caravan, where the lid blew off the biscuit tin? Well there's a safer way to show the power of steam. We heated a little water in an old, one-gallon metal can with the lid removed. When steam gushed from the top we took the flame away and screwed the lid back on tight, and..."

"Tightly. It's an adverb," Dad corrected.

"Oh, all right, tightly then!" Sharon snapped sulkily, annoyed at being interrupted. Seeing Chris grin, she hurried on. "After a while this tin, with its lid screwed on *tightly;* it buckled inwards, partly flattening itself. Teacher said when it cooled down the steam condensed leaving a vacuum inside. He also had a brass ball, about the size of a big marble..."

"Poor man," Jan whispered loudly enough to be heard.

"Mum! Stop it! How can I tell you if everyone keeps laughing? This ball passed through a hole in a piece of metal. When it was heated it got bigger and wouldn't go through the hole anymore."

"Well what use is that?" Chris, not pleased by the scorn thrown at his own subject, sought recompense. "You say history is useless. Go on then, tell us how important crumpling a tin is!"

Sharon glared at him, this was not going at all as

planned, she had thought to impress the family, not be made fun of. Drawing in a breath and opening her mouth to speak, she hesitated, hunting for an answer, but in spite of her indignation, could find none.

"Fit in the dustbins easier," Stephen muttered, a little grin on his face when his sister appeared at a loss. Another round of laughter broke the developing tension; they all understood dustbin space!

Jan smiled at him, then turned to Sharon, "Rescued by your younger brother eh? Both subjects are important. History is supposed to teach us where mistakes were made so they won't be repeated. Anyway, if you achieve something great one day, won't you want to be remembered?"

The suggestion brought a slow smile back to Sharon's face, one hand instinctively tucking the blouse a little tighter into her skirt, the other running through a loose strand of hair, flicking it behind the ear.

Gordon, concerned that a subject of such practical significance was being treated too lightly, leaned forward resting his elbows on the table. "A good knowledge of science helps you reason things out and solve problems in life. Just because Sharon can't find an example, you mustn't think the effects of heat are unimportant. If you look at a railway line on a cold day, there are gaps where two rails join; on a hot day these gaps get smaller because the metal expands. Without that arrangement, the rails might buckle. I'll tell you a little story about something similar. When I was a young Engineer in my early twenties, we were setting out a large site in London. Do you recall how we laid out this house, marking the lines on wooden profiles so we would know exactly where to build the walls? Well on busy sites where the timbers could get knocked, the ends of the lines are usually marked on the nearest building or wall or anything conveniently near and solid. One of our Engineers marked his lines on a railway bridge running alongside the site. It was very long and made of metal girders. Such bridges are fixed at one end, and all the other supports have metal rollers to allow for expansion when the temperature rises. One sunny afternoon, this Engineer used his theodolite to sight on these marks and set out a wall. They found later that it was built in the wrong position. The bridge and his mark had moved over an inch in the sunshine! Perhaps he didn't pay attention at school do you think?"

Winter rushed on. Some diver found part of a propeller from the sunken oil tanker Torry Canyon, a boy of eleven caught a Monk fish weighing 35 pound making Chris envious, then the bullion ship Princess Maria, lost in 1686, was found off Newlyn. Not all the news was so good. Early in January a headline appeared in *The Cornishman*, "Sewers but no Sewage Works." Apparently over a million pounds of contracts had already been signed for laying the sewers, but now a Government circular said the final contract, the one for the actual sewage works, should be held up.

"Typical!" Jan looked up from the paper. "Just about the mentality of politicians; spend a fortune on sewers that go nowhere! How will this affect us?"

"If they cancel altogether, then we could be in trouble. All the mess of laying the pipeline through the site and still no connection afterwards. My pipework would be wasted too – but it will never happen. They dare not. It would leave them open to too much ridicule. They might delay, but never cancel. This is not something they can sweep under the carpet, everyone will talk about it."

On site the work progressed less spectacularly but with persistent determination. Each day new lengths of trench were dug. At one point the pick struck granite, sending a shock wave up through the haft, hands and shoulders as the tool quivered to an abrupt stop. Careful probing with a crowbar found the stone extending in both directions across the trench. In spite of a desire not to disturb too much ground, Max's engine was started and the surface stripped away with the rear digging bucket; the turf of course first being removed by hand. The length extended to five feet! With a cross-section two feet wide and almost as deep, this single stone exceeded a ton in weight. Trying to lift it caused the excavator's front wheels to rise in the air, pulling the machine's rear end down rather than shifting the granite. Putting Jan in the front bucket as a counterweight also failed, she was too light. Max could however, raise one end of the granite at a time. In this way, coaxing the stone up and sideways, eventually raised the obstruction to ground level, leaving it as a bridge for the trench to pass under.

"What will we do with it?" Jan asked as she walked by later to check on the goats.

"Nothing. It's where two areas join, not in anyone's way. Leave it where it is, could be straightened up a bit afterwards when the trench is finished and filled, but otherwise let it stay. Probably still be here in a hundred years." Gordon gave a shrug, inviting comment.

"Put a standpipe nearby. People can sit on it while filling water carriers."

And so it was done; that granite looked good too, washed clean by the rain as the weeks passed. Hard work and perseverance saw the services almost finished in late February, so far as was possible that is – the final connections must wait until the main sewer's completion. Jan had continued to mix the concrete for manholes and trundle sand and building blocks around in Max's bucket, but it set things back with her own work. For the last week she had been dashing round trying to catch up, painting bits and pieces in the toilet buildings ready for opening in March. She was tired and edgy, concerned at unavoidably neglecting her housework. When they had first arrived at River Valley and lived in the small touring caravan, space had been so scarce and valuable that she formed the habit of putting everything away immediately after use and had become particular that things should be tidy. House-proud is not the word; she had no fetish for polish or cleaning, just that everything be in its proper place; the house would never be posh, but it must look presentable. That was certainly not true at the moment!

Gordon had been little help, being rushed himself and working long hours to get the final inspection chambers finished and safe. Tools and working clothes lay around in various places, together with reference books, pricelists, catalogues, rough sketches of drain runs and lists of pipe levels. Relations between the pair had already become somewhat strained on the day when, in an attempt to give visitors more privacy, he started to build a wall round the drain used for chemical toilets. His suggestion that this facility would improve if clad with the remaining Delabole slate, drew an immediate protest.

"You're not covering a place where people empty their portable loo with the same stone as my house!"

Oh dear, how best to persuade her? Under less arduous circumstances he might have been more sensitive.

"I'll put up a sign, 'Emptying Point', so people know which is which."

Not a diplomatic approach. They had both just entered the office, Jan carefully carrying her paint and brush was on the point of taking them through to the kitchen when he spoke. She was not amused. Already tired and only too well aware of the house's poor appearance, she stared back, her face a stony cast, incensed, but without the burning rage that made her eyes flash. She was searching for a telling reply, the struggle for words almost visible. There were chances here for a real result! He glanced pointedly round the room.

"You ought to be flattered. At least my emptying point is neat and tidy!"

It was wrong, he had known that before speaking, but Jan looked so pretty when really angry. These opportunities were rare; often enough she pretended anger, it was part of their games, their life together, but very seldom did she lose control entirely. And there was something deeper, the antagonism had built up all day, causing both to needle each other. For some seconds she stood, struggling with herself, eyes flaming, mouth a tight line, still holding the paint, annoyed almost to the point of madness, quite capable of throwing the tin and its contents but unable to definitely decide on any course of action. But for the carpet it would be the paint for sure; had he been a touch nearer that brush would definitely have sploshed straight in his face.

Well aware she was worried at leaving the housework undone, it was wicked to take such unfair advantage. He wanted to go to her now, give a little kiss, rest her head on his shoulder, pat the hair and offer comfort. But three steps forward would take him in range; it was obvious from the way her arm moved what would happen. Like a tiger in the zoo, she was majestic and so attractive, something you'd love to stroke, but it was more than your life was worth. Instead he took several quick paces backwards, telling himself it wasn't a retreat, just that paint and carpets were expensive!

The movement relieved Jan's tension. He was in the wrong, those backward steps admitted it. Her eyes still sparkled but no longer with rage. She realised now that he had deliberately tried to arouse her, and had succeeded momentarily, she admitted that but now it was her turn; now he must pay the price. That too, was part of the game! She moved purposefully forward. Quickly he backed through the door, jumping down the steps and running off a dozen quick paces. She followed with deliberate strides, reached the stony yard and lowered the tin of white paint to the ground, bending to balance the brush on top.

"I'm off to do housework," her words flowed with exaggerated sweetness. "*You* can finish the painting. Don't forget to wash the brush afterwards, I'll be too busy. Someone says my house is dirtier than a toilet emptying point. Dinner won't be ready at twelve-thirty; try six o'clock!"

Watching her mince off, he grinned ruefully. "Serves me right, I asked for it. Should be fun making up tonight!" He picked up the brush, walked over to a tap and let the white water run down the drain.

A day later the job was finished. Anyone calling at River Valley when down Penzance way in the following season, would see a chemical emptying point faced with Delabole slate. How did he persuade her? A little of this and that I guess, and maybe...?

Lamorna cove, so peaceful on a February morning, lay before them. A resolve to explore those places visitors regularly asked about had been thwarted through the winter months by work on pipe runs and a continuing struggle for more pitches. Even with the underground work complete, Gordon had still been reluctant to leave the site because of telephone bookings. However, the family pushed for a break, Sharon several times referring to a promise made the previous autumn. In the end he gave way, knowing Jim would be down within the hour to take any phone calls.

They had driven to Penzance, on through Newlyn, then Mousehole, both traditional Cornish fishing villages where fresh fish could be acquired straight off returning boats by those prepared to rise early enough. The harbours and tiny streets, some really narrow, attracted many holidaymakers but could hardly be recommended to anyone towing a caravan. Rising up the steep hill out of Mousehole, the famous bird hospital stood on the right near the top, overlooking the sea. This somewhat tortuous route had led on to Lamorna Cove where they now stood.

"Look," Chris pointed to a cottage high on the cliffs.

Jan followed his outstretched arm. "Great view, but what must it be like in a winter gale? I'd rather have our valley! What d'you think Dad?"

"Hm. Marvellous position. Built in those wonderful days before the dreaded planning committee existed, no doubt. Who carried concrete and building materials right up there?"

"Trust you to think of work. There must be an easier route." Jan followed the line of cliff, pivoting slowly round to gaze across the bay. Lamorna had been an inspiration to painters for generations; it was easy enough to see why.

"It *is* beautiful. There! The water's colour, that wonderful green." she pointed. "This section of the coastal path leads eventually to Minack Theatre. Derek Tangy's house is along there; some of our visitors have spoken to him, bought his books and taken them to be signed. We should walk that section one day."

Indeed they should, but not right now. Instead they drifted idly along capturing the magic of that bay, allowing the children time to dissipate their energy dashing here and there across the sands before climbing back in the car, taking the easy way to Porthcurno.

Having parked, the family walked down to Minack, that famous open air stage carved in the rocks. Normally no plays were performed in winter or early spring, both stage and seating being entirely open to the elements. As they entered from higher ground, the bowl of the theatre lay below. The backcloth was magnificent; a deep blue-green sea with white breakers smashing themselves unheard against a headland jutting seaward far across the bay.

At a signal, the children raced down, not another soul in sight regardless of the mild temperatures and bright though still weak sunshine. They had been warned on the journey not to tread on the seating, for Stephen at least would have clambered up the tiers of stone. Even so, he received a sharp command almost immediately for trying to climb out and gaze down over the drop below. The parents followed slowly; it was relaxation they sought, there was exercise enough awaiting back at the site! Wandering round, they briefly mounted the steps back-stage before returning to stand on the circular platform, gazing over the sea to the far horizon. After a while the children dashed up breathless to join them. Grasping Stephen's shirt collar as he was about to disappear again, and with an arm around Sharon, Jan guided the family to a row of stone seats – the younger children either side, Gordon and Chris standing in front. Producing a pamphlet, she extracted the relevant information, relating it in her own words.

"Someone called Rowena Cade started all this," a gesture embraced the whole of the natural theatre. "This woman, born in Derbyshire in 1893, moved to Cornwall and Porthcurno at the age of 28. Do you think she had an urge to do something different, like we had? She first started to develop the open air theatre in 1929 with a performance of The Tempest, that's a play by Shakespeare; it was staged in the garden of Minack House. From that time on, Rowena and two helpers worked to clear the huge masses of granite. New performances and constant work over the years have made it like this. Today the Minack is famous across the world. Many of the foreign visitors we get come to Cornwall especially to see a play acted here."

They wandered back towards the entrance, pausing to look out again across the sea, reluctant to leave, standing close in a family group.

"Look," Gordon called their attention to a granite pillar. "See the little black streaks in the stone; those are tourmaline striations, typical of Cornish granite."

The car whisked them on to Land's End and a lunch of sandwiches sitting on the short grass facing out towards the Longships lighthouse. A few people wandered by following the coastal path and a party of climbers was busy eastward along the cliffs. The Scilly Isles were not visible even with good sunlight and only a light breeze, though many visitors had claimed to see the islands from this vantage point.

"Probably the ones who can afford binoculars." Jan suggested, as they sat contentedly, sometimes watching the scenery, sometimes lying back on the grass close together. The children as elsewhere on the trip, had slipped away to explore, having been properly cautioned about the cliffs.

Early afternoon saw them driving homeward, but along the north coast, stopping at Sennen to see Whitesand Bay from the cliff tops, then off through St. Just with its Lapidary shops offering all types of polished stone. In a few miles, a steam engine passed, all sparkling brass and shiny red paintwork, trundling on towards Lands End.

Several steam rallies took place locally; Cornwall was sometimes called the second home of steam, from the days of the old mine engines. They had seen it coming from some way off and not fancying their chances on the narrow carriageway against such a monster, pulled onto the right hand verge for no kerbs intervened, just tarmac running straight into grass and scrub. The driver looked out from under the canopy, smoke belched from the tall funnel and its whistle blew; for the children's benefit probably. As it passed noisily by, the fireman waved. They waved back with excitement; Stephen would certainly have jumped aboard given the chance.

Cape Cornwall, then Botallack, disappeared from view behind them on the winding road, as did Pendeen where the Geevor tin mine still worked. Parts of this mine are under the sea, the surface of which rippled three to four hundred feet below the road. On the south side the land rose again, the slope strewn with giant boulders reaching up to over 800 feet in places. There were many small parking areas sufficient for a car or two, the occasional couple eating in a vehicle, gazing out at the spectacular jumble of cliffs and the sea beyond. In one of these clearings they stopped at the children's request and set about climbing the summit that towered above on the inland side. Isolated patches of gorse and heather dotted the lower slopes, intermixed with the inevitable ration of bramble and a liberal sprinkling of bracken, brown and dead from the previous season. Chris and Sharon dashed ahead, Stephen struggling to keep up. As the family climbed the vegetation thinned to a short grass, becoming more sparsely tufted and rising eventually to a cluster of enormous angular granite rocks at the summit. Here they sat recovering, gazing down at a dinky toy car far below. Beyond spread the glistening panorama of the Atlantic, a deeper blue lacking that greenish tinge seen on the channel coast at Lamorna and Minack.

Continuing homeward, the cobbled streets of St. Ives rumbled under bouncing wheels before skirting round the estuary at Hayle. Here Cornwall Bird Watchers had a hide for observing seabirds and waders. Kingfishers too, might be seen, they needed the estuary's tall sandy banks for nest burrows, probably the same birds that occasionally flew up the Hayle river to visit the caravan park. A few more miles driven on little used side roads led back to Relubbus.

Nothing stays the same forever! A week later the site opened again as March arrived and with it the new season's first ill omen; the village shop changed hands. They would miss Sampson and his wife Dorothy who had lived in the area since childhood and ran the shop for over 20 years.

"A big change for us after so long," Sampson said. He mentioned later that as a child aged around seven in the late 1920's, he had gone to the same building to buy fish and chips, done in the old way, in a pan over an oil burner. "Someone called..." he hesitated, "No, it's gone, I can't remember who ran it then; that's more than fifty years ago. One of the older villagers might know. Anyway, that was a long time before we owned the place. It went back to being an ordinary house afterwards, until we started the shop."

Sampson had driven round the site each morning since the very first season with the milk and papers, never missing a day and with a great talent for pleasing customers. A fresh pint of milk for breakfast made a big difference to many families, for none of the tents had fridges, nor indeed did many caravans. Unfortunately it soon became apparent from visitors remarks that the new man had not yet acquired Sampson's knack of keeping them happy.

Jan stood by the office door watching him one morning, "He's new, perhaps with a little time and experience…?" She left the question hanging; no need to tell this household that starting a business could be worrying and difficult; they had made enough mistakes themselves, and still did on occasions. Fortunately the house had been placed deliberately to give good vision of the entrance and adjoining areas, so an eye could easily be kept on the new man's progress, and hope for a gradual improvement.

That good vision extended to the river as well! Three children peered out through the kitchen window at a strange duck that landed on the stream near the waterwheel. Stephen reached out a hand, feeling for a dining chair and pulled it nearer to stand on. Jan entered the room, her chin steadying the top of a tall pile of loosely folded washing just removed from the line. Noticing the unmoving backs of three young heads she stepped closer.

"It's some sort of duck," Sharon offered.

"Teal I think, I'll get the book." Jan moved to the dining end of the large combined room, deposited the washing on the table, and disappeared, returning with a well-worn copy of Fitter and Richardson's *Pocket Guide to British Birds.*

"What have you done to your trousers?" she demanded, pausing inside the doorway, looking at Stephen's rear, something unnoticed before, hidden by the armful of bed linen and clothes on her previous entry. "Never mind, tell me about it after we identify the duck."

She moved to the window, laying the book on the worktop and turning the pages. "There. The teal." A finger pointed at the top picture on the right hand page, checking details. "White wing line, green stripe on head, dark chest flecks and much smaller than a mallard. A drake. Wonder where the female is? Anyway, so much for the duck. Now, what on earth have you done with those trousers?"

Stephen craned his head over one shoulder, trying to see, frowning, but said nothing. The other two looked at each other with a ghost of amusement on their faces.

"Well?" Jan asked again impatiently, eyeing the three, clearly directing the question to them all. Chris studied the ceiling with a little shrug and an expression of innocence. His mother had seen the gesture often enough to realise her eldest son knew more than he would say. She turned her attention to Sharon who seemed about to speak, glanced at her brother, then shook her head. Stephen, chin raised, mouth tightly set, stood defiant.

"Go and change. I'm angry with you! This time I'll let it pass, but if it happens again you spend the rest of the day in your room!"

March had seen a total of fifty-eight caravan days, another record, several visitors in middle management forced to come before the financial year ended in April or lose the balance of last year's holidays. Virtually all had pitched on hardstandings, which seemed favourite with the ground still soft.

One evening Sharon and Chris raced down the road. Noticing their approach, Stephen called, "They're coming."

Seconds later Sharon burst through the door, out of breath, excited, arms gesticulating. "I've found the answer!"

Walking through from the kitchen, Jan stopped in surprise, noticing Chris roll his eyes towards the ceiling in resignation.

"What answer?"

"We did it in French today!" Sharon slipped off her coat, laying it carefully on the snooker table. "Our proper teacher was away; the temporary master talked of places, cities in France, told us about Paris!"

"What about Paris?"

Sharon turned to Stephen. "*I* know why the fish are mad!"

Jan wondered for a moment what fish, then recalled Stephen's question and how annoyed Sharon had been. It was not that Stephen had refused to explain, he never tried to goad his sister with words, never said "Shan't tell you" – not his way. The little lad had sat there, lips tightly closed, staring back as Sharon had demanded the answer. The question had been asked repeatedly over those past weeks, it had become a family joke; but on each occasion little Stephen had stood or sat, lips compressed, a hint of naughty pleasure lurking elusively in his face.

"Mum!"

Jan's attention returned to the present, to the impatient

stance of the girl waiting to be asked why. There was little need to ask! Even running to the kitchen could only win a delay; Sharon would chase after, determined to tell of her discovery – there was no escape. Anyway there was something endearing about her daughter's eagerness; it would be cruel to reveal that the answer was already known. The parents had worked it out in bed that same night, but had kept silent so not to rob Stephen of his prize.

Sharon moved restlessly, anxious to deliver her punch line but wanting the satisfaction of having someone ask.

"Well?" Jan obliged.

"They're insane! In Seine; S-E-I-N-E! It's the river that runs through Paris. That's where the fish are!"

"Really? Did you hear that Chris?"

"Only a million times already. At school, on the bus home, twice when we called in at Jim's bungalow and…"

He stopped abruptly, forced to defend himself as Sharon lunged with clenched fists.

Many quiet April days were used to build more dry walls with the stone stockpiles accumulated over past years. Banks of topsoil and shrubs provided a visual break to the various terraces and raised areas. This planting was not required by the planning permission and would undoubtedly cause extra trimming work for the future, but endeavours to create the best site in the Southwest would never be achieved by being economical with effort!

During this period, Jan's front mat disappeared; the coconut fibre one kept outside the door. The stony area in front of the office crunched by many feet as time passed, had, like the rest of the site roads, grown more powdery in dry weather and more adhesive in the wet. An exterior mat, though occasionally rain-soaked, helped defend the carpet from this fine stone dust that tended to walk in. Suddenly it had gone!

"What's happened to my doormat?" she asked at tea. Although the children professed ignorance, Chris suggesting that perhaps someone had 'borrowed' it, Jan again had a feeling that the truth was being hidden. Sharon in particular had that bubbly air she often acquired when in possession of secret information, a feeling of something bursting to get out, being withheld only with the greatest difficulty. Stephen looked down, a little demonic grin passing across his face. As she stared accusingly at the lad, he turned back, defiant, meeting her gaze.

No further information was forthcoming and other matters took precedence. Visitors might still be scarce, but the livestock needed more attention. One of the goats, Olive, had been taken to the billy. She was expecting her first kid in late spring and therefore warranted special care. The ducks, now including a few Mallard, had their own problem. They had started laying again but Magpies were stealing the eggs. Crafty birds Magpies, alert enough to fly off before anyone could get near them, yet sufficiently bold to enter the duck shed in search of a meal! The eggs were for hatching, not eating, so these losses would delay the arrival of spring ducklings, for Muscovys would not start before they layed a decent sized clutch to sit on, normally at least fourteen, which might take just over a fortnight. They would then sit for five and a half weeks before hatching; that made over seven weeks in which the eggs were at risk to those long tailed, piebald robbers. Sitting should ideally begin by May, but achieving this seemed unlikely. Eggs were stolen almost as quickly as they were laid! As a temporary measure the shed door was left shut for much of the day, but had to be open long enough for the ducks to exercise, eat and swim. Still some eggs were lost; another solution must be found.

"We could blow an egg and fill it with mustard," Jan suggested.

"I'd rather fill it with gunpowder." Each egg lost was a little chick that would never to see the light of day. Magpies had become River Valley's least favourite birds!

***

Jan approached the big excavator carefully. Gordon was working farther down the valley, figuring that even though it was weekend, he might as well get in a few more days' work with so few tourists yet around. Holding a basket with the coffee, she waved, knowing it was useless to shout above the engine noise, and dangerous to approach before being seen. Shortly he noticed her, the engine died and he climbed down. Usually they drank either leaning against the machine or on a sunny bank nearby but she forestalled either, laying the basket down by the large rear wheel, then beckoning and moving stealthily back towards the office. "Follow me and be quiet."

"What…" he started, but she put a finger to her lips and continued on. He followed, content to watch as she tried to move without sound, bottom waggling nicely from side to side. He reached to touch, but at the first contact she spun round, raising a warning fist and putting one finger again to her lips before leading on. Almost within sight of the big waste heaps, she cautioned again, crouching lower and moving stealthily from bush to bush. He could hear children's voices from somewhere above, and bumped into Jan as she stopped abruptly at the edge of a large clump of willow and pointed upwards.

Looking carefully round the edge of the trees, he saw Chris climbing the steep face, not where the terraces were being formed, but nearer, at the northwest end. The other two children were already above, not right at the top but on a broad ledge some thirty feet up, the ground below sloping smoothly, having lain undisturbed maybe since mining ceased in the 1800's. Sharon called down but her words were lost on the wind. Chris was carrying something flat and squarish, the exact nature of the object not clear at that distance. More words drifted down as he reached the top, unintelligible words, just voice sounds with gestures that might have been a small argument. Shortly they saw Stephen take whatever Chris was carrying and walk towards the edge. Hesitating only long enough to say something to the others, he tossed the object on the ground, sat on it, and heaved forward. Slowly at first he slid away, then faster and faster, rapidly gathering pace until plummeting at breakneck speed down the sloping side to be lost from sight somewhere below.

Jan turned with amusement, pushing him back into the cover of the bush, and holding onto his hand as they stood close looking at each other.

"You knew they were doing that before bringing the coffee," Gordon accused. Seeing her nod, the flash of white teeth, and feeling the squeeze of a hand, he could not resist pulling her closer. After a while they leaned apart, still holding each other round the waist.

"So that's what happened to your doormat. Are you going to stop them?" he asked, curious why she had not done so immediately.

"We should. It *is* dangerous; well it might be. Stephen's still very young; did you see the speed? Sharon must be doing it too, I'm sure they were arguing over whose turn it was. She's usually so careful with her clothes. Probably pulls her skirt up round the waist and sits on her knickers. Will you speak to them?" Jan asked.

"Why me? I tell them too much already, especially when I'm tired and they do things that cause extra work; I tend to forget sometimes that they're still quite young. You tell them. Anyway, they must be allowed some risks. I don't think you need worry about Stephen, he's good at anything requiring balance."

"He is, isn't he?" Her eyes shone with pride but part of the concern remained. "If we let them carry on, others will copy. Someone's bound to get hurt?"

"There are no other children on site at the moment," Gordon prompted, still curious what she would do.

"All right I won't tell them yet; tomorrow perhaps, or next week." She made to move off. "Are you coming to drink that coffee and do some work, or just standing around wasting time all afternoon?"

He made a grab for her but she was running, keeping her head low.

A new Calor gas fridge arrived on Friday, the old one had been playing up and parts were no longer available, or so the suppliers claimed. More caravans were getting them now. Jan insisted that with summer coming and the weather already quite warm, she had no intention of tolerating kitchen facilities inferior to those of her visitors. In any case, doing without a working fridge would scarcely have paid – apart from the cost of wasted food, they could not really afford to be ill. This one was bigger, but not greatly so, still easy enough for one delivery man to carry from the lorry through to the kitchen while his driver stayed pouring over a map in the cab

"Make coffee before I start." Gordon insisted, "the gas must be off to rearrange these connections."

Unfortunately the required pipework differed from that expected and as a temporary measure, Sharon's gas light was cannibalised to get the fridge working.

"I'll pick up a new fitting when I go to Penzance on Monday and re-fix the light then. It's not worth a special journey tomorrow."

At tea Jan displayed her newly acquired fridge with delight, forgetting at the time to mention the lost gas lamp. It was later during homework that she finally remembered. Since it took at least three 24-watt bulbs to give decent illumination for reading, the family sat in one room in the evenings. This was usually the dining room during homework, and later the lounge. The use of any other lights would deplete the battery charge and reduce the current available for television. Short duration trips like using the bathroom and topping up the boiler had little effect but the boys could not for, instance, take a book to read in their bedroom. Sharon had always been free from this restriction because of her gas lamp, the only one in the house apart from the kitchen. Whether from preference or just to show off, she went often to her room in the evenings, lying on the bed to read by this light. On hearing the lamp was temporarily not working, she frowned in disappointment.

"Oh dear!" Chris spoke with exaggerated concern and obvious delight, "You could have a candle to read by, it should be enough, you're not very bright."

She lashed out, bypassing his defensively raised arms, catching him a goodly blow round the ear with her exercise book as he realised her intention a fraction late. The damage was more surprise and sound than actual injury, the book too thin to inflict much pain, but Chris stumbled and fell backwards on the floor. This major victory for the younger Sharon was viewed with equal surprise and merriment by the rest of the family. Stephen said nothing but reached for Sharon's right hand and pushed it from the elbow, high in the air; the gesture of triumph declaring a knockout.

Dad suggested that instead of bullying her elder brother she should use her new talent for swatting magpies. The ducks were nearly ready to sit, but those damn black and white robbers were at it again! For a while, a net rigged over the shed doorway reaching down to within a foot of ground level had proved successful, since for short distances ducks walk, whereas magpies invariably fly. It was, as elsewhere in nature, a matter of energy conservation. Ducks were heavy birds; getting airborne demanded more effort than walking to and from the stream. However one or more of those disgusting long tailed villains had now found a way to fly under the net. Eggs were again disappearing!

Turning the corner of the house to inspect the shed shortly after nine one morning, a Magpie thief was disturbed in the act. The bird tangled itself in the net in a rush to escape. Gordon dashed forward reaching out. Simultaneously the bird broke free, making a dive under the net towards freedom. Too late! His hand grabbed the fleeing robber, firmly grasping the feathers. A great tuft came away in his hand as the squawking, partially bald miscreant made good its escape! The eyes that followed that absconding bird should have shot it down in flames but the miserable Magpie flew on, disappearing into a distant stand of trees. Glancing down at the firmly gripped feathers, a great bunch in his hand, produced a shrug; so near and yet... Returning to the office, he walked through to the kitchen, holding out his hand for Jan to see.

"Look."

"You missed it! Should have rung its neck. Fancy getting that close and missing. Typical man!" Laughing, she tossed her head with a final "Hmm!"

Cheek! No woman could have got that near. Only the superb physical qualities of a man made it possible. Women were getting quite above their station. They were supposed to swoon with admiration when a husband displayed proof of his prowess! There *must* be an answer. Ah, yes!

"That, my dear, is exactly where male subtlety comes in! I deliberately let the bird escape. Now not only will it be deterred, afraid to come back again, but will tell the other Magpies, discouraging them as well." He stopped, pleased with the quick improvisation.

"Tell them in Morse code, will it? Hammer out the dots and dashes with its beak on a tree trunk? In case you hadn't realised, birds can't talk. And don't think I haven't heard you talking away to that robin! Poor bird. I have to put up with you, but I don't see why it should." She held out a hand inviting him to reply, the contest joined.

"The bare patch on that Magpie's rear will do all the telling; the other birds will know! I shall strew these feathers inside the shed. Magpies are so damn clever, they should be able to understand that message. Can't stand clever birds!

They smiled at each other, eyes shining; she had not missed the inference of that final sentence. Stepping close they hugged. Life together was so good. As she reached up he kissed her open lips, pulling her body more tightly against his own, neither noticing when Magpie feathers littered the kitchen floor.

Chapter 15

Personal Magnetism

The waterwheel produced many things not obvious to a casual observer. There was power of course, and oxygen for the fish; any splash or surface disturbance trapped oxygen in the water – a more efficient mechanism than those churning paddles would be hard to find. Further, wheel and weir combined to hold a pool of slow moving water which reached as far as the bridge preventing scour damaging the foundations, and in addition there was the matter of debris. Odd branches blown down after a storm, sedge uprooted by the ducks, river weed that occasionally washed free after heavy rain; much collected on the wheel's protective grid allowing its removal rather than floating on downstream. Even among regular visitors, few were aware of all these assets, but there was another; a closely guarded secret! This special feature remained virtually unknown except to the handful of people who discovered it, usually to their cost! The hidden bye-product was *fun*; provided that is, one had a fairly distorted sense of humour!

To comprehend properly what happened to certain mystified strangers walking along the footpath requires a brief understanding of how this device functioned. Basically, the waterwheel turned slowly when producing electricity, and much faster whenever no current was required. Power, though limited, was needed for many things; for lighting and TV, for the vacuum cleaner, the food mixer, the drill and other power tools, and for charging caravanners batteries. Whenever such power was called for, the alternator obligingly produced current – not always enough, but as much as it could. This made the wheel turn more slowly. However, it often happened that about mid-afternoon nothing electrical was in use and the batteries were already fully charged. Then the alternator would cut out, giving no resistance to rotation, allowing the wheel to spin much faster.

A little game developed with folk wandering along the river; a one sided game because only the family knew it was being played. Any group of people who were new to the site would invariably stop to admire the wheel; it had special qualities that attracted them. The swish and splash of moving water pleasing to both eye and ear, the comparative rarity, that nostalgic connection of waterwheels with bygone years; it was hard to resist! Provided this was a time of day when no power was needed, then the wheel would be spinning fast and spraying spectacularly. One member of the group would usually walk over and rest a hand or an arm on the guard rail. This was the cue! As hand touched rail, a cluster of lights would be switched on. The small bulbs were invisible to those outside during daylight hours, but the power they required immediately slowed the wheel. Such an incident occurred during coffee break one afternoon. Jan spotted some people crossing the bridge. She glanced at Gordon and pointed towards the window. He leaned over to look out as they both rose, standing back from the glass, a position hidden from those outside.

The chap leading the way stood out; so obviously the self-appointed group leader, formally dressed in a good quality tweed suit and matching trilby hat. He walked erect, shoulders back, a touch shorter than the rest but strutting a few paces ahead. When they stopped to gaze at the wheel it was he who pointed, clearly explaining how it worked. He had no idea, no means of knowing, that two extra pairs of eyes lay hidden deep inside the room.

"Captain Mannering?" Gordon asked.

The man led down the short bank to the water's edge and stood sideways to the wheel, a stance typical of the character.

Jan nodded agreement. "Wonder if he's bald under that hat?" Moving closer to a cord hanging from the ceiling switch, she put on a deep voice. "Now pay attention men! We have here a waterwheel and it works like this."

One could well imagine him saying those words; it only needed an army uniform. Mannering turned to his followers, at the same time waving an arm towards the wheel, a gesture implying expertise on the subject. His hand reached towards the railing as he straightened, glaring at one companion who had dared to speak, waiting for silence as he prepared to offer the benefits of superior knowledge.

At the instant his fingers touched the metalwork, Jan switched on a cluster of lights! The wheel responded immediately, slowing drastically, a change clear to those outside both by sight and by ear. The swish and splash diminished and water no longer flew vigorously off the downstream paddles. His hand came off the rail as if stung; an 'I never touched it' look appearing momentarily on his face, quickly masked with an indignant glare at the wheel, as if it had deliberately misbehaved.

"You stupid wheel!" Jan's deep voice mimicked as she switched the lights off.

Gordon smiled at her perception. The speed responded quickly. Mannering reached out again, a little less confidently but with a certain amount of bluster. The group stared intently, their thoughts not hard to guess.

"Would it slow – it wouldn't dare!"

The finger touched, the lights went on again, the wheel slowed. Mutiny! He took a quick step backwards. Another tug on the switch and the wheel's pace quickened, spraying water with abandon at the downstream side. A little conference started among the onlookers, he seemed temporarily to lose his grip, they no longer listened to him but talked among themselves. With a little shake he recovered himself, brushed an imaginary speck from one sleeve and stepped towards the chattering group, tapping a shoulder and saying something to one of the other men. The victim stepped forward reluctantly. Another word from Mannering and the unwilling male reached out a hand, touching the rail. Jan did nothing. The short pompous leader showed every sign that the wheel had offered him a direct affront, glaring at it fit to scorch the timber. The hidden watchers would not have been surprised to see steam rise from the wet paddles. He addressed the group again and several others tried. No effect whatsoever! Expressions of bafflement crossed their faces. Had they imagined the whole thing? Mannering moved forward, stretched out a single finger and placed it gently on the framework. Jan pulled the light switch, the wheel obediently slowed.

Gordon expected a scowl and a shadow of it did cross the man's face, but slowly a self-important smirk emerged and spread. Mannering's chin came up. Still touching the rail with his right hand, he pivoted round to eye his group of followers with a superior smile, somehow putting a swagger into that single sideways step. Slowly the other arm rose towards them, palm upward and open, fingers extending, wrist rotating in a little twirl.

Jan lowered her voice an octave. "Ah yes. Well, personal magnetism you see! Some of us have it, others..." she left the words unfinished but waved an arm in exact imitation of Mannering's gesture to the group.

Yes, she had that about right. Gordon nodded, and seeing the hand grasping the rail lifted experimentally, he reached over pulling the switch and the lights went off, speeding the wheel again.

With a little, 'there you are' tilt of the head, and a 'move-over' signal, Mannering indicated that the group should stand aside and allow him through. Stepping back into the lead he strutted off down the valley talking non-stop. No one seemed to reply, but at one stage he raised a pointed finger towards three people at the rear.

"Stop talking in the ranks!" Shaking her head Jan resumed a normal voice, "Wish we could tell the rest of them what we did. He would be mortified if they laughed at him."

They watched until the group disappeared from sight. Not all these little games ended so easily. Occasionally someone came to the door to ask the reason; then they felt bound to answer honestly. Reactions were mixed, but usually it caused laughter. Most people however, never asked; they just wandered off deep in conversation, probably never to solve the mystery, making their stay at least a memorable one. Who knows what hidden powers you may discover in the Cornish countryside?

Like others walking beside the stream, the departing group would no doubt look out across the site, for in May the valley was splendid. Apart from the new standpipes that now sprouted unobtrusively near every area, no marks, not even the faintest sign, now remained to indicate where those service trenches had been dug. Even the extra areas prepared over last winter for more visitors were already covered in grass, and young spring leaves in various vibrant greens clothed trees in every direction. Though daffodils were long gone, the odd primrose remained and Bluebell Wood was a carpet for the eye to behold, near violet in colour, criss-crossed with rabbit tracks and punctuated by ivy-covered trunks. Wild flowers grew in abundance along verges that edged the site's stony tracks, many more showing on those uncut grass borders surrounding all the mown areas. Campion, speedwell, patches of ox-eye daisy, bugle, herb robert, bush vetch and others bloomed chaotically, singly and in bunches. Even the track to the village was improving, the trees set along one side were all in graceful leaf, a few blooms now showing on the rhododendrons. How could any visitor resist?

The ducks were thriving; winning in their tussle with Magpies, many fewer of which now came near the shed. The reason for this success was still a matter of contention, a little battle adding spice to coffee breaks. That bird with a bare rump had disappeared completely! Gordon had pointed this out on more than one occasion, insisting the feathers, carefully collected from the kitchen floor and sprinkled around the duck shed, were responsible. Jan countered, suggesting that news of a fearful ugly monster lurking near the shed, had spread among the magpie population. Two ducks were already sitting; another two had eight and ten eggs respectively. Usually they laid at least fourteen, sometimes as many as nineteen, so some days must pass before the next started but at least all the eggs should be fertile!

"Francis Drake was busy again when I came by," Gordon called, entering the office, "that's at least five this morning, I told you men were made for more than one woman!"

"In Francis case I think it's justified." Jan called back from the kitchen.

"Why in his case?"

"Compared to some males, he's really good looking don't you think?"

Little tragedies strike most families sooner or later. In mid-May, Chris, his head covered in blood, was driven home by a motorist. Red congealing streaks ran down one side of his face from hair to chin. This, and the sickly pallid whiteness of his skin, normally so full of healthy colour, had Jan rushing out, her own colour blanching as she went, the rest of the family close behind.

The motorist had found Chris unconscious by the roadside; he was unsure for how long, but had seen another car disappearing round the corner ahead. A bicycle had lain nearby. The man intended calling an ambulance, but Chris came round and had asked to be driven home instead. Within a few minutes they had thanked the driver, transferred Chris to their own car and were on the way to West Cornwall Hospital at Penzance. The casualty doctor admitted him, a nurse quickly assigned to check pulse and temperature hourly. Later when the family crowded round his hospital bed at visiting time, he still looked a mess, his skin colour only slightly less pale.

"Don't worry," the doctor said, "what you see is superficial, it will heal quickly. We keep children in after unconsciousness to check for delayed shock or concussion. He'll be fine in the morning. I expect you can take him home then."

It was not a happy evening, both Sharon and Stephen unusually subdued while Jan couldn't stay still, jumping up continually to do something – anything; many a task unnecessary or having little purpose. Gordon disguised his worry, fearing it might make her feel worse. What could he say that would be comforting... any attempt probably increasing tension rather than easing it. Just be available and close, talk when she wanted or say nothing if she chose to be silent – but that was not easy either.

An early phone call the following day revealed all was well and by evening Chris was home again, a little the worse for wear but much better than he might have been. A car had cut him into the bank, not the one that brought him home but another that drove straight on. Whether the driver knew, or Chris had made an error of judgement not directly caused by the passing vehicle would probably never be known. Cornwall, while having less traffic than most counties, had compensating disadvantages for the cyclist. The County Council cleverly avoided roadside trimming until wild blooms had flourished and the seeds scattered, for it gave a better show next year. However, these hedges so admired for the masses of wild flowers were usually granite underneath, not made for a soft landing! Like all parents, they gave the inevitable warning.

"Let that be a lesson to you all! Go more slowly and take care."

As Chris recovered in that slack period before spring bank holiday, life was brightened by the arrival on one windy day, of Frank and Ivy, Gordon's Mum and Dad. His younger sister Jane and her husband Bill came too, their first sight of the valley – sisterly affection or curiosity?

These increased numbers presented the first real test of space since the house was built. A bed settee in the lounge for Jane and Bill solved the final sleeping problem, but the guests had an unfortunate habit of switching on unnecessary lights and forgetting them; something with which the waterwheel could not cope. At breakfast the following morning, an extra leaf that extended the dining table came into use. Evenings found the lounge crowded with chairs, and it was as the extended family sat talking that Jane, with occasional interventions from Ivy, revealed the flowerpot tale.

The matter first came to light when some extra seats from the dining room were being arranged, a nightly ritual due to insufficient chairs. Frank took one from Chris and was lifting it back to a position beside the window. In the process he nudged a glass vase. The object wobbled, and Jane shot out a hand.

"Not another flowerpot!" But her fingers steadied the glass, preventing it from falling. As the family settled to talk, Sharon asked, "What did you mean, another flowerpot?"

Jane looked at Frank, then Ivy. Probably had anyone else asked she would have brushed it aside, but Sharon was so transparently curious.

"Well, Frank had been driving for hours, we were all hungry and thirsty but he wouldn't stop. Mile after mile he drove, on and on, past pubs and cafes, not even slowing down. Mum, that's my Mum," Jane pointed to Ivy, "wasn't speaking to him any more, but I was! Bill kept out of it too, left me to do all the complaining."

"She's good at it," Bill offered.

Jane glanced at him and sniffed, "Beware Sharon, men are mean, few of them would spend a penny on a good meal if they could help it! Anyway eventually Frank did pull in to a roadside café place; not as good as many we'd passed, not very smart – not expensive looking either! There was a car park of sorts, with old flowerpots stood around. I don't know what they were for; at this time of year everything is in bloom but these were dead, no colour, neglected, just in the way. Perhaps they were a job lot bought cheap and laid out for people to run into so the owner could make a profit on the damage. Anyway, guess who ran the car into one?"

Stephen pointed at Frank, and Ivy laughed, swinging round to the little lad, "How did you guess?"

It hadn't been difficult, Frank's expression had shown disapproval of the story throughout but he couldn't help returning Stephen's impish grin, displaying as it did such obvious approval of a grown up who had been naughty.

"Yes," Jane continued, "He did; only scraped the pot gently with the side of a tyre, but it fell apart. Ivy said it was deliberate so we couldn't stay."

"I was annoyed!" Ivy prompted, glancing fiercely at Frank. "We'd passed all those nice road houses, only to stop in this dirty, run-down, place. When the pot broke I could see us driving on to Cornwall without a bite."

"Anyway," Jane continued, "We backed up and drove into another parking space, then walked in and ordered a meal. At some time the proprietor, a surly unpleasant fellow, came across and spoke. 'Have you something to tell me?' he asks. 'No' says Frank, and we all carried on eating. Ivy wanted to leave, said we should pay the chap, and we might have if he hadn't been so nasty; probably caught dozens of people that way. What other reason is there for putting disgusting old pots in a car park? They certainly weren't decorative, just a weedy mess. The one we hit may well have been broken already, propped up there for that very purpose. We carried on eating then ordered the dessert course and the chap came across again. 'Are you sure you don't have something to tell me?' it was asked with an ill-natured roughness, threatening almost. 'No' said Frank and the man slunk off again."

“What happened?” Sharon turned to Ivy wanting to know everything.

“Nothing. We paid the bill, seemed expensive for what we had, and left. I did have a word with Frank about it as he drove on.” Ivy gave him another fierce glare.

“A word?” Jane echoed. “You bent his ear on and off for the next fifty miles!”

Conversation continued for a while about the children’s school and friends. Jane asked what their father had been doing all winter.

“Not much,” Stephen offered, without elaboration.

“Putting pipes in the ground mainly,” Chris explained, Mum’s done more. She’s kept the grass mowed, planted those flowers in the wall outside, painted the toilet buildings and cleaned the showers. He glanced sideways, “Dad was going to fix the shower heads, but I don’t think he has?”

“Oh no. You’re right, he hasn’t.” Sharon remembered.

That evening passed quickly, so many new things to talk about and games to play. In the morning the three children set off, sauntering reluctantly, satchels in hand. Anticipating their intention, Jan accompanied them as far as the bridge, waiting until beyond earshot of the waving family then stopping to warn, “If you do succeed in missing the bus, don’t come back here, you walk right on to school!” Surprise and guilt on the young faces clearly indicated her suspicions had hit the mark.

Sharon, the six mile journey in mind, gave a shriek, “Come on!” starting off at a run, quickly overtaken by Chris. Stephen walked on behind; his bus was later.

Returning indoors, Jan rang Audrey in the village, asking her mother to check and ring back that everyone caught the bus. She awaited confirmation before departing with the visiting family on a trip to Mullion. Although the wind had abated somewhat from the previous day’s storm, the sea swept in spectacularly rough. No other car stood parked nearby as they left to walk round the harbour. Not a boat remained in the water, all had been dragged up the ramp, safely above a swell that rolled heavily across the protected dock. To the right, a path led the group off along the cliffs, part of Cornwall's 200-mile coastal walk. The sea breaking on rocks far below swept forward in waves, turbulent and crashingly powerful, some spray even reaching to sprinkle the walkers. They came shortly to a point where two arms of tall irregular rock jutted out to the sea, forming a narrow V-shaped inlet, concentrating the water's power between. As each wave rushed in, the breaking top frothed white over rocks on either side to finally dissipate its energy on the cliff face directly below where the six stood.

They halted at the spectacle, bringing out a camera – but stopped too long! A giant wave lashed up the passage and thudded into the wall below, flinging one great flume or water and spray over the top. Everyone ran! Jan, posed on the cliff edge for a photo against the majestic background, got caught, half drowned, catching her breath as the curtain of water first engulfed her, then dragged her bodily towards the cliff edge. Gordon dashed forward, frightened the receding wave would pull her in! As the waters slid back over that jagged escarpment she emerged, staggering unsteadily and soaked to the skin, hair plastered flat, not a dry patch anywhere. The drowned, bedraggled figure stood bemused, shivering in spite of the open coat which now clung to her body in a sodden mess like the rest of her clothes. A short burst of laughter from the family was mostly relief and though she too attempted to smile, it was half-hearted, the wind briskly cold and her body visibly shaking. Something had to be done! Telling the family to give them ten minutes start and hauling Jan by one reluctant arm, Gordon headed urgently for the car park.

Unlocking the passenger door, he pulled off her coat, forcing the clinging sleeves from each arm and draped it over the bonnet to drain. Jan stood confused, teeth chattering in the wind. Hurriedly he pushed her into the passenger seat, closing the door. Dashing to the driver's side and sliding out of his own coat, he started the engine to operate the heater, then turned to speak.

"Strip to your underwear. Quickly."

"What here?"

"Of course! It's that or pneumonia if you don't get dry and warm. There's not a soul about. Come on, hurry up, I'll help you."

How long was it since he had tried to undress a girl in a car? More years than he cared to remember. She struggled out of the jumper and blouse, then kicked away shoes and white ankle socks. They struggled together, stripping off the soaking slacks with difficulty. As her legs pulled clear, she sat in little lacy knickers and matching bra, both wet, clinging transparently to the skin. Reaching over for his coat, he pushed down between car seat and bare back as she raised herself up, allowing it to be eased under long wet legs; an erotic movement as she struggled, bending her knees forward and raising that nice little scantily clad bottom. Leaning over with an arm each side and his head somehow mixed up with her bosom, Gordon wrestled the material down into position. "Okay!"

She sank back into it.

Pulling the coat closed, his hands eased her nearer; for warmth of course he told himself but knew it was a lie. All he really wanted to do was to pull it open again and… Instead they huddled close and kissed gently. Breaking away, he removed his shoes, taking off the socks and easing them over her still damp feet, then put the shoes back on for driving. The car was heating up nicely and had become very private when the other family members arrived, evaporating moisture condensing to stipple each window with a veil of dewy droplets like frosted glass. The wet coat was slipped off the bonnet into the boot and everyone crowded inside. Rubbing windows clear with fist or handkerchief, they headed immediately for home. Gordon had a job keeping his eyes on the road, casting sideways glances at Jan, her hair in a ruffled mess where she had tried to dry it, but looking super. It was not difficult to remember, in fact it was damn hard to forget, just what she wasn't wearing under that coat. A good deal of family ribbing discussed what lengths a chap would go to, just to get a pretty girl alone in a car with him and more in a similar vein, but he only half heard it, his mind elsewhere!

Spring bank holiday arrived, and with it a new problem. Francis had taken to landing on caravan roofs. In spite of constant exercise with the females, he was now a big bird of considerable weight and would touch down with a bang in the early morning just after the ducks were first fed, usually well before 6.30am! Several people complained of great thumps on the roof waking them in alarm. Most were more amused than annoyed when told of Francis misbehaviour and shown the big drake. Their sense of humour however, might not survive too many such early awakenings.

What to do? Try feeding the ducks later; do the toilet cleaning then have breakfast before dishing out the wheat. Several more days passed, but the complaints continued. Not only did this first preventive measure totally fail, but Francis started flying onto roofs later in the day as well. It would only be a matter of time before other ducks were copying him. A more positive cure was needed, hopefully something not too drastic!

Next morning feeding proceeded as usual, the whole flock rushing for the grain. Francis was never shy but today craftily stayed on the outer edge of the gaggle, not quite within reach. Gordon knelt and beaks began nuzzling for food from his hand, but some sixth sense prevented Frances coming nearer. Why? Did he know he'd been misbehaving? No point it upsetting the rest of the ducks in a futile attempt. Better leave it and try again tomorrow. The day passed uneventfully apart from one caravanner borrowing the stepladder to remove a large turd left on his skylight. He knew the cause, for word had travelled quickly round the handful of caravans near the river. Although this man was good-humoured over the incident, he showed a certain apprehension.

“Ducks aren’t creatures of habit, are they?”

“Oh no. I’m so sorry,” Jan apologised. “We *are* trying to stop him.”

“Orange sauce?” The visitor grasped the ladder and strode off to do his work.

That evening, Stephen as usual arrived home first. He stopped near the bridge, approaching the ducks and inspecting Francis carefully, then checked the adjoining area. His young friend’s car was gone, as were all other visitors’ cars, fine weather having tempted everyone to the beaches or perhaps sightseeing. Running to enter the office door, he dodged away as a hand reached out ruffling his hair, then stood not bothering to straighten it, smiling up at Jan. He liked this time alone before the older two arrived; felt closer to his mother, sensing somehow her need to lavish attention and love on her youngest after the days absence. Sometimes she laid an arm round his shoulder as they walked across to the window; mostly he shook it off with a show of bravado but would have missed the contact had it been withheld. Today they looked at each other, happy faces, content with that brief touch.

“Francis?” Stephen asked.

Jan shook her head. “Couldn’t catch him.” Something in the lad’s expression made her ask, “You want bread?”

He nodded once and she strode off into the kitchen, rummaging in the bin. The bread was really too fresh for ducks – wasteful, but some deep feeling would not let her refuse this first request of his homecoming. Two slices were handed over and, throwing his jacket untidily on a chair, he raced off. It was on the tip of Jan’s tongue to shout at the retreating back, “Don’t get those school trousers dirty,” but the words would not come. In any case the effort would have been wasted, he would take no notice, she knew that. “Ah well, I can always wash them.”

With the visitors out, the ducks had not been fed for hours, not that they needed feeding; there was only Francis and those three ducks who were not yet sitting, with all the river and surrounding site to satisfy them. But muscovys are delightfully lazy, they prefer to be fed than to forage for themselves, so the appearance of someone bread in hand had them running quickly up the bank. Stephen tore off tiny pieces, walking slowly backwards until reaching a point near the centre of the entrance yard. Here he knelt offering individual fragments, not throwing them now but making the ducks take pieces from his fingers. Again Frances lagged behind and the second slice was already half gone. Holding the remaining bread out in one piece had the ducks surging to grab a beak-full, the drake somehow carried forward with them. In that moment Stephen launched himself horizontally, grabbing wildly, just catching the edge of one wing to end spread-eagled on the ground, ducks and feathers flying in every direction. Jan, standing watching some distance away, raised both hands involuntarily to protect her face.

Francis struggled, slipping on the dusty stone yard and Stephen seemed unable to regain his feet as the drake continued to pull away. Recovering from the minor trauma of passing ducks, Jan peeped from between spread fingers at the contest as if in slow motion, unable momentarily to grasp that she should run in and grab the bird. Then the comedy of the situation struck her and she kept the fingers in place trying to conceal her merriment, finding herself mouthing the words, “Come on Frances, you can do it!”

Abandoning attempts to stand, Stephen pulled Francis steadily backwards until within reach of both hands, then heaved himself bodily forward to throw one arm over the free wing and pull the bird closer, clamping the near wing tightly against his chest. Clasping the neck in his other hand, he rose, holding the prisoner firmly, but immediately dropped back to the ground as claws on those big webbed feet raked his chest. Pressing down on the broad feathered back disabled the feet, compressing them against the stone surface below. Stephen glanced up, triumphant but panting. Seeing his success, Jan slipped to the office still giggling, emerging again, a big pair of scissors waving in one hand.

"Dad usually does this. Shall we try?"

Stephen nodded, holding on as Francis, warned perhaps by some sixth sense, struggled anew.

Taking the right wing Jan fanned it out, trimming only the primary feathers, taking care not to cut too close and leaving the outer ones for appearance sake. Stephen hung on, the drake pinned firmly against the ground, its other wing still intact.

"Right!" Leaping back together they let go. The big bird ran a few steps and launched itself in the air fully expecting to fly. Totally unbalanced, it quickly came to grief, rolling sideways then running at full speed for the water. A definite cure! There would be no more flying onto caravans at least until the next moult. His pride might be injured, but at least it saved his freedom! Worries that he would now be more vulnerable to the fox proved unfounded, Francis sensibly stayed a little closer to the river. More people unexpectedly arriving also made him safer.

News of the Scottish petrol strike first came over the air in early June. During the second week, site numbers rose dramatically. Although each year since opening had shown a regular improvment, this sudden spectacular increase imparted an exhilaration akin to winning the pools.

"Must be the quality of the site; people are getting to know," they congratulated themselves modestly, conveniently forgetting this brief taste of glory was probably at someone else's expense. It continued through June, and whilst already anticipating another record as in the past four seasons, the final total should certainly exceed all pre-season expectations.

Most of the visitors were couples, many in retirement. Several who had been before commented on the standpipes now providing water to each area, but for most visitors these improvements passed unnoticed, becoming expected with the rising standards of sites generally. New areas by the stream developed over the past winter were already in use allowing visitors to spread along the valley, giving each a greater amount of space – for in spite of the increased trade, numbers were not nearly as high as they would be during late July and August. This aspect of the site did bring copious comments; the space, the beauty of the valley, the quietness, the birds, rabbits, squirrels and those wild flowers that peeped forth everywhere, blooming in abundance. These were so much appreciated both by older caravanners and by those younger ones seeking a restful break. That comprised everyone really, for few folk would be fool enough to visit Relubbus expecting frantic activity and loud entertainment. Even had such things been available, few of those seeking a livelier, noisier holiday would have come; most wanted a coastal site with a beach, not an inland valley by a small stream.

Chris, Sharon and Stephen were at school during the week, but a sprinkling of boys and girls of various ages on holiday with their parents provided sufficient friends for weekends and evenings. However it was one of the older men, Sam Jordan, a regular visitor, who took Chris fishing on Saturday. They left early in his yellow Ford Escort, heading for Argle Reservoir near Falmouth, leaving Sam's wife Ned sitting outside the caravan improving her suntan. Sharon and Stephen watched their brother go, waving and just a little envious, but spent the early morning happily enough with various young playmates before most departed for a day on the beach, leaving them alone.

Sharon's new companion, Paula, left too, but returned for lunch then remained on the park while her parents went off with friends. The girls, both nearly twelve years old, wandered down the valley together to find Judy and her two fully-grown offspring. Olive was herself now heavy with kid, the birth only weeks away. Untying the tethers, they let the goats run free, calling them to follow along pathways that had gradually opened with the passing of many young feet over previous seasons. Some distance downstream the new friends found a grassy bank, settled themselves and let their charges roam at will. Ivy came close, pushing between, butting shoulders gently in search of attention. Sharon fondled and scratched the goats neck, the other hand tracing a black stripe that ran from nose up over the forehead, fingers brushing against the grain, feeling the hair's rough texture. Reaching out, she pulled a bunch of grass, handing it to Paula.

"Feed her this, she likes brambles better but they're too prickly."

After a few minutes feeding and petting, Ivy wandered off in search of more interesting nibbles.

"I never knew anyone who had goats before – we live in a town. Why do you keep them, are they just pets?"

"No. Well, yes, they are pets I suppose, but Judy gives us our milk."

"You drink it?" Paula pulled a face.

"It's nice! You can't tell the difference." Sharon saw the doubt in her friend's face. "Honestly! Try some."

"When, back at the house?"

"No, now. Lie on your back under the goat with your mouth open, I'll squirt it straight in."

"You can't?" There was doubt, perhaps a little fear, and an underlying excitement in Paula's words.

"Course I can. Who do you think does the milking when Mum's busy? Judy won't mind."

"I might!" Paula, eyes wide, bit her lower lip as the two girls looked at each other. "Oh go on then, let's try. What do I do?"

Sharon ran across, taking Judy by the collar and led her into the centre of a clear circle of grass surrounded by gorse and willow. "Okay. Lay on your back, then wriggle along until you're underneath. Take a firm hold of the back legs before I touch her udder because she tends to kick forward. Don't look so alarmed, she won't hurt you. Just hold the legs tightly." Sharon was rubbing Judy's neck to stop her getting restive as Paula lay down, slid nearer, then stopped on the point of going underneath, both girls breaking out in a fit of giggles.

"Go on, it's all right!" Sharon struggled to recover.

Paula with a sigh and a shrug, dug her heels in, heaving backward until she was under the goat, then grabbed one foot, quickly bringing the other arm across her body to seize the other. Judy tried to move but had become used to having her feet held and soon submitted. Sharon, dropping on one knee, grasped a teat and directed a short experimental squirt on the ground to one side.

"Open your mouth wide! I need a big target, it's not easy to be accurate."

A long jet of white fluid gushed forth with some force. Milk splashed around the face below causing the eyes that had been staring widely upwards to blink tightly closed, but the main stream of liquid found its mark, shooting straight down inside the exposed throat. Choking, Paula rolled away, the girls ending in a pile laughing uncontrollably as Judy trotted back to her bramble patch.

"There! Could you taste the difference."

"I might – under more normal circumstances. In town we don't ordinarily take our drinks that way, you know!" Paula swallowed again, reaching up to rub her throat. "It came with such pressure it was difficult to tell. Isn't milk usually boiled first or treated somehow?"

"No, we drink it fresh, all of us, just as it comes from the goat – most of it anyway; some we use for cooking."

"Really?" Paula shook her head at the oddness of life by the river, then sighed sadly. "Cooking with goat's milk, lucky you! We're not cooking at all this week. Mostly we eat out at midday, or have salad. Breakfast is just cereal and a cold drink. Our gas started to escape yesterday, made a smell in the van. It comes from under the sink somewhere; there's lots of joints leading to the cooker, the fridge and to a gas light above. My Daddy tried to find the leak, used a match, said he would see flames coming out and know which joint it was. The whole thing went whoosh! He shot backwards, hit his bum on the corner of the bed, then staggered to one side and stood up under a ceiling cabinet. Mother and I were at the back of the caravan. When she laughed I thought he would explode!"

"Why doesn't he get it fixed?" Sharon asked in surprise. "There are details of a gas fitter on the notice board."

"We have a friend at home who will mend it free. Mother's mad, but Daddy insists. Says it serves her right for laughing. That's not really the reason. He's just too mean."

"Lots of Dads are like that! Your parents will still be out won't they?"

"Oh yes. Land's End for the afternoon then the evening performance at Minack Theatre. They've gone with a couple from the next caravan; wanted me to go, but they all talk together and I just follow them round. If I say something they nod and take no notice." Paula sighed unhappily, then broke into a grin. "They'd go mad if they knew about the goat – they think I'm not very capable. Do your parents think that?"

"They can't! I'm in charge in the school holidays!" Sharon, seeing disbelief in Paula's expression, quickly explained. "Not all the time, only when Mum goes to town and caravans arrive. Dad takes them off to pitch and leaves me to answer the phone, sell gas, or mantles or toilet fluid, see to anyone arriving – everything. Often I cook the meals too – they better not say I'm incapable! Hey, would you like to impress your parents?"

"How."

"Find that gas leak and get it fixed before they come home. Have the kettle boiling and hot coffee ready when they arrive, and the caravan lights on."

Paula sighed, shaking her head. "I'd love too! I can just see their faces; if only we could. But it's dangerous! Daddy nearly blew himself up. Who would we get to find the leak?"

"Me." Sharon stood up. "Come on, the goats have wandered off, we'll collect them and find a nice tethering place, somewhere they'll like."

"You won't burn the place down, will you?"

The goats were collected, the ropes tied to their collars, and being well fed they followed easily to a fresh position offering grass, bramble and gorse. Olive, being in kid, had prime position. Paula looked pensive and ill at ease as the girls took their time settling the goats in the new location, stroking them, rubbing cheeks and faces against the smooth hairy necks, finally standing up to take their leave and hurrying away. Reaching the caravan Paula knelt, feeling for a key that hung underneath out of sight. Sharon darted off to fetch something, returning shortly with a plastic bottle. Entering the caravan, she checked in the cabinet beneath the sink where Paula pointed, then sat on the floor and reached in, bringing the bottle close to each joint and giving a small squirt.

"What are you doing?! What is that stuff?" Paula sounded worried.

"Did you ever blow bubbles with a clay pipe? This is Dad's bottle of water with a dash of Fairy Liquid. Go and turn on the gas."

"It won't explode?" Paula was still doubtful.

"No. All the joints have this solution round them. The one that leaks will blow bubbles. Turn it on, then come and see."

Thirty seconds later they located the leaking joint; it led to the cooker. A little more liquid squirted on, frothed and foamed, bubbles rising.

"Okay, turn it off. We've finished." Sharon rose, placed the squeezy bottle on the draining board and stretched.

"Really? So simple – and father thinks *I'm* incapable! Wait 'til I tell him. What now? What do we do next?"

"We stop getting excited, go outside and turn that gas off like I said. Now! Before it makes the place smell!" Automatically Sharon placed hands on hips as she issued the order, smiling at her friend's enthusiasm, then rested on the bench seat while the job was done, speaking again as Paula mounted the caravan steps.

"Leave the door open. Good. All we need now is to tighten that nut, but the pipes are small, easily twisted. I can probably do it but my brother is better – don't you ever tell him I said that! We just need to persuade him."

"Will he do it for us?"

"Not for me, but *you* might convince him."

"How? I can't just go to a strange boy for help. I couldn't! What makes you think he'd do something for me that he wouldn't do for his own sister?"

"Doesn't your Mum teach you how to get your own way?"

"Not with strangers!"

"All you have to do is come with me. I'll say to him *'Paula has a little problem with a loose gas joint in her caravan, she wonders if you know how to fix it?'* You don't say anything, just stand there, smile at him shyly, look down, flicker your eyes a bit, pretend you think he's so great. What's the matter? It's easy! Mum does it to Dad all the while." Sharon smiled at her friend.

Paula, caught by the sheer audacity, smiled back nervously; excited but uncertain. "Will it work? You said he's good at this, so why will you ask if he knows how? Why not just ask if he'll do it?"

"Hm." Sharon shook her head. "You haven't got a brother, have you? If I say will he do it, he could just say 'No', but if I ask does he know how to, he's not going to admit he doesn't know, is he? Especially to a good looking young girl!"

"Good looking?"

"He'll think so – after we work on your hair a bit and brush that blouse, it's covered in grass. How do you get yourself in such a state!"

"If you will make me lie on my back under a goat, what else did you expect?" Paula tried to keep a straight face but the novelty of the afternoon's events and what they now planned had the two leaning against each other, giggling again.

"Have you anything else to wear?" Sharon asked, "And where's your comb?"

When they reached the office, Chris had already arrived home obviously pleased with himself. He met them in the doorway. Sharon did all the talking, Paula standing back with a coyness that had little to do with pretence. Within minutes Chris had agreed and was inside the caravan, tools in hand. Kneeling to inspect the required repair, he looked up and spoke to Sharon.

"You better go and tell Mum I'll be some time. She may need help so you don't need to come back; Paula can pass me the tools."

As his head disappeared again into the cabinet, Sharon winked at her friend, gave a little concealed wave with the fingers of one hand and saw the word "No!" form soundlessly on Paula's lips, alarm on her face at being left alone.

Sharon went quickly, promising to ask Mum to delay tea. Back at the house, she explained Chris's sudden absence, and in answer to several queries, reluctantly elaborated on the circumstances, one question leading to another. When Jan showed amusement rather than concern, and promised never to tell, Sharon was unable any longer to contain herself. The whole afternoon's tale came out to the shared delight of mother and daughter. They had finished talking when Chris entered fifteen minutes later. Sharon would have loved to gloat, but she knew secrecy was essential, the ploy would never work again otherwise. In spite of this resolve to say nothing, some comment proved irresistible.

"Took a long time to tighten one nut?"

Seeing his mother regarding him closely with her head cocked to one side in amusement, Chris shuffled his feet uncomfortably, reaching for a chair, moving it from under the table as if to sit down, then stood instead leaning against a wall.

"It was quite difficult. I think someone bent the pipe and that's what caused it to leak." Chris put his hands in his pockets, then took them out again. "You can't be too careful with gas. I repaired the joint then re-tested everything – twice. After that I showed Paula how to light all the gas lamps and check the mantles, and started the fridge going. We boiled the kettle too, to make sure. She makes much better coffee than I normally g…" He caught Jan's eye and quickly corrected himself, "…than Sharon can make!"

Sharon was smiling, secretly pleased that her friend and her brother had got on so well; glad too, that Paula would now be able to impress her parents later in the day. Aware her brother's last words were an attempt to create a diversion, she showed her thanks by obliging him and changing the subject.

"Well, did you catch a big fish?"

Chris beamed with pride and a certain relief. "We hired a boat; spent most of the day in it. Sam lent me his spare sunglasses."

"Make you handsome, did they? Pardon me while I faint!" Sharon held a limp hand to her forehead, staggering daintily against the sideboard.

"Fly fishermen wear them to protect their eyes from hooks. I learned a more professional way to tie flies. He's making me a fly tying vice – and look what we caught!" He crossed the room, swinging wide the door of the small gas fridge, stepping aside in the same motion and stretching a hand triumphantly forward. A large trout lay on the narrow shelf, its tail and part of the body cut away and lying separate to allow the main section to fit.

"We caught?" Sharon raised an eyebrow. "Did you catch it?"

"Well no, not actually. Sam did, but I was there, steadying the boat. The one I would have caught was so big the line snapped and it got away."

Even with the increased numbers, running the site was not so difficult in June, the days enjoyable, more time to gossip with customers than there would be later. Gordon and Jan did not go to bed exhausted like in the peak season, but the length of each day left them needing a good undisturbed night. One evening however, this was destined not to be so!

Falling asleep together, happy but tired, they were woken after midnight as, Boom! A loud report shattered the silence. Probably it woke everyone else on site too. If this nocturnal blast was loud enough to rouse them in the house, what chance for visitors in caravans and tents?

For some minutes they lay in the darkness listening, alert for other sounds that might indicate the cause; or had they imagined it? Gordon rose, feeling his way carefully to the window, drawing the curtain aside to peer out over the site. Many lights shone from caravan windows, and the glowing luminescence of several tents indicated lights inside. As he watched, several more flicked on.

Boom!

Again the noise echoed across the site. Four minutes later, give or take thirty seconds, another shot blasted out destroying the normal quietness of the valley, for all the world as if its source lay behind the nearest hedge. Jan switched on the light and sat up in bed. “A bird scarer?”

“Must be. Dam thing’s gone mad. I’ll have to find it.” Sleepily Gordon pulled trousers and jumper over pyjamas, and tottered downstairs, shrugging on a donkey jacket, hat, and Wellingtons. Jan appeared next to him in her dressing gown but there was nothing she could do. Waving away the offered torch, he sent her back to bed and set off alone.

Boom! The sound thundered again. Which way? To the northwest! Crossing the river and bridge his direction turned up through a wood, the sound temporarily muffled by rising ground and trees. Finding a route through in the darkness took perhaps twenty minutes, maybe more, before emerging on an open ridge. He waited, listening, needing another indication of direction. A point of light flashed briefly in the dark landscape, ahead and above, along the valley and higher up the slope. A thin crescent moon offered little illumination, it was not possible to gauge the distance by sight. Boom, the sound followed some seconds later. After a time watching in the darkness, the flash came again, exactly the same spot. He counted silently, "One and two and three..." Boom!

"Hm, half a mile. About the distance I've travelled already." The unexplained loudness now became clear. Although far off, this bird scarer faced directly towards the valley, pointing downwards from higher ground. At least it confirmed he was not hunting a real gun. Bird scarers, designed to frighten rather than to kill, did not actually fire a missile. A long tapered steel tube filled steadily with gas from a nearby cylinder. This gas, when ignited at set time intervals by a glowing wire or spark, produced an explosion similar to but louder than a shotgun. Sometimes, but not in this case, such tubes were arranged to ratchet at each firing, jumping round to face a different direction. On better models the time interval would be variable. Both refinements were designed to improve the imitation of a real gun, thereby fooling pigeons (for rabbits just move a little farther away then seem quickly to ignore these devices). Normally a clock mechanism or a light sensitive cell start and stop the equipment, causing it to operate only during daylight since pigeons don't fly in the dark. If such mechanisms existed, they were certainly not working; regular blasts still punctuated the otherwise peaceful valley. Was it accidental or deliberate? Surely the farmer had not intended it to sound all night? A faulty clock perhaps?

Stopping the apparatus presented no problem; provided it could be reached. Nothing savage or damaging needed, simply turn off the gas valve – though being woken in the small hours did offer a strong temptation to throw the whole stupid contraption in the river. It has been said that a piece of black tape stuck over the 'magic eye' of later models can preserve the quiet of an early dawn - hardly playing fair of course but for anyone being driven round the bend, far preferable to damaging the mechanism. After all, the farmer has to make a living too. Usually it's a waste of gas anyway, since most creatures quickly become immune to the noise.

Leaving the ridge, Gordon pressed on through a dark landscape, barely visible in the dim moonlight. Steady but careful steps descended a shallow gradient, a dip leading on to an almost level field where long grass swayed about his boots, evening dew soon soaking the trousers above. It caused no discomfort on the warm night as he followed the hedge round to avoid damaging crops, a wise precaution when crossing any unknown field; something to jump over if confronted by a bull.

After a while the hedge swung abruptly eastward, becoming a dense belt of blackthorn and bramble that barred the way. Its thickness was difficult to judge in the murky light and far too impenetrable for a forced passage. Another boom called from beyond but the thorny obstruction could only be followed sideways until some larger trees over-shadowing the thicket created a gap, allowing more direct progress. The opening gave almost immediately onto a steep bank dropping to a tiny step-over sized stream. Scrambling up the uneven ground and through another hedge, the target boomed noisily but seemed little closer. Following the rising valley side, led in the sound's general direction without the source ever coming into view. Eventually however, a flash of fire stabbed the night, uphill to the right, the sound booming simultaneously. Struggling hurriedly up the slope, nearing the final goal, the stillness of the night and a slight sense of guilt at interfering with someone else's property created an uneasy feeling. He slowed to look all round, making a full turn while still continuing towards the target, taking a few backwards steps up the slope at one point, then swinging on to complete the circle; checking for witnesses perhaps?

It was near now, he hurried on, the gas bottle just visible in the dim light. At the precise moment his fingers touched to turn the valve – Boom!! The noise crashed out; terrible at close quarters, shattering the silence, stunningly effective, paralysing body and brain. A bright flash from the igniting gas closely missed one leg. His heart, already pounding from the final uphill dash, took a giant leap. In that fraction of a second he knew for sure he'd been shot! He would die, remote and alone, no hand to hold, no last words to share; only this maniac contraption at his side booming on into the night and marking his grave!

Recovering, drawing in a deep breath, he muttered to himself, "Hell. It may not frighten rabbits but it shatters humans! B fool. Getting nervous in your old age!" He had felt much younger five minutes ago. Another quick glance round in the darkness brought a broad grin of relief. No one had seen his little jump as the report rang out! Reaching down again the valve was quickly turned. Job done! For some moments he stood there, continuing to breathe deeply before turning to face down hill. Only the return journey remained.

Looking back in the general direction of approach, no distinguishing features marked the landscape, no 'friendly' boom acted as a beacon; even the faint crescent moon was becoming obscured by cloud.

The distance he estimated at something over a mile, based on that time lag between flash and sound, though in terms of effort it had seemed much farther. Part of the return must be downhill, but like a lost soul on Bodmin Moor, the exact direction was unclear. The outward journey had been navigated almost solely by ear – by following the noisy reports. Little attention was paid to such landmarks as might have been visible in the moonlight, something now regretted, though in the increasing darkness they would probably have been missed anyway on this return journey. Taking a guess, he strode forward.

After a while the downward slope reduced, flattening until marshy ground squelched underfoot. Stepping back onto firmer terrain he found a tall bush, feeling among the branches for a stout straight staff then with difficulty, broke and twisted it free. Stripping the lateral twigs and snapping off the top section, his fingers brushing over large, roundish, soft and slightly furry leaves; hazel probably. Cautiously he moved forward, prodding the ground ahead; a small splash warned of water. Bending down, a hand dipped in the pool failed to detect any flow, but faint though it was, somewhere away to the left the trickling of water was discernible in the stillness of that grove. There must be movement! He tried again – which direction? The drift, hardly detectable, seemed to be left to right, but he had to be sure and the surface was quite invisible!

Glancing up, the branches of a single tree showed blacker against the dark sky. Standing, he felt for a leaf, stretching up to find and pull one free, small and olive-shaped; a willow probably on this wet ground. Squatting down, he dipped it under the surface, let go, and waited. Had the leaf merely floated, any zephyr of wind might move it erratically; submerged it must follow the flow. His left hand rested in the water twelve inches away in the direction the current seemed to drift. Nothing could be seen but after a short time something touched his palm. Plucked from the water, its shape was checked carefully with fingertips – the leaf! This seepage must flow to the Hayle; there were no other streams in the area. That put the river to the right. He was facing the correct way. Good!

Now which route to choose? Follow this tiny brook down to the main river then go upstream to locate the site, or strike out on the direct but unmarked and uncertain route straight ahead. The possibility of deeper marshes along the brook's course decided the issue; it must be straight ahead! Wading across the water, another 50 feet of soft ground and the land began to rise, to become firmer. The crest of the ridge lay some way off, but once reached it should be possible to see signs of life in the next valley. There would be a light from the house at least, if not in the caravans or tents, for now the noise had stopped any visitors' lamps would surely be extinguished; it must be approaching two o'clock. The moon faded, then disappeared completely, obscured by thickening cloud as the terrain first levelled then in a few hundred yards began to fall. From this point the house should have been visible! No glimmer of light showed ahead – or in any other direction come to that. Where was he?

There was nothing to do but plough on. Seeing had become more difficult and on entering the wood, almost impossible! Tree trunks and thickets were detected mainly by the staff that, either by chance or good sense, he had retained. Pitch black is a term easily used but seldom true; even here there must be light, but so little only a night creature could use it. Holding a hand quite close in front of his face, the shape was hardly detectable; stretched out to arm's length it entirely disappeared.

Moving with any speed was difficult to the point of being foolhardy. Each foot moved carefully forwards, testing, feeling the ground before trusting any weight on it. Generally the terrain ran downwards. That was right, the descending gradient expected. A small bank intervened, knee high when prodded with the stick. Veering left, he followed a different downhill route. Several times, unseen bramble thickets or trees with dense spreading branches blocked the intended path. Working round them, sometimes being forced upward again before finding a new way, he relied now completely on the ground's slope for guidance, having turned so often at obstructions that all other sense of direction had been lost. Not even a breeze penetrated the wood to offer a clue.

There was no denying, even to himself, that he was lost; no longer knowing for sure which way led towards the caravans and home. A rustle somewhere away to the left caused him to freeze, to stand statue-like listening intently as something approached, moving through the undergrowth close by. He remained motionless, letting it pass. Had the creature, whatever it was, detected his own presence? Could its eyes see him without being seen in return? A Badger perhaps, or… It didn't really matter, the darkness and this unknown animal caused no feeling of concern; there would scarcely be man-eaters in these woods; unless one believed in the Beast of Bodmin? Conditions were relaxing rather than the reverse – providing no one was foolish enough to jump out from behind a tree! Automatically the staff would swipe out if they did! Although he felt at home, even slightly exhilarated in the darkness, the reflexes were sharpened, in a heightened state of readiness, some portion of the mind alert for the unexpected; lost maybe, but in a strange way, enjoying himself. And he was not really alone, standing there listening to the night noises and that retreating nocturnal visitor.

How lucky were those born in the Stone Age when sparse populations lived close to nature, uncomplicated by politics and pollution, the next neighbour a hundred miles away. Would Jan have risked that too, come back to those times with him, as she came to Cornwall and lived in the valley? Yes, quite probably. As he worked gradually downward, thoughts came and went, just as obstacles did. One foot stubbed on a tree root, not hard enough to be painful, the cautious movements too slow for that. Something else hurried away as though startled, he couldn't tell what – another badger? No, it had moved fast. A fox probably, it sounded heavy for a rabbit. At least Mr Fox would know the way; should he ask it? He remained silent, content enough but somehow not wishing to reveal his presence to… whatever?

The downward slope continued, the stream must still flow somewhere to the right. Pausing to listen again he detected no sound of water. After a time, the going became easier. Underfoot no longer had that feel of leaf mould, nor the continual snap of twigs and tug of brambles, but firm, without vegetation – a path maybe? He followed more quickly, guided by the texture of the ground. Quite suddenly vision began to improve, the moon was emerging from cloud as he left the trees, and there, not 100 yards away across the river, lay the house. Not bad! A surge of pleasure from the achievement washed over him, dampened by a reluctance to lose the black unknown.

From here he could detect a faint glow in the toilet building windows where the gas lights still burned, a glow that had not been visible from afar, either too dim or more likely masked by willows. The house itself sat in darkness, not a light to be seen; Jan had switched them all off and gone back to sleep. Because of the waterwheel, switching off lights was automatic, done by force of habit! She woke quickly when he tapped on the door, appearing shortly in a gown, quite contrite. Biting one fingertip and with lowered head, she looked up at him under her eyelashes, amusement in her voice.

"Ooh! Forgot, didn't I." But she made hot coffee and a snack, and let him lie in the following morning.

When Gordon did get up, almost everyone he spoke to referred to shooting in the night. About mid-morning in a slack spell, rough calculations with the aid of a large scale Ordinance Survey map of the area, suggested a position. A trip in the car and a brief search on foot eventually revealed the device halfway down a sloping field behind the hedge of a narrow track. He tried to see the owner to advise him the device had been silenced, but the farmer was away. The old chap temporarily in charge didn't want to know. He shook his head.

"Don't understand these newfangled gadgets."

Chapter 16

The Pill

Olive's time came one Saturday in June, late in the year for a goat, but being young the mating had been left as late as possible. Her restlessness was obvious more than an hour earlier and knowing the birth to be due she had been tethered by a long cord to a bushy willow offering ample shade and conveniently near the house. Even with school holidays yet some weeks away, the site had quite a number of children, many away at the beach with parents. Chris and Stephen too, had gone off with friends for the day.

Left to tend the goat and answer any phone calls while her parents were temporarily occupied elsewhere, Sharon fetched a plastic bucket from the kitchen. Turning it upside down, she sat within sight of the office door; nicely placed to see clearly but not close enough to disturb Olive. A group of younger children, shouting and dashing towards the bridge, ran over, ever curious, wondering why someone should sit looking at a goat. Within no time at all, Sharon had the ragged band seated on the ground, watching in fascination, whispering to each other in hushed voices as two little hooves appeared.

A caravan crossed the river, drawing up in the yard. Sharon offered to book them in but the couple insisted on waiting, smiling as their two youngsters joined the group and immediately followed the other children's example of speaking with lowered voices. Eagerly, excited questions and explanations were whispered back and forth to the newcomers. This was the scene that greeted Jan and

Gordon as they rounded the toilet building to stand quietly behind, nodding briefly to Sharon and the caravanners.

Olive handled her first kidding with no real signs of concern, the small goat slipping out by degrees to lie, covered in mucous, on the grass. Stepping forward, Jan wiped the clear viscous slime from around its head with an old towel that she had slipped inside to fetch. It bleated a first cry; Olive responded, reaching to lick her baby. The watching group waited, but there was only the one kid, a male. Shortly, the small billy rose, stood shakily on tall spindly legs, moving in uncontrolled jerks, tottering, almost falling after each few steps. The learning process was rapid, stabilising the erratic movements, instinct leading it unerringly to the food supply. The little head reached under its mother and sucked greedily at the udder.

Olive now alternately browsed and licked the kid. Sharon, being familiar with the goat, moved forward, pulled irresistibly to fondle and stroke the little chap. Touching it, she looked back to Jan for approval. As neither nanny nor kid objected, Jan nodded agreement but seeing the other children rise together, held up a hand.

"Only three at a time please. Take turns. Sharon will stay because Olive knows her."

The visitors were booked in and led off to be pitched, the father calling to his children to come; prying them away from new friends, promising they could run back as soon as the caravan was sited.

By the time other youngsters began returning from the beach, the baby goat had fluffed up, very dark compared to her mother, and had become the most cuddly thing imaginable, totally captivating the younger girls. As the afternoon wore on several boys joined in, some quite good with animals, knowing where to rub and avoiding sudden movements. Even at only a few hours old the billy liked to push its head against an arm or leg, and obviously enjoyed the attention. As days passed, the little goat became more sturdy and a great favourite.

“He should have a name,” Sharon suggested.

“Let’s leave it until autumn.” Gordon shook his head.

“Why? I think John is nice.”

“Billy would be better, after all he does live in the West.” Chris offered, and seeing that the family did not understand, explained, “Billy the Kid?”

Eyes looked to Dad for agreement but he shrugged and turned away.

Later that evening when the children were in bed, Jan whispered, “I know why you didn’t want it named. What are we going to do?”

What indeed? What could they do? Both knew how smelly a full grown billy would be, and dangerous too, with so many small children about; quite capable of inflicting at least serious injury, possibly even death. Too much to risk, unfair to visitors and to the goat itself. On the other hand, not only their own three youngsters but all the visitors loved the little animal. Gordon caught Jan’s eye then looked away, but she was waiting, he must say something.

“Whatever we do will have to be after the season, in the autumn. Can you imagine the number of children crying to their mothers if it disappeared now? Sharon would be heartbroken. We’ll find a good home for the little chap once the school holidays have come and gone.”

“Yes,” Jan agree doubtfully. “It may not be that easy. By the way, that shower head was twisted again today, I stood on a footstool and forced it back. That hasn’t happened since last year. Probably the same person back again, I told you we should write all these things down in the daybook.”

“What would that tell us? Half the people here are return customers.”

“Granted, but how many were here when that shower was twisted last year. Probably less than half a dozen. It’s not school holidays until next week.”

Gordon felt he was losing but resisted. “What have school holidays to do with it?”

“People come then, only because they have to. It restricts

them to a shorter period – pretty much the same time each year. Those we have now are more free to choose; their visits are probably more variable. See, I was right, we should record anything that goes wrong."

"Okay," he agreed, realising it was true, "Go ahead, write at the bottom of each page in the daybook. I had hoped this wouldn't recur; the extra brackets are ready but I'd prefer not to have needed them; they won't be quite so neat. I'll start with the Gents showers tomorrow – early afternoon, it's least busy then."

"Those brackets, are they the chrome ones on the shelf above the vice?"

"Why?" He looked up defensively, "They'll be okay won't they?"

"Bit heavy. Why are there no chrome screws?"

"Ah. The screws they supplied were only one-inch size eight, and chrome on brass at that. Brass is weak, I'll use stainless steel instead."

"The same size?" She did not believe for a minute that they would be.

"Well no, slightly bigger, two-inch size ten; they need to be strong! I wanted size twelve but the holes are too small. I'd drill them out but it would spoil the finish."

The extra brackets were started next day, it was planned to fit all eight in a three hours period after lunch. Jim came up to help Jan in the office, so she could take any caravan to a pitch without interrupting work on the showers. The first to arrive were an elderly couple, the woman in a smart dress and wide brimmed hat more suitable for Ascot than for holidays, and carrying a small dog. The office was part of the lounge, and obviously a normal lived-in room of the house. Customers seldom entered with dogs and those that did were usually asked to leave them outside, hitched to a special tie-up point provided for that purpose. Jan, never completely at ease dealing with strangers, hesitated, about to speak when the woman, still clutching her dog, tilted a chair to one side, brushed the seat with a gloved hand as if it were contaminated, and sat down. The movement had an aristocratic touch, the manner in which she regarded Jan then looked pointedly in the other direction, suggested, 'I don't deal with people in trade. My man will see to it!'

An elderly gent with greying hair who had followed respectfully a few paces behind as she entered, nodded to Jim sitting in the adjoining lounge before stepping forward to the desk. He booked six nights and paid, then quickly moved to the door, holding it open for the woman and her dog. They walked away towards a caravan that had been expensive once but was now showing its age.

Jan rose, glancing towards Jim but he had noticed nothing. With a shrug she left the office, catching the visitors, asking them to follow and leading on to an area adjacent to the river. Two pitches were empty, one at the far end, one near at hand by the gate. The couple climbed from their car, the man nodding agreeably.

Jan swept an arm, "This is the dog area, that gate..."

"Dog area?" The woman interrupted disapprovingly.

Jan was reminded again of Lady Bracknell and the handbag, but pushed the thought aside and pointed, "Yes. That gate gives access to the riverbank; it makes a splendid walk. That's why we reserve these pitches for people with pets. Everyone on this area has a dog."

"Pugh dislikes other dogs. We'll take a different paddock."

Jan sighed. This was going to be difficult. Why did the awkward ones never come when Gordon was pitching? "I'm sorry, this is the only area available, the others are dog free so children and babies can play safely. Why don't you take that corner pitch, you'll have more privacy there."

"And pass all those nasty caravans whenever Pugh needs walkies? Really!" The woman sniffed, turning to step away a few paces as if dismissing a maid.

Hurrying forward, the man took Jan's arm apologetically, guiding her to the pitch right next to the gate.

"Could we have this one, that might be satisfactory. If

we can, you stay here and I'll talk to her?"

"This pitch..." Jan hesitated again, wondering about the man; was he a husband, some chauffeur or perhaps a paid companion? It had been on the tip of her tongue to warn that this was the least favoured pitch on the whole area. Everyone must walk their dog right past the caravan window to reach the gate. Whenever possible this space was left vacant. Glancing over one shoulder, undecided, she saw the woman turn sharply away as if not prepared to acknowledge menials.

Right! Jan swung back to the man, her mind made up. "I was going to say this pitch is booked, but the other caravan is not due until tomorrow. You can have it, I'll give them the corner instead. Go and talk with madam." The words were said with such sweetness, he might have guessed they offered a poison chalice.

Jan was angry! She stood waiting, one foot tapping on the grass while the visitors conferred. Shortly the man signalled agreement, pointing to the pitch, climbing into the car and making a creditable job of reversing – but he placed the caravan centrally rather than to one side, then turned the engine off and climbed out. Fine! That would force people to walk even closer. Serves her right! Realising that madam would soon discover her mistake and either arbitrarily change pitch or send the man, her servant, to arrange it, Jan sought a way to forestall such action. Yes! With a snort of satisfaction she strode determinedly towards the woman.

"I hope you will be comfortable there. If not, don't worry, you can always come to the office and tell me you've made a mistake."

The words had forced the visitor to turn, and having said them, Jan walked away without a backward glance. That would fix her wagon! Never in a hundred years would her ladyship come to the office and admit to a mistake, nor would she send the man, for that too would be an admission! Only when well out of sight did Jan allow herself to smile, flexing the fingers of one hand like a claw. "Meow!" She felt better, much better! But what of the other caravan, the one she said would now go in the corner? It did not exist. Never mind, surely someone would arrive – and if they did not and madam realised? Well..." she shrugged, flexing the fingers again, "Perhaps that would be even better!"

Life's pace was rising – the bustle of many people plus one important addition. The sewer with its mess, noise and big machinery crept steadily closer, following the river upstream from St Erth. This additional worry could well have been done without! Would it reach the site during the peak season? They prayed it would not, but there was little time to speculate for the days were very full. Each evening on arriving home from school, the three children dashed down the riverbank to report on progress, on how much trench had been dug that day. Any hold up, a machine breaking down or any difficulty that impeded the sewer's progress, was hailed with cheers as the family devoured a quickly eaten tea.

Fortunately, a week later when the school holidays hit the sewer was not yet in sight. A wave of new visitors pushed away all thoughts of big excavators and the accompanying devastation. Busy days swept future worries aside; never mind tomorrow – today demanded full attention!

"Now I know your friends are back and you'll make new ones as the season goes on, but we'll still need help sometimes." Jan warned at breakfast. "Any afternoon you're free, not going out with your pals, let me know. I'll try to go shopping then, so you needn't stay in on other days! Don't forget your regular chores though."

The reminder was scarcely necessary. They had become used to helping, grown up with it; Sharon cooking, the boys shovelling coal, removing ash, shifting dustbins and the various jobs they all shared like serving gas bottles, helping customers, tending the goats and ducks. These chores were taken in their stride, done mostly before any friends awoke. Heads around the table acknowledged their mother's words while continuing to attack the bacon and eggs before them.

"The goats are getting difficult to find new places for." Chris complained. "All the good grass is covered with caravans. Three goats are really too many in summer. I'm still giving Olive the best patches with Billy to feed."

"Four goats, not three," Sharon corrected, reaching for more bread. "Goats are supposed to like rough ground. Walking with me they always prefer brambles."

"When did *you* last take them out in the morning when they're most hungry? They each need a clear patch, room to move without getting tangled; there aren't that many. There are less each year as more pitches are made." Chris turned to his father. "What will we do eventually?"

"Let's worry about that when the season's over. Good thing you children are home now, it does help to have you tend the goats." Dad looked round the table. "I know Chris does the mornings, but you all walk them and move their places in the daytime. Not getting a real problem is it?"

Stephen shook his head once but said nothing.

"My friends like helping, we take one goat each and Billy follows. Usually I don't have to do a thing," Sharon sat back with a grand gesture, "they all want to hold the tethers, I just lead the way."

Jan could imagine her daughter issuing instructions, those friends so much taken up with the goats as not to notice they were following orders. How would she do it? A picture formed of Sharon, head back, arm outstretched pointing a finger. 'Sally, tie it to that bush there! Make sure the knots are tight! Of course there are brambles, Judy needs them to eat! Never mind if you scratch yourself a bit.'

"Mum, what are you smiling at?"

"Oh? Nothing Sharon, just thinking of Billy."

Chris would have liked to offer an opinion on his sister's ability with goats, but wisely held his own counsel, aware that she might stop helping if he ridiculed her efforts. Instead he pursued another line. "There is one problem; at least I think it's a problem. Judy's droppings are not little spheres any more, they come out in big squashy blobs, more like the muscovys. You said they get worms if the same place is used often but I can't help it, there aren't enough new places. Should we give her those green pills?"

"Why must goats not feed often in the same place?" Sharon interrupted. "I never know where Chris has already used when I move them."

"Most goats are thought have some worms," Dad explained, "It's mainly the next generation, the eggs or larva, I'm not exactly sure which, that get ejected with the droppings. In a short time new worms develop in the dung, climb the grass and can survive for a while on top of the stems. If goats re-use that grass too soon, they eat the worms and get re-infested to a level their bodies can't cope with. I think Chris is probably right."

Further discussion was prevented as the doorbell rang. It was hardly surprising, they had all been eating as they talked, no one finding the subject unusual during a meal. Feeling lucky to finish before this interruption, Gordon hurried off to find a man at the door and a caravan standing in the yard. He booked it in and was leaving to choose a pitch as another man walked up with a gas bottle. Sharon dealt with it while Jan greeted an attractive young lady who had arrived yesterday, booking for one night, and now wanted to stay longer. Many people did that.

"Do you know anywhere local that repairs awning rails?" the woman asked. "My husband drove too near an overhanging tree and squashed it; scratched the caravan side a bit as well. Your Cornish lanes are quite narrow aren't they!"

Chris had been hovering in the adjoining corridor, waiting to finish the discussion of Judy's health. He stepped forward, "I might be able to fix it, Mum."

Now fourteen and growing rapidly, the lad looked almost a young man. The woman smiled at him, pleased but a little doubtful, flicking a glance back at Jan.

Chris flushed slightly, waiting for his mother's nod of approval, not rushing off as he would have in earlier years, but with a studied air of coolness that he had begun to adopt. “I need a few tools,” he said, stepping into the corridor and reaching for the basement door. In the workroom the necessary equipment was collected together; a flat piece of timber some fifteen inches long, a hammer and an inch wide wood chisel that was old, blunt, and often used as a lever.

Sharon, having found the man a gas bottle and received the correct change, carried the money back to the office in time to see the lady and Chris, tools in hand, walk off side by side chatting together. “Going for older girls now, is he?” she commented to her mother.

Jan found the thought amusing. “That girl as you call her, is over twenty and married; at least they signed in as Mr and Mrs. You don’t think her husband will object when she brings a toy boy to the caravan.” Mother and daughter smiled at each other before Jan added, “He’s gone to do a little job.”

“I saw the tools.” Sharon cast another glance as Chris disappeared round the toilet building.

On reaching the caravan, the woman called to her husband, “Harold, this young man thinks he may be able to help with the awning rail.” A casually dressed man appeared in the doorway; the hand that gripped the door-frame had long slender fingers showing no sign of manual work. He pointed to where the rail was partly flattened.

“A tree branch caught it. This is only a second-hand caravan, most of the rail is so slack the awning tends to slip out, but at this point it’s now too tight. I tried to force the material in, but its hopeless.” He rubbed his fingers together uncomfortably, as if the canvas had made them dirty.

Chris set to work, gently levering the closed section open, then with the hammer and piece of wood, forced those parts that had opened too far, back into line. A piece of emery paper from his pocket smoothed off the rough places leaving a faint residue of black powder. Finally, going along the entire rail with the wood strip and carefully tapping to adjust several wider places to the proper width, he finished the job, accepted the lady's thanks, and left.

More caravans arriving down the road with little dust clouds following, prevented any resumption of the goat discussion until lunch. As they ate, it was agreed that Judy should be given one pill, the first time these had been used.

"Are there any instructions how to give them?" Chris asked.

"No, that man who breeds goats gave us a few in an unmarked tin," Gordon shrugged. "Up to you to find a way of administering it, but only use one. At least you won't lose it in the grass, they're big enough to see."

"It, um..." Chris glanced uncomfortably at his mother. "It… does go in the top end?"

The parents regarded each other with suppressed smiles, seeing puzzled expressions on the younger children's faces.

"Yes, you can rely on that. Try offering it in the palm of your hand."

Late that afternoon a little group approached the office. Chris led the way, with Judy walking at heel, the rope held close to her collar avoiding any slack on which the goat might trip. Behind followed Sharon, Stephen and six other children. Arriving at the house, Judy was led round to the rear while Sharon slipped inside for the single pill. She slid past several visitors talking in the office, soon to rejoin those waiting outside. Chris held out a hand but she moved in quickly, offering it on the open palm. Judy took the green sphere, rolled it over in her mouth and spat it out!

As Sharon made to grab it, Chris obligingly stood back. A shadow of a grin crossed his face as his sister jerked backwards, withdrawing the hand and wiping her fingers on the grass. Passing the rope to a friend Chris took a few paces, plucked a large leaf, picked up the slimy pill without touching it and wrapped the leaf ends over. Judy took the whole green parcel, unwrapped it with her tongue, spat out its contents and retained the leaf. While chewing, the goat placidly regarded Chris with her oblong TV-shaped pupils, as if saying "One of us is a fool, and I don't think it's me?"

Two girls in the group knelt down, stroking the coarse black hair; one tentatively holding a horn had her hand quickly thrown off with a toss of the dark head.

A conference of low voices eventually sent Sharon back inside for a bucket of oats. This ploy proved equally unsuccessful as might have been guessed. Any goat that could locate something inside a leaf was scarcely likely to find difficulty avoiding the same object in a bucket. Never mind, Judy enjoyed both the attention and the oats!

Stalemate! Sporadic suggestions were offered, thought over and discarded. Chris tried to open the goat's mouth with his hands but after nearly loosing a finger, abandoned the attempt. As the group rested, looking at each other with blank faces, ideas exhausted, Stephen suddenly took off at speed without a word. Jumping into the service passage he re-emerged, clippers in hand, to dash round the building out of sight. He was back shortly with a cow-parsley-like stem, more probably from hogweed for it was thick, more a beanshooter than a peashooter. The clippers were not to be seen, left, cast aside somewhere in the hurry to return.

The little band needed a hungry goat if they were to succeed; the bucket had been removed from Judy's reach. Looking inside, Stephen picked up the pill, its green colour almost concealed by a flaky coating, and pushed it into the tube. Particles of crushed oats and sticky goat saliva now adhered to the end of the oversize peashooter.

"You can't put it in your mouth!" Sharon warned aghast.

With a deliberate rebellious stare, Stephen raised the stem firmly to his lips, pointing it in his sister's direction. Uttering a little shriek, she leapt to one side. Satisfied, the young lad knelt, carefully keeping the tube horizontal for the pill was a loose fit and promised to roll out. Unable to speak he beckoned for the goat to be pulled forward.

"Don't breathe in through you mouth!" a boy warned.

"Be sure you blow before Judy does," Chris cautioned.

A bearded chin lifted towards the green stem, sniffing it, the teeth opened to bite… "Whooosh!" Stephen blew.

Jan, in the office, wondered about the great cheer that sounded clearly from behind the house but was too busy to investigate. A visitor standing waiting his turn for attention, popped outside, went to the corner and returned.

"What was it?" another waiting customer asked.

"Only a bunch of children and a goat."

As always, the site became even more busy during the second school holiday week. Stephen struggled with dustbins each morning, helped sometimes by Chris after his own chores were complete. Dad usually carried the heavier ones when he finished cleaning. Rubbish had become a real problem, the lines of bins beside each toilet building were filling too quickly; they sometimes failed to cope with the morning rush. As an emergency solution, extra lines of empty bins were placed at the entrance to the storage area which had previously been used only for those that were full. It solved the problem, but this concentrated mass of rubbish standing out in full sun began to attract a little army of wasps. Gordon was away pitching tents when an inspector from the local authority arrived, parked his car in front of the office then knocked at the door to introduce himself.

At first Jan suspected the Council had finally discovered the absence of tents on their Planning Permission! Learning with relief that this was a routine inspection, she watched him march off round the site with a clipboard, then remembering the mass of dustbins, worried in case they were declared a health hazard. She was even more concerned when the man reappeared moments later, asking her to accompany him. He strode off, leading her round the first toilet building and stopped as she had feared, directly in front of the bins, perhaps as many as eighty, heat shimmering above the black lids, a faint whiff on the air and the whole area alive with buzzing insects.

"This is it!" she thought silently, wondering what in the world they could do to improve the situation.

The man regarded her sternly.

“That,” he raised an arm and pointed, “does not comply with the regulations!”

Her heart sank as he paused, tapping a pencil on his board before continuing.

“It should have a sign that says Dustbins!”

Jan surveyed the sea of bins, the wasps, various bags and an open box of rubbish that had not been there when the area had been tidied only three hours ago, and she wondered? Several lids were off towards the back; crows had no doubt removed them in a hunt for tasty morsels of food that had nicely started to decay. And all he wanted was a sign!

Moving only her eyes, she glanced sideways and saw his expression; a schoolmaster telling a naughty child. The world had gone mad! Here were dustbins as far as the eye could see, well not quite, but a great mass of them – and he wanted a sign. Of course, how would people know otherwise? An urge to laugh gripped her; an insane desire to run through the site screaming “Must have a sign!”

She lowered her head, pretending to cough to cover the tears of glee forming in her eyes, fighting for control, saved from failure as a wasp zoomed round them and they both stepped smartly backward. The inspector continued his round alone, calling at the office as he left to congratulate them on the site, the cleanliness, the new standpipes, and particularly that the minimum twenty feet spacing between caravans and tents was everywhere observed and so well exceeded. Not to worry about the dustbin sign during this busy period, but he’d expect to see it on his next inspection. When? He had no idea, next year probably. Watching him drive away, Jan thought, “What a nice man.”

The family were discussing the visit later in the office when Sharon pointed.

“Dad, look!”

He saw a caravan leaving and moved to the door intending to wave goodbye to the car’s occupants. Hearing Sharon shout again and seeing her still pointing, he glanced again at the caravan, then jumped across, clearing the steps and raced to stop it, holding out a hand to intercept the towing vehicle as it approached the bridge. A woman in the front passenger seat turned to the driver, said something and the car rolled to a halt. Two windows wound down, the occupants leaning out with concern.

"Your jockey wheel is still down."

"Thanks." The man climbed out and walked round to the caravan. "I thought for a minute we'd forgotten to pay. Thanks again for noticing. I promised myself I'd never do this after reading a magazine article about a man who lost his caravan that way. It hit a bump and unhitched itself somehow." He wound the wheel up, hit the handle hard twice with the palm of his hand to lock it, and climbed back in. A few pleasantries were exchanged through the passenger side window before the caravan drew away. As Gordon headed for the house, Sharon and another young girl were leaving.

"The man says thanks for spotting it," he called to them.

"I had one with a leg still down just like that," Sharon shouted back as another voice called, "Gordon!"

Jan was standing by the office door with a woman.

"Do we have anything else besides Elsan Blue? The lady wants tablets."

"Tablets?" He walked across to them.

"Yes, for our chemical toilet. We first used them last summer." The woman paused, thinking, shaking her head. "No, I can't remember the name, Aqua-something; they were so much easier than measuring out the fluid. Is there anywhere local I might get some?"

"Try Bennetts in Penzance if you're going that way; the Calor gas suppliers at the bottom end of town, or GB Caravans at Scorrier on the way to Truro."

The woman offered her thanks and left.

"I've not heard of tablets." Jan shrugged as they re-entered the office. "Should we arrange a supply?"

"Yes, probably. I'll enquire. There are several caravan accessories we've been asked for, maybe a few of each would be a good idea, and some waterproof spray for the tents. We can't expect the village shop to stock that sort of thing."

The day, as each day at this time of year, continued busily, a midday meal snatched between arriving caravans. There would be no respite for many weeks yet, but the pressure was exhilarating – when one had time to think about it! Perhaps it was the ability to deal with these constant demands that provided the stimulation; the satisfaction of managing abrupt changes, from welcoming and pitching a constant flow of people, to dashing back and unblocking a drain, or settling a dispute between neighbours. There were gas bottles or mantles to provide, taps to re-washer, dustbins to change, innumerable question to answer on beaches, birds, shopping, local places – a hundred other things. When several of these occurred simultaneously, as happened constantly, then the strain increased, but so too did the gratification of successfully handling those many demands.

The Scottish petrol strike that increased trade so dramatically earlier in the season was over, but numbers remained well up on last year. Although extra pitches had been made last winter, a few short stayers were still forced to accept hardstanding with a promise of grass if they decided to stay longer, but again nobody had been refused; barring that is, a few that were considered unsuitable. Only when late August approached and the shorter evenings began to set in did pressure for grass pitches ease. Most people were again happy with the site, apart from comments by some teenage girls on the lack of hairdryers. To avoid spoiling people's holiday, any visitors in this category were now warned before their money was taken, and this shortcoming explained. Some decided to move on, but most were so taken with the valley that they stayed anyway.

This general site happiness was not achieved without care. One day two couples had dropped in at the office for no other reason than to say how pleased they were with the valley. As they chatted a large old car drew up in the yard. This vehicle had great rolls of canvas, obviously several tents, tied to a roof rack together with surfboards and other gear, including what might have been a guitar case. Six young men emerged, jostling each other in fun, full of life and vigour. One picked up a large stone edging the yard. Disregarding the ducks, he heaved it like a shot-putter into the river near the bridge to shouts of approval from his companions.

The couples in the office showed alarm. As these six lads walked across the yard, Jan looked questioningly at Gordon, who quickly snatched an old hat and Jim's spare walking stick from the hall. Bending slightly, the stick in one hand apparently supporting him he opened the office door and limped down one step to meet the new arrivals.

"How much a night, six of us with three tents?"

Gordon standing slightly bent over, shook his head slowly, appearing to have trouble drawing breath; then spoke in a shaky voice, "I'm sorry. This is an old people's site."

The young men stopped, hesitated, then were off back to the car, swinging round to speed up the road, stones flying from the wheels as if old age was catching! Back inside the office, the four visitors expressed profound relief.

"We had a crowd like that close to us at a site on the way down. When we left early next morning, they had just gone to bed. Terrible night! Why didn't you say outright that you wouldn't take them?"

Gordon shrugged.

"I'll tell you why," Jan smiled seeing his embarrassment. "This is new; something he's never done before. We do refuse people occasionally but he tries to find ways that won't make them feel personally disliked or not wanted." She turned, holding out a hand, palm upwards, putting him on the spot, inviting him to deny it. For a moment they looked at each other, the company forgotten, both smiling, pleased with the private little duel and the relief it brought from pressures that always built up at this time of year.

"Okay. Yes I do try to send them away happy, even if they're laughing at me. We have something special here in our valley, but it wouldn't be special to them. They'd hate it;

try to change it. Young men like that want activity, action, girls! They aren't bad, just so… so energetic!" Gordon wondered how to explain better.

"When the dustmen come, I help them throw the rubbish on the cart; there's a lot of it, a hundred bins in all and they're pushed for time in midseason. We have a laugh and a joke; the driver hates rats and the men keep telling him one is hiding at the back. There was one once, it created havoc. He shoved the other chaps out of the way and leapt clear – should have been in the Olympics! You've noticed the pile of building blocks at the back corner of the dustbin area?"

One of the visitors nodded and Gordon continued.

"Well, when we put extra water points all round the site last winter, I had to build inspection chambers below ground near each one. We had a load of building blocks for the job, full loads are cheaper; those are the ones left over. We stacked them behind the bins to be out the way but if you look closely, the bottom row is not stacked neatly together, there's a gap about three inches wide between two of the blocks. Well, the dustmen told their driver that I'd made that hole deliberately to let the rat hide in so it could lie in wait for him. The funny thing is a rat did start to come in that way; they could tell because bits of loose rubbish had been dragged over there, paper bags that were nibbled to get the things inside. It wasn't so surprising really, rats prefer hidden places like that rather than being in the open. I usually stand in that corner now and pass the bins to them, tucking my trousers in my socks just in case. The point is this, we work together well – like each other. If I have a piece of rubbish that won't go in a bin as it's supposed to, they take it anyway. They say the quicker turn round which my help gives is more important than bothering about an odd item of rubbish that isn't in the proper bin. We had a set of lounger chairs once, left by someone because the material was rotten. They shoved them on the dustcart; no trouble, good crowd of lads. I bet we load a hundred dustbins quicker than anyone else in the county!"

Gordon paused again, realising that he'd strayed from the subject. "Sorry I'm digressing; the dustmen are just an example. Far nicer to get on with people. Now take those young men; I *had* to send them away, they want different things. But why should I make them think we're snooty, or that we find them in some way undesirable? You realise they now believe everyone here are a lot of old fools, and not only me, that also includes you! They've gone away laughing at the lot of us – but we're laughing at them too – no one is upset. Wish I could always pull it off."

The couples stayed talking for a while, then left the office in great good humour. After they had gone, Jan stepped away and scanned him up and down.

"That stick and old hat suits you; it isn't often someone still in their thirties pretends to be sixty." She took three further backward steps to stand near the hall doorway, looked him over again then pulled the office chair nearer and lifted a foot onto the seat. Leaning to the side in a suggestive stance, the dress fell back around a shapely leg. "I suppose you're too old now for desires of the flesh?"

He stood for a moment, taken aback, then made a grab for her waist but she was gone, fleeing through the hallway and into the bathroom. He arrived as the door slammed shut, hearing the bolt slide across inside. Simultaneously the office bell rang. "Damn!"

By late September there was more time for such distractions. The sewer had already reached the boundary, and was starting to make its way through the site. Most visitors had gone, several leaving prematurely, others turning round in front of the office to drive away again; put off by heavy lorries on the entrance road. Sadly, the goats were to be sold. Sewer laying had proved even more destructive than feared. Many of the parts so far grassed lay in a long narrow strip following the valley bottom, and those sewer pipes must be laid through the site's entire half-mile length. Much of this grass would be churned up, possibly most of it. No one knew how little would remain or what level of danger the big lumbering machines and frequent lorries might present. With three fully-grown goats and one kid, this lack of grass would be serious, for as they had already found, feeding too frequently in the same place invariably led to worms. There remained also the time factor. Clearing up work afterwards would almost certainly be a rush. Returning the site to condition ready for the following season could prove almost as difficult as opening on time in the first year. Any construction delays and it might even become impossible. This could well lead, not exactly to neglect, but to the goats no longer receiving the attention they had come to expect and which every goat deserves. Better for them if the offer of a good home was taken up, at least until the work finished. Later, when the site returned to normal the goats could be repurchased, or failing that, a pedigree goat bought with a view to serious breeding.

A local farm where they would be well cared for wanted goats to help clear some wasteland, a project in which they revel. It had been agreed that the new owner would bring them back if they failed to settle in happily. So they were to go, all except Billy; nobody wanted him. The whole family watched the departure. Chris stood holding Judy, gently stroking and rubbing her coat for over half an hour before the trailer arrived. He had tended her more than anyone else, she liked him best; a bond had developed between the two. Chris didn't cry, though his eyes were very bright. For once he said nothing, choked for words, hating to see her go, yet knowing, having agreed beforehand, that it was best for Judy. He led her up the tailboard of the trailer, kneeling to lay his head against her neck, one hand resting on her side, the other gently rubbing her back. Judy leaned towards him twisting her head over his shoulder.

"Damn the sewer!" Jan thought, witnessing the poignant farewell with sorrow.

When the trailer disappeared up the road, Chris didn't return to the house; he walked off alone round the corner of the toilet building. His father took a tentative step, wondering whether to follow, but Jan shook her head.

Days passed and the sewer crept forward, but standing on the bridge near the house, those big machines were not yet in sight. The billy, too young to require tethering but no longer needing mother's milk, ran up, still missing the other goats after his first week alone. Looking down at him sadly, Gordon saw Jan do the same and lightly took her hand; they bent together to fuss the little goat, stroking the lustrous, almost black hair.

"What else could we do? Poor little fella," he ruffled the head as it jumped up, placing two small dainty forelegs on his bent knees. It had not proved possible to sell or even give him away, though they tried hard. Billy of course would get strong and unsociable as he grew, dangerously so and smelly too, but at the moment was still so cuddly and affectionate. Perhaps different tactics might induce someone to take him; a used car salesman could have done it.

"He'll be a lovely milker when he grows up."

But it didn't ring true somehow, so finally, sadly, Dad decided they would eat him.

"Cannibal!" Chris muttered, somewhat incorrectly when the subject was discussed with the rest of the family.

Mutiny hung in the air!

"Well I won't eat him," Sharon protested, "if you kill him I may never eat again." She turned her back, sniffed, and walked to the other side of the room, as far from her father as it was possible to get.

Chris asked, "Couldn't we let him loose somewhere?"

Stephen made a grimace.

Gordon gazed back at three rebellious faces. Jan had already insisted they could not possibly keep a male goat, but offered no solution. She shrugged, what could she say?

"Let's be reasonable," Gordon appealed. A stubbornness

entered their expressions, but he continued. "I'll explain how I see it. There is no way we can keep a fully grown billy goat on a caravan park; you know what Judy smells like when she comes back from the billy. It would be dangerous too, for other children; the mother's would worry. Another thing, no one else wants him, we can't even give him away. No need to look like that, you know we've tried – none of your friends will take him either." The last words were defensive, passing some blame perhaps. He turned to Chris. "About your idea; it would be cruel just to leave him in some deserted place, he's too young to survive alone, might die slowly and in pain. He has to be put down properly. He mustn't suffer. I'm having him killed the most humane way possible; the slaughterhouse have promised he will feel nothing. So he's not frightened they even say I can go with him."

The children's faces remained sullen. When they heard the "Go with him," Sharon and Chris exchanged glances. Sharon, her lower lip trembling, said, "Good!"

Chris nodded agreement. Stephen didn't understand.

Shaking her head, Jan stepped in.

"When they said Dad could go with him, they meant for company, not to be put down as well."

"Pity," Sharon said softly under her breath.

Gordon heaved a sigh, he wasn't feeling good about it himself, but he tried again.

"Goat they say, is good to eat. If we are to eat meat, then while we eat Billy we are not eating another animal which need not then be killed."

It was his last attempt; reason had failed. He had always held a personal belief that killing for sport was wrong. Even when it served a useful purpose the idea of finding pleasure from slaughter was repugnant; but killing for food was different, it happened naturally among carnivores and man was certainly a carnivore to some extent. Indeed such action throughout the food chain held the balance of nature. What would happen to mice without any owls or cats? And rabbits, what about them? Without the foxes, buzzards and stoats, they might cover the landscape a foot thick in no time at all and perhaps start walking into the sea off Lands End like Lemmings. He told himself all this; it was logical, proper, and there was no escaping that over ninety percent of all billy goats were put down, especially non-pedigree ones, and this one must be too! But it made no difference; both he and Jan were still utterly miserable driving to the abattoir. Parking, they sat for sometime in the car outside, neither speaking, both stroking the little goat as it stood patiently on the back seat, blissfully ignorant of what lay ahead.

Eventually the doors opened and they got out, bending to tie a rope round the furry neck – it might as well have been a noose! Billy accepted it gladly, rubbing against the hands that tied it on. Trusting them, allowing itself to led, the little goat followed happily at heel, small white hooves running along the tarmac, young and innocent, head turning this way and that curious at anything that moved, prancing and full of life, enjoying the warm sunshine it would never see again. Along one side of the building a large door lay open; approaching at an angle they made to enter but Billy shied backwards, fighting against the lead as a river of blood swept past, still warm and steaming in a channel just ahead. Quickly Gordon stooped to pick him up rubbing the shiny fur but it was unhappy now, frightened; they almost turned back... but stepped quickly across that river of death and moved on – there was little alternative – it would be no easier another day. Moving down the building, a man in a bloodstained white overall and cap bent over a carcass lying prone on the floor. He straightened as they approached, more blood dripping from a large knife in one hand.

What a relief to hear the slaughter man's request to buy the goat as a pet for his daughter. He understood the habits of a grown billy but thought the vet could help him there, and offered £5.

“Yes!” they agreed, almost simultaneously, a surge of elation lifting them as the lead was passed over and the note taken; stooping together to stroke Billy for one last time before leaving the building. Outside they looked at each other, then raced for the car, Gordon jumping, punching one fist in the air, “Yes!” Fumbling through pockets for the key, unable to contain the jubilation, he continued to talk – had to, just could not stop. “Great! I never thought about the vet, I wonder if it would work? Actually that chap could have made his purchase for nothing, I might even have paid *him*!”

But the money seemed to guarantee the goat really was wanted and would be cared for. Arriving home, three sullen unfriendly children waited by the door. Jan waved excitedly to them. They didn’t wave back, but turned away. She had no right to be happy.

“Dad sold him!” Jan called, bursting with delight. The children’s heads lifted, expressions changed, half hope, half doubt.

“Alive?” Chris asked, wanting to believe but unsure.

Jan replied simply, “Yes!”

They rushed forward to hug her. Gordon stood in the background, leaning against the car. They looked at him, undecided.

“It was Dad who saved Billy,” Jan encouraged, telling at least half the truth.

He stepped forward, heading for the door. No one rushed towards him as they had for Jan, but on entering the house, Sharon quietly took his hand and the boys gathered closely round. As evening progressed it became apparent that his rating had changed from being a sensible but slightly hateful Dad, to a soft and loveable one.

He liked it.

<u>CHAPTER 17</u>

The Dreaded Sewer

A vehicle headed down the track, slowing as it approached the bridge. Jan heard the heavy engine noise, stopped eating and leaned sideways to peer through the window.

"A damn great lorry, where's that going?"

Gordon rose, hurried to the office door, yanking it open as the vehicle rolled forward across the yard. "Hey!" He held out a hand, racing in front, bringing it to a halt.

A window in the cab wound down. "What's up?"

"That's what I'd like to know," He stepped back a few paces, stretching sideways to see the coarse granite chippings piled high behind the cab, wondering about the tonnage. "Where are you going with that lot?"

"It's for the sewer. I was told, follow the track to the bottom of the site. Is that straight on or turn right? Will the road take this weight, am I likely to get stuck?"

"You're the biggest so far, but yes, it will take the weight; just don't get mud all over it. Keep to the centre, don't go putting your wheels on the grass at the corners. I'll show you." Gordon ran round and climbed up to the cab.

Jan, seeing him wave and clamber aboard, returned to the almost finished meal. Five minutes or so later a heavy engine noise pulled her to the kitchen window. The same lorry was reversing up the riverbank towards the north end of the house. It stopped fifty feet away, the driver running round to release the tailgate before tipping its load. Gordon stood to one side as the stones fell, then headed back to the house. Shortly the office door opened and he slipped in, returning to the kitchen but waved the now cold food aside. It was almost finished anyway.

"Didn't expect that did you?" she asked.

"No, and there are more to come. They'll be running all day and tomorrow, several of them shuttling back and forth with more chippings. Rain is forecast later in the week the foreman says – he wants to get it in before the bank softens. We can't argue with that."

"I suppose not. Why are they going right down the site, then backing up the riverbank again?"

"Can't get in from this end, the ground slopes right up to the house. They're reaching the river by crossing that last cleared area, the one farthest downstream and not grassed yet. Less chance of getting stuck; those are heavy vehicles!"

Jan cast a glance through the window at the lorry now driving away. "That one's off again. Come for a walk before the next arrives."

They strolled over, pausing at the stony heap, then walking hand in hand beside the river. The bright flowers of summer, yellow rattle, ragged robin, the southern marsh orchid, were gone, replaced by a continuous belt of heather, pinkish-mauve, stretching off into the distance. In bloom for a month already, its beauty shone still, edged by bushy willow and gorse with the occasional taller tree. Near at hand the glossy leaves and bright red berries of black bryony twined round a branch, attractive but poisonous; and there not far ahead, a cluster of red rose hips defended themselves with stout hooks to snag the unwary. But neither poison nor barbs could protect from what lay ahead.

"Will it all be destroyed?" Jan asked, squeezing his hand, her sad eyes following two ugly streaks where the vehicle's twin rear tyres had squashed the living heather.

"Bound to be. What the lorries don't get, that excavator will. Could be twenty years if ever, before it grows like this again. Most of these trees will go too."

The sound of another engine approaching sent them away – they didn't want to know; Jan back to the house,

Gordon off to build stone walls far from the river. As the day progressed, an armada of lorries assailed the valley. Other machines worked busily away, the contractors digging steadily onwards were now two hundred metres into the site. The trail left by pipes already laid stretched off into the distance, all the way to the Sewage Works, located thankfully some two miles down river.

A new wave of stone arrived the following day. Dozens more lorries all loaded with granite chippings backed along the riverbank tipping their great piles. Sorrow at the mounting destruction left little room for anger. The sewer was necessary, people needed it; sewage should be treated before being discharged to sea. How sad that work designed to protect the environment should cause such devastation. The Local District Council appeared to be in charge, apparently acting as agents for the Water Board, the exact arrangements never totally clear.

The following week a letter came from the same District Council, this time from the footpath section. It threatened prosecution for obstructing the footpath with piles of stone! Gordon had opened the mail that morning, read the letter, then suspecting an elaborate hoax, had inspected the heading, the envelope and every small detail. All appeared genuine. Scanning it again he nudged Jan.

"Read this!"

For a while they discussed the possibilities; think of the publicity if it actually came to court! There would be articles in newspapers and magazines, possibly even on TV! Caravanners everywhere would read about the site. Campers too, but the mention of tents brought more sombre thoughts. Could it lead the Council finally to notice they had no proper permission for these?

"Dangerous." Gordon shook his head. "We need another three years at least to be safe; two more years after being connected to the sewer – then they can't do a thing! Whatever they discover then, it will be too late! At least, I think that's right. Mind you, they might not mind anyway, they do like the way we run the site, they've said so. But better not take the risk."

So letting the Council sue them in Court was out, and with it the accompanying publicity. Pity! A letter perhaps, a little note to the footpath department? That might not be too risky. It offered welcome relief; chances to laugh had been rare lately! With a certain relish and gleeful sarcasm, several drafts were concocted. These handwritten notes complimented the department on their vigilance, speed and organisation in moving to prevent inconvenience to the public, agreeing that the perpetrator of this dastardly act should be severely punished. Didn't the Council think prosecution a bit lenient? Wouldn't persecution be more appropriate? How long since St Hilary had seen a good burning at the stake? What was the Cornish equivalent of the Bastille – the 18th century Bodmin jail perhaps? Could it be reopened? A final request suggested all writs be sent to their own Chief Executive! Had no one noticed the Council themselves were responsible for placing these piles of stone on the path? Why bother to check? Blame the landowner!

Much of the passion felt at the riverbank's desecration went into these notes; an outpouring of pent up feelings, a harmless, much needed release valve. For over an hour they sat together scribbling. From these numerous slips of paper, the final reply was selected, discarding the more outlandish suggestions but still retaining sufficient biting sarcasm to leave them feeling content. Tea that evening seemed more happy and relaxed than for several weeks. Another letter dropped through the door a few days later. Although Jan had felt both amused and indignant at the time, her opinion of the footpath department improved after reading the apology. A little over-enthusiasm was forgivable, and probably quite rare!

Work on the sewer continued at full pace. Excavating, hoisting the large pipes into position, covering them with chippings then re-filling the trench were all messy operations. However, it was the lorries that caused more widespread damage. The site's carefully prepared stone roads were the only access for vehicles. These surfaces and the adjoining areas had already deteriorated to a terrible state, worsening by the day. As each lorry backed across to the riverbank to deposit its load of granite or pipes or other essentials, the wheels sunk in, leaving deep channels. Mud clinging to the tyres was flung off in chunks along the road as the vehicles left, then crushed to a slurry by the next incoming lorry. The cycle repeated endlessly. No amount of asking could persuade the drivers or anyone else to clean their wheels before commencing the return journey.

As work moved upstream, little dumps of pipes were made at intervals, new tracks churning across the grass. A surprisingly wet winter caused some lorries to sink in the soft wet ground and be hauled clear by the heavy tracked vehicle which was otherwise busily employed in tearing up the riverbank. These pipes were 24-inch diameter; in places the engineers made their inspection by crawling along inside, from manhole to manhole!

The family was powerless to prevent this devastation, even the children suffered, no longer able to play without returning covered in mud. However, as the bosses in charge pointed out, at least it would now cost nothing to offer all caravans a sewer connection if that became fashionable in the future. Jan and Gordon walked round every evening after the men had gone home, fearful of the extra problems each day revealed. However, as the damage mounted, so did the sewer's progress, for they were working quite fast.

"Good," Jan murmured as the pipework passed another area, "We're going to need every day possible to clear this havoc before next season starts. Thank goodness Judy and the other goats are safely off on a farm!"

Already Gordon worked regularly at the downstream end of the site, but even after the pipes were laid and covered in, further damage could recur as materials were brought in for the large inspection chambers giving access to the sewer.

Weeks passed and the big machine approached their home, creeping daily nearer until it entered the narrow strip of land between house and river. A sea of mud showed in its wake, marking its passage up the valley. A whole swathe of trees and heather had now been lost, pipes and other bits and pieces lay about everywhere. Farther down the bank another track vehicle churned around. Jan saw this depressing scene each time she returned to the kitchen. Even the birds seemed to have gone. One event however did raise a small chuckle. Preparing to start washing-up, she stepped back quickly from the window as a man, the digger driver possibly, relieved himself directly into the stream, adding fractionally to its flow.

In spite of warning the contractors about various service pipes and cables, that first morning saw the electric supply from the waterwheel torn apart. No lights were on inside the house, but Jan glancing again through a window at the chaos outside, saw the wheel had suddenly increased speed as it did when not producing power. Strange? She had used the food mixer not long ago; could the battery be full already? Pulling the switch to a cluster of lights did not slow the wheel. "Sugar!" She swore under her breath; turned them off quickly and hurried to disconnect the battery, preventing what current remained from draining away.

Shortly after lunch, an arc of water sprayed up as the main to the house was severed. She knew the telephone cable ran in the same duct, and stepped through to the office, lifting the receiver. The phone too, was dead – that was worst of all. Thank goodness the pipe from the house loo went in the other direction! The children could collect buckets of water from the stream to flush it when they arrived home from school.

The Engineer in charge visited the following evening after dark. Surprised to be met with a candle at the door, he accepted an invitation to come in for a coffee, and expressed his regret for the loss of power.

"We've lost our television hour too." Sharon frowned

resentfully as she slipped away to light the gas under the kettle.

"Well thank goodness we missed your other services."

"Oh, but you didn't. Water main and telephone have both gone; yesterday afternoon. Very thorough your men – cut the lot!" Jan moved to sit down, signalling the visitor to a chair.

"No water? No one told me that either. How are you managing?" He sat down.

"We get some in the village but most is drawn direct from the river in buckets, the boys fill them early in the morning or late at night. We try to avoid taking any during the day now everyone is working nearby. Sometimes your men..." Jan hesitated, waving a hand self-consciously, "Sometimes they use the stream... add to the flow."

"You drink it? The river water? Use it to make..." The Engineer looked up apprehensively as Sharon re-entered the room. "Er... I won't stay for that coffee after all, I don't deserve one. I'm really sorry about all this." He held both hands up, palms outward in apparent repentance, rising and stepping back towards the door. "I'll get straight on to it, hurry construction forward and get that water main reconnected. Then if you invite me, I'll be happy to take coffee with you."

Gordon rose from his chair, "Never mind the water, it's a nuisance of course but get the phone reconnected first! Losing that is more than inconvenience – we'll be losing bookings!"

The men went out still talking. Jan stood waiting on the threshold but a gust of wind almost blew the candle out; she closed the door, returning to the children waiting in the darkness.

"There you are. How to get rid of a visitor quickly. Don't think he fancied river water coffee! Slip out and take the kettle off, Sharon." Jan put the waxy saucer down on the low table in the room centre, reaching to snip a ragged piece off the wick with a pair of scissors then spoke again as Sharon returned. "Did you hear what Dad said? *Get that telephone back on in case we lose bookings!*" A facetious touch of panic laced her deep voiced imitation, before continuing in a normal tone. "Lose money he means. Never mind about the water I struggle to lug from the village, or you draw from the stream! Typical! Ah well, another ten days the Engineer said, then they should be clear of the house and the trench backfilled. We can work at reconnecting the services then."

"Why should we have to mend everything?" Sharon demanded. "They cut them, why don't they fix the damage? All those repairs Dad's doing down the site..." she stopped, twisting round and addressing the question to her father as he entered after chatting outside before the Engineer drove away. "Why do you work so hard? Make them do it!"

Gordon moved across to sit down, gathering his words to reply, but it was Jan who answered.

"Yes Sharon, they should do, I expect we could insist. But how long do you think it would take before they started. What will your friends think if the site is like this when they arrive next season? Will their parents ever bring them again?" Jan watched her daughter nod thoughtfully, then directed a question to Chris. "Another thing, you've seen the mess they make; what sort of job would be done, how would it look afterwards?"

"Worse than now, probably." Chris shook his head. "But if it's really their job, why should Dad do it all free?"

Gordon regarded his children thoughtfully in the soft flickering light, casting a glance at Jan. How many times had he discussed this with her over coffee? What depth of depression had the two felt as winter progressed? But they had hidden it from the children; or rather attempted to; it was difficult to appear happy under present circumstances. Strive as they might, evenings lacked the spontaneous good feeling that they previously had. Should he now try to make them understand? Clearing his throat, he addressed young Stephen who had so far not entered the conversation.

"Do you think they should pay me?"

"Yes." The little head tilted once in a brief nod.

"They may, but I can't be sure. Let me try to explain. We could hire help, get a receipt, that's a piece of paper to prove that we've paid, then ask the sewer people to give us back the money. I may *have* to pay someone anyway, however hard I work. It *has* to be finished for next spring, at least most of it must. The finer points might be left, it can never be fully restored in one season, but it has to be ready for visitors. The trouble is, if we do pay for some help, we may never get the money back. We can't really afford that yet. We've some savings but not much. That extra pipework, the blocks and cement, the manhole lids; it took quite a lot. Bookings have already been lost with the phone cut off, and people may not stay so long if the site is still poor. It could affect many things; like when we can start the next toilet building, our food, even what new clothes you have."

"They should *have* to pay!" Sharon swung indignantly to her mother, "They must!"

"In a way that's true," Jan agreed. "And they will; they are legally bound to add up all the damage done and pay for it; but there's a catch, a thing called betterment." she held out a hand, "Dad will explain it."

Gordon started to speak; his mouth moved but no sound came forth, and he clasped his throat suddenly with a look of alarm. The children moved forwards on their chairs, straightening up, tense, unsure, turning to their mother to find her smiling.

"Stop hinting!" Jan reached for a cushion and pitched it, making the candle flicker. "Sharon, go and put the kettle back on. He wants that coffee."

Dad caught the cushion and sat holding it defensively, in case she threw another. "A good woman should anticipate her husband's needs, I should never need to ask."

Sharon, having risen and crossed to the door, swung round at the words, placing hands on hips and drawing a deep breath, but Jan stopped her.

"Go on, he's only teasing you. Get the coffee. If he hints next time we'll all scrag him!"

Stephen nodded vigorously, rising ready for action but his parents were grinning at each other. Jan held up a hand, catching the cushion that was tossed gently back, then rose. "Come on, into the other room all of you and sit round the big table; I made scones this afternoon."

With coffee and scones at hand and everyone settled comfortably again, Dad commenced his explanation.

"Betterment. It's a legal term, supposed to measure the advantage we get from anything they do which leaves our site better than it was before. They might argue the sewer will be more convenient, will save us work. Therefore it must be worth a certain amount to us. They can take that amount off any damage done to the site. The trouble is, we don't know how much they may say betterment is worth. Anything we spend putting the damage right may never be recovered. That's why I must do as much as possible myself, work everyday – Mum is helping too. Even getting nothing for our efforts, it's better than paying someone with money we can't afford. As I said, we'll probably have to pay for some things to be done anyway. There's too much for the two of us alone. We'll never fix it all by March."

"What about the road?" Chris asked.

"Ah. That's the *real* problem. I just don't know."

Within a few days, the open trench extended past the house, across the yard and into the grassy plot known as Area 1, the first area ever to have caravans on it. This trench passed in front of the bridge, so entering or leaving the site by car entailed steering very accurately over lengths of steel sheet piling laid loose on the ground. They were perhaps fifteen inches in width and well over six feet long.

"What about that open trench after dark?" Chris asked. "Supposing someone walks down the road without a torch, they're bound to fall in. It should be covered."

"The workmen haven't let that bother them anywhere

else. Must have laid well over a mile of pipes since we started watching, without a single rope or fence, or a lamp or anything. What makes you think they'll do it differently here?" Jan asked.

"I didn't say they will," Chris corrected, "just that they ought to. Nobody walks down the valley, that was fairly safe, but hundreds of people come as far as the bridge."

He was wrong so far as actual numbers were concerned, only a handful of walkers ever came down the track at this time of year. In spirit however, what he said was true; most people did stop at the bridge, or crossed it only to examine the waterwheel then headed back towards the village. It really was more dangerous to leave this trench open.

"Well there's nothing we can do," Jan rose, collecting up the plates. "If we put up a rope to stop people falling in, either someone will hang themselves on it or the Council will be after us for blocking the footpath – probably jump at the chance after the letter we sent last time. Now enough chatter, get on with your homework, we can talk afterwards."

Lighting another candle, Jan signalled Gordon towards the lounge, leaving more room for the children to spread their work. It was unusual; normally they stayed in the dining room until all the homework was finished.

"Okay, what did you want?" Gordon asked as they settled down.

"What makes you think I want anything?" She spoke defensively, as if having nothing particular in mind.

He knew it was untrue. She certainly wanted something, would get round to it in her own way in time no doubt. A mischievous thought occurred. He leaned closer to whisper, "Are you after my body?"

"Your… Hm! You should be so lucky!" She leaned to the far side of the chair putting up two hands defensively. "Actually, now you mention it, there is something. Have you noticed Sharon lately?"

"Why?"

"She's growing, her clothes are tight. I noticed when

she reached up to the tall food cupboard this evening; the top hinge is loose by the way, getting dangerous, the door is hard to close. Can you cure it?"

"Okay, sure. Isn't it nice to have a man who can fix things for you?"

"Oh it is."

Something about her reply triggered an idea, he smiled and waved a finger "Stop thinking '*I had what I could get*!'"

She stared at him, smiling back in surprise. "How can you tell exactly what's in my mind?"

They sat for a time caught in each other's eyes. She was wearing slacks and a dark blue, high polo-necked jumper that for some reason, knowing there was no blouse beneath, he wanted to take off. The candle flickered darkly in her eyes, and he reached out a hand. She met it halfway, leaning forward, lips slightly apart. "Can I change my mind about your bo… No!" She sat suddenly upright. "One of the children may come in with a question. Anyway, don't change the subject, we were discussing Sharon's outfits. They're too tight. She needs new ones."

"Girls like their things tight – like your jumper."

"Not at twelve they don't! And keep your eyes off my jumper, it's not the only thing that's tight around here! Some people wouldn't even pay for their daughter's clothes! Has this sewer business really made us so poor we can't afford anything new?"

"Difficult to say, that's the trouble. We don't have any real idea of what it will cost. Even if a settlement does give part of the money back, it could be years before we see a penny. Much depends how hard I can work myself. Go ahead and buy her an outfit, but be economical. The road is the real worry."

Shortly after, voices from the other room indicated homework was finished. Jan rose to make coffee. Gordon followed, joining the children. "Any problems."

"Yes." Stephen replied quietly.

"Well?"

"Decimals. We've started them."

"Okay. Shall I see what I can remember? Anyone else interested?" Dad looked at the two older children.

Sharon indicated that she was, and Chris nodded vaguely, retaining that macho, 'I'm not really bothered, but go ahead if it pleases you' stance.

"Okay then a quick run through. Adding up and taking away first. Always keep the decimal point under each other, and if you're taking away and want to check the result, then add it together again and see if it comes to what you started with. Decimal multiplication next? Right, it's the same as ordinary multiplication except you have to know where the point goes. Just count the total number of decimals in both figures, that's how many the answer should have. Remember to show all the noughts when you do the sum." Dad stopped to show a few on paper.

"Now here's a special trick. When two numbers that end with point five, are multiplied together, they always end .75 if one is an odd number and one even, or .25 otherwise." He scribbled a few more examples. "There. Is that enough?"

"Unless you know how to learn tables?" Stephen asked.

"Well, not really. Having trouble? There is something special about the nine times table. All the answers if you add them up come to nine."

"How do you mean?"

"Two nines are eighteen, one and eight add up to nine. Three nines are twenty-seven, two and seven make nine. It goes like that all the way."

"What about… fourteen times nine?" Sharon picked a figure out of the air.

"One hundred and twenty six. Go on, add the three figures up." Dad waited. Both Sharon and Stephen reached for pencil and paper before believing.

"Eleven doesn't," Chris challenged. "That's ninety nine, adds up to eighteen!"

"And what does eighteen add up to?" Dad held out a questioning hand palm upward, before continuing. "Nine is the only special one; if you can't do the eight times table, then do the four times, and double the answer. It's slower but it works."

"Coffee coming up," Jan called, "bring the other cups and the candle, we'll go in the lounge."

November was passing and there remained half a mile more sewer to reach the village. That half-mile might isolate the site completely, for much of the planned pipe route lay under the entrance road. Progress however, was being made. Nobody had fallen in that open trench by the bridge, and this length together with the narrow section between house and stream were now covered in. Work had moved on to the grassy area beyond, or rather, what had previously been grass. It now lay under attack by the Contractor's best storm troopers, a friendly enough bunch of lads with a real talent for wrecking chaos; or perhaps it was the weather? Great mountains of soil, heaps of granite chippings and a sea of mud created a spectacle like some backwater gold rush where soil and stone were scattered in a mad scramble for the yellow metal.

"We could sell this scene to a film company," Jan suggested as they took photos.

A lorry struggled by delivering another cargo of stone. From the front house windows, the yard remained a mess even though work there had supposedly finished! Close at hand stood a yellow compressor, apparently no longer required, the ground around it adorned with yellow five-gallon diesel cans. Farther over, a great concrete inspection chamber section and its heavy capping stood beside a 40-gallon drum; a haphazardly strewn pile of old metal sheet piling resting on the other side. More pieces of the metal lay elsewhere together with digger buckets not in use. On the far side an enormous excavator was now manoeuvring to park. The driver climbed down and ran for the canvas shelter where the other men sat, a brazier burning near the entrance. The weather had turned cold, a biting north wind blew up the valley.

"It's ready!" Sharon called from the kitchen. She was stirring a mixture in a large pan on the stove, the pan Jan used for making jam. Alongside on the sink's draining board lay half a dozen extra large cans of Heinz vegetable soup, all empty. A handle was attached at both sides of the big utensil, pivoting like a bucket, but twice the width. Folding a teacloth into a wad to insulate his hand, Gordon lifted it and headed for the door. This was the first time, perhaps the only time, such a gesture would be made. Carrying the soup to the canvas shelter; he heaved the steaming cauldron onto the ground between the circle of feet. Six men sat hunched over against the cold on a fixed wooden bench that ran round the thin walls; such low temperatures were rare.

"Do you need dishes?"

"Not me!" One man drained his coffee and dredged a mugful, cupping the warmth in his hands and lifting it to his lips, sipping carefully. "Hot, but damn good!"

Others quickly followed, the level falling rapidly.

"What about Ernie?" Gordon asked.

"Blow him. If he can't get to tea break on time that's his hard cheese!"

The answer came as no real surprise. Nobody in the building trade expected any great show of politeness or consideration; any that did were doomed to disappointment and should choose another occupation.

"Hey, this is the best thing you done since we got here. Growing on you, are we? Do it again tomorrow if you like," a man declared. Murmurs and nods of approval sounded round the shelter.

"Don't bet on it! Growing on me, Huh. Just can't have you catching cold and slowing up. All I really want is to see your backsides disappearing into the next field and on down that road! Bring the pan back when you've finished."

The outside might look an absolute shambles, but inside the house things were improving – a little at least! An argument over the level of one manhole cover had prevented the waterwheel being reconnected, so the candles were still in use. However, Gordon had dug a trench and replaced the severed water pipe slipping it into a new duct that also had room for the new telephone line, and that too was now working. The news on other fronts was not so bright. Repair and reshaping of damaged areas was not progressing well. It was tedious, and exhaustingly manual, for Max could not run on the soft winter grass. The roads however, were worse; their condition pitiful! Digging away the top layer and carting the mud-laden rubble off to some low ground farther downstream, gave only limited improvement. At least here Max could help; just as well, for re-laying with fresh stone would clearly be required over the entire length. One short stretch had been completed as an experiment with depressing results! Thin layers of the available material proved impossible to level well but nothing better could be done; there was no time. Both Gordon and Jan were working themselves to a standstill each day already.

All this would have been enough on its own, but a greater setback lay in store. The big excavator, digging well ahead of pipe laying, broke through the hedge and into rough land beyond the site. The ground there tended to be marshy, and within a few metres the trench line breached either an old mine adit or some natural drainage channel, releasing a continuous flow. This water found its way along the now covered trench to bubble up, flooding an area in front of the office.

Young Stephen noticed first, on arriving home from school. He said nothing to anyone but dropped his satchel on the doorstep, then waded about in the miniature lake, socks in his pocket and shoes dangling from his neck, the laces tied together behind. Jan, checking through the window to see if Chris and Sharon were coming down the road, saw him and called out, making him come inside.

"Must be mad in this weather," Sharon shuddered as the tale unfolded at tea. "How deep is it?"

"About eighteen inches in the middle as far as we can

tell using a long stick," Jan answered. "We've rung the engineer."

The following day several men in suits, one actually wearing a bowler hat, descended on the site and trod warily out to cluster round the trench in deep conversation. A man detached himself from the circle, and came to the house.

"Yes," he said, "There is water running along that trench. We're looking into it." After more conversation and some arm waving, the group departed with the far from reassuring statement that they intended using a seal to stop the flow.

That afternoon a lorry loaded with china clay arrived. It backed towards the open excavation with great difficulty even though approaching from the drier side, then tipped the soft putty-like substance into the trench. It slipped out in a cohesive mass to surround the pipe; an attempt to stem any further water flow. A good geologist could have forecast in advance that this tactic would be useless. It is a feature common to rivers that over geological time the stream moves back and forth across the valley floor. This leaves lenses of sand and gravel scattered everywhere. Water running along the pipeline easily found a porous strata to bypass the sticky china clay plug. Consequently, conditions continued rapidly to deteriorate. Land drains seemed the only solution. Driving Max out onto this area with the intention of digging an escape channel, the whole machine started to sink! Only the power of its hydraulic rams saved the situation. Pulling with one bucket, digging teeth into soil and heaving forward, inched Max towards the firmer ground. Forcing the rear jib down, pushing mightily until the bucket almost disappeared under the surface, finally extricated the machine.

Something had to be done! Waiting for the contractors to act was no longer an option. A track vehicle and two lorries were hired for several weeks, clearing the existing topsoil, digging channels for land drains, laying down up to three feet of stone, then spreading the topsoil again. In all, a very expensive operation.

"You've finished at last?" Jan asked as the track vehicle finally left.

"Only that section, and there's still the grass to set. Somebody one day in the future is going to dig a hole and wonder how ten tons of pure white china clay comes to be lying in that field. We may even find some special varieties of plants start to grow, it's happened before. One of the orchids, the Bee Orchid I think, has sometimes appeared in unexpected places, thriving on lime mortar left over from Roman times, nearly 2000 years ago."

For many weeks, no more damage occurred as the sewer moved on southward through gorse covered land still on the west bank of the river. The site entrance road lay safely on the east bank – but all that was about to change. Those pipes were approaching the crossing point! The construction gang fought for several days to sink the sewer below the riverbed, signalling success with memorial posts stuck in the ground, one on each bank. Overnight, some wag added a note stuck on with selotape; it read, "Here lies a dirty great sewer. RIP." At the moment these markers were unnecessary, a great swathe of disturbed earth indicated the crossing point. In future years however, nature must surely claim back its own and camouflage the scars. The posts would be handy then, if ever that pipe needed to be found. This significant stage, this crossing, was treated with both relief and apprehension by the family. Only a quarter mile remained, but that length lay entirely under the track that formed the only vehicle access to their home. They badly needed this section to be finished, for the new season was fast approaching; but they also knew access would now be more difficult. Neither children nor parents had the slightest idea of how difficult.

Chaos! That first section of trench collapsed completely; one could hardly call it a trench any more, the unsupported sides falling in over a lengthy stretch. The big machine reached out, clawing up the debris of muddy soil, trying to clear the fallen material, but another collapse occurred, and yet another. The 'trench' ended up not four feet wide, but the entire track width and beyond. From opposite sides of this broad crater projected the shattered ends of the three inch water main. Alongside, the severed telephone cable hung limply down, all fifteen lines of its multicoloured strands masked drably brown, each liberally covered with sticky silt. The site was completely cut off; deprived again of water, of telephone, and in addition, no vehicle could enter or leave! Goodness knows what would happen in the case of a fire. The nearest a fire engine could approach was nearly half a mile from the house. Even if firemen ran up on foot with a hose it would have been no good; with the water main cut the hydrant would not have worked. Things were fairly desperate!

"What will happen if that pipe under the river leaks at some time in the future? How will they repair it while the sewer is live?" Chris asked.

"Most likely no one would know – you wouldn't see a wet patch underwater. It would just percolate slowly up through the soil. Hope we never need use river water then! If we do, Sharon can try it first." Gordon suggested.

"Wouldn't work," Chris shook his head. "Whatever it did to her, you probably couldn't tell."

Dad and Stephen solemnly nodded agreement.

"I'm the one who makes most of the coffee," Sharon warned, "I know what goes into it – but you don't! You want to be careful."

"You don't really think it will leak?" Jan addressed the question to Dad.

"No chance; not under ordinary circumstances. The other way around perhaps; river water more likely to leak in than sewage leak out. The pressure from above is greater."

Repair work too, was behind schedule and going badly. The quality of road surface being achieved could only be classed as awful. When originally laid, the roads had been made with eighteen inches of fresh stone; under those conditions a decent surface had been possible. Now, with only the top few inches of muddy material being removed, the fresh stone replacing it refused to level well. In a long discussion that evening after the children had gone to bed, there seemed only one solution. Gordon had a policy with a Life Insurance company, a policy designed to give the family protection in the event of his death or injury. It would also provide a lump sum at retirement age for they had no other pension prospects. The amount involved was not large, for no payments had been possible since the site was first started, but it was all they had – and it would have to be cashed in. This money must be used to surface the roads with tarmac, blacktop as most builders call it. The layer of clean stone they were laying would form a sound enough base, but they had to make the surface more acceptable to visitors. Now the family would be without insurance cover and had nothing towards retirement. If the sewer was not finished and the entrance road could not be opened on time, or if the grass was not re-established quickly, then they were quite likely to go bust! Truly, this was a dark time.

One morning, struggling past the gaping hole before any workmen had arrived, Sharon slipped and fell, soiling her skirt and jumper. Time prevented her returning home to change; the school bus to Penzance was due! In any case it would have entailed climbing twice more over the piles of mud. She continued on her way, returning that evening greatly distressed. Being still a youngster at the senior school, her standing within the class remained insecure, affected by appearance and self-confidence, the latter having fallen close to zero that day.

"People were watching me Mum, you could see them talking, staring in my direction, and when I went towards them they stopped and turned away." Sharon wasn't cross with her friends, that was never her nature, just embarrassed and upset.

Remembering her own school days and the importance of appearance to a girl, Jan looked at her young daughter with compassion. "Go and change into a clean skirt. You can have a bath later. I'll boil two big saucepans and send the boys for an extra bucket of water each from the river. It's their job but they'll hate it when they know what it's for. We won't tell them until afterwards."

At least the gas was still working, but dirty clothes and bathing now presented a real problem again. With no water in the taps a normal bath was not possible, and of course nothing in the toilet buildings worked either. Those buckets from the river and a couple of saucepans heated on the stove would combine to offer a few meagre tepid inches in the bath. The soiled skirt could be washed in the same water afterwards. Sharon brightened at her mother's suggestion and slipped away.

The boys had come in and were sitting at the table arguing over some new game Stephen had learned at school when their sister reappeared. She wore a fresh skirt, another tartan, swinging it from the hips with obvious satisfaction as she crossed the kitchen, then stopped with sudden concern to whisper, "Mum. What should I do if it happens again?"

"Come into the lounge a minute," Jan moved away from the stove slipping into the corridor, leaving the boys sitting at the table. "We can talk now, they won't notice if we don't take too long." She spoke quietly, sinking into a chair. "Why don't you leave ten minutes earlier, you'll have time to get back and change if anything happens."

"Won't Chris and Stephen want to know why?" Sharon knew they would laugh.

"Tell them you're calling on Jim and Audrey," Jan hesitated, thinking. "Why don't you keep a spare skirt and jumper up at Jim's, you wouldn't need to leave so early then; you could change down there."

Dismissing the matter that had been weighing on her young mind, Sharon beamed, "What are we cooking?" She rose and heading towards the door.

Later, after the meal, everyone returned to the lounge. With coffee still too hot, the boys were playing snooker and Gordon sat reading, while Mother and daughter were talking together.

"Mum, what will happen if the road is still blocked when we open, and visitors can't get in?"

"If that big machine is still working I don't suppose many will try. Even if it was possible to get by they would probably not fancy the risk, and go elsewhere."

Some excitement from the boys had the whole family stepping through the big opening into the adjoining room.

"I just potted a black," Chris explained, "and now I'm going for that plant." He pointed with pride, indicating two reds to the left of the black spot, the pair neatly lined up with the corner pocket.

A hush fell over the room as he bent down, carefully cueing up, keenly anxious to pull it off and aware everyone was watching. The small group of spectators understood the game well and stood unmoving, the interest intense. With a crisp action, Chris hit the cue ball, his head remaining low as it contacted the first red, sending the second straight for the pocket. A little cheer sounded. This table was hard to play with cue room on only two sides. A black then a plant was rare enough! Following this success, the boys laid down their cues, returning to the lounge for coffee.

"I heard you talking about the road," Chris looked towards Mum, "What *will* you do if they don't finish? Suppose it continues to fall in like the big crater they're working on now?"

"Dad will probably charge Max up the road at full speed, push all the workmen into their own hole and fill it quickly with that mountain of soil!"

"End up in the Old Bailey!" Sharon warned.

"What are you smiling at young lady?" Jan asked. "At burying the sewer men, or at seeing Dad in the dock? Anyway, where did you hear about the Old Bailey?"

"A teacher was telling us about the justice system,

juries and that. What would a jury do to Dad?"

"Offer me a medal probably," Gordon interrupted, having seen broad smiles at the previous question.

"Why?" Sharon pointed with one finger outstretched in accusation.

"Well, it's a long story, but I saved the Old Bailey from collapse once. Drink your coffee."

They drank for a while in silence, then Dad spoke again. "It was several years ago. Let's see, must have been in my early-twenties at the time and…"

"Several years ago?" Jan echoed loudly, raising her eyebrows.

"As I was saying before I was so rudely interrupted, must have been, uh… fifteen years ago; I was working in central London, right near Fleet Street where they print all the newspapers. I actually worked on the Daily Telegraph offices for a while, an impressive organisation. I was calculating the strength of beams because they wanted to extend their cuttings library. Storing paper creates heavy loads on buildings, people don't always realise; but that's another story. At the time I'm talking about we were constructing a large office block with deep basements. The site was split into two parts. I was the young engineer for the half in front of the Old Bailey. My friend, a little older and more experienced, managed the other half; that part stretched all the way to Ludgate Circus. Now I need to explain about foundations. Big buildings are supported on piles. Any of you know what piles are?"

"Andrew, a boy at school, said his father had some but that may be a different type?" Chris grinned.

"Witty tonight aren't we? Many cities are built on rock, New York is I believe, but London stands on blue clay. Did you know the whole of London is sinking? Near the Bank of England ground levels have sunk seven inches over a period of 68 years. However, in spite of that, this blue clay is a strong layer. It will carry lots of weight, but it's a long way down. To reach it, they drill holes in the ground then fill them with concrete and steel. Not little holes like we drill in wood, but big ones, the size of those sewer pipes up the road, big enough for a man to go down. Of course, piles are expensive! I was in a lot of trouble with the boss because I had made sure the piles on my side of the site were concreted several feet longer than was really needed, so they stuck up out of the ground.

"We were already thirty or forty feet below normal ground level, depth enough for several layers of basement; even underground space is valuable in London! We had a heavy timber retaining wall holding up the sides, massive timber buttresses coming down like this." Gordon held a book upright to represent the wall, and leant a pencil against it.

"Think of this pencil as stopping the book falling over; our buttresses did the same thing for the wall, but they were massive timbers, so heavy only the crane could lift them into position. On my side of the site I had extra buttresses built to rest against the piles; those ones I just told you about that stuck up in the air several feet higher than they should. Well, a long spell of wet weather made everything on the site soft and muddy. The buttresses on my friend's half fell in. The narrow road to the Old Bailey lay right beside our site and part of that road fell in too. People can be stupid! Small crowds gathered, standing as near the edge as they dare, peering over at the devastation, ignorant of the danger, unaware the ground they stood on might give way at any moment. Perhaps a few did know and their own boring daily routines made the risk worthwhile. Anyway, large service pipes under the road had ruptured – like ours have where the sewer men are working, only in London there were more underground pipes and much bigger. Some young girls, office workers I believe, were caught by a mass of escaping gas! They passed out, lying unconscious on the edge of that precipice. Ambulances rushed to the scene, men were dashing about trying to see if anyone was trapped under the fallen debris, the road was closed; pandemonium! Everyone expected the whole length to fail as cracks appeared and spread along the tarmac surface. If it did, part of the Old Bailey might well fall, killing people inside. Police whistles were blowing, ambulance bells, the fire service, people being evacuated – it was chaos." Dad paused watching the young faces.

"Well!" Sharon prompted urgently, "What happened?"

"My half held! Remember the piles, the ones I got in trouble for deliberately making a few feet higher than they need be? Well, because of those Old Bailey was saved! You could say I've done more for that building than any judge ever has. Let's hope I never have cause to regret it!"

Gordon stopped, spreading hands in a 'what do you think,' expression. For a moment there was silence before a torrent of questions flowed from Sharon and Chris. Stephen said nothing but quickly disappeared, returning with paper and pencil, pushing them towards his father. The drawing as it developed showed tall buildings, a road with tiny matchstick people, and a deep excavation with wooden retaining wall and buttresses. "My side!" Dad said, then drawing a collapsed shape over the top, he pointed, "That's my friend's side!"

More questions and answers, flashed back and forth for a while, explanations and further doodles on the drawing illustrating various points before Dad pushed the paper and pencil aside, and spoke again.

"For many weeks after that, everyone was asking my advice. It was marvellous for a young man. I could do no wrong! The expense of an extra few feet on those piles saved thousands, perhaps millions of pounds. Pity they never paid me a bonus!" He turned to Jan, "You see how important it is to build strong!"

Much later, with the children already in bed, the parents sat together in the lounge. It had been a good evening, they had pushed aside sombre thoughts, hiding deep worries from the children, but now, sitting together, those thoughts returned. The door was closed so their voices would not carry, but undetected by either parent a small figure sneaked along the corridor and now crouched behind that door, listening intently.

"We never did answer Sharon's question, for all your elaborate story." Jan spoke quietly. "Okay, I know it was true, I remember that evening paper you brought home with the details, but your tale only diverted attention from the real question. What *will* we do if the road is still blocked when the season starts?"

"I think it's bound to be. It's February already; March and April will certainly be lost, and who knows how much longer? Since that last big collapse they're hardly moving forward at all."

"How badly will it affect us? You said to go ahead and buy Sharon new clothes; can we still afford to?"

Behind the door, the crouching figure tensed, holding her breath, fists clenched in concentration.

"Is it essential?" Gordon frowned.

"She thinks so. I do too, really. No mother likes to see her daughter in clothes she's growing out of, but I could delay. Are things really that serious?"

"Could be, if our road is closed for long. We need the visitors, need gas too, but the lorry can't get through. You've only one bottle left for cooking; you seem to be using it quicker lately?"

"Boiling water – it mostly comes from the river now. How did the repairs go today."

"The topsoil work is coming on but no way I can finish in time and there's seed to set everywhere when the ground warms. I'm doing all I can, but it's not enough. I need help, and that means cash. The new road surface is poor; thin layers won't level properly. I know we intend to tarmac, but if the base is rough that may increase the cost. Even with the cash from my life policy, things will be tight – and how long since we had a day off?"

"I forget, not since Christmas anyway." Jan sighed, "Tight you say – how short of money is that? Not really in danger, are we?"

"Not immediately, depends how much I have to spend to get things right, but we need a good season. Do what you can to economise, food, clothes, you know, like when we first came down."

Behind the door Sharon rose silently, creeping away back to her bedroom. For a long time she could not sleep and lay thinking of her school friends, of the clothes they wore, of other more shapeless fears, not just the words she had overheard, but the tones, the concern in her parent's voices. As she twisted restively the thoughts churned but always returned to clothes. When sleep did come it was shallow, she was fleeing down the valley, chased by an enormous excavator, its bucket snapping open and shut, gnashing like some modern day dinosaur. The vegetation was thick, holding her back, brambles ripped her clothes to shreds, gouging red streaks across the skin. On and on she ran, until suddenly the pursuit stopped and she broke free into a clearing filled with people. They were her school friends, standing around, each immaculately dressed. She stumbled and fell, tired and bleeding but her friends turned, walking away, speaking secretly to each other behind raised hands. She tried to follow but they faced her with outstretched arms, fingers pointing beyond the fringe of willows, sending her back to where the machine waited. She sagged, beaten, head hanging, and trod with dragging feet back into the jungle. The huge bucket arched over, smashing its way through the trees as she had seen it do along the riverbank. It was reaching towards her, swinging downwards...

"Aaah!" the cry screamed in her brain as she sat bolt upright in the darkness... nobody came. For some moments the young girl sat there, shaking uncontrollably, then a tear rolled down one cheek and she fell on her pillow sobbing. What did the future hold?

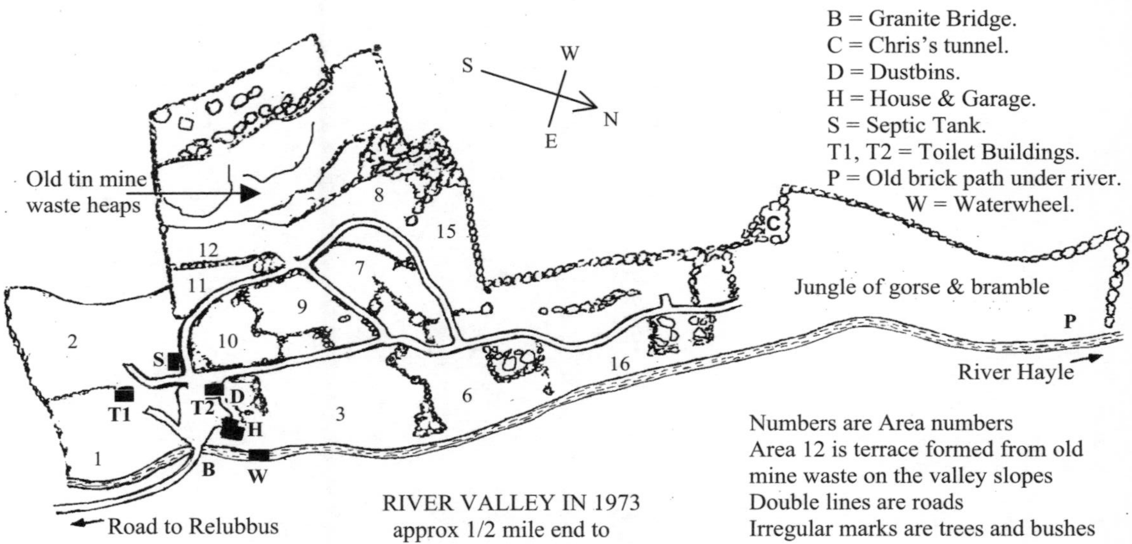
B = Granite Bridge.
C = Chris's tunnel.
D = Dustbins.
H = House & Garage.
S = Septic Tank.
T1, T2 = Toilet Buildings.
P = Old brick path under river.
W = Waterwheel.
S
W
N
E
Old tin mine waste heaps
Jungle of gorse & bramble
River Hayle
Road to Relubbus
1
2
3
6
7
8
9
10
11
12
15
16
T1
T2
S
D
H
B
W
C
P
Numbers are Area numbers
Area 12 is terrace formed from old mine waste on the valley slopes
Double lines are roads
Irregular marks are trees and bushes

RIVER VALLEY IN 1973
approx 1/2 mile end to

The author thanks readers for their letters
on books in the series
and may be contacted through the publisher's address
or Email Gordjan@AOL.com

The first Waterwheel
- but will it produce electricity?

The shark

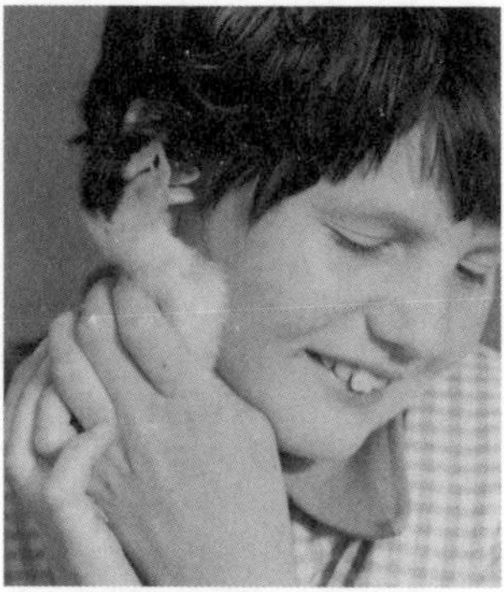

Sharon with duckling

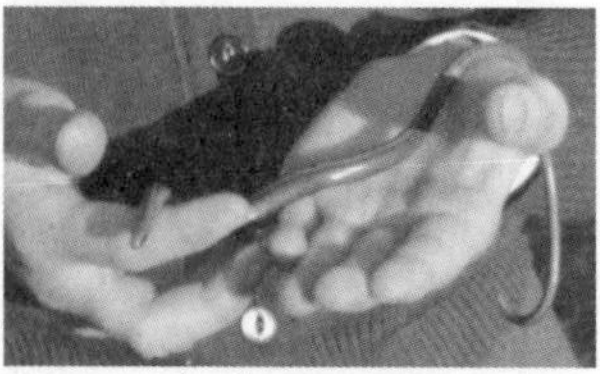

A slowworm

Sharon and Chris with the goat kids

The Goats, from the left Olive, Judy, Ivy.

Rough Sea at Mullion - Jan

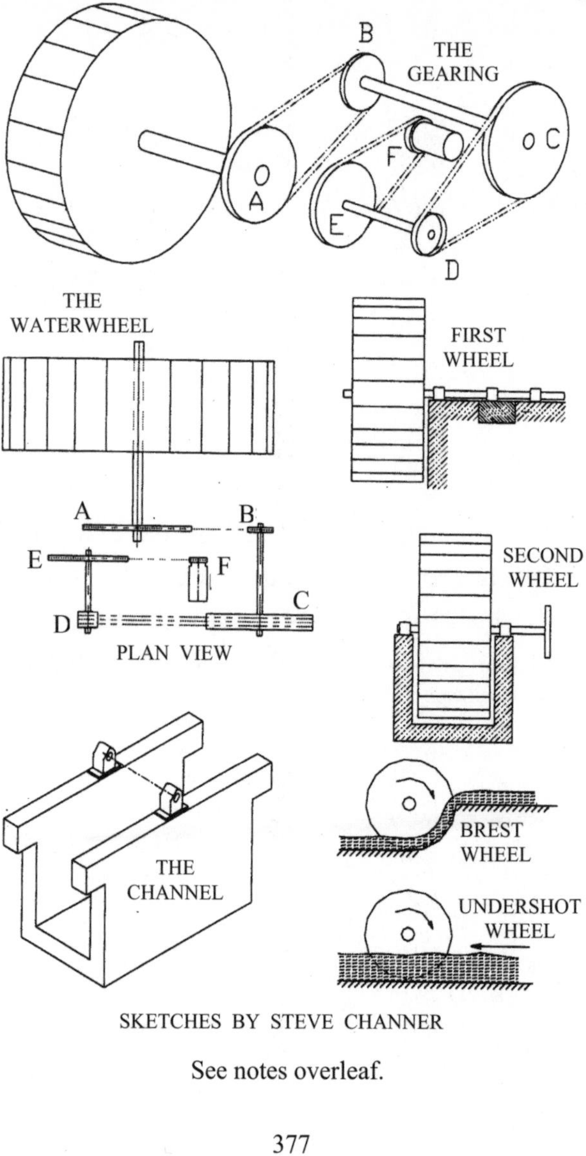

SKETCHES BY STEVE CHANNER

See notes overleaf.

The Valley of Dreams Series.

by Gordon Channer

Village by the Ford	£6.95	0-9537009-1-7
House by the Stream	£7.95	0-9537009-2-5
Wheel on the Hayle	£7.95	0-9537009-0-9
A Buzzard to Lunch	£6.95	0-9537009-3-3
Follow that Caravan	£7.95	0-9537009-4-1

Book sizes:- 309 374 372 368 427 pages.
Best enjoyed if read in the order given above.

This is a novel, not a work on waterwheels, but the sketches overleaf show there really is a Wheel on the Hayle, a wheel that is very much part of the story

For the technically curious, remember two things. Wheels on the same shaft must turn at the same speed. When a chain or belt connects two wheels, the smaller wheel turns faster.
Try it with your bicycle.

Web page with photos:- www.Cornishbooks.co.uk

The series is available through your local bookshop or can be ordered direct (post free in UK) from:- Cornish Books, 5 Tregembo Hill, Penzance, Cornwall, TR20 9EP
Email Dreams@Cornishbooks.co.uk